THE AUTHORIZED LEFT BEHIND HANDBOOK

THE AUTHORIZED
LEFT BEHIND®
HANDBOOK

TIM

LAHAYE / JERRY B. JENKINS
WITH SANDI L. SWANSON

Tyndale House Publishers, Inc.
Wheaton, Illinois

Visit Tyndale's exciting Web site at www.tyndale.com

TYNDALE is a registered trademark of Tyndale House Publishers, Inc.
Tyndale's quill logo is a trademark of Tyndale House Publishers, Inc.

Discover the latest about the Left Behind series at www.leftbehind.com

Written and developed in association with Tekno Books, Green Bay, Wisconsin.

Left Behind series designed by Catherine Bergstrom

Designed by Julie Chen

Published in association with the literary agency of Alive Communications, Inc., 7680 Goddard Street, Suite 200, Colorado Springs, CO 80920.

Material for "Facts behind the Fiction" taken from *Are We Living in the End Times?* Copyright © 1999 by Tim LaHaye and Jerry B. Jenkins.

Library of Congress Cataloging-in-Publication Data

LaHaye, Tim F.
    The authorized Left behind handbook / Tim LaHaye, Jerry B. Jenkins, with Sandi L. Swanson.
        p. cm.
    ISBN 0-8423-5440-9 (pbk.)
    1. LaHaye, Tim F. Left behind series—Handbooks, manuals, etc.   2. Christian fiction, American—History and criticism—Handbooks, manuals, etc.   3. Apocalyptic literature—History and criticism—Handbooks, manuals, etc.   4. Rapture (Christian eschatology)—Handbooks, manuals, etc.   5. End of the world in literature—Handbooks, manuals, etc.   6. Second Advent in literature—Handbooks, manuals, etc.
I. Jenkins, Jerry B.   II. Swanson, Sandi.   III. Title.
    PS3562.A315L443 2005
    813'.54—dc22   2004026540

Printed in the United States of America

09 08 07 06 05
8   7   6   5   4   3   2   1

DEDICATION

TO MILLIONS OF READERS who have helped make these books so successful. As many have said, "At last I can finally understand the study of the last days, including the book of Revelation." For many it was the first time they saw the prophecies for what they were. Jesus is coming back to this earth to set up his thousand-year kingdom and will use believers to help him rule and reign over it, just as he promised. We're so grateful that many have written to say that after reading our series they enjoy getting back to reading their Bibles, particularly the prophetic passages.

Most of all we dedicate this special edition to our Lord and Savior who purchased our salvation and reveals in his Word the wonderful plan he has for our eternal future: rapturing his church (all believers) to "his father's house" while those left behind go through the seven worst years in human history, "the Great Tribulation" (Matthew 24:21; John 14:1-3; 1 Thess. 4:13-18 and Matthew 24:29-31).

T. L & J. B. J

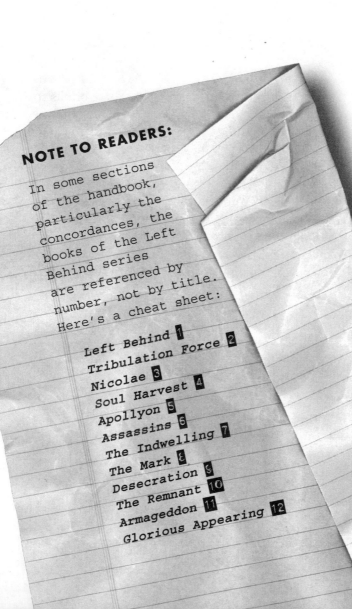

NOTE TO READERS:

In some sections of the handbook, particularly the concordances, the books of the Left Behind series are referenced by number, not by title. Here's a cheat sheet:

Left Behind **1**
Tribulation Force **2**
Nicolae **3**
Soul Harvest **4**
Apollyon **5**
Assassins **6**
The Indwelling **7**
The Mark **8**
Desecration **9**
The Remnant **10**
Armageddon **11**
Glorious Appearing **12**

CONTENTS

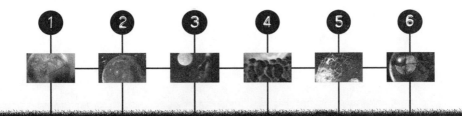

BEHIND
LEFT BEHIND:
AN INSIDER'S LOOK

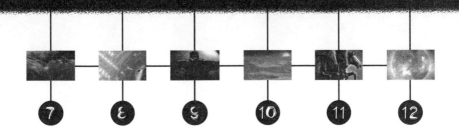

HOW *LEFT BEHIND* CHANGED THE FACE OF CHRISTIAN PUBLISHING

NEARLY 2 DECADES AGO, pastor and author Tim LaHaye was on a plane when he witnessed a pilot flirting with a flight attendant. The interplay between them caught his attention because the pilot was wearing a wedding ring. It was a passing moment of temptation, one that has undoubtedly been repeated thousands of times, but this time was special. Dr. LaHaye wondered what would happen to the pilot if the Rapture occurred at this very instant. Unknowingly, that pilot and flight attendant had just provided the trigger point for something that would revolutionize Christian publishing and Christian discourse in public and private. In fact, this tiny moment is proof that the Lord works in mysterious ways.

There's no denying that this encounter created the first tiny ripple of something that would become a tidal wave. The Left Behind series and its related books have sold over 62 million copies. Tim LaHaye and Jerry B. Jenkins have become the best-selling novelists in America, displacing writers like John Grisham and Tom Clancy along the way. The Left Behind books have cumulatively spent hundreds of weeks on every major best-seller list in America, including (much to everyone's surprise, at least initially) the *New York Times* list. The first print run for the hardcover edition of *Desecration* was over 2.9 million copies. That's a whole lot of books. And readers everywhere have responded with passion to the saga.

Thanks largely to the Left Behind novels, Christian fiction sales have quadrupled in the last decade. The number of Christian fiction titles released has doubled in the same time. The Left Behind series has also inspired a highly successful line of young adult books, and young adult Christian fiction is increasing in sales and number of titles being released too. The series is published in multiple languages, so the message is getting out all across the globe. It's a new world out there for Christian fiction, a world with vibrant, exciting new stories hitting the shelves daily. And most industry experts believe that the bulk of that growth was spurred by the success of *Left Behind*.

But it isn't just about the books. It isn't even mostly about the books. The real impact of the Left Behind series is on souls. Tim LaHaye and Jerry B. Jenkins get many letters every day from readers who have had their relationships with Christ strengthened through reading the books. The authors also get letters from people who came to Christ because they read the books. The official Left Behind Web site gets thousands of hits every day as readers look for a place to discuss the books and get answers to the questions they raise. There's a Left Behind Prophecy Club that looks at the biblical basis for the Left Behind series, complete with interpretation by leading biblical scholars and bulletin boards for the members to discuss the issues. The whole field of end-times prophecy has been given a major boost by these books, and the discussion of the various interpretations of biblical prophecy has become more mainstream and intense since the release of the series.

And all of this is just what's occurred in the world of Christians. The Left Behind series has been exceptionally effective at taking the Word of God into high-profile, non-Christian media venues and triggering a serious discussion of Christianity in places where Christ is otherwise rarely given a passing mention. In the last decade, the Left Behind phenomenon has resulted in front-page articles in *Time* and *Newsweek* and lead articles in most of the major daily newspapers, including the *New York Times*. The books even broke into the rarified air of top-level television and radio. Stories about the books and their authors have been featured on the *Today Show, 60 Minutes*, CNN, MSNBC, the Fox News Channel, *The Morning Show, Good Morning, America,* and thousands of talk radio stations. Through these stories broadcast by the mass media, millions of people who have never seriously considered their need for God have been brought face-to-face with the concept of redemption through Jesus Christ. The success of the books has driven the opportunity for an unprecedented harvest of souls. By bringing the message of Christ's love to the worldwide media, the Left Behind series has spread the discussion of Christianity from church confines into the whole world. What people are talking about, they are thinking about. And what they are thinking about might change their minds and hearts. Through the widespread discussion of the Left Behind books, the opportunity has been created for millions of people to seek and find God.

TALKING ABOUT LEFT BEHIND WITH TIM LAHAYE AND JERRY B. JENKINS

THE AUTHORS of the Left Behind series, Dr. Tim LaHaye and Jerry B. Jenkins, love to communicate with readers of their books. They've spread the books' message through the official Left Behind Web site, leftbehind.com, through personal appearances and national tours to meet their fans, and through interviews with the media. In a series of interviews for Tyndale and for this handbook, both Dr. LaHaye and Jerry Jenkins gave candid answers to many questions readers have raised about their novels.

Question: I understand, Dr. LaHaye, that you were the one who came up with the idea for this series, and you are the prophecy consultant. When and where were you when you developed this book scenario?

Tim LaHaye: On the way to speak at a prophecy conference, I watched the captain of a plane come out of his cabin and begin flirting with the head flight attendant. I noticed he had a wedding ring on and she didn't. As the sparks flew between them, I thought of a remark by one of my lifetime friends to the effect, "Wouldn't it be interesting if the Rapture occurred and the pilot recognized that the hundred people that suddenly were missing from his aircraft meant that his Christian wife and son would be missing when he got home?" That was when the title hit me; knowing his loved ones were missing, he knew before he got home that he was left behind. From that we made the pilot the hero who becomes a Tribulation believer living during what our

Lord described as "great tribulation, such as has not been since the beginning of the world until this time, no, nor ever shall be" (Matthew 24:21). Though there are many prophecies concerning that time, the book of Revelation contains the most complete details of that period. So we have followed it carefully, using fictional characters of newly converted believers to fulfill the detailed events in the book of Revelation.

Jerry B. Jenkins: That really was the germ of the story. When we met that's basically what Dr. LaHaye shared with me, and I recognized that it would be a great idea and something I wanted to be involved with. The follow-up question, the one that resulted in the whole series, is "what happens next?"

Question: When you envisioned this series, what reader audience were you targeting? Have you been surprised by its popularity?

Tim: I envisioned both Christians and unsaved souls as the primary audience. I was hoping to see Christians rededicate their lives to Christ in light of his coming and for the unsaved to receive him. And, yes, I have seen my dream of reaching half a million people multiplied over a hundred times.

Question: How did the LaHaye/Jenkins team come together?

Jerry: I was aware of Dr. LaHaye and his ministry, but I had never met him. I had even heard, probably back in the mid-eighties, that Dr. LaHaye had this idea called *Left Behind*, but I didn't give it another thought until our mutual agent at the time introduced us back in 1992. I had signed with Rick Christian just a few months before, and I didn't know that he represented Dr. LaHaye. Rick organized a meeting and introduced us, and we hit it off immediately. Dr. LaHaye is about the age of my mother, so there is sort of a father/son-dynamic relationship between us. I'll never forget that day we met. After we started talking, it just seemed like the right combination of an idea person and a resource person. The whole thing just blossomed from that meeting.

Question: How did the books find a home at Tyndale?

Tim: Our agent, Rick Christian of Alive Communications, shopped *Left Behind* to about a dozen publishers, and five of them bid on it. It came down to two, and Tyndale won out. Mark Taylor of Tyndale House is the one who really saw the book's potential.

Question: How has the phenomenal popularity of this series changed your life?

Tim: It has broadened my entire ministry in ways I could not imagine.

Jerry: I have had much the same reaction as many readers. I have become more aggressive about my faith, more conscious of the return of Christ, more serious about my spiritual disciplines. Needless to say, it is a writer's dream to find out that your novel is the best-selling novel in the world for 2001, which was true of *Desecration*. We got that word from *Publishers Weekly*, and what made it even more special is that on the nonfiction list the number 1 title was also by a Christian—Bruce Wilkinson's *The Prayer of Jabez*. And I was mentioning to Bruce on the phone that I know that John Grisham is also a man of faith, and he had the number 2 novel for 2001. I said, "Do we know who's number 2 on the nonfiction side? If it's a Christian, we'll have the top 4 spots." He said, "Well, actually I am, for *Secrets of the Vine*." I don't know if that will ever be duplicated—4 books by believers on top of the best-seller charts.

As we have said from the beginning, our purpose is not to have best sellers, but it is great to have that kind of coverage when the ministry is inherent in the story and people are seeing their lives changed through it. It's not just lip service when we talk about the purpose of the series. When we get letters from people who say they received Christ, it's so much better than any best-seller list or royalty check that you can imagine. If this had happened half my life ago, I might have been more impressed with the material blessings from it. Reaching those souls was our reason for writing. Nothing compares with that, and so this is clearly head and shoulders above everything else I do.

Question: In how many languages does this series appear? What kind of world market exists?

Tim: I have heard that the series has been translated into more than 30 languages.

Question: What kind of feedback are you receiving on the series?

Tim: All the feedback has been great. The books have gotten people into the habit of having daily devotions. One lady has read the series all through and plans to reread it again and again. Others have written to say what an encouragement it has been to them. This is great news to an author and the reason we write books.

Question: What book have your readers most responded to?

Jerry: People have responded most, of course, to the first book. It's got that sort of music and magic of the Rapture happening in the first chapter and setting up the whole tone of the series. I'm hoping I've grown as a writer over the years and that the books and the story have gotten better. Twenty-one judgments come from heaven during the end times and each is worse than the previous, so there is more for the novelist to work with as the series goes on. It's been gratifying to see that each book becomes more popular than the previous. Readers did respond really dramatically to *The Mark* and the idea of people facing the guillotine because of their faith. People often vote for their favorite book in the series, and the results are pretty evenly divided. Some will say, "I didn't like that one at all; I didn't think it worked. But I love this one." Then others will have the opposite view, so it's pretty even.

Question: Have you received any hate mail about the series, and if so, what are they angry about?

Jerry: Less than we expected. But I recall an irate letter from a woman who said she picked up the book not realizing it was "religious propaganda." She said she would be telling all her friends and acquaintances to avoid it. I wrote her back, telling her she had as much right to do that as we did in producing a novel with a message in it that we believe. I added that I didn't want to be flippant but that she might consider keeping the book around, just in case we proved to be right.

Question: How do you interact with people who don't believe what you write?

Jerry: Dr. LaHaye is often fond of saying that we don't separate from fellowship with people who disagree with our interpretation of the end times. He says he is confident that they will get their minds changed "in the air."

Question: What would you tell someone who claims that the Left Behind series is leading people to incorrect doctrine that will eventually disillusion them if Christ doesn't return soon?

Tim: Of course we don't say when he is to come, but in the first place, I think Rapture before Tribulation is the correct position, and I have defended it in several of my nonfiction books on prophecy. Believing the coming of Christ is imminent, which pre-Tribulationism inspires in the heart of the believer, produces three things: 1) holy living in an unholy age, 2) greater evangelism, and 3) a stronger world missions outlook. Do you think the Christians of the first 3 centuries who were motivated by this belief have any regrets that it affected the way they lived? Not at the judgment seat of Christ when they receive their rewards.

Question: What event in the series produces the most questions for readers, excluding, perhaps, the Rapture itself?

Tim: Probably the 2 signs on Chang's forehead. Some have gotten downright nasty about it. I just point them to Revelation 14:7-9 and ask them to think of Chang in the light of those Scriptures, and then we never hear from them again.

Jerry: I agree with Dr. LaHaye. It's where the Chang character is a believer, having the seal of God, and is still forced to take the mark. Some have said that scenario may be huge mistake on our part, giving people the idea that maybe they could fake the mark, or take the mark but not really mean it. I think everything was made clear in the follow-up book, where Chang got the second mark and the reader finds out that it was done against his will. He didn't worship the Beast or the Beast's image. By the time he got to the mark application station he was drugged and virtually unconscious and unable to resist.

That worked for the story because now we've got a mole who is not suspected because he has the mark of the beast. Critics say because he has that mark he's lost his salvation, but our contention is that he didn't receive it or accept it; he got it against his will, and that makes the difference. Maybe it would never happen that way, but I think we've covered the theological problems of it in the story.

Question: Will there be "bi-loyal" people (like Chang) going through the Tribulation period? If so, what evidence is there in the Bible to back this up?

Tim: Chang was not a "bi-loyal" person. The mark of the beast was forced upon him. He never bowed before the Antichrist or worshiped his image. I'm sure you are aware of the Scripture that establishes the principle that "man looks at the outward appearance, but the Lord looks at the heart" (1 Samuel 16:7). No man will spend eternity in hell because of what someone else does to him, but for his own choices every man "shall give account of himself to God" (Romans 14:12).

The mark that causes someone to be damned is something they do voluntarily as an act of rebellion against Christ and calling on the Antichrist to be their Lord. It is a symbol of their voluntarily worshiping Antichrist. Clearly, Chang did not do that! The fact that he still has the believer's seal that only other believers can see seems to be ample evidence that he is a true believer.

Frankly, I would not be surprised if something like that happens to many others during that last three-and-a-half years, which will be a time when fiendishly evil people do everything they can to persecute, humiliate, and murder true believers in our Lord. Further confirmation of our position is found in Revelation 16:1-2, where the first Bowl Judgment produces a grievous sore like a boil on "the men who had the mark of the beast and those who worshiped his image." It is obvious that those who received the mark did so as a testimony that they worshiped the Beast. By no stretch of the imagination could Chang, who resisted the mark, be in that category.

Question: What kind of impact has this series had on the world's Jewish population, since so many key characters are Jewish and Ben-Judah's declaration on international TV converted so many?

Tim: An interesting question. When you say "the Jewish population," you must understand there are many kinds of Jews, from Orthodox rabbis to liberals, conservatives, secularist skeptics, Zionists, and atheists. Actually, I have heard that some Jewish fiction lovers actually urge their Jewish friends to read the book. Some will say, "Don't pay any attention to the Christian propaganda, but they make a good read." We believe the books in the series are Jewish friendly, and some Jews see them as such. It is our prayer that the Jews who do read the books will come to find the Messiah as their Savior.

Question: Have you had any notable response from the Catholic population, considering that in the series the pope vanished and Peter Mathews was so self-serving?

Tim: Actually, far less than we expected. We went out of our way to show that the Rapture is not limited to Protestants, but as we believe, many Catholics have accepted Christ by faith as the only means of salvation. There are some Catholic purists who refuse to think any ill of their church or their popes. We have tried to point out to them that Peter Mathews was a renegade priest—and history shows there have been many...just as there have been renegade Protestant ministers. We try to stress that "the church," which is raptured, is made up of all true believers in Jesus and, let's face it, only God knows who they are.

Question: In light of the events of 9-11-01, why do you think the Left Behind sales jumped so significantly afterward?

Tim: Because millions of people suddenly became interested in prophecy, hoping God had some answers to the unsettled and fearsome future that exists in our world. Whenever world tragedy hits, people look to the Bible for answers.

Question: Okay, Jerry, if you can just share your thoughts about all the other Left Behind projects? Not just the 12 books, but all of the associated material . . .

Jerry: I'm really excited about the graphic novels that are covering the Left Behind story. I feel the work that has been done on those is the closest to the original of any ancillary product that we have. One of the things that Dr. LaHaye and I have been very firm about is that we don't want products to come from Left Behind that are just there for the sake of sales, or to try to capitalize on the popularity of this series. We want to make sure that each derivative from the original has ministry value intrinsic to it. And of all those products, I think the graphic novels are some of the best. As you know, that type of artwork, comic artwork, is very dramatic, and it really helps the story come alive. I enjoy reading them, and I am excited about how they're going to expand the audience for these books. People who have difficulty reading enjoy that kind of pictorial rendering. Graphic novels are very popular in prisons, with hobbyists who collect them, and, of course, with children.

Question: What was your original vision when you came up with the idea of a kids' series?

Jerry: The idea for a kids' series based on Left Behind really came from the publisher, and at first blush it seemed to make sense. I'd written a lot of kids' fiction in the past. The idea was to not just dumb down the product so it would be easier to read, but actually start with new main characters and have them be in the age group of the reader. So we start with 4 kids from 12 to 16. And over the period of 7 years of the Tribulation, they age by that much, of course, so it's an interesting dynamic to watch these kids grow up. They become believers early in the story, and then they have their own adventures and exiting times fighting the Antichrist while trying to keep from being exposed as believers.

Question: All the children in the Left Behind series were raptured, including unborn babies. What Bible verses support the idea in the books that 12 could be the age of accountability?

Tim: There is no specific age of accountability in Scripture. Because Jesus was 12 when he separated from his parents and discussed with the rabbis in Jerusalem, the church traditionally assumed it was about that time a child reaches the point he knows right from wrong.

Jerry: Well, we were arbitrary in the story. You don't see anybody in the books left behind under the age of 12. As a matter of fact, I think there probably will be kids under that age who are left behind because I was 6 years old when I became a believer, and I think if I knew enough to become a believer then, I could have known enough to be not a believer as well. Dr. LaHaye was 7 or so when he became a Christian. We made the decision to rapture all the children in the books just for the sake of avoiding controversy. There is, we believe, an age of accountability, which is not necessarily a biblical concept. But it just seemed to make sense to us that, with the character of God, a child would not be responsible for an eternal decision like that until he was old enough to know what the consequences are for that decision. The age of accountability would be different for every individual. When is a person old enough to understand God's grace? Only God knows. If there really is an age of accountability when Christ returns, it's going to be in God's hands. God knows a person's heart and knows a person's mind, and he knows when that person is old enough to make a decision for Christ.

Question: Some of your fans wrote you letters asking you what happened to all the pets. What did you tell them?

Jerry: One of the reasons we don't deal too much with pets in the story is that the Bible doesn't either. People always ask me, "Is my dog going to be raptured?" "Will I see my cat in heaven?" There is imagery of animals in heaven, but we don't know if they are our personal pets, and so since we don't know, we just don't say. But there are animals in the books. When earthquakes take place, animals hear it or sense it first. We see dogs running in circles and roadkill-type animals running across the street.

The reason we are not more specific is because we don't know what's going to happen. But because God is a God of love, there is a very real possibility that there will be animals that we have as friends in heaven. Whether they are our own pets, that I don't know.

Question: Dr. LaHaye, when were you convinced that the Bible taught the pre-Tribulational view, and what are your key Bible verses to substantiate this view?

Tim: Very early in life I saw the Rapture of the church happening before the Tribulation, and different from the Glorious Appearing. My parents were saved in a Bible-believing church that took the Bible literally. Once you see that even prophecy was intended to be taken literally, you discover 15 specific differences between the Rapture (1 Thessalonians 4:13-18; John 14:1-3; 1 Corinthians 15:50-58; Revelation 4:1-2; and others) and the Glorious Appearing (Matthew 24:30; Revelation 19:11-21; and others). If readers would like a more thorough discussion of this and the 15 differences between the two, they can look at Chapter 9 of our book *Are We Living in the End Times?*

Question: Who personally challenged you to study biblical prophecy?

Tim: Actually several people . . . My mother, while I was in high school. While attending Moody Bible Institute, I studied under the great scholar Wilbur Smith, then later Dr. M.R. DeHaan and Dr. David L. Cooper. I also did an enormous amount of reading prophetic literature. Looking back, when you ask who challenged me to study prophecy, I like to think the Holy Spirit, who Jesus promised "will guide you into all truth."

Question: With your love for prophecy, have you prepared a videotape, like Dr. Vernon Billings did, for those left behind to view after the Rapture? Or do you know of one that someone else has produced?

Tim: Yes, we did it through Tyndale, with an actor playing Pastor Billings. I have done several 1-hour lectures on Bible prophecy that are included in the Tim LaHaye Prophecy Institute. The 20-minute video that Tyndale produced is the one I recommend to readers, but I have heard of local pastors making such a video for their own congregation.

Question: Bruce Barnes is an associate pastor, and yet he is left behind. Do you believe there are people who think they are Christians who will be left behind?

Jerry: Yes, I do, and so does Dr. LaHaye. That's the reason for the Bruce Barnes character. We believe there are people who are putting their faith in their works or their church attendance or are phonies who have no relationship with Christ. That's the deal with Bruce. He knew the lingo, but he also knew down deep that he had never really made the transaction with Christ to become his personal Savior. When his family disappeared he knew immediately what had happened. The Rapture had occurred and he had been left behind. It happens that *Bruce Barnes* is also a first and last name of a friend of mine—a very dear, close friend. I finally heard from him, and he was really tickled that his name was in there, but he said, "Why did you have to leave me behind?" Of course, if he wasn't a believer, I never would have used his name in that context. My friend Bruce is one who won't be left behind.

Question: How did you decide that all 144,000 Jewish witnesses would survive the Tribulation?

Jerry: That's up for debate as well. Dr. LaHaye's position is that they will be protected until the end. We really vacillated on that, because there is some evidence that they are protected only for a certain amount of time. But, in the books, we have decided we're not going to depict the deaths of any of the 144,000.

Question: Who are Eli and Moishe?

Jerry: Eli and Moishe are Elijah and Moses sent back from heaven. That's an area open for interpretation. Dr. LaHaye's belief is that those would be the two prophets, because they were at the Transfiguration with Jesus. A lot of people ask why it wouldn't be Elijah and Enoch, because they are two who never died. Dr. LaHaye doesn't believe that's necessary, working from the Scripture. Some say, as the Scripture says, that "it's appointed unto a man once to die." Yet Moses died, and then in our story is killed again at the middle of the Tribulation. It's an interesting debate. It could really have gone either way.

Question: What is the significance of the rebuilding of the temple?

Tim: Look at Revelation, particularly chapter 11:1-3. Our book *Are We Living in the End Times?* has some very interesting information on the rebuilding of the temple. The Israeli government has clamped down on news of progress on that subject. And because it would ignite an unholy war, they try to keep Jewish extremists from doing something that would rock the boat.

Question: Who came up with the believer's seal, and which Scriptures describe it?

Tim: We invented the believer's seal. Scripture doesn't say one way or another. However, God sealing his servants is not a new thing. He commanded it for believers in Ezekiel 9:4, so we used that as a precedent. Anything done in the Old Testament could happen in the New. In fact, the book of Revelation quotes the Old Testament 400 times.

Question: Where did you get the idea for a global, uniform currency?

Jerry: The one global currency idea is one that Dr. LaHaye believes is also prophetic. He thinks we'll eventually get to one currency and a one-world government. So in the books I do it in stages, where the world starts by going from all the various currencies down to 3, then down to 1. It's not that far-fetched anymore. Some people think that the series itself is prophetic when they see the Eurodollar, which may be a precursor to a one-world currency.

Question: Are you aware of anything new occurring in the New Babylon, Iraq area that would make the U.N. moving there more likely? Some Bible prophecy teachers have indicated that with the United Nations located in New York City, someday it would be destroyed. With the World Trade Center buildings destroyed and the anthrax scares that impeded New York City's activities and profits, do you think it's possible that New York City could be the biblical New Babylon?

Tim: No. Babylon means Babylon. There is too much prophecy that would not be fulfilled if Babylon is not rebuilt. One thing to keep in mind, however, is there could be a space of time between the Rapture and the start of the Tribulation period. The Rapture does not start the Tribulation; the signing of the covenant between the Antichrist and Israel does. Consequently there could be sufficient time during the dreadful chaos after the Rapture to start the rebuilding and moving to New Babylon. One thing seldom mentioned is that from one half to a billion people could suddenly go up in the Rapture, leaving glaring holes in government, finance, health care, education, military, law enforcement, and every other legitimate industry in the country. That will be the most drastic shock in the history of the world. During which I believe many will turn to Christ in faith.

Question: Where did you come up with the idea of a Russian Pearl Harbor?

Jerry: The idea of an attack on Israel from the north is based on Dr. LaHaye's interpretation of what the biblical prophecies say. How it plays out in the story is, of course, just a matter of imagination. I knew that the result had to be miraculous, that God had to save his people. According to Dr. LaHaye, Israel had to be overpowered by an enemy from the north that is just unbeatable, and because of a surprise attack they really should have no chance to fight back, none whatsoever. And, as you read the incident in the series, that's the way it appears. In *Left Behind*, the Russians attack Israel with an overwhelming force, but then no damage is done to anyone or anything but the invading force. The invaders are just wiped out and their planes crash and burn. I started from Dr. LaHaye's prophecies and took off from there, and that's how the idea for a Russian Pearl Harbor came about.

Question: Do you think we are currently living in the end days predicted in the Bible?

Jerry: It's very possible that we are. I know Dr. LaHaye believes that we are. I like to tease him. He says he thinks the Lord could return in his lifetime, and then I say, "It's going to have to happen soon, then." Dr. LaHaye has a great sense of humor. As far as the timing of Christ's return, nobody knows. It could happen today. Could happen tomorrow. But I also think that God in his mercy could wait one more day, and in his economy of time that could be a thousand of our years. It would be just like him to wait until every last person has had a chance to receive Christ. But we are instructed to live as if his coming could be today. We are supposed to live in the light of Christ's imminent return, and that should make us more aggressive about our faith and more eager to make sure nobody gets left behind.

Question: How do your beliefs impact your writing?

Jerry: From the very first time I met Tim LaHaye, he made it clear that his purpose in wanting to have novels written about the end times was twofold: He wanted to encourage believers and persuade unbelievers. Basically, we're saying that we believe what the Bible says. People are born in sin, apart from God, but God loves you and wants to have a relationship with you. He has sent his only Son to live a perfect life and then to die as a sacrifice for your sins. We believe that he was resurrected the third day and sits at the right hand of the Father and that all you have to do is pray and receive Christ and tell him that you know you are a sinner and believe that he died on the cross for your sins. He will save you and you will be secure for eternity, knowing that you will go to heaven and won't be left behind. And our prayer is that you will do that and that you will find someone who can walk you through that prayer or explain it to you from the Bible. That's the whole purpose of what we are writing about, and we've heard from many people who have done just that.

Question: What's the process of writing one of these novels? They are biblically based, so how do you plan for that? And at the same time you're writing a thriller with locations all over the globe. That's got to be tricky. And how do you handle the deadline pressure of working on such massive best-sellers? Do you have any special tips?

Jerry: I just do my best, and I keep the deadlines sacrosanct. There were times when I asked for an extra week or 10 days, but I always did that early enough so that it became the new deadline. It's important to get each manuscript done on time because it takes a long time to print this many books after Tyndale does its work. It's obviously a major thing in their publishing calendar.

I get a fairly ambitious workup from Dr. LaHaye in notebook form. It lays out the Scriptures we're going to cover in the next novel. It includes his commentaries on those Scriptures, so besides having several different versions of the Bible open on my desk (and on my computer) at once, he also reproduces them in his notebook, along with his own commentary, commentaries from other people, things he's read, things he's written. I immerse myself in that stuff.

I also have an atlas, including a time zone chart. Sometimes novelists make the mistake of writing a scene in the middle of the day in China and then saying in the United States at the same time some character was having lunch. Obviously, it would be a different time in the States. I've got a pretty good amount of table space on both sides of me, with all that stuff open and available at the same time, and I'm constantly referencing the prophecies and the commentaries and interpretations of Dr. LaHaye.

Question: Jerry, how difficult is it to sit down and write each new volume?

Jerry: I have to say that each succeeding book is harder to write. I feel significant opposition with every new one, and each seems to get more difficult than the last. I count on much prayer support. As difficult as they are to write, they can also be thrilling and rewarding. I tell writing students, "If there are no tears in the writer, there will be no tears in the reader." There is tremendous pressure in writing a book that you know will sell at least 3 million copies. You could write a mediocre, or worse, book, and your career could be over in one fell swoop.

As far as technique goes, I tend to do them all in about the same amount of time. I write a certain number of pages per day, and if I finish writing by noon, fine, I can relax and prepare for the next day. If it takes me until midnight, I do that, whatever it takes. I dread the process of going in the cave and going to war as it were, but it's fun to be able do it and to finish and know it worked. But it's grueling, and it gets harder all the time.

Question: What book in the series did you enjoy writing the most and why?

Jerry: I always look forward to the next book. But, realistically, probably the first one, because it really sets the stage and introduces all the characters and starts with the Rapture. I had a lot of fun with *The Indwelling*, too, because that's such a huge dramatic event and covers just a few days, which lends itself to my style. I like a reportage style, where I cover every second in all these different places and then come to this huge climax when the Antichrist is inhabited by Satan himself. It was traumatic and fun to write. Got a lot of response to that.

Question: Which book was the toughest? Which challenged you the most?

Tim: *Soul Harvest* . . . I love the fact that our merciful God is going to use the terrible Tribulation period to win "a great multitude which no one [can] number, of all nations, tribes, peoples, and tongues" to faith in his Son (Rev. 7:9).

Question: The books are so moving and real. How do you do it?

Jerry: Not to sound overly spiritual, but that is a work of God. It's the hardest writing I do, and it's the hardest thing to make real. That's my biggest fear every time I sit in front of the blank screen—the first time and every time—because one of the things Dr. LaHaye wants in every book is what he calls a believable, reproducible conversion experience. We've all read made-up stories that can come across hokey. To avoid that, it takes longer to write these than any other scene, but I surrender that and ask God to work. All I can do is try to imagine that I'm that person. That's what novelists do. Given everything I know about this person—a skeptic, lost, they don't believe, they are desperate, afraid— what would they say? How would they respond to the truth? Would they want to believe but worry that they're just doing it to save themselves or protect themselves? What will convince them? Often, we know, it isn't in the mind where the truth penetrates; it's in the heart. God has to do the work before a person can make that decision. So it's hard, grueling, front-lines work, and the fact that readers say these scenes do work in the books is very gratifying. We hear from people all the time who say they prayed the prayer of salvation right along with the character.

Question: One of the most memorable experiences I have had regarding this series was on a flight home from Nashville. A gentleman from Alaska and I were discussing the just released *The Mark*. He had listened to the audio, but had not specifically remembered the scene at the loyalty mark center in Greece where many believers gave their lives rather than receive the mark. So we were reading it together, both in tears at the power of those last strong words of testimony from Mrs. Miklos, and Mr. and Mrs. Demeter. Jerry, how long does it take for you to write such moving scenes? And I know that you get lots of mail regarding people coming to Christ because of these books, but do you also get letters from born-again people who are stirred to live more holy lives and to speak more boldly for him? In other words, what kind of spiritual impact have these books had on your readers, other than testimonies of rebirth?

Jerry: We do get those kinds of letters, and primarily because of the very scene you're talking about. I recall many instances of writing through tears (the guard blessing Tsion rather than arresting him on the bus in *Nicolae*, the guillotine martyr scenes in *The Mark*, etc.). Dr. LaHaye himself is a great encourager and cheerleader, always asking to see more manuscript so he can find out what happens next. He believes that martyr scene was inspired and sent a note saying that he himself was challenged and emboldened by it.

Question: Why'd you set so much of the series in the Chicago area?

Jerry: From my freshman year in high school through college, I lived in the Chicago suburbs, and my first newspaper job was in Mt. Prospect, and so I know those suburbs. I grew up in Elk Grove, I drove through Arlington Heights, I knew Northwest Community Hospital, so I wanted to write about places that I know. That way I don't wind up having somebody go the wrong way down a one-way street and readers go, "Wait, that makes no sense." I read a novel once where a guy drove east out of the Chicago Loop for so many miles. Of course he would have been drowning in Lake Michigan, so that ruined the credibility of that story for me. Fiction has to be believable. You want your reader to willingly suspend disbelief, and most will do that until you just shock them with something totally irrational.

In a way it's ironic that much of this is set in Mt. Prospect, Illinois. As a teenager I worked for the *Prospect Day*, a daily. Somebody was challenging the editor's rule that all the news in this paper had to be local. A reporter said, "What if something major happens in Chicago?" The editor said, "Listen, I don't want you to write about the Second Coming unless it happens in Mt. Prospect." That always stuck with me, so I had it happen in Mt. Prospect.

Question: Do you have a personal fascination with airplanes or exotic weapons?

Jerry: The latter more than the former. Dr. LaHaye is the former pilot, so I put the plane stuff in there for him. As the first adult male in my family who didn't go into law enforcement, I have all the weapons consultants I need.

Question: Do you do a lot of research or use consultants when you write about things like weapons or airplanes?

Jerry: Yes and no. I learned the hard way I do need to do a lot of research on airplanes, because I had a consultant I thought was careful. I was guessing with a lot of the aviation stuff and assumed he was checking it, and then I started getting letters from pilots and mechanics pointing out stuff that was clearly inaccurate. I eventually got a new consultant who flies 747s and is really an expert. He has gone through all the books, and in the reprints of the early books we fixed things. That helped with consistency and accuracy.

As far as the weaponry, some of it I made up. If people write in and say there is no gun that will do that, I say you've got to remember this is set in the future. It could be 10 years, even 50 years from now. I've talked to consultants, especially on the high-tech stuff, who say that if you can imagine it, it will be here in a few years.

Question: How much research do you do on the political components of your fiction? Things Nicolae's government and the "council of ten" do seem to have a "ripped from the headlines" feel.

Jerry: I didn't use that term in the books, but people assume that's what it is. It satisfies the curiosity of people who believe in the conspiracy theories and believe there are groups like the Illuminati and the Trilateral Commission and the Bilderbergers—all those secret organizations. I'm not sure where I stand on all that stuff. There is some evidence that there could be those kinds of groups, but I didn't want to use those actual names and say they exist. But some group like those is certainly possible, and I can see an Antichrist rising out of that sort of organization. So if people think that's how it's going to happen, there is enough there in the story for them.

Question: What is something in the book that you have written so skillfully that most people haven't even recognized it yet?

Jerry: Well, my skill is rarely recognized, that's true. And I do embed lots of personal stuff that no one would recognize but my own family. For instance, the 6-digit code that Sebastian uses in Greece (0-4-0-3-0-1) is the birth date of my grandson (4/3/01).

Question: Have many of your readers noticed what you did with Viv Ivins? You know, the whole name thing? Is there significance to it?

Jerry: Yes, a lot of them have. I thought it was obvious, and I had fun with it on the Web site. If somebody would say, "Do you realize that the first 6 letters of her whole name in Roman numerals come out to VIVIVI, like 666, man?" And I'd write, "No way! Really? What a coincidence, eh?"

Question: What is the significance of 216? When do you reveal it?

Jerry: Um, I don't. And that's another one I think is really obvious. Many readers have caught it, but we still get the question every few days. It's the product of a simple equation, and that eventually gets around. It's a lot more fun to have them discover it than to have us tell it. They can just play with it for a while. People should realize that 666 is such a well-known number that it's unlikely a fast-rising new world leader would boldly use it without people saying, "Hey, wait a minute. . . . "

Question: Which book reveals the meaning of the numbers of the world map?

Jerry: Again, it's left to the reader to figure out, and many do. There are 10 regions of the world and names for them like the United Asian States, the United European States—that type of thing. Each area has also been given a number, and those numbers are very similar to 216. When you figure that out, it all comes together and makes sense.

Question: What is your favorite scene in the Left Behind series?

Jerry: I have 2, actually. The first is the scene in *Nicolae* where Buck is helping Tsion escape from Israel. They are driving across the desert in the middle of the night, having to go through checkpoints, and they finally get into a situation where there is no possibility of escape. While Buck is being processed, Tsion is hiding on the bus under one of the seats, and the guard is going to find him. When writing that scene, I didn't know what was going to happen. I write as a process of discovery. The guard finds Tsion and drags him out, but instead of arresting him, he blesses Tsion. It was a moving thing to write, and for a long time was my favorite scene in all the books. Now that I've written 12 books in the series, the one that rivals it is probably in *The Mark* where the first people face the guillotine. Men and women sing, they get smacked to the point where their skulls are broken and their teeth are shattered, but they still sing and face death with peace and courage. I get more letters about that scene than any other in the whole series.

Question: Do you have fun developing the gaudy garb for the religious leaders in the series? Where do you come up with this stuff?

Jerry: I make it up. It's crucial to have comedic breaks as some sort of tension easer because these books get darker and darker all the time. The times get terrible, and comic relief comes in the form of a buffoon in a position of authority working for the Global Community. And then if they are "religious" leaders, too, the ultimate pharisees, worshiping themselves and Carpathia and ignoring God, they deserve it.

Throughout history a lot of people have done this. The bigger they get, the more they justify more braids and buttons and hats and all kinds of adornment, so I just ran with the concept and had fun. It does make them look ridiculous, taking themselves seriously, thinking they are solemn and important and devout and sacred.

Question: You did a fantastic job of making the judgments of Revelation so vivid. Which judgment was the most challenging to write?

Jerry: They get more severe as they go, and so each one has more to offer a novelist. In one sense they become easier to write because they are so dramatic—you can really let your imagination run. One in *The Remnant*, for instance, is the utter darkness. I had a lot of fun with that because we interpret that to mean not just that the sun doesn't appear, but also that you don't see the moon, you don't see the stars, you don't see any lights, not emergency lights, not even the glow from an iridescent watchband. Nothing. I mean, people are seeing blackness and that's it, and Scripture says that they claw themselves from the pain. Now, why would darkness cause pain? I don't know, but that's what it says, so that is in the story.

I would have to say the horde of demonic horsemen was a tough one, because we're not really sure if they are real and will trample people, or if this is something spiritual that takes place only in heaven. I depicted it as visible to believers so they see what's happening. But it was a tough thing to write.

Question: Where did you come up with the idea of Dr. Rosenzweig's formula?

Jerry: The easiest answer to that is that I made it up. We needed a reason for this attack from the north, and in the scenario in the books it becomes a jealousy thing. Russia has a crucial need for this formula that allows deserts to bloom like a hothouse. And when you think of the real world, we're talking about enemies from the north, in this case Russia. They've got vast wastelands like Siberia where it's difficult to grow things, and so that seemed the right vehicle for me to use in the story.

Question: Why did you choose an airline pilot and a journalist for your main viewpoint characters?

Jerry: The airline pilot was Dr. LaHaye's idea. He used to fly small planes and is fascinated by aviation, so that fit. In the proposal, when we first shopped the opening chapter of *Left Behind* to publishers, Buck didn't even exist. That sample first chapter consisted of the conversation with the pilot and the flight attendant and the Rapture happening. But as I got into the writing, I realized I needed to have another viewpoint character to observe the events of the Rapture. I could then switch back and forth between the pilot and this new character and show the story much more easily. I chose a writer with a news weekly

magazine so that the character would have access to government leaders and get to travel all over the world.

Question: Which character do you relate to the most?

Jerry: I'd have to say Buck, because he's a journalist and that was my
background too. Plus he's young and handsome and, you know, I just
look in the mirror and I see Buck.

Tim: Rayford Steele. And the fact that I joined the U.S. Air Force to be
a pilot at 17, became a gunner on a B-29—they had too many pilots—
then took up flying at 40 years of age, became instrument and twin-
engine rated, and started a missionary aviation school has nothing to
do with it.

Question: I've heard that your readers really bond to your characters.
What death precipitated the most reader questions?

Jerry: I am often surprised at who lives and who dies. I know it still
comes from my imagination and is planted in there somewhere by
the subconscious. But my defense then to people who complain is
that I say, "I didn't kill them; I found them dead."

Bruce Barnes obviously was the first, and he was such a major
important character to all the new believers that even Dr. LaHaye
said he wished we could bring him back to life. But I convinced
him that I had another character in mind to take over as spiritual
leader of the Tribulation Force. Dr. Ben-Judah is also a beloved
character now.

Another unpopular death was that of Ken Ritz. He was a great
character. A very earthy guy. Friend of everybody. A lot like the Mac
McCullum character, but Ken was funny, he was irreverent, and his
death came very quickly and surprisingly to the reader and to me.
People wondered how you replace a guy like that. There have been
other characters, orbital characters, some that appeared for only a few
pages and seemed like fun personalities and people you would like
to know. The reality is that's how it's going to happen in those times.
People are going to die, and you can't pretend that they are not. I
couldn't keep characters just because they are favorites.

Question: When did you decide that only 1 of the first 4 Tribulation Force
members would remain until the Glorious Appearing? It appears
that as this story evolved, you were just as disappointed as your

readers when you found out which of your characters did not survive. At what point did you even know which one of the main characters would still be alive at the end?

Jerry: Basically that was extrapolated from the figure Bruce Barnes quotes; with the percentage of the world that is wiped out in plagues and famines and wars, only 1 in 4 who are alive at the Rapture will still be alive at the Glorious Appearing. Of course, statistics being what they are, that doesn't necessarily mean that only 1 of the original 4 would live. . . . But there is that implication that of our protagonists, only 1 of the 4 will be left.

Near the end of the story there would be 1 person left standing, and I always knew who it was. I do write as a process of discovery, so I suppose there was a possibility that I thought I knew who it was and would get there and discover it was somebody else. And I could have been overruled by Dr. LaHaye or my editor. But in the end, what I expected to happen did happen. I'll leave it to readers to judge how effective my choices were.

Question: Do any of the main characters resemble significant people in your life?

Jerry: Not specifically, but my mother made an interesting point. Someone asked her if she saw me in any of the characters. She said, "I see him in all the characters." I think that's insightful, and how could it be otherwise? I use composites of friends, relatives, acquaintances. A character might have someone's first name, someone else's last name, someone else's height, someone else's coloring, someone else's personality, someone else's manner of speaking. But there's going to be a little of me in there somewhere. I have to imagine how I would react and what I would say if I were that person, be he a young man or she an old woman.

Question: Is there any reason for the names you choose for your characters?

Jerry: I like names that are memorable. I don't go usually for dramatic or ethnic names unless it's like Tsion, who clearly is an Israeli, and Carpathia, who is from Romania—that type of thing. I do try to choose character names that are different from each other. I want people to be distinctive. I often combine names of people I know, using one's first name with somebody else's last name. That keeps the character alive in my mind and causes me to picture them. In some cases I use both the first and last name of someone I know, and I often hear from them eventually.

Question: Where does the name *Nicolae* come from?

Jerry: We get a lot of questions about that, because there is a verse in the Bible, Revelation 2:6, that refers to the Nicolaitans, which has nothing to do with Nicolae. People wonder why we picked that name, and why we made Nicolae a Romanian. Based on Bible prophecies, we know the Antichrist will have Roman blood. And the cliché would have been to make him Italian. We wanted to do something different. The root word of *Romania* is *Rome*, and there are Roman ancestries represented in its population. Having visited Romania, I knew Nicolae is as common a name there as Joe is in America. Nicolae's last name, Carpathia, I took from the Carpathian Mountains in that region. I didn't realize that the name of the ship that picked up survivors from the sinking of the *Titanic* was the *Carpathia* until I saw it on the screen in James Cameron's movie. I sometimes wonder if the name stuck in my memory from studying the history of the *Titanic* when I was a kid. But, in the end, I made up the name *Nicolae Carpathia*.

Question: How did you decide what type of person Carpathia would be in the Left Behind series? Was it difficult to describe the Antichrist? to decide how he would act in various situations?

Jerry: In a way, it was easy, because Scripture is clear on this. And I know Dr. LaHaye's interpretation is clear that the Antichrist, especially in the first three-and-a-half years of the Tribulation, is going to be so attractive and so articulate and so deceptive that people won't even think that he is evil at all. Some will even think he *is* Christ. And so he had to be dramatically handsome, good looking, articulate, know lots of languages, and be very smart. That was easy. I made him the epitome of a model person, someone everyone would love to be like or look like. I tried to make him completely charming. . . . When Antichrist comes, he's going to be somebody people won't even suspect at all. The Bible says that the very elect—believers—would be deceived if they weren't already sealed by God.

Question: What biblical texts support that this international leader will have Roman ancestry?

Tim: Daniel 9 is a very important passage of prophecy. In verse 26 it says after the Messiah is "cut off" (crucified) "the people of the prince who is to come shall destroy the city and the sanctuary." In AD 70, the Romans destroyed the city of Jerusalem and the sanctuary; therefore we believe the Antichrist will be a Roman.

Question: What were you thinking when you wrote about the meeting at the United Nations in which Carpathia commits murder in front of everyone, alters the memories of the unbelievers, and in the process reveals himself as the Antichrist?

Jerry: I put myself in Buck's place. He is close to making his decision, and Bruce Barnes has told him not to go into that meeting without the protection of Christ in his life. So Buck is agitated and feels the presence of evil in the room. He's scared to death. He has come to believe that Carpathia is the Antichrist, and if there is an Antichrist, there is a Christ. Buck realizes he needs to be on the right team when he goes in there. So Buck makes his decision. When Carpathia commits the murders and tells people they didn't see what they saw but rather makes them remember what he wants from his perspective, Buck is the only one protected against that, because he had the Spirit of Christ in him.

Question: Why did Carpathia want to move his seat of government to Babylon?

Jerry: We think that it is clear in Scripture that the new head of the world government is situated in Babylon, and eventually Babylon is destroyed. We don't see any evidence of any mention of America or of the United States in prophecy. That made it impossible to have an international headquarters in the USA. We just think it's unlikely that Antichrist's HQ would be in America. Of course, we don't know that the biblically predicted seat of world government will be the United Nations either; that was strictly a vehicle for me as a novelist. I had to imagine a person suddenly coming into power over the whole world and what structures might already be in place that could allow that to happen. So I picked the U.N. Of course, the United Nations is not a governing agency—it's a representative agency—and some readers said, "Are you shooting at them, saying they are part of this evil structure?" I'm not. I suppose there are things to criticize about the U.N., but in these books I use it strictly as a literary device. Whoever the Antichrist is and whatever structure he uses to govern the world, we believe his headquarters will be in Babylon.

Question: Jerry, at what age did you know you had a love for writing? Who influenced you the most in your writing career?

Jerry: Writing always seemed to come easier to me than to my friends. In high school, when others moaned about having to write papers, I felt a little guilty because I preferred that to other kinds of projects. There were a lot of influences on my writing career. I'd have to say my mother the most because she is a lover of words. She loved to do anagrams, and my dad liked the cross-word puzzles, and we played a lot of word games. My mother saved a poem I wrote when I was 12, among other little things I wrote to her when I was a kid. But I didn't think of it as a career until I was in high school and got injured playing sports. I had thought I wanted to be a professional baseball player. It's all I ever wanted to do. Whether I ever had the ability for it, nobody will ever know, but when I got hurt, I went into sports writing for the school paper. I realized almost immediately that I had found my niche. It was just a perfect fit for me. I don't think I was a good writer then, but I was sort of natural at it, and better than most, and it wasn't hard for me. I had a lot to learn, but I loved it. I was soon stringing for local papers (even at 14 and 15 years old), and I was a full-time sports editor of a suburban Chicago daily by the time I was 19. For several years I did do that, until I branched out into other kinds of writing.

Question: If you weren't a writer, what would you be doing?

Jerry: I'd like to be involved in the sports world. Probably in the front office of a major league baseball team, something like that. It sounds like fun.

Question: Jerry, how did you become a Christian?

Jerry: I personally came to faith in Christ when I was 6 years old in March of 1956. My 2 older brothers were with my father at a father-and-son banquet at church. I was too young to go, and so I was home playing in the living room. My mother was a good mom. She let me ride the back of the couch like a horse. She always says that really says more about the couch than it does about her parenting, but being up there and pretending like I was a cowboy put me at eye level with a famous painting of Christ knocking at the door. I asked my mother what that was about because, having been a church kid all my whole 6 years, I thought I knew all the Bible stories, but I didn't know what story that was. And she explained to me that it wasn't actually a story from the Bible, but it was symbolic and I, of course, had never thought symbolically up to that point—and maybe haven't since either—but I caught what she meant. She said that door was actually the door to my heart, and there is no handle on the outside because Jesus won't open the door. He just knocks, and it's up to me to open the door, and I did that night. As young as I was, I understood that I needed God's forgiveness and Christ in my heart. And so I trace my salvation to that day.

Question: What is your favorite Scripture?

Jerry: I have several favorite verses, and the one I use most often when I sign a book is Matthew 5:16: "Let your light so shine before men, that they may see your good works and glorify your Father in heaven." It's a verse that I try to take personally. I also love Psalm 91:1-2. And rather than try to quote it for you, which I probably wouldn't be able to do because it always makes me emotional, I just urge you to look that up, and you'll find probably the 2 greatest phrases ever translated into English.

Question: What are some of your hobbies?

Jerry: I play tournament and club Scrabble, and I like to play online occasionally, when I have time. I also play Boggle online. I play racquetball and I play at golf. I've been playing too long to still be as spectacularly bad a golfer as I am, but I still enjoy it.

Question: What do you do in your spare time?

Jerry: I really like to visit my kids. My oldest son and his wife live in Los Angeles and have given us our first grandchildren—a grandson named Samuel Dallas, whom we call Sammy D., and Maya Rachel, and they have another on the way. Our second son, Chad, is a college baseball coach in the Midwest. And our youngest son, Mike, is a student at Colorado Christian University, about 80 miles from us.

Question: Has someone special ever made you the cookies with the chocolate hearts on them?

Jerry: You betcha. My wife of more than 3 decades.

Question: Could you share some information with the fans on some of the other projects you are involved in?

Jerry: In 2001 my oldest son, Dallas, and I formed a film company called Jenkins Entertainment. And our first movie, *Hometown Legend*, came out in January 2002. (There is also a novel from Warner Books, which I wrote.) It's a high-school football picture. We try hard in this movie to avoid the typical sports clichés, and we are proud of the film. It opened theatrically in the South on about 30 screens and then we expanded a little bit to the North. Warner Brothers Home Video distributes the video and DVD and has also sold it to HBO and ABC Family Network.

Our main purpose is to do quality work and compete in the general marketplace. We don't want to surrender the arts, especially movies, to the world. Rather than curse the darkness, we want to light a candle. While we may disagree with Hollywood's messages, we have to acknowledge that they make the best movies on the planet, and so we just hope to make more and better films, striving for their level of achievement but with our message.

Question: Could you talk a little about your work with other writers?

Jerry: For many years I admired the work of an old friend, Norman Rohrer, who founded and had been the sole driver behind the Christian Writers Guild, an association of writers learning the trade and trying to get published. I bought the Christian Writers Guild from Norm and kept him on as dean of instruction. Meanwhile we have rewritten the material—a 2-year, 50-lesson course—and we have done a fairly heavy advertising campaign. We now have nearly 2,000 students and are adding about 100 new students a month. We team each with a widely published mentor; we have more than 3 dozen seasoned veterans who coach these people via e-mail. If people would like to see what it's all about, check us out at www.christianwritersguild.com. It's been a way to give back to the writing field, which has been so good to me. I want to restock the pool of Christian writers.

Question: So what have you done with the organization?

Jerry: The first conference for the Christian Writers Guild under the new management was in San Diego in May of 2002. I spoke at the Friday night banquet of the local Christian Writers Guild there and then the next day we had a 1-day seminar.

Our national conferences are held at the Broadmoor Hotel in Colorado Springs every February. We have a spectacular lineup of speakers and some of the best-selling writers in all the Christian market. These are people who write their own books and who also challenge writers to holiness. And we have a lot of individual workshops in various specialty areas, so these really are fantastic conferences.

Question: So, really, what is your favorite book in the series?

Jerry: It's like choosing a favorite among one's kids, though the first title has a certain amount of music to it. It sets the stage and the tone, and starting with the Rapture in the first chapter gave me a real advantage as a novelist. All those characters who knew the evangelical lingo were gone, and those left behind are desperately searching for truth. And they find it in their own language, not ours. I think that has been one of the secrets of the success of the series. Even the skeptical reader finds credible characters he can identify with and who speak his language. Readers have their own favorites, and most say it's *Left Behind*. After that, the polls are pretty even.

Question: Do you have something that you'd like to say directly to your fans who will be reading this handbook?

Jerry: I'd just like to take this opportunity to thank all you readers and fans of the Left Behind series for supporting it. As we said all along, this is about a lot more than sales and best-seller lists. These books are really about persuading unbelievers and encouraging believers with the story of what is going to happen in the end times, based on our interpretation of Bible prophecy. And so many of you have written and encouraged us and passed the books along and shared your faith. It has been the privilege of a lifetime to be involved in a project like this. Thank you very much.

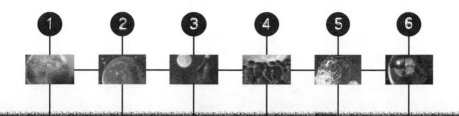

ARE YOU A LEFT BEHIND EXPERT?

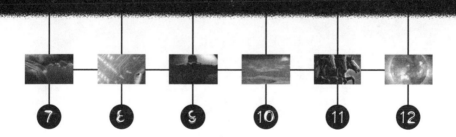

THE SERIES IN BRIEF

The 12 volumes of the Left Behind series were written over many years, and even the most ardent fan can forget a few details of such an epic along the way. If you are reading or rereading the series and need a quick refresher, here are the basic story lines of the books, stripped to their bones. These synopses obviously contain spoilers, so read only the appropriate portions to refresh your memory.

1

LEFT BEHIND

In one cataclysmic moment, millions around the globe disappear. Vehicles, suddenly unmanned, careen out of control. People are terror stricken as loved ones vanish before their eyes. In the midst of global chaos, airline captain Rayford Steele must search for his family, for answers, for the truth. As devastating as the disappearances have been, the darkest days may lie ahead.

WHO WOULD GUESS that a transatlantic flight from Chicago to London could end so bizarrely? One minute Rayford Steele is entertaining lustful thoughts about his attractive senior flight attendant, Hattie Durham. The next he is involved in a global crisis that will change his life and the world forever. Although happily married for over 20 years, Rayford has recently grown tired of his wife's incessant talk of religion and begins to toy with temptation. At the very moment Rayford is thinking about her, Hattie is busy serving the passengers, including world-famous reporter Cameron "Buck" Williams, an award-winning writer for *Global Weekly* magazine.

In that instant, everything changes. Rayford, Buck, and Hattie are left behind, along with everyone else in the world who does not have a personal relationship with Jesus Christ. Those left behind are faced with the dilemma of figuring out what just happened. But Rayford has a pretty good idea—his wife's Rapture talk must have been true.

Suspecting he will find his house empty and his wife and son gone, Rayford turns the plane back to Chicago. As soon as he lands, he goes on a desperate journey for answers. Irene and Raymie, his 12-year-old son, are indeed missing, and Rayford frantically seeks out someone from their church for help. He meets grief-stricken visitation pastor Bruce Barnes. Bruce was a pastor for years, talking the talk of a Christian but never internalizing the message taught at New Hope Village Church. Through Bruce's guidance and Dr. Billings's Rapture tape, Rayford finds peace amidst his heartache and accepts Jesus Christ as his personal Savior.

Rayford sets out to share the Good News with everyone he meets. First he presents the truth to his 20-year-old daughter, Chloe. Just home from Stanford and resistant at first, Chloe's excuses melt when God meets her needs in a very personal way. In the middle of her spiritual decision making she is introduced to Buck Williams, who is curious about her father's slant on the disappearances. Rayford in turn introduces Buck to Bruce Barnes. Bruce shares the truth about the Rapture and prophecies from the book of Revelation. The renowned newshound is now in hot pursuit of the story behind the disappearances, searching for meaning and spiritual truth to share with his readers.

In the meantime, Rayford also shares Christ's message with Hattie, trying to right their relationship. Hattie refuses the message and feels spurned and alone, leaving her vulnerable when Buck introduces her to rising political figure Nicolae Carpathia. An unexpected career change leaves Hattie at the side of the man Rayford and his friends believe may be the Antichrist. Buck attends a meeting where he sees Carpathia murder 2 men and brainwash witnesses to forget what they saw. Having become a believer just before the meeting, Buck is protected from Carpathia's mind control and left with no doubt about the identity of the Antichrist.

Despite everything, Rayford has reason for hope. Armed with the truth and knitted with Bruce Barnes, Chloe Steele, and Buck Williams, he determines to live on in these perilous times with resolute faith and new purpose. As members of the Tribulation Force, the 4 friends seek to tell as many people as possible about the message of hope in Christ and the coming events of the Tribulation.

2

TRIBULATION FORCE

Rayford Steele, Buck Williams, Bruce Barnes, and Chloe Steele band together to form the Tribulation Force. Their task is clear, and their goal is nothing less than to stand and fight the enemies of God during the 7 most chaotic years the planet will ever see.

ENLIGHTENED BY THE BIBLICAL TEACHINGS of Bruce Barnes, Rayford, Buck, and Chloe thrive in their newfound faith. They attend New Hope Village Church, where Bruce shares his discoveries about the biblical prophecies for the coming 7 years of tribulation. Their faith and knowledge prepare them for the trials to come. The members of the Tribulation Force share their faith and biblical perspectives with coworkers, though many refuse to listen.

Bruce becomes an evangelist and travels the world, while the other Tribulation Force members witness to Hattie. But Hattie is on top of the world—involved with the most powerful man on earth, wearing his diamond on her finger, and pregnant with his child—and she remains spiritually unresponsive.

As the Tribulation Force members grow in their faith, their relationships also develop. Buck and Chloe's friendship blossoms into love in spite of several misunderstandings. Rayford also meets someone special—the very attractive Amanda White, who attended a Bible study with Irene Steele prior to the Rapture. Over the course of 18 months, between good-byes and hellos, these romances bloom. Both couples tie the knot in a simple double ceremony officiated by Bruce.

With Buck and Rayford working as Carpathia's employees, the couples manage to get through the first year and a half of the Tribulation. Rayford flies Carpathia around the world, while Buck travels worldwide in his new position as publisher for *Global Community Weekly*. Buck conducts fascinating interviews with 2 rabbis, Marc Feinberg and Tsion Ben-Judah, and with the Archbishop of Cincinnati, Peter Mathews. He even has a meeting with the two witnesses, Eli and Moishe, who preach at the Wailing Wall in Jerusalem. Although Carpathia generously fills their pockets, Rayford and Buck both miss their loved ones as they jaunt all over the world and are increasingly uncomfortable working for the Antichrist.

When the Tribulation Force gets together again, their peaceful world is destroyed and worldwide chaos erupts. Just as Revelation predicted, World War III rides in on a red horse. The final pages of the book reveal the unbelievable: Bruce Barnes, the Tribulation Force's spiritual leader, is dead.

3

NICOLAE

The 7-year tribulation is nearing the end of its first quarter, when prophecy says that "the wrath of the Lamb" will be poured out upon the earth. Rayford Steele becomes the ears of the tribulation saints at the highest levels of the Carpathia regime. Meanwhile, Buck Williams attempts a dramatic all-night rescue run from Israel through the Sinai.

AFTER THE DEATH of Bruce Barnes, Rayford Steele humbly accepts his new role as leader of the Tribulation Force. Rayford still pilots for Carpathia, and thanks to Earl Halliday's secret bugging system on the Condor 216, he keeps the Tribulation Force abreast of Carpathia's doings. Rayford gets wind of the coming Chicago bombings and is able to warn his family. Chloe barely escapes—in fact, she ends up in a tree. Buck frantically searches for her and finally rescues her.

While Rayford pilots Carpathia, other members of the Tribulation Force are home in Mt. Prospect comforting Loretta and planning Bruce's memorial service. They make sure that Bruce's teachings continue with the help of Donny Moore, the computer and phone expert.

Soon Buck hears from his good friend, Dr. Chaim Rosenzweig, an Israeli statesman and inventor. Chaim is distressed to report that Tsion Ben-Judah's wife and children have been murdered. Using the assumed identity Herb Katz, Buck heads to Israel for a dramatic rescue. Even in the midst of his grief, Tsion draws strength from his new Christian faith. Michael Shorosh, along with Ken Ritz, Buck's pilot friend, assists in the harrowing but successful escape from Israel.

Meanwhile, Rayford meets with Hattie in New Babylon. She feels spurned by Carpathia even though she is carrying his child. Rayford makes another attempt to share his faith with her, but she refuses to listen and is offended when Rayford urges her not to get the abortion she seeks. Buck, Chloe, Loretta, and Amanda also meet with Hattie. They continue to love her unconditionally, but Hattie distances herself from the Good News and remains troubled by her pregnancy.

Tsion and Buck make it back to Mt. Prospect just in time for Bruce's memorial service. Under the questioning eye of Verna Zee, Buck's boss, Loretta has to avoid revealing Tsion's identity. Tsion hides out in New Hope Village Church's secret shelter.

Rayford is back in New Babylon when the wrath of the Lamb earthquake strikes, and he barely escapes with Nicolae Carpathia. Cities are leveled, millions are killed, loved ones are unaccounted for . . . and the Tribulation Force members know that more death and destruction lie ahead.

4

SOUL HARVEST

**As the world hurtles toward the Trumpet Judgments
and the great soul harvest prophesied in Scripture,
Rayford Steele and Buck Williams begin searching
for their loved ones from different corners of the world.
Soul Harvest ranges from Iraq to America, from 6 miles
in the air to underground shelters, from desert sand to
the bottom of the Tigris River, from hope to devastation
and back again—all in a search for truth and life.**

THE WRATH OF THE LAMB earthquake shakes an already chaotic
world. Tribulation Force members are isolated and trapped in its
aftermath, unable to discover who has survived. In one corner of the
world Rayford frantically searches for Amanda. On the other side of
the globe, Buck travels from one makeshift hospital to another in his
hunt for Chloe.

Buck discovers that death has struck New Hope Village Church.
Loretta and Donny Moore have fallen, but Tsion Ben-Judah is miraculously found alive amidst the rubble. Finally Buck finds Chloe and
rescues her from the GC's clutches. Although Chloe is badly injured,
Buck rejoices that she is alive and is shocked to learn that she is pregnant.

In his search for Amanda, Rayford secures the assistance of Mac

McCullum, Carpathia's copilot. Although Carpathia tells Rayford that Amanda is dead in a plane crash, Rayford refuses to believe it. Carpathia also insinuates that Amanda was a GC plant. Rayford is desperate to know if his wife is alive and if she was genuine and true to her faith and to him. He and Mac take a dive in the Tigris and find Amanda's body in the wreckage of the plane.

Mac is spiritually hungry after living through several of the judgments, and he picks Rayford's brain and heart about the catastrophic world events. Rayford worries that Mac could be a spy for Carpathia, but he also knows Mac could be a true seeker. Mac becomes a believer and starts going on missions for the Tribulation Force.

The whereabouts of Hattie Durham are unknown until she contacts the Tribulation Force. Again they reach out to her, rescuing her from a reproductive clinic and the GC forces trying to harm her. With bullets flying all around them, Buck and Ken barely escape with their lives and take Hattie back to the safe house. Dr. Charles looks after her health, but her spirits remain low. While suffering from strange symptoms, she still refuses to accept God's forgiveness.

The first 2 Trumpet Judgments devastate the earth's population, and the meeting of the witnesses is postponed for 10 weeks. Wormwood also splashes upon the earth, poisoning the water supply. But in the midst of this chaos, believers find joy in the realization that God has sealed his own with the mark of the cross on their foreheads, visible only to fellow believers.

5

APOLLYON

The world holds its breath as the Tribulation Force ventures to Jerusalem for the great Meeting of the Witnesses, where tens of thousands defy the Antichrist to sit under the ministry of their pastor-teacher, Tsion Ben-Judah. The fifth Trumpet Judgment—a plague of scorpion-like locusts led by Apollyon, chief demon of the abyss—is so horrifying that men try to kill themselves but are not allowed to die.

GREAT EXCITEMENT HOVERS over Teddy Kollek Stadium in Israel as over 75,000 believers gather to hear Tsion Ben-Judah teach. Although Leon Fortunato and Nicolae Carpathia make an unwelcome appearance, many believe Tsion's message that Jesus is the Messiah. Chaim Rosenzweig, however, remains skeptical, and his Jewish background keeps him from receiving Jesus as Messiah. Although Chaim remains unconvinced of the truth despite Buck, Chloe, and Tsion's witness, he continues to extend them warm hospitality.

While most of the team is in Israel, Rayford receives welcome news from Hattie. She confirms that Amanda was a true believer and that she loved Rayford dearly. Carpathia and his cohorts had planted the incriminating information, and none of it was true. Hattie also reveals that Carpathia poisoned Bruce Barnes—and Hattie herself!

Rayford continues to reach out to Hattie with spiritual truth, but she wrestles with her unworthiness and can't believe that God could forgive her.

The Tribulation Force members make another harrowing escape out of Israel, but this time tragedy strikes. Ken Ritz is killed by the GC, and Buck barely escapes death as he falls while trying to board the plane.

Later, Dr. Charles and Leah Rose assist Hattie as she miscarries. She becomes more depressed than ever and reveals to Rayford that she wants to kill Carpathia. Rayford secretly desires to kill him too. Hattie's heart remains hardened to the gospel, and even world-renowned spiritual leader Tsion Ben-Judah cannot penetrate her refusal to see the truth. The pain of a locust sting—the scourge of unbelievers around the world—does not draw Hattie to a personal relationship with Christ.

At the safe house, Chloe, pregnant and concerned for Buck's safety, begins to implement Ken Ritz's plans for an International Commodity Co-op.

In Jerusalem, Carpathia embarrassingly negotiates with the two witnesses to have the fourth Trumpet Judgment lifted. He has to admit that his accusations concerning the Tribulation Force were false and announces that the members of the Tribulation Force are now free to travel.

An angel makes an announcement, causing many to be terrified, including Chaim. But this heavenly messenger is still not enough to convince Chaim of his need for Jesus. Even after Chaim gets stung, the loving care of Hannelore, Hannelore's mother, Jacov, and Buck fails to break open his heart to the gospel.

Apollyon ends with Abdullah Smith, a pilot friend of Mac's, hurrying to get Buck home from Israel for the birth of his first child. Chloe is having complications in the last days of her pregnancy, and Dr. Charles is concerned. Buck makes it just in time to share in the birth of a healthy baby boy, Kenneth Bruce Williams.

6

ASSASSINS

The Tribulation Force hurtles toward the 4 murders foretold in prophecy. Antichrist himself is prophesied to suffer a lethal head wound. As a supernatural horde of 200 million demonic horsemen slays a third of the remaining population, the Tribulation Force prepares for a future as fugitives. Yet another Force member dies, and others join as crises draw them around the globe.

RAYFORD, CHLOE, and Buck are all stateside in the Mt. Prospect safe house, along with Tsion, Dr. Charles, and 10-month-old Kenny Bruce. Hattie is still recovering from her poisoning and locust sting, while Chloe finds joy in her new experience of motherhood. Rayford is edgy, seething with anger, and filled with despair over so many lost lives. The Tribulation Force members also voice concern for Dr. Charles's health—his eyes are yellow and his energy is waning. When Dr. Charles dies, Rayford's rage against Carpathia erupts and he begins to pray that he will be the one to fulfill the prophecy of Antichrist's death.

Tribulation Force members learn that Hattie has run off with Bo's brother, Samuel Hanson. Although her plane was reported down, they know she faked her own death.

In the meantime, Mac and Abdullah deliver 144 computers to believers in Kuwait. When they set out again to meet Mwangati Ngumo, the 200 million horsemen wreak havoc. A forced landing and an ambush leave many on the Condor 216 dead. Both Mac and Abdullah require medical attention, but they are glad to be alive.

When gathering stashed cash from Leah Rose's garage, Rayford and Leah meet up with GC Peacekeepers. A demonic intervention by the horsemen allows them to escape back to the muggy Mt. Prospect safe house, where their nerves become more frayed.

Back in New Babylon, Carpathia and Leon plot against the two witnesses and Peter the Second. David Hassid even hears Carpathia praying to Lucifer. Peter ridicules Carpathia for not being able to control the two witnesses, which adds more fuel to the fire. Plans are made to assassinate the leader of the Enigma Babylon One World Faith.

Tribulation Force members continue to travel the globe. Buck flies to Israel and checks on his good friend, Chaim. He finds Rosenzweig in good spirits but exhibiting strange behavior, like purchasing a wheelchair and spending long hours filing metal in his workshop. Rayford, along with his new believing friends, Dwayne and Trudy Tuttle, heads for Europe to find Hattie. They narrowly escape a GC ambush. When Rayford flies to Al Basrah to obtain a Saber, he returns to the café to find the Tuttles murdered by GC troops.

Three months later, Tribulation Force members are traveling again. Rayford drops Leah off in Brussels to check on Hattie; then he heads to Israel for the Global Gala. Buck brings honored guest Chaim Rosenzweig to the Gala, although Chaim appears incapacitated by a stroke. The Global Gala opens with speeches, fanfare, partying, and the assassination of the two witnesses. True to Scripture, they rise again after 3 days and ascend into heaven. An earthquake follows but does not halt the rest of the week's activities.

In the crowd at the Gala, Rayford aims his Saber at Carpathia but finds himself unable to fire. He is bumped and the gun goes off accidentally. The next thing anyone knows, world potentate Nicolae Carpathia lies on the stage, mortally wounded. But who is the assassin?

7

THE INDWELLING

The members of the Tribulation Force face their most dangerous challenges. Some are murder suspects; others test the precarious line between subversion and being revealed. It's the midpoint of the 7-year tribulation. A renowned man is dead, and the world mourns. In heaven, the battle of the ages continues to rage until it spills to earth and hell breaks loose.

CHAOS BREAKS LOOSE in Israel following the assassination of Nicolae Carpathia. Rayford barely escapes from Israel to Greece, and Buck happens upon a gruesome scene at the Rosenzweig estate. As Leah searches for Hattie in the Belgian Facility for Female Rehabilitation, tensions mount for Chloe and Tsion at the safe house. Chloe fears that her precious son will fall into the GC's hands and prepares to commit infanticide before allowing this. Tsion tries desperately to dissuade her.

The news reports that Rayford is Carpathia's assassin, but Buck soon learns the truth that Chaim killed Carpathia. Buck and Chaim hide out until they can get back to the States. Chaim finally accepts Christ as their plane crashes. Buck and Chaim survive, but their pilot, T, is killed.

While Buck and Chaim are being rescued, Greek believers bring refreshment and rest to soothe Rayford's soul before he heads for home.

In New Babylon, David busily works to assist the Tribulation Force despite being sidetracked by requests for a giant statue and phenomenal funeral plans for Carpathia.

Tsion reaches new heights in his prayer life. He experiences a vision in which he sees the angels Michael and Gabriel and images from Revelation.

Word gets out that the safe house in Illinois has been compromised, and the Tribulation Force goes into high gear. Albie, posing as GC Deputy Commander Marcus Elbaz, saves the day, but not without tension. The Tribulation Force relocates to the Strong Building in downtown Chicago.

Back in New Babylon, the sun is not the only thing cooking. At Carpathia's funeral, his statue begins to speak, commanding the crowds to worship it. Leon Fortunato calls down lightning from heaven, frying 3 of the 10 potentates. But all this is overshadowed when movement is detected in the casket. As the crowds watch, astonished, the assassinated potentate rises from the dead. Now indwelt by Satan, Carpathia speaks Jesus' words, then gives dire warnings for those who oppose him.

THE MARK

His Excellency Global Community Potentate Nicolae Carpathia is back. Resurrected and indwelt by the devil himself, the Beast tightens his grip as ruler of the world. Terror comes to the believers in Greece as they are among the first to face the benignly named but hideous guillotine death contraption, the loyalty enforcement facilitator. The gloves are off, and the battle is launched between the forces of good and evil for the very souls of men and women around the globe.

AS THE GREAT TRIBULATION BEGINS, Rayford, Chloe, and Buck reside in the new safe house, the Strong Building. Chaim is taking in the teachings of Tsion Ben-Judah while recuperating from injuries sustained in the plane crash. After a heroic rescue in a Humvee, Z busily supplies new IDs to Tribulation Force members for their missions.

In New Babylon, David frantically searches for the love of his life, Annie. In his search he suffers heatstroke and collapses. His hospitalization opens a new friendship with another believer, Hannah Palemoon. Through Hannah, David learns the devastating news of Annie's death.

Stateside, Tribulation Force members again find themselves rescuing Hattie Durham. Hattie tries to commit suicide, but God is not finished with her yet. Rayford and Albie rescue her with the help of Buck's old boss Steve Plank, now known as Pinkerton Stephens. On the way back to the Strong Building, Hattie makes the decision Tribulation Force members have prayed and hoped for: she makes peace with God through Jesus Christ!

As soon as Albie returns, he is off to Greece with Buck as they try to bring encouragement and aid to the incarcerated members of the underground church. While there, they see firsthand the brutality of the loyalty enforcement facilitators. It is almost too much for them to bear as they watch Mrs. Miklos, Pastor and Mrs. Demeter, and other church members walk the road to martyrdom. But their deaths are not without hope, for the martyrs lead many to Christ within their last earthly moments. Albie and Buck succeed in saving 2 teenage believers from the blade, then leave Greece, bringing Ming Toy, a former GC employee now AWOL, with them. She joins the other Tribulation Force members at the Strong Building.

The Mark ends with Rayford outlining the next mission: Operation Eagle. On the other side of the world, Mac, David, Hannah, and Abdullah stage their own deaths in the crash of the remote-controlled Quasi Two. They head for Mizpe Ramon to assist in Operation Eagle. Chaim and Buck arrive in Israel for a face-off with Carpathia. Hattie also arrives in Israel on her first Tribulation Force mission.

DESECRATION

Believers in Jerusalem must flee or take the mark of the beast. Nicolae Carpathia, no longer pretending to be a pacifist, has ordered every Morale Monitor armed as he prepares to travel along the Via Dolorosa and then onward to the temple, where shocking surprises await. The lines are drawn between good and evil as God inflicts the first Bowl Judgment upon the flesh of those who have taken the mark, while his chosen ones flee to the wilderness.

OPERATION EAGLE soars into motion in the first pages of *Desecration*. Albie introduces a new believer, military pilot George Sebastian. George comes heavily equipped with firepower, and although Rayford declines it at first, it eventually comes in handy at Petra. David Hassid is killed by GC Peacekeepers outside Petra, and his death rocks everyone, especially Hannah and Chang.

Back in New Babylon, Chang struggles with his loyalty mark. Peace of mind finally arrives when he discovers that he was drugged and given the mark against his will. He hopes he can somehow convince his parents to forget Carpathia and give their allegiance to Christ.

With the sores judgment striking Carpathia's worshipers, most of them itch without relief. Many are incapacitated so severely that they can't meet the demands of their jobs. As they seek medical relief, they leave the Global Community even more poorly staffed than before.

In the meantime, Carpathia mocks the Stations of the Cross by riding a pig down the Via Dolorosa and speaking at Calvary. Prompted by a visit from the archangel Michael, Hattie speaks out at Calvary against both Fortunato and Carpathia. Fortunato calls lightning from the sky and kills her. Chaim gathers her ashes for a remembrance, and her death prompts both Chaim and Buck to action.

Another desecration occurs when Carpathia sacrifices the pig in the temple. Many of his followers lose respect for him, horrified by his lewd and murderous behavior. Even some of his own staff sharply disagree.

Chaim, as Micah, negotiates with Carpathia for the release of Jews from Israel. Although Carpathia reverses his promise of safety, Operation Eagle is successful and a million are transported to Petra.

As the 2 teenage escapees from the Greek detention center, Marcel Papadopoulos and Georgiana Stavros, eagerly await freedom in America, Georgiana is killed and replaced by a GC plant, Elena. She kills K, Miklos, and Marcel, and George is taken captive.

Stateside, Chloe brings a new group of believers to the Strong Building. The believers of The Place offer prayer support and colorful praise and song to the safe house. Happy to be back in action, Chloe leaves for Greece with Mac and Hannah to rescue George Sebastian.

Those in Petra watch anxiously as GC fighter-bombers appear overhead. As Tsion prays and Carpathia watches with glee, the bombs begin to fall.

10

THE REMNANT

Global Community Supreme Potentate Nicolae Carpathia has his enemies right where he wants them: massed at Petra, a million strong—within reach of 2 bombs and a missile no one could survive without a miracle. The Trib Force's aliases and even their Strong Building safe house have been compromised, forcing Rayford Steele, Buck Williams, and all members to flee for their lives while trying to maintain their overt opposition to Antichrist. All pretense is gone as the planet hurtles toward Armageddon and the ultimate showdown between good and evil.

TO NICOLAE CARPATHIA'S HORROR, Petra is miraculously protected from his attack. The bombs fall, but believers are able to stand in the flames unharmed and give glory to God.

In Greece, Mac, Hannah, and Chloe work courageously to rescue George Sebastian. They are aided by the believers of the Greek co-op. George is finally able to escape his captors and meets up with the Tribulation Force members. With the intervention of the angel Michael, the rescue team gets safely out of the country. Later they are devastated to learn that the GC raided the Greek co-op and killed all the believers on the night of their escape.

Back in the States, Ming Toy disappears. She travels to China with Ree Woo in search of her parents. Ming learns that both became believers before her father was killed by the GC. She witnesses the angels Christopher, Nahum, and Caleb preaching and is promised that she and her mother will live to see the Glorious Appearing.

In Petra, God supplies manna and water for residents and even keeps their clothes from wearing out. Tsion and Chaim continue their teaching ministries from there.

The Tribulation Force learns that the Strong Building has been compromised and they evacuate, relocating to Long Grove, Illinois, and San Diego. Chloe continues to run the co-op from San Diego, and Rayford and others go on a mission to exchange wheat from Argentina for water from India.

As God pours out more Bowl Judgments, Carpathia's followers suffer. The bloody waters, blast-furnace temperatures, and painful utter darkness add to their disillusionment with their once-revered leader. Spiritual warfare rages as Tsion has a face-off with Leon Fortunato, and Carpathia's false messiahs perform miracles all over the globe.

11

ARMAGEDDON

The scattered Tribulation Force is drawn inexorably toward the Middle East, as are all the armies of the world, gathering for the battle of the ages. By the time of the war of the great day of God the Almighty, homes have been uprooted, new alliances forged, and the globe has become a powder keg of danger. Who will be left standing when the battle leaves the Tribulation Force on the brink of the end of time and the Glorious Appearing?

IN BLINDING DARKNESS, with Naomi close at hand, Rayford and Abdullah rescue Chang from New Babylon. While on the rescue, Rayford meets a talkative new character, Otto Weser, who has a small band of believers residing in this evil metropolis.

Back in San Diego, Chloe sees something on the motion detectors and goes outside to investigate, where she is picked up by the GC. Although her dad and husband lament their inability to intervene on her behalf, God graciously ministers to Chloe through his angel Caleb. She is able to give a testimony to the world before her execution, and Caleb appears to blind those watching as she goes to the guillotine.

On the other side of the world, Albie meets with Mainyu Mazda for a wiretapping job. The deal sours, and Tribulation Force members learn that Albie has been murdered.

San Diego believers evacuate their underground compound and travel to Petra. The Whalums, Leah Rose, Hannah Palemoon, and Z also arrive for Albie and Chloe's memorial. These Tribulation Force members express great love for their martyred friends, and they reminisce about Albie's and Chloe's love for Christ.

On a happier note, Ree and Ming are married soon after the memorials. Another romance blossoms as Chang and Naomi run the tech center within the walls of Petra.

Nicolae Carpathia relocates his government from the darkness of New Babylon to Al Hillah. Soon after, New Babylon is destroyed as prophesied. For over 6 years Carpathia has stashed nuclear weaponry in Al Hillah. Under his command, GC forces now distribute these weapons. Six months later Baghdad becomes Carpathia's new headquarters, the place where he gathers world leadership and commissions Ashtaroth, Baal, and Cankerworm. Their mission is to go forth and gather all the armies of the world to fight against God and his people.

As the book comes to a close, everyone is gearing up for the Battle of Armageddon. As prophesied, the Euphrates River dries up and armies amass. Against Rayford's advice, Tsion and Buck fly to Jerusalem. Tsion teaches here, leading many to Messiah. But in the siege on Jerusalem, Tsion is killed, and Buck is gravely wounded

Many key Tribulation Force members man the perimeter of Petra. Although Sebastian has fun ordering the firing of the DEWs at the GC army, now known as the One World Unity Army, his smiles fade as the real shells blast. Rayford is badly injured on an ATV outside Petra. The battle draws closer, with the welfare of Buck and Rayford unknown.

GLORIOUS APPEARING

Antichrist has assembled the armies of the world in the Valley of Megiddo for what he believes will be his ultimate triumph of the ages. With a victory here he would ascend to the throne of God. The Tribulation Force has migrated to the Middle East, most ensconced at Petra with the Jewish remnant. But only 1 of the 4 original members of the Force remains alive, and he is near death. It's been just over 7 years since the Rapture and almost exactly 7 years since Antichrist's covenant with Israel. Believers look to the heavens for the glorious appearing of Christ, as the world stands on the brink of the end of time.

THE REMAINING TRIBULATION FORCE members attempt to find and assist their beloved comrades in the faith. In the Old City of Jerusalem, Mac McCullum finds Buck's body and must report the news of his death. Meanwhile, Leah, Abdullah, and Razor rescue the badly injured Rayford and return him to the safety of Petra.

As the Unity Army advances, the residents of Petra restlessly await the coming of Christ. Believers are reassured as clouds, meteorites, and finally a massive cross appear in the sky. This long-awaited sign of the Son of Man brings miraculous healing to all in Petra.

Finally, the heavens open and Jesus Christ appears. Believers watch in awe as the Unity Army is massacred at Jesus' words. No matter where they are in the world, believers are able to speak to Jesus face-to-face and hear him speak to them personally.

Ashtaroth, Baal, and Cankerworm are brought before Jesus for judgment, as are Nicolae Carpathia and Leon Fortunato. The Antichrist and the False Prophet are thrown into the abyss. Finally, Lucifer is brought for judgment, and after declaring that Jesus is Lord, he is chained and thrown into the lake of fire.

One final judgment separates the sheep from the goats. Then believers witness the rewarding of Old Testament saints and tribulation martyrs. The final pages of *Glorious Appearing* rejoice in the reunions of those parted by the Rapture or death. Believers eagerly await the beginning of the millennial reign of Christ.

But there is one last ominous threat: "But after these things [Satan] must be released for a little while" (Revelation 20:3).

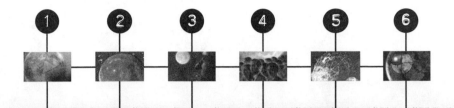

THE
LEFT BEHIND
TRIBULATION
TIMELINE

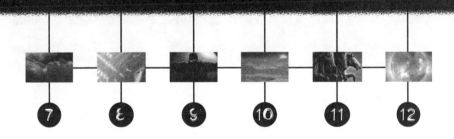

FIRST HALF
OF THE TRIBULATION
3½ YEARS
(1,260 DAYS OR 42 MONTHS)

RAPTURE OF ALL CHRISTIANS (I THES. 4:16-17; REV. 3:10)

 SEAL JUDGMENT #1
White Horse—Antichrist comes in conquering power and promises peace (Rev. 6:1-2).

ANTICHRIST MAKES A COVENANT WITH ISRAEL

THE TRIBULATION BEGINS

THE TWO WITNESSES OF REVELATION BEGIN THEIR MINISTRY (REV. 11:3)

 SEAL JUDGMENT #2
Red Horse—war and bloodshed (Rev. 6:3-4).

SEAL JUDGMENT #3
Black Horse—famine and disease (Rev. 6:5-6).

SEAL JUDGMENT #4
Pale Horse—pestilence and death (Rev. 6:7-8).

SEAL JUDGMENT #5
The martyrs of the Tribulation (Rev. 6:9-11).

 SEAL JUDGMENT #6
Great earthquake (Rev. 6:12-17).
144,000 witnesses (Rev. 7:1-8).

 SEAL JUDGMENT #7
Trumpet Judgments—silence in heaven (Rev. 8: 1-2).

LEFT BEHIND
(BOOK ONE)

TRIBULATION FORCE
(BOOK TWO)

NICOLAE
(BOOK THREE)

THE LEFT BEHIND

TRIBULATION TIMELINE

TRUMPET JUDGMENT #1
Hail, fire, and blood—a third of the earth, trees, and grass is burned (Rev. 8:7).

TRUMPET JUDGMENT #2
A mountain of fire—burning mountains plummet into the sea (Rev. 8:8-9).

TRUMPET JUDGMENT #3
A star called Wormwood (Rev. 8:10-11).

TRUMPET JUDGMENT #4
Darkness descends—sun, moon, and stars darkened by ⅓ (Rev. 8:12).

TRUMPET JUDGMENT #5
The locusts of Apollyon attack (Rev. 9:1-11).

TRUMPET JUDGMENT #6
The 4 angels released—plague of horsemen kills ⅓ of the people (Rev. 9:13-19).

TRUMPET JUDGMENT #7
Loud voices in heaven—worship of Christ in heaven; lightning, earthquakes, and hailstorms on earth (Rev. 11:15-19).

THE MARK OF THE BEAST BEGINS (REVELATION 13:16-18)

MIDPOINT OF THE TRIBULATION

SOUL HARVEST
(BOOK FOUR)

APOLLYON
(BOOK FIVE)

ASSASSINS
(BOOK SIX)

THE INDWELLING
(BOOK SEVEN)
THE MARK
(BOOK EIGHT)

SECOND HALF
OF THE TRIBULATION
3½ YEARS
(1,260 DAYS OR 42 MONTHS)

ANTICHRIST ENTERS AND DESECRATES THE TEMPLE— ABOMINATION OF DESOLATION (DANIEL 9:27; MAT. 24:15)

BOWL JUDGMENT #1
Foul and loathsome sores (Rev. 16:2).

BOWL JUDGMENT #2
The sea turns to blood (Rev. 16:3).

BOWL JUDGMENT #3
The rivers and springs turn to blood (Rev. 16:4-7).

BOWL JUDGMENT #4
The sun scorches men (Rev. 16:8-9).

BOWL JUDGMENT #5
Darkness on the Beast's kingdom (Rev. 16:10-11).

DESECRATION
(BOOK NINE)

THE REMNANT
(BOOK TEN)

ARMAGEDDON
(BOOK ELEVEN)

THE LEFT BEHIND

TRIBULATION TIMELINE

BOWL JUDGMENT #6
The Euphrates dries up (Rev 16:12).

BATTLE OF ARMAGEDDON, ARMIES OF THE WORLD DESTROYED *(REV. 19:19-21)*

RETURN OF CHRIST TO EARTH *(REVELATION 19:11-21)*

BOWL JUDGMENT #7
The greatest earthquake in history (Rev. 16:17-21).

BEAST AND FALSE PROPHET THROWN INTO THE LAKE OF FIRE *(REV. 19:20)*

SATAN BOUND IN THE ABYSS *(REV. 20:1-3)*

THE MILLENNIAL KINGDOM—1,000 YEARS

CHRIST RULES FROM JERUSALEM *(REV. 20:4-6)*

"BUT AFTER THESE THINGS [SATAN] MUST BE RELEASED FOR A LITTLE WHILE" *(REV. 20:3)*.

GLORIOUS APPEARING
(BOOK TWELVE)

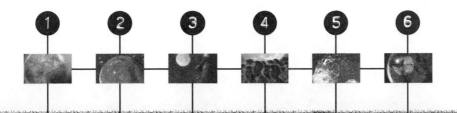

FACTS
BEHIND
THE FICTION

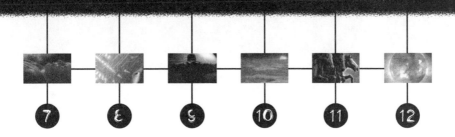

WHAT ARE THE
END TIMES?

Behind the fiction of the Left Behind books are
more than 1,000 verses of biblical prophecy. Here's
a brief overview of the prophecy behind the events
portrayed in the Left Behind series. For a more
thorough discussion of any of these topics, check out
Are We Living in the End Times? by Tim LaHaye and
Jerry B. Jenkins or go to leftbehind.com.

"THE LAST DAYS," "the time of the end," and "the end of the age"
are terms used in discussing the end times. To what do these terms
refer and when will they occur?

In most cases the terms for the "last days" or "end times" refer to
a period of time predicted in the Bible that may encompass no more
than 7 to 10 or so years. No one can pinpoint it more accurately
because no one is certain how much time will elapse between the Rapture, which ends the church age, and the beginning of the Tribulation,
begun by the signing of the covenant between the Antichrist and Israel
(Daniel 9:27). Some prophecy scholars think the end times will be just
a matter of days, but other estimates go as high as 50 years (though
that opinion was written over 75 years ago. Many modern scholars are
confident that if that writer were living today he would shorten his estimate to about 1 to 3 years, in view of the many new signs of the end
that have come to light during the last century). If one assumes that
the Antichrist's covenant with Israel follows the Rapture by a very short
time, an estimate of 3 to 10 years is reasonable.

A similar expression ("afterward") from Joel 2:28-32 refers to that same period of time. It is included here because it is so significant, for it prophesies that during those "last days," just before and during Israel's seventieth week (the Tribulation), from the Rapture to the Glorious Appearing, the Holy Spirit will again be poured out on the earth like on the day of Pentecost, leading millions to the Savior. Like the other passages, one must examine the context to see what is meant. In this case believers expect the Holy Spirit to move in the hearts of people at the beginning of the Tribulation and culminate with the second coming of Christ. This outpouring will occur during the ministry of the 144,000 Jewish witnesses spoken of in Revelation 7 who see "a great multitude which no one could number" come to faith in Christ.

In short, the "last days," "end times," the "latter days," or even "afterward," usually refer to any point from just prior to the Rapture to the Glorious Appearing itself. While some references may refer to trends during the church age, most of them point to the 7 to 10 or more years, a period that pinpoints the end of "the times of the Gentiles" to the end of the "Great Tribulation."

Jesus rebuked the people of his day for failing to recognize the "signs of the times" that heralded his first coming, calling them "a wicked and adulterous generation" (Matthew 16:3-4). They should have discerned the times, for centuries before, Daniel and other Hebrew prophets had predicted his coming. Simeon and Anna, mentioned in Luke 2, found in their studies of these prophecies sufficient cause to prompt them to go to the temple where they found the Christ child.

How much more reason do people have today to recognize the signs of his second coming! We are surrounded by so many obvious signs that one would have to be blind not to see them, yet some fail to recognize them even when they are called to their attention. Never in history have so many legitimate signs of Christ's return existed.

Of course, there is a difference between true signs of his coming based on Scripture and those that are inferred or imagined. In 1996 a popular TV preacher wrote a best-selling book, prompted by the cruel assassination of Israeli statesman Yitzhak Rabin. The book, based on the author's imagined significance of Rabin's signing the peace accord 2 years before, considered Rabin's untimely death to be a sign of the end. The truth is that the death of Rabin or any other world leader signifies only the anarchy predicted by the Bible for the end of the age. No significant Scripture links any specific leader to any peace treaty until the Antichrist is revealed and signs a 7-year peace accord with

Israel (Daniel 9:27). That *would* be a sign of the end, but not the assassination of any current world leader, no matter how prominent.

For more than 1,900 years God has largely refrained from unmistakably intervening in the affairs of men as he did in the days of ancient Israel. That will change as history enters the end times. There have been many miracles in that time, of course, but they have been confined mostly to believers, and even then he has not always intervened in a way that would cause skeptics to acknowledge his existence. During these years he has confined his expressions of his existence primarily to creation, the Scriptures, his Son's life and teachings, and the power of the Cross as it changes the lives of those who come to him in faith.

While we hear a lot about the shortcomings of the church today, there are thousands in the body of Christ who are doing a good job of getting his message out to the people of the world. That is why there is such an incredible turning to God today in many parts of the world. The church is considered the "lampstand," or light of the world, in this age, and some in the church have done an extraordinary job of fulfilling their destiny.

That is about to change as we enter "the time of the end." As soon as the church is raptured, God will again begin to visibly intervene in the affairs of mankind. Russia and her allies will go down to destroy the nation of Israel but will themselves be destroyed supernaturally by God (Ezekiel 38–39). No one knows for sure whether this precedes or follows the Rapture; a case can be made either way. One thing is apparent: Russia's attack and the Rapture are the number 1 and 2 end-times events. They are followed by the rise of Antichrist, the day of God's wrath, the two witnesses, the 144,000 Jewish evangelists, and many other acts of divine intervention during the Tribulation. There will be so many signs that atheism will not be widespread during that period; amazingly, it will be supplanted by open and blatant rebellion against God.

The Tribulation will be followed by the majestic intervention of God in the glorious return of Christ to the earth to set up his thousand-year kingdom, followed by heaven or eternity.

The "time of the end," as Daniel called it, or "the last days," as the apostles referred to it, is that short period of 7 to 10 or more years of enormous change for this world as almighty God brings this age to an end by his supernatural intervention. God's people need to study the prophetic Scriptures so they can both be prepared themselves and help others prepare for his coming.

The good news is that this world will not end in chaos as the secularists predict. The Bible says Christ will come to solve the world's problems by introducing the greatest period in world history, the millennial kingdom of Jesus Christ. No one knows for certain when Christ will return or whether we are really living in the end times. We believe, however, that Christians living today have more reason than those of any generation before us to believe that Christ could come in our lifetime. For example, all prophecy scholars agree that the generation that saw Israel restored to her land in 1948 could well be the "generation [that] will certainly not pass away until all these things have happened" (Matthew 24:34, NIV). In other words, before this strategic generation passes from the scene, time, as we know it, will come to an end.

When you examine all the "signs of the times" that have been fulfilled in our lifetime, you have to believe the coming of Christ is very near. As Jesus said, "Near—at the doors!" (Matthew 24:33). This generation does indeed have more solid reason to believe Christ could come in our lifetime than any before us. Yes, we could indeed be living in the end times!

We hope that everyone who reads this book will be prepared for his coming at any moment. Don't be like the majority, "ashamed before Him at His coming" (John 2:28). We pray that you will be ready when he comes!

The story is told of a little girl who had trouble sleeping one night. Her bedroom was upstairs, and her parents were downstairs reading. First she asked for a glass of water, then a cookie, and then she wanted to know what time it was. Finally her parents' patience ran out, and they warned her to go to sleep, threatening to punish her if she called them again.

The best she could do was lie there, watching the ceiling and listening for the striking of the grandfather clock downstairs. When the clock struck 11, something must have gone wrong mechanically, because as she counted the hours, the clock tolled 11 and kept on going: 12, 13, 14. When the clock tolled 18, she threw caution to the wind, jumped out of bed, ran downstairs, and cried, "Mom, Dad—it's later than it's ever been!"

That is what we are saying to you—prophetically, it is later than it has ever been. We pray that you will live every day as though Jesus could come at any moment, because no generation of Christians ever had more reason for believing he could come in their lifetime than does ours!

THE RAPTURE

CNN showed via satellite the video of a groom disappearing while slipping the ring onto his bride's finger. At a burial, three of six pallbearers stumbled and dropped a casket when the other three disappeared. When they picked up the casket, it too was empty.

—Left Behind

ONE OF THE MOST compelling prophetic events in the Bible is called the "rapture" of the church. It is taught clearly in 1 Thessalonians 4:13-18, where the apostle Paul provides us with most of the available details:

"The Lord Himself will descend from heaven with a shout, with the voice of an archangel, and with the trumpet of God."

"The dead in Christ will rise first."

"Then we who are alive and remain shall be caught up together with them in the clouds."

We shall "meet the Lord in the air."

"We shall always be with the Lord."

The word *rapture* comes from a fourth-century Latin vulgate translation of the Greek word *harpadzo* (occurring in 1 Thessalonians 4:17) and has been picked up by many as the best single word to express the event it describes. Some translators have rendered that word "caught up," which is a good term.

In 1 Corinthians 15:51-52 Paul unveiled what he called a "mystery" —that Christians "shall all be changed [transformed]—in a moment, in the twinkling of an eye." This mystery was revealed primarily by the apostle Paul; it is not mentioned either in the Old Testament or by Jesus in the Olivet discourse. Some think John alludes to it in Revelation 4:1-2.

Enoch in the Old Testament provides an illustration of this transforming experience. The Bible says, "Enoch walked with God; then he was no more, because God took him away" (Genesis 5:24, NIV). A day is coming when all believers will be transformed like the godly Enoch, whose earthly body was suddenly made fit to be in heaven with God. In Paul's terms, this happens when "this corruptible [our bodies] has put on incorruption, and this mortal has put on immortality" (1 Corinthians 15:54).

The Rapture, then, is not only for those Christians who "are alive and remain" at the coming of Christ, but includes all believers from the day of Pentecost (when the church began) to the day Christ returns for his church.

We prefer to call this miraculous event of the Rapture "the blessed hope," the term Paul uses in Titus 2:13: "Looking for the blessed hope and glorious appearing of our great God and Savior Jesus Christ." That is exactly what the Rapture is—a blessed hope.

When the Bible uses the word *hope* here, it does not mean a nice thing we earnestly suspect might happen, but rather a certified fact of the future, promised by God's unfailing Word. In this case, *hope* means a present, confident expectation of a certain future event. It is this hope that has characterized believers in Christ for 2,000 years. When a loved one dies he awaits this resurrection when the dead rise first and then those believers who are still alive are transformed to go to be with the Lord. And this is no temporary respite, a brief vacation from earthly difficulties! Paul adds, "so shall we *ever* be with the Lord." Now *that's* hope!

As for what happens during the Rapture, the Bible has a lot to say. The best passages to describe the Rapture are John 14:1-3; 1 Thessalonians 4:16-17; and 1 Corinthians 15:50-58. Note these details carefully!

1. The Lord himself will descend from his Father's house, where he is preparing a place for us (John 14:1-3 and 1 Thessalonians 4:16).

2. He will come again to receive us to himself (John 14:1-3).
3. He resurrects those who have fallen asleep in him (deceased believers whom we will not precede; 1 Thessalonians 4:14-15).
4. The Lord shouts as he descends ("loud command," 1 Thessalonians 4:16, NIV). All this takes place in the "twinkling of an eye" (1 Corinthians 15:52).
5. We will hear the voice of the archangel (perhaps to lead Israel during the 7 years of Tribulation as he did in the Old Testament; 1 Thessalonians 4:16).
6. We will also hear the trumpet call of God (1 Thessalonians 4:16), his last trumpet for the church. (Don't confuse this with the seventh trumpet of judgment on the world during the Tribulation in Revelation 11:15).
7. The dead in Christ will rise first. (The corruptible ashes of their dead bodies are made incorruptible and joined together with their spirit, which Jesus brings with him; 1 Thessalonians 4:16-17).
8. Then we who are alive and remain shall be changed (made incorruptible by having our bodies made "immortal"; 1 Corinthians 15:51, 53).
9. Then we shall be caught up [raptured] together (1 Thessalonians 4:17).
10. With them in the clouds (where dead and living believers will have a monumental reunion; 1 Thessalonians 4:17).
11. To meet the Lord in the air (1 Thessalonians 4:17).
12. To "receive you to Myself." Jesus takes us to the Father's house "that here I am, there you may be also" (John 14:3).
13. "And thus we shall always be with the Lord" (1 Thessalonians 4:17).
14. The judgment seat of Christ (2 Corinthians 5:10). At the call of Christ for believers, he will judge all things. Christians will stand before the judgment seat of Christ (Romans 14:10; 2 Corinthians 5:10), described in detail in 1 Corinthians 3:11-15. This judgment prepares Christians for . . .
15. The marriage supper of the Lamb. Just prior to his coming to earth in power and great glory, Christ will meet his bride, the church, and the marriage supper will take place. In the meantime, after the church is raptured, the world will suffer the unprecedented time of the wrath of God, which our Lord called the Great Tribulation (Matthew 24:21).

A QUICK HISTORY OF THE PRE-TRIBULATION VIEW OF THE RAPTURE

For several years opponents of the pre-Tribulation position have argued that the position was invented by John Darby in the mid-1800s and was never mentioned before that. Quite simply, this argument is false.

The Reverend Morgan Edwards was a Baptist pastor in Philadelphia who described a pre-Trib return of Christ for his church in his 1788 book *Millennium, Last Days Novelties*. Although he saw only a 3 ½-year tribulation, he definitely saw the Rapture occur before that Tribulation. What is even more interesting is that he claimed he had preached and written the same thing as early as 1742. He may have been influenced by John Gill before him or by others whose writings or teachings were available at that time but have not been preserved.

What is known for certain is that the Protestant Reformation resulted in a proliferation of Bibles being translated, printed, and made available to common people. The gradual development of prophetic understanding through history is understandable; it progressed along with the availability and study of the Bible.

By the nineteenth century, it is said that "prophecy was in the air," particularly at Trinity College of Dublin, Ireland, where John Darby and other prophecy scholars attended between 1800 and 1830. Darby claimed he got the inspiration for his understanding of a pre-Trib rapture in 1828 after he saw the distinction between Israel and the church in his study of the book of Ephesians. Few scholars who do not make that distinction see a pre-Trib rapture of the church. In fact, separating Israel and the church is one of the major keys to rightly understanding Bible prophecy. Second is taking the prophetic Scriptures literally whenever possible.

Most (if not all) premillennialists believe in a Rapture. They differ in that some think they will be raptured in the middle of the Tribulation; the "pre-wraths" think the Rapture will occur about three-quarters of the way through; and the post-Tribs believe in a yo-yo type of Rapture (snatched up to come right back down). We are convinced that the only view that takes into consideration all the Scriptures on the Blessed Hope and the Glorious Appearing is that Christ will rapture his church before the Tribulation. What is at stake here is whether the church will go through any, part, or all of the Tribulation. (Note: Only the pre-Tribulation position allows sufficient time for the judgment seat of Christ and the marriage supper of the Lamb.)

Consider these 4 reasons why we believe that the Rapture will occur before the Tribulation begins:

1. The Lord himself promised to deliver us. One of the best promises guaranteeing the church's rapture before the Tribulation is found in Revelation 3:10: "Because you have kept My command to persevere, I also will keep you from the hour of trial which shall come upon the whole world, *to test those who dwell on the earth*" (emphasis added). Adherents to the mid- and post-Trib positions suggest God will keep us on earth *through* the Tribulation. This is difficult to reconcile, however, with other passages that teach that few, if any, believers will populate the earth when he comes "with power and great glory" at the end of the Tribulation. Instead, the saints who have been kept from wrath are with him as he descends to this earth.

2. The church is to be delivered from the wrath to come. The promise in 1 Thessalonians 1:10 ("Jesus . . . delivers us from the wrath to come") was given by the Holy Spirit through the apostle Paul to a young church planted on his second missionary journey. He had only 3 weeks to ground this church in the Word of God before being driven out of town. Many of his teachings during that brief period evidently pertained to Bible prophecy and end-time events, since this letter— one of the first books of the New Testament to be written—emphasizes the Second Coming, the imminent return of Christ, the Rapture, the Tribulation, and other end-time subjects. These topics may indicate what subjects Paul considered essential for new converts.

3. Christians are not appointed to wrath. First Thessalonians 5:9 makes it clear that God did not "appoint us to wrath" (the Tribulation) but to "obtain salvation," or deliverance from it. Since so many saints will be martyred during the Tribulation, there will be few (if any) alive at the glorious appearing of Christ. This promise cannot mean, then, that he will deliver believers *during* the time of wrath, for the saints mentioned there (the tribulation saints) will *not* be delivered; in fact, most will be martyred. To be delivered out of it, the church will have to be raptured before it begins. Since the Tribulation is *especially* the time of God's wrath, and since Christians are not appointed to wrath, then it follows that the church will be raptured *before* the Tribulation. In short, the Rapture occurs before the Tribulation, while the Glorious Appearing occurs after it.

4. The church is absent in Revelation 4–18. The church is mentioned 17 times in the first 3 chapters of Revelation, but after John (a member

of the church) is called up to heaven in chapter 4, he looks down on the events of the Tribulation, and the church is not mentioned or seen again until chapter 19, when she returns to the earth with her bridegroom at his glorious appearing. Why? The answer is obvious: *She isn't in the Tribulation*. She is raptured to be with her Lord before it begins!

THE GREAT LIE

Scripture teaches that a great lie will be published and believed by the masses left behind after the Rapture. The apostle Paul describes it like this:

> The coming of the lawless one [the Antichrist] is according to the working of Satan, with all power, signs, and lying wonders, and with all unrighteous deception among those who perish, because they did not receive the love of the truth, that they might be saved. And for this reason God will send them strong delusion, that they should believe the lie, that they all may be condemned who did not believe the truth but had pleasure in unrighteousness. (2 Thessalonians 2:9-12)

This passage teaches that the people left behind on earth after the Rapture will believe "the lie," a gargantuan, bald-faced untruth presented to the public with "all unrighteous deception."

No one knows for sure what this "lie" will be, but in *Tribulation Force* we imagined that it would be a carefully designed fabrication created to "explain away" the Rapture. We imagined that the religious-minded would be given an "explanation" like this: "Those who opposed the orthodox teaching of the Mother Church were winnowed out from among us. The Scripture says that in the last days it will be as in the days of Noah. And you'll recall that in the days of Noah, the good people remained and the evil ones were washed away."

For the more secular and irreligious crowd, we created another "explanation": some confluence of electromagnetism in the atmosphere, combined with an unknown atomic ionization process generated by the world's nuclear power and weaponry stockpiles, was triggered by some natural cause such as lightning, resulting in the instantaneous disappearance of millions of persons worldwide.

The actual lie that will be perpetrated is unknown to us, but we do know its purpose: to discount and discredit the work of God in the world and to allow men and women to follow their own evil lusts. Whatever the lie is, that's what it does.

IS THE RAPTURE CLOSE?

One of the chief characteristics of the Rapture of the church is that it will be sudden, unexpected, and will catch people by surprise. Some students of Scripture will anticipate "the season" or general period, but as our Lord said, "No man knows the day or the hour." Which is why we should so live as to "be ready, for the Son of Man is coming at an hour when you do not expect Him" (Matthew 24:44). Only the pre-Tribulation rapture preserves that at-any-moment expectation of his coming.

God, in his wise providence, has designed Bible prophecy in such a manner that the Rapture has appeared imminent to Christians of every generation. Nothing is a better motivator than to believe Jesus could come at any moment! An imminent Rapture moves us to greater consecration, to holy living in an unholy age, and to evangelism and missions (both giving and going). None of the other Rapture theories have such an effect on the body of Christ.

While we do not assert that our brethren who are looking for the Savior after the Tribulation are deceived by the devil, we do not think their positions do anything to motivate the body of Christ to heed the Savior's words "occupy till I come" (Luke 19:13, KJV).

Since the Scriptures teach that the Rapture occurs prior to the Tribulation, it is reasonable to ask how much time will pass before the Tribulation. The answer is simple: no one knows! One of the greatest misconceptions about the pre-Trib rapture is that it starts the Tribulation. It does not. Daniel 9:27 is clear: the signing of the covenant between the Antichrist and Israel begins the 7-year tribulation, *not* the Rapture. The Rapture could happen a day, a week, or several years prior to the signing of that covenant.

In *Left Behind* we arbitrarily put the Rapture 2 weeks prior to that signing. We must confess, we just assumed that would give Nicolae Carpathia (the name we gave to the Antichrist) time to organize his takeover of the One World Government. In actuality, it may take 2 months or 2 or more years.

> Therefore, beloved, looking forward to these things, be diligent
> to be found by Him in peace, without spot and blameless; . . .
> but grow in the grace and knowledge of our Lord and Savior
> Jesus Christ. (2 Peter 3:14,18)

This "blessed hope" of ours contrasts sharply with the "no hope"
of the unbelievers referred to in 1 Thessalonians 4:13. What a vast gulf
stretches between that "blessed hope" of Christians and the "no hope"
of non-Christians! And the gulf can be bridged only by a true salvation
experience.

This "no hope" lifestyle is unnecessary for anyone reading this
book. For as the apostle said, "If we believe that Jesus died and rose
again, even so God will bring with Him those who sleep in Jesus"
(1 Thessalonians 4:14). And what is it that all must do to have this
blessed hope? Believe in the death of Christ for our sins and his
resurrection! If you do not believe that, we urge you to confess
your sins directly to Christ and invite him into your life to become
your Lord and Savior. If you would like to receive Christ by faith
but are not sure how, we suggest you pray the following prayer or
one like it:

> Dear Heavenly Father, I believe you sent your Son Jesus to
> die on the cross for my sins and the sins of the world. I also
> believe you raised him from the dead and that he is soon com-
> ing again to set up his kingdom. Therefore, today I confess my
> sin of rebellion to you and invite Jesus into my heart to become
> my Lord and Savior. The best I know how, I give myself to him
> and declare that I would like to serve him as long as I live.
> Amen.

This matter is of such great importance that we urge you to examine
your heart to make sure you have invited him into your life. If you
have any doubt about ever having done so, erase it today by calling
on the name of the Lord, and receive his salvation. Accepting Christ's
offer of salvation helps you avoid the traumas of the Tribulation on
earth even as it allows you to enjoy eternity with Christ.

If you already are a Christian, may we suggest that in light of what
you have just read, you surrender your life to him and cooperate with
him in making you holy. As the apostle Peter looked ahead to the
coming of the Lord, he gave the following advice to all Christians:

Therefore, since all these things will be dissolved, what manner of persons ought you to be in holy conduct and godliness, looking for and hastening the coming of the day of God, because of which the heavens will be dissolved, being on fire, and the elements will melt with fervent heat? Nevertheless we, according to His promise, look for new heavens and a new earth in which righteousness dwells. Therefore, beloved, looking forward to these things, be diligent to be found by Him in peace, without spot and blameless; . . . but grow in the grace and knowledge of our Lord and Savior Jesus Christ. To Him be the glory both now and forever. Amen. (2 Peter 3:11-14, 18)

THE ANTICHRIST

IN THE BIBLE, we find a number of descriptions of Antichrist, the last ruler of this world:

The Son of Perdition
The phrase "son of perdition"("man doomed to destruction" in the NIV) is applied to only 2 people in the Bible: Judas Iscariot and the Antichrist. And while nowhere in Scripture does the Bible ever explicitly say that the Antichrist is indwelt by the devil, a careful reading of Revelation 12 and 13 leads many Bible scholars to believe that after the devil is defeated by the angelic forces and forcibly ejected from heaven at the midpoint of the Tribulation, he enters the body of the Antichrist and in God's temple declares himself to be God.

The Little Horn
The wicked activities of the Antichrist were first foreseen by the prophet Daniel, who saw him as a "little horn" (see Daniel 7, 9). These passages describe his arrogance, egomania, blasphemy . . . and ultimate

destruction. From Daniel we also see that Antichrist will be a descendant of those who destroyed the temple in A.D.70. In *Left Behind* we imagined that the Antichrist, whom we named Nicolae Carpathia, would come from Romania, a former eastern-bloc nation that retains much of its ancient Roman heritage. Daniel 9 is also where we hear for the first time of the "abomination of desolation," in which Antichrist halts the sacrifices in the rebuilt temple and proclaims himself to be God, thus starting the Great Tribulation.

The Man of Sin
The apostle Paul tells us a little more about the coming Antichrist. His name for this wicked ruler is "the man of sin." Paul agrees that the Antichrist will sit in the temple of God and there proclaim himself to be God (2 Thessalonians 2:3-4).

The Beast
The apostle John gives us many more details about the Antichrist in the book of Revelation. John's special name for this godless world leader is "the Beast," although he first introduces the Antichrist not as a beast but as a conquering king (Revelation 6:2,4). He is a master diplomat and resolves disputes between countries by charisma and tact. But soon he turns his fearsome military machine on his enemies in a horrific World War III, and the result is a catastrophic loss of human life: a quarter of the world's population is wiped out. Can you see why he is called "the Beast"? In Revelation 13 John makes it plain that the Beast's power and authority and kingdom are given to him by Satan (verse 2).

A Poor Imitation
The Antichrist is scheduled to be the last ruler of this world—just before Jesus comes. While the unredeemed people of the world will fall down to worship him during the second half of the Tribulation, by the end of the Tribulation only one name will be worshiped: Jesus Christ, the King of kings and Lord of lords. At his return, the whole world will know it made a gargantuan error by mistaking Satan's cheap imitation for the real thing.

THE TRIBULATION

With handshakes, embraces, and kisses on both
cheeks all around, the treaty was inaugurated. . . .
Only two men on the dais knew this pact signaled
the beginning of the end of time. The seven-year
"week" had begun. The Tribulation.
—Tribulation Force

THE FIRST HALF OF THE TRIBULATION

Former president George Bush did not originate the idea of a "new
world order." He merely popularized the phrase. Satan, the master
conspirator, had just such a world government in mind centuries ago.
God revealed that hellish plan to his servant-prophet Daniel more than
5 centuries before Christ was born; and history has unfolded exactly
as predicted.

Daniel's Prophecy of the End
Daniel was the first prophet to write about the Antichrist's one-world
government, and interestingly enough, the prophecy was given in a
dream to the man whom historians consider the most absolute dictator
in world history.

In his dream King Nebuchadnezzar saw a beautiful statue with 4 distinct parts, each part inferior to the section above it. Under pain of death, the king demanded that his astrologers and soothsayers tell him the vision and its interpretation, something they could not do. Daniel the Hebrew prophet, however, inquired of the living God, who revealed both the dream and its interpretation. Daniel prefaced his remarks to the king by saying, "There is a God in heaven who reveals secrets" (Daniel 2:28). He then predicted there would be 4 successive world governments, and in the last days just before the Messiah came to establish his kingdom, 10 kings would form one final world government. This prophecy is so significant that it would be worth your time to read both the vision and its interpretation. . . . You'll find it in Daniel 2:31-45.

The Accuracy of Daniel's Tribulation Prophecy

When prophecy is accurate, critics often suggest that it must have been written after the events occurred. But Daniel wrote his book long before this prophecy came to pass; yet here we are, 2,500 years later, and it has been fulfilled exactly as he predicted. In fact, his prophecy was so specific that for many years it was fashionable to suggest that an unknown author wrote it long after the 4 world governments were in place. Skeptics said the reason the prophecies were so accurate was that the writer (whoever he was) was merely writing history, not prophecy.

Unfortunately for those skeptics, archaeologists have discovered copies of Daniel's prophecy dated from well within the period of the second (or Medo-Persian) kingdom. There is no question today that Daniel's prophecy was accurate history written in advance. And that, of course, can happen only by divine revelation.

It is important to note that many have tried to conquer the world and become a fifth world leader. Genghis Khan, Napoleon, Adolf Hitler, Joseph Stalin, and many others have tried, all to no avail. The Bible said there would be 4 world governments, and history reveals there have been only 4.

Babylon, the first kingdom in the prophecy and the one that made Daniel a captive, was to be the most despotic empire that ever existed, and it was. It was to be followed by the Medo-Persians, then the Greeks under Alexander the Great. When Alexander died, his generals divided the world into 4 kingdoms, which eventually were absorbed by Rome, the fourth kingdom "made of iron" that stamped its imprimatur on all forms of government. Today, even though Rome is no longer an empire, virtually all western nations have taken their basic principles of government from Rome. The laws, statutes, senate, and other debating bodies have continued in what is called "Cesarean imperialism."

THE GREAT TRIBULATION

Rayford wanted to vomit. "So now you're some sort of deity?"
"That is not for me to say, though clearly, raising a dead man
is a divine act. Mr. Fortunato believes I could be the Messiah."
—Soul Harvest

In the first half of the Tribulation, vicious plagues sweep the earth, flaming meteorites poison a third of its water, warring armies kill millions, demonic beings torture the unredeemed, darkness swallows a third of the sun, and half the world's post-Rapture population dies horribly.

And then it gets worse.

As it is the Antichrist who begins the terrors of the Tribulation by signing a godless 7-year treaty with Israel, so it is the Antichrist who starts the Great Tribulation by using the rebuilt temple in Jerusalem as the stage to proclaim his divinity. In so doing he breaks the treaty after 3 ½ years and brings upon his kingdom the terrible wrath of God. So unspeakably dreadful is the period he triggers that Jesus said of it, "Then there will be great tribulation, such as has not been since the beginning of the world until this time, no, nor ever shall be. And unless those days were shortened, no flesh would be saved; but for the elect's sake those days will be shortened" (Matthew 24:21-22).

Chapter 15 of Revelation provides a fitting introduction to the Great Tribulation, which we might rightly call 42 months of hell on earth. The chapter begins and ends with the wrath of God, a holy wrath so intense and hot that verses 7-8 tell us, "one of the four living creatures gave to the seven angels seven golden bowls full of the wrath of God who lives forever and ever. The temple was filled with smoke from the glory of God and from His power, and no one was able to enter the temple till the seven plagues of the seven angels were completed."

Imagine! The rebellion and arrogance of the Antichrist and his followers has reached such staggering proportions that neither angel nor man can enter the temple in heaven until God's wrath is poured out in full strength.

While it is the "abomination of desolation" (the defiling of the temple by Antichrist) that triggers the Great Tribulation, it is not this vile event alone that merits the divine judgments to come. The sins of the "man of sin" have been piling high ever since his appearance on the world scene a few years before.

But even in the midst of this hell on earth, there is hope. The Scriptures do not tell us much about believers in Christ during the time of the Tribulation, but what they do say both thrills and chills us. We thrill to the prophecies about millions of men and women coming to the Savior during this period of wrath. Still, a cold wind chills our soul when we read of the shocking persecution and martyrdom that will fill those years. For a glimpse into what to expect, read Daniel 7 and Revelation 6:9-11; 13:7; 14:13-14; 17:6.

Several important points should be emphasized from these texts to help us understand God's program for his people during the Tribulation.

The Tribulation Will See a Great Soul Harvest

The Holy Spirit will be alive and well on planet earth during the Tribulation, convicting all who are open to the gospel. The key then will be exactly what it is today and always has been: repentance and faith.

God Is Still in Control

Despite the horrific numbers of saints who will lose their lives in the Tribulation, God is still very much in control throughout the whole period. Note the careful language both Daniel and John use to describe the Antichrist's power over the people of God. Daniel: "The saints shall be *given into his hand*" (Daniel 7:25, emphasis added). John: "*It was granted to* him to make war with the saints" (Revelation 13:7, emphasis added).

The Death of a Believer Is Blessed

"Blessed are the dead who die in the Lord," declares Revelation 14:13. The world will believe these martyrs are ignorant, foolish, idiotic. They will be thankful (if that word fits) that they are not among the ones marked for death. Some of the more tenderhearted (if there be any) may even pity these saints who would rather die than deny their Lord. But God does not pity them. He blesses them!

God Will Avenge the Death of His Children

When the slain saints cry out in heaven, "How long, O Lord, holy and true, until You judge and avenge our blood on those who dwell on the earth?" (Revelation 6:10), the Lord does not rebuke them. Instead he tells them to wait a little while longer. In many ways throughout Scripture God says, "It is mine to avenge; I will repay" (see Deuteronomy 32:35; Romans 12:19; Hebrews 10:30).

TRIBULATION, JUDGMENT, AND MERCY

If the Rapture didn't get your attention, the judgments will. And if the judgments don't, you're going to die apart from God. Horrible as these judgments will be, I urge you to see them as final warnings from a loving God who is not willing that any should perish.

—Tribulation Force

The Tribulation is a terrifying period of 7 years in which God pours out his wrath on a rebellious and unbelieving mankind. It is also "the time of Jacob's trouble," in which the Lord will once again deal specifically with the nation of Israel, bringing the Jewish people to faith in Jesus Christ, the Messiah they rejected almost 2,000 years ago.

Yet while this period is primarily a time of wrath and judgment, it also features a very strong note of mercy and grace, a note that too often gets overlooked.

We believe with all our hearts that the Tribulation judgments of God serve a dual purpose: to punish hardened sinners *and* to move others to repentance and faith. The Tribulation will be God's ultimate illustration of the truth found in Romans 11:22: "Therefore consider the goodness and severity of God."

The Old Testament prophet Joel clearly saw these 2 aspects of God's nature working side by side in the Tribulation. In Joel 2:28-32 the Lord said through him, "And it shall come to pass afterward that I will pour out My Spirit on all flesh. . . . And I will show wonders in the heavens and in the earth . . . before the coming of the great and awesome day of the Lord. And it shall come to pass that whoever calls on the name of the Lord shall be saved."

We believe these verses teach that there will be a great "soul harvest" during the Tribulation. Uncounted millions of men and women and girls and boys will recognize that, although they missed the Rapture and thus will have to endure the terrors of the Tribulation, God is still calling them, wooing them to his side. And through the ministry of the Holy Spirit, these individuals will respond in repentance and faith and will choose to forsake their rebellion and instead commit their lives and their futures into the hands of the Lord Jesus Christ. That is why the apostle John could write, "After these things I looked, and behold, a great multitude which no one could number, of all nations, tribes, peoples, and tongues, standing before the throne and before the Lamb, clothed with white robes, with palm branches in their hands" (Revelation 7:9).

We believe these "Tribulation saints" could well number into the billions. And do not forget, every one of these new believers will have been left behind after the Rapture precisely because he or she had (to that point) rejected God's offer of salvation. Yet even then, the Lord will not give up on them.

Far from being a stomach-turning display of divine meanness, the Tribulation demonstrates beyond all doubt that our holy God is also a God who loves beyond all human reckoning. No wonder Jesus himself told us, "For even the Son of Man did not come to be served, but to serve, and to give His life a ransom for many" (Mark 10:45)!

Yes, the Tribulation is a time of fury and wrath and terrifying judgments, but it is also a time of long-suffering grace and mercy. Only God could hold both extremes in perfect balance. And in the Tribulation, he does exactly that.

THE TWO WITNESSES

No one ever saw them come or go; none knew where
they were from. They had appeared strange and weird
from the beginning, wearing their burlap-like sackcloth
robes and appearing barefoot. They were muscular
and yet bony, with leathery skin; dark, lined faces; and
long, scraggly hair and beards. Some said they were
Moses and Elijah reincarnate, but if Buck had to guess,
he would have said they were the two Old Testament
characters themselves.

—Apollyon

TWINING THROUGHOUT the Left Behind books is the story of
2 men who stand at the Wailing Wall in Jerusalem and perform impossible feats while sharing prophecies that can be understood by all listeners, whatever their native language. The profoundly moving and
disturbing story of these men is biblically founded and is at the core
of the series' prophetic message.

Revelation 11:3-4 describes these two witnesses: "And I will give
power to my two witnesses, and they will prophesy one thousand
two hundred and sixty days, clothed in sackcloth. These are the two
olive trees and the two lampstands standing before the God of the
earth."

Some identify one of the witnesses as Enoch (because he never died—Genesis 5:24) and the other as either Elijah (who also never died—2 Kings 2:11-12) or Moses. But for the following 3 important reasons, many are inclined to think they are Moses and Elijah.

1. Moses and Elijah were two of the most influential men in the history of the Jewish people. Moses introduced God's written law to Israel. Elijah was a leading prophetic figure. Whenever the Jews said, "Moses and Elijah," they usually meant "the law and the prophets."

2. Moses and Elijah appeared with Jesus and the 3 disciples on the mount when Jesus was "transfigured before them" (Matthew 17).

3. The two witnesses will have the power to kill with fire from their mouths those who try to harm them, "shut heaven, so that no rain falls," "turn [the waters] to blood," and "strike the earth with all plagues, as often as they desire" (Rev. 11:5, 6). These are the very miracles performed by Moses and Elijah. Elijah was famous for calling down fire from heaven, the best-known occurrence appearing in 1 Kings 18:36-38 during the contest between Elijah and the prophets of Baal. He is also connected to divinely caused droughts and judgments of fire. Moses, of course, is intimately connected to the 10 plagues that struck Egypt before the Exodus (Exodus 7–11).

The two witnesses of Revelation 11 will play a vital role in producing the enormous soul harvest of the first 42 months of the Tribulation. They will provide the millions of Jews in the Holy Land a theological and spiritual bridge to the Christian gospel.

The supernatural works entrusted to these two witnesses will be a testimony to the existence and power of the living God. The Antichrist will have no power over them until the due time.

We might wish for these two witnesses to oppose and finally overthrow Antichrist, as Moses did Pharaoh and Elijah did Ahab and Jezebel. But that is not their destiny:

> When they finish their testimony, the beast that ascends out of the bottomless pit will make war against them, overcome them, and kill them. And their dead bodies will lie in the street of the great city which spiritually is called Sodom and Egypt, where also our Lord was crucified. . . . And those who dwell on the earth will rejoice over them, make merry, and send gifts to one another, because these two prophets tormented those who dwell on the earth. (Revelation 11:7–8, 10)

For reasons known only to God, the Lord will allow the Antichrist to overcome and kill the two witnesses once they "finish their testimony." Before that time they will be untouchable; anyone who threatens them must be killed by fire coming out of their mouths.

After the deaths of the witnesses, the unsaved people of the world who so hate them will refuse them a decent burial, leaving their dead bodies to decay in the streets of Jerusalem. Then they will "rejoice over them, make merry, and send gifts to one another" in celebrations of the witnesses' deaths (Rev. 11:9).

John prophesied that "those from the peoples, tribes, tongues, and nations will see their dead bodies three-and-a-half days" (Revelation 11:9). How could the whole world see their dead bodies? Even as recently as [15 years ago] it seemed impossible to fulfill that prophecy, but today the technology exists to broadcast news across the globe. The prophetic significance of this capability cannot be overstated.

As the unredeemed "peoples, tribes, tongues, and nations" gaze on the putrefying corpses of the two witnesses, no doubt they will think, "Ha! Take that, you miserable troublemakers!" But they rejoice too soon. John predicted that while the world is watching, God will do a mighty miracle.

> Now after the three-and-a-half days the breath of life from God entered them, and they stood on their feet, and great fear fell on those who saw them. And they heard a loud voice from heaven saying to them, "Come up here." And they ascended to heaven in a cloud, and their enemies saw them. In the same hour there was a great earthquake, and a tenth of the city fell. In the earthquake seven thousand men were killed, and the rest were afraid and gave glory to the God of heaven. (Revelation 11:11-13)

Among other things, the resurrection of the witnesses will be a loving gesture by God Almighty to make his existence and power known around the world. Millions spoken to by the 144,000 Jewish witnesses and convicted by the Holy Spirit will see this demonstration of divine power and respond to the Savior. The people of Jerusalem will have even more reason to respond, for John tells us of a mighty earthquake that will topple a tenth of the ancient city and kill 7,000 people. Often in Revelation, after a divine judgment hits the earth, we read that the people refuse to repent and even blaspheme God (Rev. 16:9, 11). But not this time. John tells us that "the rest were afraid and gave glory to the God of heaven." The significance of this verse is central to the story, and to the end times. God intends the plagues and judgments of the

Tribulation to cause the people of the world to repent and turn to him. He tells us over and over in his Word that he has "no pleasure in the death of the wicked" but instead desires that they turn from their sin and place their trust in him (Ezekiel 33:11).

In the Left Behind novels, a pastor makes the following speech in a videotape for any of his flock who missed the Rapture:

> *"Strange as this may sound to you, this is God's final effort to get the attention of every person who has ignored or rejected him. He is allowing now a vast period of trial and tribulation to come to you who remain. He has removed his church from a corrupt world that seeks its own way, its own pleasures, its own ends."* —Left Behind

The resurrection of the two witnesses will allow those who remain to take stock of themselves, leave their frantic search for pleasure and self-fulfillment, and turn to Christ for salvation.

144,000 JEWISH WITNESSES

"Ladies and gentlemen," Tsion continued, spreading his feet and hunching his shoulders as he gazed at his notes, "never in my life have I been more eager to share a message from the Word of God. I stand before you with the unique privilege, I believe, of addressing many of the 144,000 witnesses prophesied in the Scriptures. I count myself one of you, and God has burdened me to help you learn to evangelize. Most of you already know how, of course, and have been winning converts to the Savior every day. Millions around the world have come to faith already."

—Apollyon

ONE OF OUR LORD'S well-known promises about the end of the age is found in Matthew 24:14:

> "And this gospel of the kingdom will be preached in all the world as a witness to all the nations, and then the end will come."

Most prophecy scholars assume this feat will be accomplished during the Tribulation through the ministry of the 144,000 witnesses described in Revelation 7.

This passage suggests that before the world is plunged into the plagues and disasters ushered in by the sixth Seal Judgment at the end of the first quarter of the Tribulation, God will raise up an army of 144,000 Jewish evangelists to spread across the globe and bring in a soul harvest of unimaginable proportions. Each of these servants of God will receive a seal on his forehead. In our novel *Soul Harvest* we speculated that the believer's mark would be visible to other believers but not to its owner or to unbelievers.

Whatever the seal is, it affords these 144,000 Jewish witnesses supernatural protection—at least until the great soul harvest can be accomplished. Some interpreters have a hard time believing that the Tribulation could usher in such an enormous soul harvest, but we are convinced this text shows that more men and women will be won to Christ in this period than at any time in history. That God could pour out his Spirit in a flood of conversions, even in an Old Testament setting, was proved in Jonah's day when the Lord spared the city of Nineveh after the prophet Jonah warned of their destruction (Jonah 3). The Bible says the inhabitants of that wicked Assyrian city "heard Jonah and believed God, proclaimed a fast, and put on sackcloth, from the greatest to the least of them" (verse 5). And how did God respond to such earnest repentance? "Then God saw their works, that they turned from their evil way; and God relented from the disaster that He had said He would bring upon them, and He did not do it" (verse 10).

A partial fulfillment of this prophecy took place on the day of Pentecost (Acts 2:16-21), but its full manifestation awaits the day of these 144,000 Jewish witnesses of Revelation 7. Their preaching of the everlasting gospel will be so clear and so powerful that it will result in the conversions of a great multitude, which no one will be able to number, from every people group on the face of the earth!

ANGELS

Rayford suddenly heard a voice, as if someone were in the car with him. The radio was off and he was alone, but he heard, "Woe, woe, woe to the inhabitants of the earth, because of the remaining blasts of the trumpet of the three angels who are about to sound!"
—*Apollyon*

AT ALL THE MOST CRUCIAL periods in the history of the world, angels were in the middle of the action: the creation of the earth, the destruction of Sodom and Gomorrah, the giving of the Law, the birth of Christ and throughout his ministry, at the empty tomb to announce his resurrection, and at the Ascension to announce his return.

What Are They?
The Bible presents angels as "powerful, ministering spirits" (Hebrews 1:14), created by God sometime before he called the universe into being (Job 38:7) to serve and worship him (Hebrews 1:7).

Angels differ from one another in power and glory and function. There are messengers (Gabriel), protectors (Michael), destroyers (during plagues), and those associated with the presence of God (cherubim and seraphim). God's angels are powerful, wise, swift, efficient, and devoted to doing the will of the Lord.

Scripture distinguishes between "the holy angels" (Mark 8:38) who serve God, and the "demons" who answer to Beelzebub, the devil (Mark 3:22). Demons are apparently fallen angels (Revelation 12:4) who long ago chose to rebel against God and join Satan's unholy insurrection.

During the days of his earthly ministry, Jesus had frequent confrontations with demons, whom he also called evil spirits. He forbade them from announcing his divine identity (Mark 1:34) and cast them out of those whom they were possessing (Luke 11:20). What the Gospels make clear (and what Acts amplifies) is that these fallen angels are no match for Jesus Christ.

Angels in Revelation

Angels, both holy and fallen, are mentioned in the book of Revelation no less than 77 times. They are seen acting in various capacities throughout the book and throughout the time periods outlined in the book. Many times a holy angel is pictured as making a proclamation.

It is through the angels that God executes most of his judgments in the Tribulation. According to the prophet Daniel, Michael the archangel has special duties in the Tribulation. He will be tasked with protecting the nation of Israel.

God even uses fallen angels to accomplish his purposes in the Tribulation. In all these things, however, the fallen angels merely carry out the will of God. They are never "on the loose."

The book of Revelation offers us an awesome picture of the power and supernatural abilities of the angels, both holy and fallen. But it never allows us to be so taken with them that we forget the main personality of the book, God Almighty and Jesus, his Son.

THE JUDGMENTS

> Loretta raised her hand. "Why do you keep saying 'if we survive?' What are these judgments?"
>
> "They get progressively worse, and if I'm reading this right, they will be harder and harder to survive. If we die, we will be in heaven with Christ and our loved ones. But we may suffer horrible deaths. If we somehow make it through the seven horrible years, especially the last half, the Glorious Appearing will be all that more glorious. Christ will come back to set up his thousand-year reign on earth."
>
> —*Left Behind*

READERS OF THE SERIES know all too well that the last days after the Rapture aren't pretty. All people, believers and unbelievers alike, have to struggle with the changed world left behind after the Rapture and the steadily escalating attacks upon that world by God himself. Here are the biblical bones for the terrible trials that the earth must endure.

THE SEAL JUDGMENTS

In order, they are:

1. White Horse
2. Red Horse

3. Black Horse
4. Pale Horse
5. Martyrs
6. Great Earthquake
7. Trumpet Judgments

One of the worst horrors of the Tribulation is the many plagues that will strike the world's people, particularly those who reject the Savior and refuse to have their name written in the Lamb's Book of Life. The Greek word translated "plague" appears 8 times in the book of Revelation and is a part of the first "birth pain" mentioned by Jesus in his Olivet discourse. Most of these plagues are the result of man's inhumanity to man, like the plagues that usually follow wars.

The many plagues of the Tribulation will be so extensive that only a small percent of the world's population will remain by the time Christ returns. Considering together the Rapture, the 4 horsemen of the Apocalypse, the many judgments of God, and the martyrdom of the saints during the second half of the Tribulation, it is unlikely that half a billion people will still be living on the planet when Jesus Christ returns. Probably billions will die of the plagues. Others will die from wars, earthquakes, changes in nature, and the other judgments of God. Unsanitary conditions will be everywhere during that time, doubtlessly exacerbating the many infectious diseases that already will be out of control.

Seal Judgment 1—White Horse (Revelation 6:1-2)
The first seal introduces the initial member of the famous "4 horsemen of the Apocalypse." The rider is said to have a bow but no arrows, indicating that although he is militarily strong, in the beginning he does his conquering by diplomacy. Since he wears a crown, we know he is successful in his efforts. And who is this rider on a white horse? There can be no doubt that it is the Antichrist, who through deceit and clever maneuvering will bring a false peace to the world. But that peace will not last.

Seal Judgment 2—Red Horse (Revelation 6:3-4)
John writes of the second horseman, "It was granted to the one who sat on [the red horse] to take peace from the earth, and that people should kill one another; and there was given to him a great sword." We believe this seal represents a great conflagration we might call World War III. When Daniel's "3 kings" oppose the Antichrist, he will respond in deadly fashion, swiftly crushing his enemies and bringing death to earth on a massive scale never before known.

It is easy for modern readers to imagine the reality behind this second seal. The ability of modern armies to inflict staggering casualties on their enemies is well known but almost beyond comprehension. Only since the advent of the atomic age has it been possible to bring this kind of unimaginable, swift destruction to bear on widely scattered portions of the globe.

Did you know that the Soviet Union at the time it collapsed had 30,000 atomic or neutron warheads, many aimed at population centers? Since the breakup of that "evil empire," no one knows what has happened to all those weapons. A case could be made that the world is in a much more precarious condition today than when the Soviet Communists controlled all their weapons!

Former president Ronald Reagan was once quoted as saying, "We see around us today the marks of a terrible dilemma, predictions of doomsday. Those predictions carry weight because of the existence of nuclear weapons and the constant threat of global war . . . so much so that no president, no congress, no parliament can spend a day entirely free of this threat." Our leaders fear not only rogue nations but also world domination by another Joseph Stalin. In addition, there is always the threat of nuclear proliferation by some terrorist group that could blackmail cities or whole countries, a possibility not as far-fetched as some people might think. And, of course, nuclear weapons are not the only technological threat to mankind today.

We are not suggesting that these doomsday prophecies will be fulfilled in our lifetime or even before Christ returns; in fact, they most assuredly will not. My point is that since Christ is going to return to a *populated* earth, he will have to return soon, or some man or nation will try to destroy all humankind. Such a holocaust is now conceivable for the first time in human history. Certainly this must point to a soon coming of Jesus Christ!

Seal Judgment 3—Black Horse (Revelation 6:5-6)

Rampant inflation—a common aftermath of war—is suggested by John's words, "A quart of wheat for a denarius, and three quarts of barley for a denarius; and do not harm the oil and the wine." Since in biblical days a denarius was a common wage for a day's work, and a quart of wheat or 3 quarts of barley are basically subsistence diets, John is indicating that a man will have to work all day just to get enough food to eat, with nothing left over for his family or the elderly. On the other hand, the call to not "harm the oil and the wine"—symbols of wealth—indicates that the rich will do just fine.

The third horseman of the Apocalypse, who rides out early in the Tribulation, will take a heavy toll in deaths and sickness. The black horse he rides is an obvious symbol of famine and disease, which often follow war.

Although we don't have medical descriptions of these Tribulation plagues, already today we have identified some diseases, such as the Ebola virus, AIDS, and STDs (sexually transmitted diseases), which have similar effects. Four decades ago, the medical profession thought it had eliminated sexually transmitted diseases. Yet today these scourges have returned with a vengeance. Sexually transmitted diseases aren't the only ones spreading; there are many others. Penicillin and antibiotics worked for a time, but the diseases developed stronger strains, too powerful for the usual drugs to contain, and today they are worse than before.The golden day of medical cures for man's sins seems about over.

All that is needed for Tribulation plagues to sweep this earth, as Scripture teaches they will, is for Christ to rapture his church, the Antichrist to sign his covenant with Israel, and the 4 horsemen to begin their march to doomsday. Many of the Tribulation-type plagues are already here!

Seal Judgment 4—Pale Horse (Revelation 6:7-8)

Why is the fourth horse pale? Because its colorless appearance symbolizes death. John says the rider who sat on this horse "was Death, and Hades followed with him. And power was given to them over a fourth of the earth, to kill with sword, with hunger, with death, and by the beasts of the earth." One quarter of the earth's population—well over a billion people—will die as a result of World War III. That Hades follows Death shows that those slain are unbelievers, for upon death believers do not go to Hades but straight to the Savior's side.

One man who heard about these first 4 seals was so impressed with the possibility of the soon second coming of the Lord that he said, "I sometimes think I hear the hoofbeats of the four horsemen of the Apocalypse." Our reply should be, "Don't listen for hoofbeats, because the shout of the Savior from heaven to call his church to be with himself comes first!" It can't be far off!

Seal Judgment 5—Martyrs (Revelation 6:9-11)

When the fifth seal is opened, John sees "under the altar the souls of those who had been slain for the word of God and for the testimony which they held." Shortly after the beginning of the Tribulation there will be a great "soul harvest" in which millions will come to faith in Christ, many as a result of the preaching of the 144,000 witnesses described in Revelation 7. Most of these tribulation saints will be killed by the forces of Antichrist. These martyred souls will cry out for God to avenge their deaths, but they will be told to "rest a little while longer, until both the number of their fellow servants and their brethren, who would be killed as they were, was completed." Imagine! Despite the desperate evil of the Antichrist, despite the horrors of war and famine and pestilence and death, God is still so much in control of earthly events that even the number of believing martyrs has been fixed by divine decree. Astonishing!

Seal Judgment 6—Great Earthquake (Revelation 6:12-17)

The first 4 seals described judgments that are largely inflicted by man; the sixth seal describes a judgment clearly supernatural in origin. John tells of an earthquake so massive that "every mountain and island was moved out of its place." Probably he also has in mind enormous volcanic activity, for he says, "the sun became black as sackcloth of hair, and the moon became like blood." Particulate matter scattered in the atmosphere after a volcanic eruption has often turned the sky black and made the moon seem to turn red; recall the 1980 eruption of Mount St. Helens in Washington or the gigantic explosion of Krakatau on August 27, 1883. John also foresaw meteorites crashing into the earth (verse 13) and what may be huge mushroom clouds of undetermined origin (verse 14). The people of earth will recognize these phenomena as coming from the hand of God, for they are said to cry out to the mountains where they take cover, "Fall on us and hide us from the face of Him who sits on the throne and from the wrath of the Lamb! For the great day of His wrath has come, and who is able to stand?" (verses 16-17).

Seal Judgment 7—Trumpet Judgments (Revelation 8:1-2)

The seventh seal is different from all its predecessors in that it introduces the next series of divine judgments, the 7 Trumpet Judgments. While 5 of the Seal Judgments feature devastations wrought by man, all of the Trumpet Judgments come directly from heaven. They are so severe that verse 1 says, "When He opened the seventh seal, there was silence in heaven for about half an hour." In the rest of Revelation heaven is seen to be a joyous and worshipful place, with choruses singing, trumpets blaring, celestial beings crying out—but suddenly there comes this ominous silence. As horrible as the Seal Judgments were, the Trumpet Judgments will be worse

THE TRUMPET JUDGMENTS

The Trumpet Judgments are:

1. Hail, fire, blood
2. Mountain of fire
3. Wormwood
4. Darkness descends
5. Locusts of Apollyon
6. Four angels
7. Loud voices

From Bad to Worse
While the Seal Judgments occur in roughly the first 21 months of the Tribulation, the Trumpet Judgments take place in the second 21 months. In the first period of the Tribulation the earth has known the wrath of the Antichrist; now it will begin to feel the wrath of God Almighty.

Trumpet Judgment 1—Hail, Fire, Blood (Revelation 8:7)
In this opening salvo, ice and fire rain from the sky, burning up a third of all the earth's trees and all of its grass. This is an ecological disaster without parallel to this point in the history of mankind; its results are incalculable. To make matters even worse, John also adds that "blood" arrives with the hail and fire, as the prophet Joel had predicted: "And I will show wonders in the heavens and in the earth: blood and fire and pillars of smoke" (Joel 2:30). And this is but the first trumpet!

Trumpet Judgment 2—Mountain of Fire (Revelation 8:8-9)
When the second trumpet is blown, John sees "something like a great mountain burning with fire"—likely an enormous meteorite crashing through the atmosphere—"thrown into the sea, and a third of the sea became blood." As a result, a third of everything living in the sea dies, and a third of the ships on the sea are destroyed. We shudder to think of the plagues that will be spread when the water supply turns bitter, then to blood in that "great and terrible Day of the Lord."

Trumpet Judgment 3—A Star Called Wormwood (Revelation 8:10-11)
When the third angel blows his trumpet, another meteorite crashes to earth, "burning like a torch." It does not fall on the sea but on a third of the earth's rivers and springs, turning them "bitter" and poisonous. As a result of this plague, "many men" die.

Trumpet Judgment 4—Darkness Descends (Revelation 8:12)
All life on this earth depends on the sun. If it were to explode, the earth would incinerate; if it were to go cold, the earth would freeze solid. Neither of those extremes is in view with the fourth Trumpet Judgment, but in some way God does reduce by a third the amount of radiant energy reaching earth from the sun and all other celestial bodies. John writes, "A third of the sun was struck, a third of the moon, and a third of the stars, so that a third of them were darkened; a third of the day did not shine, and likewise the night."

This naturally reminds us of the plague sent on Pharaoh as described in Exodus 10:21: "Darkness over the land of Egypt, darkness which may even be felt." And it gives detail to our Lord's prediction, "There shall be signs in the sun, and in the moon, and in the stars; and upon the earth distress of nations, with perplexity; the sea and the waves roaring; men's hearts failing them for fear, and for looking after those things which are coming on the earth: for the powers of heaven shall be shaken" (Luke 21:25-26, KJV).

Trumpet Judgment 5—Locusts of Apollyon (Revelation 9:1-11)
The fifth Trumpet Judgment is also the first of 3 "woes" pronounced by the angel of Revelation 8:13—a frightening sign of the ferocity of the coming judgments. When this trumpet is sounded, an angel unlocks the "bottomless pit," and out of the pit belches smoke and "locusts" with the scorpion-like power to sting and torment unbelievers for 5 months. Their sting is never fatal—in fact, John says, "In those days men will seek death and will not find it; they will desire to die, and death will flee from them"—but the pain they cause will be unbearable. Victims of scorpion bites say the animal's venom seems to set one's veins and nervous system on fire, but the pain is gone after a few days; not so with these locusts. They are given power to torment "those men who do not have the seal of God on their foreheads" for 5 long months. Yet unlike normal locusts, these beasts attack only unregenerate human beings, never foliage.

The appearance of these locusts is both frightening and repulsive (verses 7-10), and they do not act in an unorganized way; in fact, John says, "They had as king over them the angel of the bottomless pit, whose name in Hebrew is Abaddon, but in Greek he has the name Apollyon" (verse 11). Both names mean "Destroyer."

This seems to be one of the plagues that God sends on the followers of Antichrist to hinder them from proselytizing among the uncommitted of the world. It may also give tribulation saints some time to prepare themselves for the horrors of the soon-to-come Great Tribulation. In our novel *Apollyon* we used the attack of the locusts for just this purpose. A character named Mac writes to a fellow tribulation saint:

> A few of us believers have been able to pretend we are simply recuperating more quickly, so we don't lie around the infirmary twenty-four hours a day listening to the agony. Carpathia has sent me on some missions of mercy, delivering aid to some of the worst-off rulers. What he doesn't know is that David has picked up clandestine shipments of literature, copies of Tsion's studies in different languages, and has jammed the cargo hold of the Condor 216 with them. Believers wherever I go unload and distribute them.

Trumpet Judgment 6—Four Angels (Revelation 9:13-19)

At the blowing of the sixth trumpet, the second "woe" is unleashed: the release of "the four angels who are bound at the great river Euphrates" (verse 14). These angels apparently lead an army of 200 million "horsemen" who kill a third of mankind through the plagues of fire and smoke and brimstone. When you combine this third with the quarter of humanity killed in the Seal Judgments, by this point in the Tribulation half of the world's population (after the Rapture) already has been destroyed.

Who are these 200 million horsemen? In the May 21, 1965, issue of *Time* magazine, the author of an article on China threw a hand grenade into the laps of prophecy preachers by stating that the Chinese had the potential of raising an army of "200 million troops."

That this number of troops matches exactly the number found in Revelation 9:16 triggered an outbreak of speculation that caused some interpreters to suggest the 200 million would come with the kings of the east to do battle with Christ at the consummation of the end of this age, known as the Battle of Armageddon. But while there is no question that the armies of the Orient coming to that battle at the very end of the Tribulation will be enormous, due to the incredible population of those countries, they definitely are *not* the Revelation 9:16 army. Consider the following reasons:

1. The 9:16 army goes out during the sixth trumpet, which occurs near the middle of the Tribulation; the 16:12 army goes out at the end of the Tribulation.

2. The 200 million in 9:16 are not humans but demons, doing

things men cannot do. These "horsemen" have a supernatural effect on the earth.

3. The *Time* article included all the men and women under arms in China, including their local militias or defense forces. There is no way the communist government could risk committing *all* its military and armament to the Middle East. Besides, the logistics of moving an army of 200 million from the Orient across the Euphrates and the Arabian Desert to the little land of Israel seems impossible. Such an army would consist of 4 times as many troops as were utilized in all of World War II—and that stretched from the South Pacific through Europe and into the Near East and lasted over 5 years. This battle is over in a matter of days.

Thus, it is not realistic (and scripturally unnecessary) to assume that the armies of 16:12 are synonymous with those of 9:16.

The 200 million horsemen who come on the scene in this text will obviously be supernatural—creatures that are so awesome to look on, as we portrayed them in *Assassins*, that they actually frighten some people to death. Their sting "is in their mouth and their tails"—and with them they kill a third of the world's population of those who reject Christ and commit themselves to Antichrist (9:4).

Trumpet Judgment 7—Loud Voices (Revelation 11:15-19)

The third "woe," the blowing of the seventh trumpet, is like the breaking of the seventh seal in that it introduces the next series of divine judgments. The seventh trumpet is not in itself a judgment but rather shows all heaven rejoicing at the soon-to-be consummated victory of Christ over the Antichrist. John records that "loud voices" in heaven shouted, "The kingdoms of this world have become the kingdoms of our Lord and of His Christ, and He shall reign forever and ever!" (verse 15). Great rejoicing and loud worship fill heaven, and on earth many lightnings, noises, thunderings, hail, and an earthquake announce the approaching end.

THE BOWL JUDGMENTS

The Bowl Judgments are:

1. Sores
2. Sea turned to blood

3. Rivers and springs turned to blood
4. Sun scorches men
5. Darkness
6. Euphrates dries up
7. Greatest earthquake in history

Bowl Judgment 1—Sores (Revelation 16:2)

When men choose to worship Antichrist rather than Christ and demonstrate their allegiance by accepting the mark of the beast, God responds by sending on them a plague of "foul and loathsome" sores. The Greek word for these sores is the very term the Septuagint (the Greek translation of the Old Testament) used to translate the Hebrew term for "boils" in the story of the Egyptian plagues in Exodus 9. John makes it clear that these awful sores afflict only those who worship the Antichrist and who have accepted the mark of the beast; no tribulation saint suffers from the least hint of them.

Bowl Judgment 2—Sea Turns to Blood (Revelation 16:3)

Earlier in the Tribulation God had turned a third of the sea into blood; now he commands that the entire sea become "blood as of a dead man"—that is, corrupt, decaying, stinking, putrid. No wonder "every living creature in the sea died"! How is it possible to imagine a disaster this enormous, this all-encompassing? Dead sea creatures rise to the surface, spreading their corruption to the 4 winds. Think of an ocean full of such filth! It staggers the imagination. And this is only the second of the 7 bowls of judgment!

Bowl Judgment 3—Rivers and Springs Turn to Blood (Revelation 16:4-7)

By this point in the Tribulation the Antichrist and his forces have martyred millions of believers. Therefore God seems to say to him, "You like blood? Very well. Then you may have it to drink!" Is this literal blood? Who knows for sure? But if Jesus could turn water into wine at the marriage feast of Cana, surely he would have no problem turning water into blood. Whatever the case, because of its rebellious, murderous ways, the world will find itself without drinking water. And so the prayer of the martyred saints in Revelation 6:10 will be abundantly answered. They asked, "How long, O Lord, holy and true, until You judge and avenge our blood on those who dwell on the earth?" This plague of blood is God's answer.

Bowl Judgment 4—The Sun Scorches Men (Revelation 16:8-9)
Their mouths already parched from lack of water, those who are unrepentant suffer even more intense thirst when God causes the sun to "scorch" them with "great heat." But even this does not drive the rebels to their knees in repentance. Instead, they blaspheme the name of God "who has power over these plagues; and they did not repent and give Him glory." How right the angel was who said to God, "true and righteous are Your judgments" (16:7)!

Bowl Judgment 5—Darkness on the Beast's Kingdom
(Revelation 16:10-11)
Is it God's mercy that causes him to follow the plague of scorching heat with cooling darkness? Perhaps, but even this does not cause rebellious mankind to repent, for verse 11 says: "They blasphemed the God of heaven because of their pains and their sores, and did not repent of their deeds." This verse reveals that the sores of the first bowl still afflict the people, and verse 10 appears to indicate that the darkness exacerbates their pain: "And they gnawed their tongues because of the pain." This is a special judgment focused particularly on the "throne of the beast" and on his "kingdom," thus demonstrating to the whole world where the source of its trouble lies. When the Antichrist proclaimed himself God, he made himself the focus of God's wrath. And now the world will see without question who the real God is.

Bowl Judgment 6—The Euphrates Dries Up (Revelation 16:12)
The sixth Bowl Judgment comes in 2 stages: the drying up of the Euphrates River, in preparation for the armies of the kings from the east (verse 12), and the activity of demonic forces in bringing the armies of the world to the valley of Megiddo, where they will try vainly to oppose the Lord Jesus (verses 13-14).

It is likely that when the Euphrates River, the natural boundary between east and west for 1,600 miles, is "dried up," the "kings from the east" will march a sizable army across to battle with the King of kings. That army will probably be 3 to 5 million strong. These forces will be joined in the valley of Meggido by huge armies from all over the world, and while that valley is vast (as Napoleon has said, "the most ideal, natural battlefield in the world"), even it has a limit to how many people it can hold.

These "kings from the east" have befuddled Bible prophecy scholars for many years, for few scholars mentioned anything about them. That is, until the Communist takeover of China after World War II. Since then it has become apparent that this largest of all countries (by population) has a prophetic role, however minor it may be, in end-time events. While China had been content to stay within its vast borders for thousands of years and keep largely to itself, its communist dictators have changed all that. They seem to have the same obsession that characterized Communists before them; world conquest.

One hundred eighty years ago Napoleon Bonaparte said, "When China awakens, the world will tremble." You don't have to be a prophet to recognize that time of trembling has already come to Asia and soon will probably come to the whole world.

Bowl Judgment 7—The Greatest Earthquake in History (Revelation 16:17-21)

With the pouring out of this final Bowl Judgment, a voice from the heavenly temple cries out, "It is done!" But what a finish it is! The most severe earthquake the world has ever known "since men were on the earth" shakes the planet to its foundations, crumbling Babylon into 3 parts and leveling the cities of the world. Babylon is struck particularly hard, for it is "remembered before God, to give her the cup of the wine of the fierceness of His wrath" (verse 19). And that is not all! Enormous hailstones weighing about 135 pounds each rain out of the sky, striking men all over the planet. But do they repent? No. They "blasphemed God because of the plague of the hail, since that plague was exceedingly great" (verse 21).

And with that, the Bowl Judgments are over. With the cessation of this plague, only one significant event remains before the kingdom of Christ can be established. The most famous battle in history is about to be fought.

ARMAGEDDON

"Armageddon comes from the Hebrew Har Megiddo, which means Mount Megiddo."

"You have been doin' your homework, boy."

"Experts say Megiddo has been the site of more wars than any other single place in the world because it is so strategically located. Thirteen battles by the end of the first century A.D. alone. Some say Megiddo has been built twenty-five times and destroyed twenty-five times."

"Isn't Jesus' hometown up there somewhere? Nazareth?"

"On the northern side of the valley," Abdullah said. "Imagine how it will feel for Him to fight an entire army that close to home."

—Glorious Appearing

JOHN SAW IN HIS VISION the most famous engagement in history, the Battle of Armageddon. The Antichrist and the False Prophet and all the godless armies of the world will gather there to fight each other, but when they see Christ "coming on the clouds of heaven," they will turn their feeble weapons against the King of kings and Lord of lords. The word *battle* in Revelation 19:11-21 really means "campaign" or "war," and several other Bible passages indicate that the "battle of that great day of God Almighty" (Revelation 16:14) actually consists of at least 4 "campaigns" and spreads over almost all the land of Palestine.

The Lord first goes to Edom to rescue Israel from the hand of the Antichrist; here he soils his clothing in the blood of his enemies (Isaiah 63:1-6). The Lord then goes to the Valley of Megiddo, where he defeats many of the armies of the world (Revelation 16:12-16). Next the Lord defeats most of the remainder of the world's evil forces in the Valley of Jehoshaphat (Joel 3:1-2, 9-17; Revelation 14:14-20). Last, the Lord will come to Jerusalem to defeat the advance guard of the Antichrist, who will attempt to wipe out the Holy City (Zechariah 12:1-9; Revelation 16:17-21).

On the great day of his return, Christ will defeat all his enemies, capture alive the Antichrist and the False Prophet, and cast them into the lake of fire, where they will be tormented day and night forever and ever (Revelation 20:1-3). The birds of the air and the beasts of the field will feast on the corpses of the slain, and no one who resists Christ will remain alive.

THE GLORIOUS
APPEARING

On the border of the city, Carpathia stood exposed atop his personnel carrier, sword at his side, stared at by saints standing side by side.

"You can see them now! Charge! Attack! Kill them!"

But as his petrified, lethargic soldiers slowly turned back to the matter at hand, the brilliant multicolored cloud cover parted and rolled back like a scroll from horizon to horizon. Rayford found himself on his knees on the ground, hands and head lifted.

Heaven opened and there, on a white horse, sat Jesus, the Christ, the Son of the living God.

—*Glorious Appearing*

WHEN CHRIST CAME to earth the first time, he came to live as one of us; when he returns again he will come "with power and great glory"(Matthew 24:30)—a truly Glorious Appearing! Here are the highlights from Revelation 19:11-21 (NIV); you'll want to read the entire passage:

> I saw heaven standing open and there before me was a white horse, whose rider is called Faithful and True. With justice he

judges and makes war. . . . Then I saw the beast and the kings of the earth and their armies gathered together to make war against the rider on the horse and his army. But the beast was captured, and with him the false prophet who had performed the miraculous signs on his behalf. With these signs he had deluded those who had received the mark of the beast and worshiped his image. The two of them were thrown alive into the fiery lake of burning sulfur. The rest of them were killed with the sword that came out of the mouth of the rider on the horse, and all the birds gorged themselves on their flesh.

John here calls Jesus a righteous Judge, a righteous Warrior, and a righteous King. He is accompanied by the armies of heaven but they are dressed as no other army in history. They are all in white, symbolizing both their purity and Jesus' unconcern that their "uniforms" would be soiled. Jesus will accomplish all by the power of his almighty word.

The world will never be the same after Jesus' glorious appearing! When Jesus returns to our planet, his feet will touch down on the Mount of Olives, and it will split in two. Geological reports indicate there is a fault under the mount; the touch of our Lord's feet upon the ground will cause that fault to split the mountain wide open, yet another powerful announcement of his coming.

After he destroys the armies of the Antichrist on the mountains of Israel, he will chain Satan in the bottomless pit for the duration of the Millennium, judge the nations of the world according to the way they have treated his chosen people (Matthew 25), and finally usher in a time of peace that men and women of goodwill have yearned for throughout the centuries.

When the more than 300 Bible references to the Second Coming are carefully examined, it becomes clear that there are 2 phases to his return: the Rapture and the Glorious Appearing. There are far too many conflicting activities connected with his return to be merged into a single coming.

Since we know there are no contradictions in the Word of God, our Lord must be telling us something here. Most scholars who take the Bible literally wherever possible believe he is talking about 1 "coming" in 2 stages. First, he will come suddenly in the air to rapture his church and take believers to his Father's house, in fulfillment of his promise in John 14:1-3. There they will appear before the judgment seat of Christ (2 Corinthians 5:8-10) and participate in the marriage supper of the Lamb (Revelation 19:1-10). Second, he will finish his second coming by returning to earth gloriously and publicly in great power to set up his kingdom.

We believe that Scripture describes these as 2 distinct events. One is a select coming for his church, a great source of comfort for those involved; the other is a public appearance when every eye shall see him, a great source of regret and mourning for those whose Day of Judgment has come. Imagine, if you can, that these events are simultaneous; we think you will see there *must* be a period of time between them. Seven years would allow sufficient time for all these things and the Tribulation to take place.

The coming of Christ *must* occur in 2 installments because they are for 2 different groups of people and fulfill 2 different purposes. The first is the Rapture, when all living and dead Christians will be snatched up to be with Christ in the Father's house. The second is for all the people of the world, who will be judged for rejecting Christ. The first is secret, for a special group; the second is public, for everyone left on the earth. They are entirely distinct events!

Dr. David L. Cooper often compared the Second Coming to a 2-act play separated by a 7-year intermission (the Tribulation). The apostle Paul distinguished these 2 events in Titus 2:13 by designating them "the blessed hope and glorious appearing."

EVEN SO, COME QUICKLY

The apostle John ends the book of Revelation with several pointed reminders of Christ's return:

"Behold, I am coming quickly!" (22:7).

"And behold, I am coming quickly, and My reward is with Me, to give to every one according to his work" (22:12).

"Surely I am coming quickly" (22:20).

Friends, he is coming again, and he will do so quickly! Are you ready? John was, so he could write with gladness, "And the Spirit and the bride say, 'Come!' And let him who hears say, 'Come!'" (22:17). But he wasn't content to leave it at that. He knew some might be reading his book who weren't ready for the Lord's return. So to them he writes, "And let him who thirsts come. And whoever desires, let him take the water of life freely" (22:17).

Are you thirsty? Then come to Christ, so that you will be ready for him when he comes. Do you desire to quench your thirst at the great fountain of God? Then come and take that water "freely." Drink deeply of his cool, refreshing waters. Cast yourself wholly upon his grace, and ask Jesus to satisfy your soul.

Then you too will be ready to say with John, "Even so, come, Lord Jesus!"

THE TRIVIA CHALLENGE

SO YOU'VE READ all the books, you've made your peace with God, you've invited Jesus into your heart, and you're living like the Rapture is coming tomorrow. Not only that, you're sharing the Good News with everybody you know. That's the central message and mission of the Left Behind series. And it's a very serious goal of the writers, editors, and publishers of the books to make readers of the series think about salvation and the state of their souls.

But you've also got a head stuffed full of characters and stories from all the books you've read. What do you do with it? Why not have a little fun with your fiction? If you paid attention to details as you read the Left Behind series, here's the ultimate insider's trivia challenge.

BOOK 1: *LEFT BEHIND*

1. What was Buck doing on the airplane when the vanishings occurred?
a. Talking on his phone
b. Working on his laptop
c. Talking with an older lady next to him
d. Sleeping

2. What is a Rapture Special?
   a. Free stitches for a head wound
   b. A sale at the church thrift store to get rid of the clothes left by the raptured
   c. A half-price deal on towing a wrecked car
   d. A television show about the disappearances

3. Prior to the Rapture, what was Rayford Steele's stock answer to the question, "What is God doing in your life?"
   a. "Changing my mind."
   b. "Guiding my heart."
   c. "Blessing my socks off."
   d. "None of your business."

4. What did the girl at the Pan-Con ticket counter say when Buck asked for help?
   a. "Go away."
   b. "What can I not do for you?"
   c. "Don't you have anywhere better to be?"
   d. "Closed for repairs."

5. Buck's frequent flyer miles have accumulated at Pan-Con. What level of reward card did he say he has?
   a. Silver
   b. Gold
   c. Platinum
   d. Kryptonite

6. Rayford Steele loved his wife, Irene, very much. What personal items of hers did he collect and pack away after the Rapture?
   a. A locket with a picture of him inside, her wedding ring, and her nightgown
   b. A cookbook and chocolate chip cookies
   c. A Bible and a study guide
   d. Her nightgown and pillow

7. What periodical did Buck write for before *Global Weekly*?
   a. *Boston Globe*
   b. *Newsweek*
   c. *People*
   d. *The National Enquirer*

8. The week after the Rapture, how much had crime increased?
   a. 200 percent
   b. 400 percent

c. Not at all

d. Too much to count

9. What tip did Buck give to Mack at the Midpoint Motel?

a. "Stay off the freeways."

b. "Be careful out there."

c. "Buy from Walmart."

d. 20 dollars

10. After the Steele home was vandalized, what did Rayford buy?

a. A security system

b. A television and a video player

c. A home theater system with all the bells and whistles

d. A pit bull

11. Which of these are part of the prayer Rayford repeats when he is saved?

a. "I admit that I'm a sinner."

b. "I am sorry for my sins."

c. "Please forgive me and save me."

d. All of the above

12. What were the two witnesses' names?

a. Elijah and Caleb

b. Eli and Moishe

c. Moses and Aaron

d. Elisha and Daniel

13. Who was the first to use the term *Tribulation Force*?

a. Bruce Barnes

b. Rayford Steele

c. Chloe Steele

d. Buck Williams

BOOK 2: *TRIBULATION FORCE*

14. When did Irene Steele witness to Amanda?

a. The day of the Rapture at a women's Bible study

b. The day of Amanda's wedding

c. After Amanda's husband vanished

d. The Sunday before the Rapture

15: When Carpathia wanted the two witnesses silenced, what did the Israeli prime minister say?

a. "Sir, we have become a weaponless society, thanks to you."

b. "You want them killed, kill them yourself."

c. "Believe me, we've tried."

d. None of the above

BOOK 3: *NICOLAE*

16. After her Chicago home was bombed, where did Verna stay?

a. Loretta's house before moving in with friends

b. The Strong Building

c. Buck's spare bedroom

d. Chloe's old room at Rayford's house

17. What was the significance of the word *trigger*?

a. It was the name of Roy Roger's horse.

b. It was the signal from Carpathia to bomb San Francisco.

c. It's one of the moving parts on an AK-47.

d. All of the above

18. Where did the two witnesses tell Buck to go?

a. To Petra to hide from the GC

b. To Galilee to find Tsion Ben-Judah

c. To Greece to contact the Christian community there

d. To New Babylon, where the new GC government is located

19. Which of these are prophecies about the Messiah fulfilled in Jesus Christ?

a. Descendant of Abraham

b. From the tribe of Judah

c. Born in Bethlehem

d. All of the above

20. Which of these are words spoken by Tsion Ben-Judah?

a. "I know that my Redeemer lives."

b. "The joy of the Lord is my strength,"

c. "The glory of the Lord was our rear guard."

d. All of the above

21. What cities did Carpathia plan to bomb after leaving San Francisco?
   a. San Diego and Oakland
   b. Los Angeles, Chicago, and Seattle
   c. Oakland, Los Angeles, and San Francisco
   d. Los Angeles and Houston

BOOK 4: *SOUL HARVEST*

22: What was the password into Carpathia's shelter?
   a. Operation Wrath
   b. Abracadabra
   c. Armageddon
   d. Shazaam

23. What not-so-subtle request did Leon make to Rayford on behalf of Carpathia?
   a. "Keep this plane out of turbulence or I'll have you fired."
   b. "Inform Hattie Durham that accidents happen."
   c. "Do what I say or I'll have your head."
   d. "If you want Chloe to live, you'd better keep working for me."

24. Who asked, "Am I still a member of the Tribulation Force, or have I been demoted to mascot now?"
   a. Chloe
   b. Buck
   c. Rayford
   d. Albie

25. What did Mac say about the plummeting tongues of fire in the hailstorm?
   a. "Time to find another safe house!"
   b. "This is like the ultimate fireworks!"
   c. "Run for cover!"
   d. "That reminds me—did I turn off the stove?"

26. How many other homes in Donny Moore's neighborhood survived the wrath of the Lamb earthquake?
   a. None
   b. Two
   c. Four
   d. Three

27. Who drove to the GC Hospital in Kenosha to find Chloe?
a. Buck and Tsion
b. Buck and Ken
c. Buck and Rayford
d. Buck and Albie

BOOK 5: *APOLLYON*

28. What was the litmus test for whether someone was a true believer during the locust attack?
a. If someone had not been stung in the first 5 months
b. If they survived after being stung
c. Both of the above
d. None of the above

29. Who were the two exceptions to this?
a. Carpathia and Fortunato
b. Viv Ivins and Hattie Durham
c. President Fitzhugh and Brad Benton
d. Buck and Rayford

30. What was the only place that looked normal from the air after the wrath of the Lamb earthquake?
a. Brazil
b. Canada
c. Israel
d. Syria

31. How did Buck answer when Chaim said, "A man cannot become what he is not."
a. "Oh, that's where you're wrong, Chaim!"
b. "A man is made new in Jesus."
c. "Old dogs can't learn new tricks."
d. "Sure he can."

32. What did Abdullah tell Buck when Buck asked him if the airport was too small for him?
a. "Now you tell me!"
b. "I could land on an envelope and not cancel the stamp."
c. "Beggars can't be choosers."
d. "Maybe for you, but not for me."

33. When was Kenneth Bruce born?
    a. Broad daylight
    b. High noon
    c. As the sun was setting
    d. In the darkest hour of the morning

34. What was described as being like "someone pulled a shade down on the heavens"?
    a. Ken being buried in the earthquake
    b. Rayford scuba diving in the Tigris River
    c. The fourth Trumpet Judgment
    d. An avalanche caused by the earthquake

35. Before Eli and Moishe bring rain, how long had Jerusalem been dry?
    a. 3 years
    b. 15 months
    c. 24 months
    d. 30 months

BOOK 6: *ASSASSINS*

36. What words did the Tuttles wear as a badge of honor?
    a. "You are a disgrace to the Global Community!"
    b. "You have been a thorn in my side."
    c. "That was a job well done."
    d. "We couldn't do it without you."

37. What was the GC's official version of what happened to the two witnesses?
    a. Zealots made off with their bodies.
    b. They gave up and went home.
    c. "Witnesses? What witnesses?"
    d. "We disposed of them like the garbage they are."

38. Why couldn't Rayford lock Leah's garage door like she asked?
    a. The safe was in the way
    b. He broke the door
    c. A dead GC body lay there
    d. The horsemen were in the way

39. Who was killed with the assistance of an angel?
   a. Bo
   b. Peter the Second
   c. Ernie
   d. Dr. Charles

BOOK 7: *THE INDWELLING*

---

40. Why was there such concern about the method of Carpathia's assasination?
   a. Prophecy said the Antichrist would be killed by a sword
   b. It implicated Tsion Ben-Judah
   c. Rayford's Saber gun was illegal
   d. It made the crowds queasy

41. Who did Carpathia quote at his death?
   a. Franklin Roosevelt: "This is a date that will live in infamy."
   b. Jesus: "Father, forgive them for they know not what they do."
   c. Thomas Paine: "These are the times that try men's souls."
   d. William Shakespeare: "Parting is such sweet sorrow."

42. Who besides Carpathia has mind control powers?
   a. Walter Moon
   b. Leon Fortunato
   c. Vivian Ivins
   d. Tsion Ben-Judah

43. When Hattie called Rayford to warn him about the safe house, what did he tell her?
   a. He warned her not to wait any longer in making a decision.
   b. He told her about Dr. Rosenzweig's decision.
   c. "We'll be praying you do the right thing."
   d. All of the above

BOOK 8: *THE MARK*

---

44. What was the resurrected Carpathia's view of the Bible?
   a. "This is the playbook of those who oppose me."
   b. "This is the holy book of those who do not recognize me and who will not, despite what they saw with their own eyes."

c. "This holds the lies about the chosen people of God and the supreme lie that there is one above me."

d. All of the above

45. What did David want to call the "loyalty enforcement facilitators"?

a. The unkindest cut of all

b. Cranium and trunk separators

c. Height reducers

d. The ultimate haircut

46. While in conversation with Buck, what caused Chaim to shake?

a. He had a slight seizure from his head injury.

b. Leah opened the window and let a chill in.

c. The realization that Carpathia had deceived everyone at the United Nations meeting.

d. He was terrified of the GC finding the safe house.

47. According to Carpathia, what did Leon order destroyed?

a. Every Vatican relic

b. Every religious icon

c. Every piece of artwork that paid homage to the "impotent God of the Bible."

d. All of the above.

48. What did Carpathia call "three days of the best sleep I've ever had?"

a. The time he took off to vacation in Jerusalem

b. The time he took off to vacation in the Vatican

c. The time he spent dead

d. The time he was knocked unconscious for 3 days as a kid

BOOK 9: *DESECRATION*

49. At the temple, what did Carpathia do with the long knife he pulled from his belt?

a. Attacked Hattie.

b. Judicious editing on the uniforms of the potentates.

c. Sliced the veil covering the Holy of Holies.

d. Tried to skewer Buck because of the amount of bad press he was getting.

50. What did Chang type to get his laptop running again after Lars paid a visit?
a. "Millennium Man"
b. "Christ alone"
c. "Word of God"
d. "Excelsior"

51. What did God provide the Petra occupants for sustenance?
a. TV dinners
b. MREs
c. Quail, manna, and water
d. All of the above

52. How did Carpathia end up on the temple floor?
a. He slipped in pig blood
b. He tripped on his white robe
c. The slashed pig dumped him
d. He caught his gold sandal on the temple stairs

53. What did the Jerusalem image look like?
a. Gold and life-size
b. Marble, 4 times life-size
c. Silver and 40 feet high
d. Gold and 40 feet high

54. When told that even the loyalists were protesting Carpathia, what did Fortunato decree?
a. The protestors should be shot.
b. The image must be worshiped 6 times daily.
c. They would be publicly shot 9 times as examples.
d. They would be given a second chance to worship and then be sent to the guillotines.

55. When the GC missile was coming toward the helicopter, what did Chaim say?
a. "The God of Abraham, Isaac, and Jacob is with us."
b. "We belong to God. His will be done."
c. "He will never leave us, nor forsake us."
d. "You men of little faith."

BOOK 10: *THE REMNANT*

56. What did Carpathia no longer need?

  a. Food

  b. Water

  c. Sleep

  d. All of the above

57. What was the Carpathian statue in Zhengzhou made of?

  a. Gold

  b. Silver

  c. Jade

  d. Alabaster

58. What happened after Christopher spoke to the crowd in Argentina?

  a. The GC shot the undecided.

  b. The GC guillotined the undecided.

  c. The GC ran for their vehicles and their lives.

  d. The GC beat up the town leader.

59. What words of Jesus did Tsion teach from John 14?

  a. "Let not your heart be troubled."

  b. "I go to prepare a place for you."

  c. "I will come again and receive you to myself."

  d. All of the above

60. When Zeke left the Strong Building, what did he take?

  a. His files

  b. His wardrobes

  c. The tools of his trade

  d. All of the above

61. What caused Carpathia to pant?

  a. Sunbathing during the fifth Bowl Judgment

  b. Watching Petra residents survive the bombings

  c. Getting stuck in utter darkness in his office

  d. Learning that the rivers were now blood

62. Who were the last to leave the Strong Building?

  a. Buck, Chloe, and Kenny

  b. Zeke and George

  c. Albie and Mac

  d. Enoch and a carful of The Place people

63. What new policy extended to unmarked residents?
  a. A loyal citizen could kill an unmarked resident on sight
  b. Daily trials that ended with firing squads
  c. Raids held nightly
  d. None of the above

64. What happened to Mecca?
  a. The GC turned the Muslim holy place into a Carpathian worship center.
  b. The GC and Carpathianism leveled the sacred city.
  c. The earthquake left it in ruins.
  d. None of the above

65. Why couldn't Muslims become Carpathia-worshipers?
  a. Their faith called for monotheistic worship.
  b. Carpathia was not Allah.
  c. They were not idol-worshipers.
  d. All of the above

66. What did the false christ wear?
  a. White robe with sandals
  b. White shoes, slacks, and shirt
  c. Black dress suit with gold tie
  d. Casual white sweater with khaki pants

67. What was the first miracle of the false christ?
  a. He provided water.
  b. He provided manna.
  c. He provided a cloud.
  d. He healed the feverish.

68. What did the false christ's microphone and cord become?
  a. One hundred small asps that slithered out to the crowd
  b. One long snake that hung out the whole performance
  c. A slithering cobra that bit several members of the audience
  d. A quickly disappearing snake

69. What happened when Michael drew the bottle from the bloody river?
  a. His robe became dry.
  b. His bloodied face and arm were clean.
  c. The bottle was filled with pure, clean water.
  d. All of the above

70. What did Akbar propose to help with the water shortage?
  a. Use a missile to tap into a spring east of Petra
  b. Desalinate the Mediterranean

c. Tap into the polar ice caps

d. Try a rain dance

71. During the fourth Bowl Judgment, how did Carpathia's physical appearance change?

a. He wore the strongest sunglasses available.

b. He got second-degree burns.

c. His hair, including his eyebrows, was bleached white.

d. He wore shorts to work every day.

72. When Tribulation Force members felt they might not make it through the mission alive, what do they say? "I'll see you . . ."

a. At the Strong Building

b. On the other side

c. At the Eastern Gate

d. At the party in the sky

73. What happened to Elena's phone?

a. George threw it out the truck window.

b. Mac ran over it with K's truck.

c. Chloe left it on the roof of a storefront 2 miles from the co-op.

d. Hannah DEW-ed it.

74. How did Mrs. Pappas respond to Chloe and Hannah's "Jesus is risen"?

a. "What?"

b. "Who are you?"

c. "He is risen indeed."

d. "I almost killed you."

75. How did Chang receive a warning that someone was checking his computer?

a. Stefanich ordered all palace computers to be monitored.

b. Lars was hacking Chang's computer.

c. Naomi used David's program to check the palace computers.

d. None of the above

BOOK 11: *ARMAGEDDON*

76. What did Mainyu use to apply his first double-M tattoo?

a. A sharpened paper clip, heated by a cigarette lighter

b. A cattle brand

c. A tattoo needle

d. His bare hands

77. How did Rayford know to relocate everyone to Petra?
a. He was told by an angel.
b. The GC called and warned him.
c. Tsion Ben-Judah sent him a message.
d. Chloe called from prison and told him in code.

78. When New Babylon went dark, how were the loyalists to worship Nicolae?
a. They had to worship his statue by crawling in the dark to touch it.
b. They were to sing "Hail Carpathia."
c. They had to set up altars in their homes.
d. They had to face New Babylon and fall to their knees 5 times a day.

79. Who did the Israelis declare their only potentate?
a. The two witnesses
b. The God of Israel
c. Nicolae Carpathia
d. Jesus Christ

80. What was the only area not destroyed by the worldwide earthquake?
a. Jerusalem
b. What was left of Chicago
c. Petra
d. Meggido

81. Who were Carpathia's secret trio?
a. Ashtaroth, Baal, and Cankerworm
b. Rayford Steele, Buck Williams, and Chloe Steele Williams
c. Albie, Tsion, and Chaim
d. Leon Fortunato, Viv Ivins, and Peter the Second

82 What happened to the GC missile heading toward Rayford and George's chopper?
a. Boom!
b. It went through it and hit the GC's own transport.
c. It hit New Babylon.
d. It hit Jerusalem.

83. Why did Tsion hand Buck a yarmulke?
a. Buck's bald spot was getting sunburned.
b. Buck needed a disguise.
c. They were going to a holy place.
d. Tsion had an extra.

84. Why was Chang ashamed at Petra?
- a. He'd packed the wrong clothes.
- b. He wore the mark of Carpathia.
- c. He didn't bring enough food to help with the famine.
- d. He wanted to do more for the community.

85. What became Tsion's most prized possession?
- a. A Bible with both the Old and New Testaments
- b. A copy of one of Bruce Barnes's sermons
- c. An autographed copy of *Left Behind*
- d. A private plane

86. What city did the GC news largely ignore?
- a. Petra
- b. Jerusalem
- c. New Babylon
- d. The smoking ruins of Chicago

87. Who felt called to Jerusalem to preach?
- a. Tsion
- b. Albie
- c. Bruce Barnes
- d. Chaim

88. What did Chloe think when the makeup artist came to work on her?
- a. *Why should I care what I look like for an occasion like this?*
- b. *What a comforting thought. I have a chance at having the best-looking head in the Dumpster.*
- c. *Maybe I can get a manicure. I'd like both pieces of my body to look their best.*
- d. *She shouldn't bother. My friends will come to rescue me before I get to the platform.*

89. Which original Tribulation Force member is still alive at the end of *Armageddon*?
- a. Rayford Steele
- b. Buck Williams
- c. Chloe Williams
- d. Bruce Barnes

BOOK 12: *GLORIOUS APPEARING*

90. What happened when Jesus said, "I AM WHO I AM"?
a. Leon fell off his horse.
b. Carpathia swung his scabbard.
c. The Mount of Olives split in two.
d. Carpathia yelled, "Charge!"

91. Where did the ark of the covenant appear?
a. On the Temple Mount in Jerusalem
b. On the Mount of Olives
c. In the temple of God in heaven
d. In Petra's main cave

92. Who do the rebels build a shrine to at the Pools of Bethesda?
a. Tsion
b. The Shivte brothers
c. Buck
d. Carpathia

93. Why were Leah and Hannah out of work?
a. There were no more co-op supplies to manage.
b. Everyone in the infirmary got healed.
c. Whalum had to fire them for goofing off.
d. They got hurt during the attacks.

94. Carpathia announced that, by his order, all the sanitation facilities emptied into what?
a. The Holy of Holies
b. The Cradle of Jesus
c. Petra
d. Golgatha

95. After Jesus came to earth, why did the manna stop?
a. The people ate the sacrificed bulls.
b. The people fasted and prayed for deliverance.
c. The Bread of Life was there and no one hungered.
d. Everyone was overcome with nausea following all the bloodshed.

96. What happened to Ashtaroth, Baal, and Cankerworm?
    a. They declared, "Jesus Christ is Lord."
    b. Their reptilian bodies burst from their clothes and exploded.
    c. Their scaly skin burst into flames and was carried away
       by the wind.
    d. All of the above.

97. Who said, "You're permitted one cosmic I-told-you-so" and to whom?
    a. Chaim to Rayford
    b. Buck to Chloe
    c. Chang to Mr. Wong
    d. Rayford to Irene

98. What happened to the "goats"?
    a. They were butchered in the Holy of Holies.
    b. They ran free among the GC army.
    c. A yawning chasm opened up and swallowed them.
    d. The GC stallions stampeded them in their madness.

99. Where did Rayford, Abdullah, and Mac plan to meet in Jerusalem?
    a. Eastern Wall, Golden Gate
    b. Western Wall, Jaffa Gate
    c. Southern Wall, Herod's Gate
    d. None of the above

100. What did the condemned shout?
    a. "Hail Carpathia! Hail Carpathia!"
    b. "Jesus is Lord! Jesus is Lord!"
    c. "Faithful is the Lord of this world!"
    d. "Praise God from whom all blessings flow!"

101. In Jerusalem, why was "Hail Caparthia" barely heard?
    a. A million were on their knees praying.
    b. The horns wouldn't play with blood in them.
    c. The earthquake had devoured most of the instruments.
    d. None of the above

DONE? TIME TO TALLY YOUR SCORE!

ANSWERS

1. d	26. a	51. c	76. c
2. a	27. b	52. a	77. d
3. c	28. a	53. a	78. b
4. b	29. a	54. d	79. b
5. d	30. c	55. b	80. a
6. a	31. a	56. d	81. a
7. a	32. b	57. c	82. b
8. a	33. d	58. c	83. c
9. d	34. c	59. d	84. b
10. b	35. c	60. d	85. a
11. d	36. a	61. b	86. c
12. b	37. a	62. a	87. a
13. c	38. b	63. a	88. b
14. a	39. b	64. b	89. a
15. a	40. a	65. d	90. c
16. a	41. b	66. b	91. c
17. d	42. b	67. c	92. a
18. b	43. d	68. d	93. b
19. d	44. d	69. d	94. b
20. d	45. b	70. a	95. c
21. c	46. c	71. c	96. d
22. a	47. d	72. c	97. d
23. b	48. c	73. b	98. c
24. a	49. c	74. c	99. a
25. b	50. b	75. c	100. b
			101. a

How did you do?

75-101 right
Genius reader. You're a Left Behind prodigy. You probably know more about the books than the authors. Amazing!

50-74 right
Grand master reader. You paid attention and remember the fine points of the story. Good job!

25-49 right
Big picture reader. You concentrated on the plot, not the details. That's okay.

0-24 right
Whoops reader. You're out of RAM. Maybe it's time to go back and reread the series.

But don't worry—only one question in this trivia quiz really counted. Question 11—the words of the sinner's prayer—are all you need to put your life in Jesus' hands. If you've learned that, you've learned everything you need to from the Left Behind books. Now it's time to help pass that knowledge on to others.

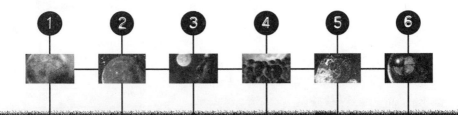

THE PEOPLE OF
LEFT BEHIND

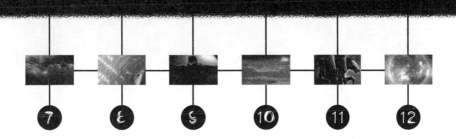

ANY SERIES is only as good as the strength of its characters. One of the reasons for the success of the Left Behind series is its cast—the memorable characters who portray the story of the end times. Every character, even a bit player who appears in a single scene, lives vividly on the pages of the series. But reading the Left Behind series over time, it is possible to forget someone. If you need a little reminder when a.character pops up again in a later volume, or simply for the fun of looking back at the cast, here are the many wonderful characters of the Left Behind universe.

NOTE TO READERS:

This section of the handbook contains spoilers. If you don't want to know a character's fate, stop reading now. Characters are organized by last name, unless the last name is never mentioned in the series, in which case they are listed by first name. Names printed in bold type are defined at the appropriate place in the concordance.

DOSSIER:

RAYFORD STEELE

Given Name:
Rayford Steele

Nicknames:
Rafe—**Irene**, his wife of 21 years, often called him that. `1`; **Dwayne Tuttle** also shortens his name to Rafe. `6`
Ray—His airline connections, **Amanda**, and other believers know him by this name. `1FF`

Aliases:
Agee, Thomas `7`
Berry, Marvin `7`, `8`
Fitzgerald, Sergeant `5`
Gonder, Jesse `6`
Naguib, Atef `10`, `11`
Pafko, Andrew `6`

Age at Rapture:
42

Physical Appearance:
6 foot 4, clean-cut. `1FF`
Flight attendant once called him a hunk. `1`
Turned gray before 30. `1`

Clothes:
Pan Continental captain's uniform with trench coat. `1`
GC pilot's uniform—navy suit with gaudy gold braids and buttons and dress shoes. `2`
Ill-fitting wet suit. `4`
Khaki shirt and shorts. `9`
Full Egyptian regalia for **Atef Naguib** alias. `9FF`

Residences:
Fashionable home in Mt. Prospect, Illinois. `1`
Sprawling two-story condo in New Babylon. `2`, `3`
Donny Moore safe house, Mt. Prospect. `4-7`
Strong Building safe house, Chicago. `7-11`
Mizpe Ramon. `8`, `9`
Petra. `9FF`
San Diego. `10`

Occupation:
Airline captain for Pan-Continental Airlines, flies **747**s. `1`
Trains to be pilot for *Air Force One*. `2`

Chief pilot for **Nicolae Carpathia**. `2-4`
Pilots the Tribulation Force members. `5FF`
Senior flyer of the International Commodity Co-op. `6FF`

Claims to fame:
In the top 5 percent of Pan-Continental Airlines pilots. `2`
After **Bruce Barnes**'s death, becomes the Tribulation Force's leader. `3FF`
Practical, analytical, scientific mind that makes him a good airman. `4`
Flew solo before high school graduation and by doing so, secured college scholarships. `4`

Marital Status:
Married to **Irene** for 21 years. `1`
Marries **Amanda White** in double wedding ceremony. `2`
Widower after **Amanda** confirmed dead. `4`

Children:
One daughter, **Chloe Steele**, college age, returns to Mt. Prospect after the Rapture. `1FF`
One son, **Raymie,** raptured. `1`

Family Background:
Rayford's and **Irene's** roots were from the Midwest. Both their grandparents celebrated their fiftieth wedding anniversaries. `1`
Rayford was raised in a decent, hardworking family, though formal and higher education was only possible in **Rayford's** generation. `4` His parents were older than those of his peers, and when they died, within 2 years of each other, it was in many ways a relief to **Rayford**. Though he loved them, they had not been well or lucid prior to their deaths. `1`

Religious Background:
Before the Rapture, **Rayford** always considered himself a Christian, mostly because he was raised that way. He attended various churches socially with **Irene**. `1`

Before the Rapture, **Rayford** was repelled by his wife's obsession with religion. She had started attending a small congregation with weekly Bible studies. **Irene** tried to tell him about the coming Rapture and his need to be saved. `1`

Post-Rapture Journey:
Rayford is piloting a 747 to Heathrow and contemplating an affair with flight attendant **Hattie Durham** when

passengers suddenly vanish. He understands immediately that the Rapture **Irene** told him about has taken place, and his conclusion is confirmed when he finds **Irene** and **Raymie** gone. **Rayford** feels he owes it to his daughter, **Chloe**, also left behind, to find out what they missed. He begins to read **Irene's** Bible, talks to **Bruce Barnes**, and watches **Pastor Billings's** Rapture tape. Finally, he prays to receive Christ. **Rayford** meets **Buck Williams** and tells his story to **Buck** and **Hattie**. He rejoices when **Chloe** makes a decision for Christ, and **Rayford**, **Bruce**, **Chloe**, and **Buck** become the founding members of the Tribulation Force. **1**

Despite his new faith, **Rayford** still experiences mood swings and misses his wife and son badly. He is threatened with 2 complaints for witnessing at work—one from pilot **Nick Edwards** and another from Pan-Con certification examiner **Jim Long**. **Edwards'** complaint goes away when he is promoted, and **Hattie Durham** confesses to **Rayford** that she created the **Jim Long** complaint, claiming it was meant as a joke. He is offered a job piloting *Air Force One*, and **Bruce** and **Chloe** encourage him to take it. He becomes chief pilot for **Nicolae Carpathia**, with his first assignment flying **Carpathia** to Israel for the peace-treaty signing. **Rayford** meets **Amanda White**, a new believer who came to Christ through her memories of **Irene Steele's** teachings, and they begin a relationship. They are married in a double ceremony with **Buck** and **Chloe**. The **Steeles** move to New Babylon, and **Rayford** continues to fly for **Carpathia**. Back in Chicago for a reunion with the Tribulation Force, **Rayford** witnesses the outbreak of WWIII and is devastated to find **Bruce** has died. **2**

Rayford learns that he is to pilot **Carpathia's** new plane, the Condor 216. Despite his anger and suspicion that **Rayford** set him up to be bombed in the New York attack, **Earl Halliday** teaches **Rayford** to fly the Condor 216 and shows him the intercom that can be used to listen in on **Carpathia's** conversations. **Rayford** meets with **Hattie Durham**, who is pregnant with **Carpathia's** child and unhappy with their relationship, and pleads with her to seek counsel before having an abortion. **Carpathia** later meets with **Rayford** and asks him to pass on the message to **Hattie** that their relationship is over and he thinks an abortion is the best choice. **Rayford** speaks at **Bruce's** funeral, giving a bold message for Christ. Back in New Babylon, he and **Carpathia** are rescued in a helicopter by **Mac McCullum** as the wrath of the Lamb earthquake hits. **3**

Unsure his wife is alive, **Rayford** learns of rumors that **Amanda** secretly worked for **Carpathia**, which infuriate him. His hatred of **Carpathia** grows, and he begins to hope that God will use him in the Antichrist's death, but **Carpathia** threatens imprisonment unless he stays in his employ. **Rayford** witnesses to **Mac**, who becomes a believer. He searches frantically for **Amanda**, finally going on a dive into the Tigris River and finding her body inside a crashed plane. He is inconsolable and wants to die, but **Mac** saves him. Finally **Rayford** finds peace in the blood raining from the sky, a reminder to him that God keeps his promises. ◼4

    Rayford learns from **Hattie** that the evidence against **Amanda** was planted by **Carpathia**. He is with **Hattie** when she miscarries. **Rayford** flies with **Ken Ritz** to rescue **Buck**, **Chloe**, and **Tsion Ben-Judah** from Israel. The plane gets out safely, but **Ken** is killed by the GC and **Buck** falls from the plane as it takes off. **Rayford** lands in Greece and meets the **Mikloses**. Back in the States, he collects **Ken's** belongings and meets **T Delanty**. **Rayford** cares for **Chloe** at the safe house and joyfully welcomes his grandson, **Kenny**. ◼5

    Despite the blessings in his life, **Rayford** becomes consumed with rage against **Carpathia**. He is the senior flyer for the co-op and continues to go on missions for the Tribulation Force, including flying to Europe with **Dwayne** and **Trudy Tuttle** to find **Hattie**, but his desire to kill **Carpathia** is always present. He contacts **Albie** for a weapon and is given a Saber gun. Leaving **Leah Rose** in Brussels, **Rayford** goes to the Global Gala in Jerusalem. He tries to shoot **Carpathia** but is unable to fire until he is bumped and the gun goes off. **Rayford** wonders if he has unintentionally caused the Antichrist's death. ◼6

    Rayford escapes the Gala and goes to Greece, where members of the underground church take him in and minister to him. They give him a disguise and an alias, **Marv Berry**, which allow him to get home safely. He learns from **David Hassid** that it was **Chaim Rosenzweig** who killed **Carpathia**. Back in Chicago, **Rayford** and **Chloe** check out the Strong Building, which becomes a great gift to the Tribulation Force. When the **Donny Moore** safe house is compromised, **Rayford** rescues **Tsion** and **Kenny**, and they all relocate to the Strong Building. ◼7

    Rayford and **Albie** (as **Marvin Berry** and **Marcus Elbaz**) go to Colorado to rescue **Hattie Durham**. There they meet **Pinkerton Stephens** (**Steve Plank**), who reveals his true identity to them and helps them with **Hattie**. They revive **Hattie** after her suicide attempt, bring her to the Strong Building, and see her become a believer. As the leader of the Tribulation Force, he plans Operation Eagle. 8

Operation Eagle is successful, though **Rayford** kills two GC soldiers in Petra. He goes to rescue **Buck** and **Chaim**, and when his hearing is damaged, the archangel **Michael** appears and restores him. Back in Petra, **Michael** speaks as the GC attacks the city. 9

Rayford rejoices with those in Petra as the bombs fall without harming believers. He meets the elders in Petra and agrees to continue leading the Tribulation Force, though he is uncomfortable being a leader to **Tsion**. Though he loves being in Petra, hearing **Tsion's** and **Chaim's** teachings, and learning from **Naomi Tiberias**, **Rayford** returns to San Diego. He flies for the co-op to Argentina for the wheat/water exchange with India and sees the angels **Christopher**, **Caleb**, and **Nahum** preach. 10

On another Tribulation Force mission, **Rayford** flies with **Naomi** and **Abdullah Smith** to rescue **Chang Wong** from New Babylon. While New Babylon is under the darkness judgment, he sits in on one of **Carpathia's** meetings undetected and sees the potentate's glow. **Rayford** learns that **Chloe** has been captured by the GC, and she gives him a coded message to get believers to Petra. **Rayford** tries to learn **Chloe's** whereabouts, but finally must give up. After **Chloe** is executed, he returns to Petra for the memorial service honoring her and **Albie**. He reorganizes the remaining Tribulation Force members as the Battle of Armageddon approaches and flies **Tsion** and **Buck** to Jerusalem. **Rayford** is on an ATV outside Petra when enemy fire causes him to lose control and he crashes. 11

Though badly injured, **Rayford** is found and brought back to Petra by **Abdullah** and **Leah**. He watches for the Glorious Appearing with **Chaim** and **Mac** until his wounds are miraculously healed. As the only original member of the Tribulation Force still alive, **Rayford** witnesses the glorious appearing of Christ. He has a personal audience with Jesus and is reunited with **Irene**, **Amanda**, **Raymie**, **Chloe**, and **Buck** after the sheep and goats judgment. 12

DOSSIER:

BUCK WILLIAMS

Given Name:
Cameron Williams

Nicknames:
Buck (because he's always bucking tradition and authority). 1FF
Bucky—*Global Weekly* coworkers. 1
Verna Zee, Lucinda Washington, Chaim Rosenzweig, Abdullah Smith, Albie, and Tsion Ben-Judah call him by his given name, Cameron 1FF

Aliases:
Jensen, Corporal Jack 8, 9
Katz, Herb 3, 4
McGillicuddy, B. 2
North, Greg 6-8
Oreskovich, George 1
Staub, Russell 6, 7

Age at Rapture:
30

Physical Appearance:
Longish blond hair. 1
Several inches shorter than **Ken Ritz**, about a foot taller than **Chaim Rosenzweig**. 4
Red facial wounds. 5FF

Clothes:
Travels and works in jeans. 1, 2
Denim shirt, dressy jeans, ankle-high boots, leather jacket to meet **Tsion Ben-Judah** in Israel. 2
Heavy wool sports coat to see the two witnesses in Jerusalem. 2

Residences:
Apartment in Manhattan. 1, 2
Beautiful condo in Chicago area. 2
Loretta's beautiful home in Mt. Prospect. 3, 4
Donny Moore safe house when not traveling worldwide. 4-7
Strong Building, Chicago. 7-10
San Diego underground compound with the **Sebastians**. 10, 11
Petra. 11

Occupation:
Senior staff writer and later executive editor of *Global Weekly*. 1
Demoted to cubbyhole in Chicago office, then to his own home office. 2

Nicolae Carpathia hires him as publisher of the *Global Community Weekly*. **2**

Anonymous publisher of cybermagazine *The Truth*. **3FF**

Claim to fame:

Youngest-ever senior writer of the prestigious *Global Weekly*. **1**

More than 3 dozen of his stories appeared on the front cover of *Global Weekly*. **1**

Wrote the *Weekly's* "Newsmaker of the Year" story 4 times. **1**

Won the Ernest Hemingway Prize for coverage of the Russian Pearl Harbor. **1**

Ivy League educated (Princeton). **1**

The Truth's Web site is visited by more than 90 percent of GC employees every time it comes out. **6**

Marital Status:

Marries **Chloe Steele** in double wedding ceremony. **2**

Children:

One son, **Kenneth Bruce Williams.** **5FF**

Family Background:

At the Rapture, his father and brother in Tucson were left behind. His brother **Jeff's** wife, **Sharon**, and their 2 kids were raptured. While **Buck** was in college and didn't have enough money to get home to visit his family, his mother became ill and died. His absence during her illness caused family friction. **1**

Religious Background:

From the time he was a baby, **Buck** was raised in Sunday school and church, but he saw no connection between his family's church attendance and daily life and quit going as soon as he could. **1**

While in Israel during the Russian Pearl Harbor, **Buck** experiences the miraculous protection of God. In light of this traumatic experience, **Buck** admits to **Lucinda Washington** 3 days before the Rapture that he is a deist, but would not go so far as to say he was a Christian. **1**

Post-Rapture Journey:

Like most of world, **Buck** searches for an explanation for the disappearances of the Rapture. His search for answers, however, is regularly interrupted by the high-pressure life he leads as senior staff writer for the national news magazine

Global Weekly. In the days following the Rapture, **Buck** pursues a lead that results in his being accused of murdering Scotland Yard investigator **Alan Tompkins** and London Exchange worker **Dirk Burton**. His connections as a journalist, however, garner him the support of rising world leader **Nicolae Carpathia**, who protects **Buck** from the false accusation. In the midst of the turmoil of **Buck's** post-Rapture life, he meets **Chloe Steele** and her father, **Rayford**. **Chloe** and **Rayford** explain the gospel to **Buck**. He does not accept the gospel message immediately, but before he goes into a meeting with **Carpathia** and his new staff, **Buck** asks Christ to be his Savior. In the meeting, **Carpathia**, a man **Buck** quickly realizes is the Antichrist, murders ambassador-appointee **Joshua Todd-Cothran** and international financier **Jonathan Stonagal**. **Carpathia** then brainwashes witnesses to remember the murder as a tragic suicide, but with God's strength, **Buck** is able to resist **Carpathia's** mind-controlling power. ∎1

 ·**Buck** is unable to convince anyone that he was a witness to what really happened to **Todd-Cothran** and **Stonagal**. As a result, **Carpathia** continues to gain power, eventually brokering a peace agreement between Israel and the new one-world government known as the Global Community. As a journalist for *Global Weekly*, **Buck** travels to Israel. There he witnesses the signing of the peace treaty and meets with celebrated Jewish scholar **Tsion Ben-Judah**. **Buck** also sees the preachers at the Wailing Wall send fire from their mouths to burn men who try to attack them. Less than 6 months after **Buck** returns to the States, *Global Weekly* is bought by **Carpathia**, and **Buck** becomes publisher of the new magazine, *Global Community Weekly*. Meanwhile, **Buck** strengthens his relationship with **Chloe Steele**, eventually marrying her in a double wedding ceremony with **Rayford** and **Amanda White**. ∎2

 Buck is startled to hear that **Tsion** has been forced into hiding after his wife and children are brutally murdered. **Buck** travels to Israel under the alias **Herb Katz**, and with the help of an angel, a vision from God, and other believers, **Buck** leads **Tsion** out of Israel and to safety in the States. While visiting **Tsion's** shelter one day, **Buck** gets the idea to publish an online magazine to counter the propaganda he publishes in **Carpathia's** magazine. He decides to call his magazine *The Truth*, and in the years following, the magazine's Web site becomes the second-most-visited site on the Internet, exceeded only by **Tsion Ben-Judah's** site. ∎3, ∎8

 After the wrath of the Lamb earthquake, **Buck** conducts an intense search for **Chloe**, finally rescuing his badly injured wife from the GC, who want to use her as a bargaining piece in negotiations for **Tsion** and **Hattie Durham**. **Buck** is able to celebrate both **Chloe's** safety and the news that she is pregnant with their first child. Before **Chloe** is fully recovered, though, **Buck** leaves for another rescue attempt—this time for **Hattie**, **Carpathia's** former fiancée. The rescue is successful, but during the mission, **Buck** accidentally kills a man, causing him to endure a fierce struggle with guilt. 4

Buck takes **Chloe** and **Tsion** to Israel to attend the Meeting of the Witnesses, and when trouble breaks out on the first night of the meeting, **Buck** gets **Tsion** to safety. When the meeting is over, GC authorities threaten to arrest **Chloe**, **Tsion**, and **Buck**, who becomes an international fugitive because of his association with **Tsion**. Though **Chloe** and **Tsion** safely board the plane **Rayford Steele** is piloting to America, **Buck** falls as it takes off, badly scarring his face. Keeping out of sight of the GC, **Buck** makes his way to Jewish scientist **Chaim Rosenzweig's** house. When the demon locusts begin stinging unbelievers, **Buck** takes care of **Chaim** and tells him about Christ. After a stay of several months in Israel, **Buck** is able to get back to America, and he arrives just in time to witness the birth of his son, **Kenneth Bruce Williams**. 5

Buck stays in hiding with his family, concentrating only on publishing *The Truth* for 10 months after Kenny's birth. When **Tsion** suggests that **Chaim** might be convinced to accept Christ if someone visits him, **Buck** goes back to Israel to see the old scientist. 6 While visiting **Chaim**, **Buck** watches **Carpathia** murder the two witnesses at the Wailing Wall, and he sees the resurrection of the witnesses 3 days later. **Buck** also attends the Global Gala and helps **Chaim** escape the GC after **Chaim** assassinates **Carpathia**. **Buck** leads the old man to Christ during a crash landing in Greece. 6, 7

Once back in the States, **Buck** briefly leaves his family to help **Z** get to safety in the Strong Building. He leaves again to travel to Greece on a journalistic assignment for *The Truth*. While there he visits the GC detention center where members of the underground Greek church are being held. With his disguise as GC official **Corporal Jack Jensen**, he is able to help 2 Christian teens escape. Though **Buck** fervently wants to save the lives of the other Greek believers, he is forced to return to the States with news of their deaths. When Operation Eagle is launched, **Buck** accompanies **Chaim** back to Israel, and he is present in the crowd when the Quasi Two goes down. **8**

As **Chaim's** escort, **Buck** is present when **Loren Hut** tries unsuccessfully to shoot **Chaim**, when **Hattie** is burned to death by fire called down by **Leon Fortunato**, and when **Chaim**, as **Micah**, negotiates with **Carpathia** for the safe passage of all Jews to the desert city of Petra. After returning to America to be reunited with his family, **Buck** takes time to remember **Hattie** and **David Hassid** with the other believers in the Strong Building. When **Chloe** leaves on a mission to Greece to rescue **George Sebastian**, **Buck** stays behind to take care of **Kenny**. **9**

Soon after **Chloe** returns from Greece, the Strong Building safe house is compromised. **Buck**, **Chloe**, **Kenny**, and **Rayford** relocate to San Diego. **10**

In San Diego, **Chloe** is captured by the GC when she leaves the safe house on an unapproved outing. **Buck** frantically tries to rescue her, but though he has been able to rescue so many during the Tribulation, he is unable to save his wife. He watches her televised execution as he flies with **Rayford** to Petra. Once in Petra, **Buck** learns that **Tsion** wants to travel to Jerusalem to preach to the remaining undecided Jews. Three days before the Glorious Appearing, **Buck** travels with **Tsion** to Jerusalem. He is unable to save **Tsion** when he is wounded in the fighting, and shortly after **Tsion's** death, **Buck** is killed defending one of the walls of the Old City. **11**

Buck is reunited with his family and meets his mother-in-law and brother-in-law for the first time after the sheep and goats judgment. **12**

DOSSIER:
CHLOE STEELE WILLIAMS

Given Name:
Chloe Irene Steele Williams

Nicknames:
Chlo' —she liked her dad calling her that when she was a little girl. **2**
Buck also calls her Chlo'. **3**, **5**, **7**, **8**, **11**

Aliases:
Ashton, Annie 4
Irene, Chloe 10
Mother Doe 4
Evangelista, Phoebe 11

Age at Rapture:
20

Physical Appearance:
5 foot 7, 125 pounds, blonde hair, and green eyes. **4**
Appearance altered by the wrath of the Lamb earthquake. **Buck** notes in his
new bride a severe limp and a strange cuteness from the unique reshaping
of her cheekbone and eye socket. **5**

Clothes:
Sophisticated evening gown for dinner with her dad, **Hattie**, and **Buck**. **1**
Sweatshirt, jeans, coat, cap, and tennis shoes for "talk" walk with **Buck**. **2**
Off-white shift dress when the wrath of the Lamb earthquake occurs. **4**

Residences:
Stanford University campus, California. **1**
Steele family home in Mt. Prospect. **1**, **2**
Spacious apartment in New York with **Buck**. **2**, **3**
Loretta's beautiful home, Mt. Prospect. **3**, **4**
Donny Moore safe house when not traveling. **4-7**
Strong Building, Chicago. **7-10**
San Diego compound with the **Sebastians**. **10**, **11**

Occupation:
College student. **1**
Bruce Barnes's researcher. **2**
Mother. **5FF**
CEO of the International Commodity Co-op. **5-11**

Claims to fame:
Knows how many 1,000-ton or larger oceangoing vessels there are in the
world before the seas turn to blood. **10**

CEO of the International Commodity Co-op. `5-11`
Her beheading and final testimony get global television coverage. `11`

Marital Status:
Marries **Buck Williams** in double wedding ceremony. `2`

Children:
One son, Kenneth Bruce Williams. `5FF`

Family Background:
Chloe is the firstborn child of **Rayford** and **Irene Steele**. She was a good student but occasionally worried her parents by staying out too late and drinking. **Chloe** stopped this behavior once her dad confronted her—she was deeply affected by seeing how much he cared about her. At the Rapture, **Chloe's** mother and little brother, **Raymie**, disappeared, and she and her father were left behind. `1`

Religious Background:
As a child, **Chloe** attended a church that was good for meeting her family's social needs. Like her father, she was a skeptic, never embracing the Christian message that her mother's new church preached. She attended church with her family but fought against having to go, and eventually **Rayford** and **Irene** stopped forcing her to. Chloe's believe-only-what-you-can-see-and-feel attitude distanced her from those "saved" and "Rapture-talking" folk at New Hope Village Church, ultimately leaving her left behind when most of them vanished. `1`

Post-Rapture Journey:
When the Rapture occurs, **Chloe** leaves college and returns home to find only her father, **Rayford**, left. She doesn't believe his religious theory on the disappearances and is skeptical when she meets **Bruce Barnes**. **Chloe** and **Rayford** meet **Buck Williams**, and **Chloe** hears her father witness to **Buck** and **Hattie Durham**. On a flight with **Rayford**, **Chloe** prays that God will show her that he cares for her personally, and she opens her eyes to find **Buck** sitting beside her. **Chloe** receives Christ after her prayer is answered and becomes one of the original Tribulation Force members. `1`

Chloe's growing relationship with **Buck** is shaken when she believes that he is engaged, but the misunderstanding is resolved. She begins a job studying and researching for **Bruce**. **Chloe** and **Buck** are married in a double ceremony with **Rayford** and **Amanda White**. **Chloe** moves to New York with **Buck**, where she continues to work with **Bruce** by e-mail. In Chicago for a Tribulation Force reunion, WWIII breaks out and **Chloe** learns of **Bruce's** death. **2**

Chloe grieves for **Bruce** but works to copy and distribute his writings and teachings. She is injured when Chicago is attacked, but **Buck** rescues her and she returns to **Loretta's** house. When **Verna Zee** threatens to reveal **Buck's** beliefs and claims to have seen **Tsion Ben-Judah** at **Bruce's** funeral, **Chloe** goes with **Buck** to confront **Verna** and forces her to back down. Together with **Amanda**, **Buck**, and **Loretta**, **Chloe** meets with **Hattie** to offer her support and counsel her against having an abortion. **3**

When the wrath of the Lamb earthquake strikes, **Chloe** is badly injured. **Buck** finds her and learns that she is 2 months pregnant. With **Ken Ritz's** help, **Buck** gets her out of the hospital and away from the GC. Back at the **Donny Moore** safe house, **Chloe** tries to do things for herself despite her injuries and fights to go to Jerusalem for the Meeting of the Witnesses. After **Hattie** is poisoned, **Chloe** helps care for her and witnesses to her. **4**

Chloe travels to Jerusalem for the Meeting of the Witnesses, staying at **Chaim Rosenzweig's** house. She is forced to flee the stadium and narrowly escapes the GC. Although **Chloe** safely boards the plane home, **Ken** is killed by the GC, and **Buck** falls from the plane as it takes off. After flying to Greece with **Rayford**, **Chloe** returns to the States, where she develops the International Commodity Co-op from **Ken's** business ideas. She also cares for **Hattie** after she is stung by the demon locusts. **Chloe** is uncomfortable toward the end of her pregnancy and worries that **Buck** will not make it home from Israel before the baby's birth. He arrives just in time, and despite developing complications, **Chloe** gives birth to a healthy baby, **Kenneth Bruce**. **5**

Although she misses being in action, **Chloe** keeps busy caring for **Kenny** and running the co-op. **6** She is terrified by the idea that **Kenny** could fall into the GC's hands, and she decides that she will commit infanticide before allowing this to happen. She tells **Tsion Ben-Judah** of her plan and begs him to carry it out if she is away, but **Tsion** refuses, and eventually **Chloe** sees that he is right. She goes with **Rayford** to check out the Strong Building, and the Tribulation Force relocates there after the **Donny Moore** safe house is compromised. **7**

Continuing her work with the co-op, **Chloe** arranges planes and fuel for Operation Eagle. **8** Still frustrated by being stateside and out of the action, **Chloe** goes on an unapproved outing and meets the believers of The Place. Although her actions have positive results, **Chloe** is reprimanded by **Rayford** for endangering the safe house. **9**

As **Chloe Irene**, **Chloe** goes to Greece with **Hannah Palemoon** (as **Indira Jinnah**) and **Mac McCullum** (as GC Commander **Howie Johnson**) to rescue **George Sebastian**. She meets **Costas** and his mother, members of the Greek co-op. With the help of the archangel **Michael**, **Chloe**, **Hannah**, **Mac**, and **George** escape from Greece. When the Strong Building is compromised, **Chloe** moves to San Diego with her family. She arranges the wheat/water exchange with India for the co-op. **10**

On watch in San Diego, **Chloe** sees something and goes outside to investigate. She is captured by the GC and interrogated by **Jock Ashmore**. **Chloe** is able to make a phone call to **Rayford**, and she gives him a coded message to get believers to Petra. She is drugged and taken to Stateville Correctional Center in Illinois. The angel **Caleb** appears to her, quoting Scripture and encouraging her to sing. She witnesses to others waiting for execution. **Caleb** appears again, standing 15 or 16 feet tall and preaching, and 6 prisoners receive the mark of the believer. Before she is executed, **Chloe** has an opportunity to give a bold message about Christ before a TV audience. **Caleb** appears again in a brilliant white light, blinding the world from seeing **Chloe's** beheading. **11**

At the judgment, **Chloe** receives a martyr's crown and a hug from **Caleb**, and she is reunited with her entire family. **12**

DOSSIER:

NICOLAE CARPATHIA

Given name:
Nicolae Jetty Carpathia

Nicknames:
Abbot—**David Hassid** calls **Carpathia** and **Fortunato** Abbott and Costello. 5
A.C.— **Hattie** suggests to **Rayford** that he call **Carpathia** A.C., short for Antichrist. 3
Nicolae the Great—In talking with **Steve Plank**, **Buck** sarcastically uses this name. 2
Roman kid—**Marge's** husband calls **Carpathia** this. 1
Saint Nick—Nickname given on world news coverage. 1 The Tribulation Force also uses this name. 3

Age at Rapture:
33

Physical Appearance:
Over 6 feet tall, trim, athletic, and tanned, with a strong Roman nose and jaw, neatly trimmed blond hair, and piercing blue eyes. 1
Appearance changes dramatically when Lucifer abandons his body. 12

Clothes:
Always formally dressed and perfectly coordinated no matter the circumstances. 2
Conservative navy pinstripe suit and matching tie for speech to the Assembly of the United Nations. 1
Black suit, white shirt, electric blue tie, and gold stickpin for meeting to introduce his leaders. 1
Black suit, white shirt, and bloodred tie with gold stickpin on the Condor 216. 3
Cashmere sport coat, open-collar shirt, and expensive slacks and shoes at the assassination of the two witnesses. 6
Dark suit, white shirt, striped tie, and gleaming shoes put on him for his burial. 7
Jet-black pinstriped suit, white shirt, and red tie for confrontation with **Chaim Rosensweig** in Jerusalem. 9
White robe, silver belt, and gold sandals for his pig ride down the Via Dolorosa and the overseeing of mark applications; he puts it back on after he washes up from the pig sacrifice. 9

Residences:
Romania. 1
Plaza Hotel, New York City. 1

New Babylon, Iraq. [2-11]
Al Hillah, Baghdad. [11]

Occupation:
Wealthy import-export businessman from Romania; he made a killing when Romanian markets opened to the West. [1]
Member of the lower house of Romanian government. [1]
President of Romania; important issues include disarmament, empowerment of the U.N., move to one currency, establishment of the world as a global village. [1]
Secretary-General of the United Nations. [1]
Self-appointed Global Community potentate. [2FF]

Claims to fame
Knows at least 9 languages: Arabic, Chinese, French, English, German, Russian, Spanish, Romanian, and Hungarian. [1]
Initiates the peace-treaty signing with Israel, starting the 7-year tribulation period. [1]
President of the Young Humanists before he was 12 years old. [7]
Unusually gifted student, earning valedictorian honors in both high school and college. [7]
Celebrated debater and speaker, with an outstanding memory for names and details. [7]
Selected as *People's* Sexiest Man Alive. [1]
Usually works 18 to 20 hours per day. [3]
Normally gregarious, smiling, confident, and charming. Can even feign grief and empathy; short tempered only when it serves his purpose. [4]

Marital Status:
Engaged to **Hattie Durham**. [3]
Single with immoral relationships. [1FF]

Children:
Hattie Durham is pregnant with his child, but he has her poisoned and she miscarries. [3-5]

Family Background:
His ancestors descend from Rome. [1] He is the only child of parents who were also only children, and he has no known living blood relatives, though it is rumored **Vivian Ivins**, who helped raise him, is his aunt. [7], [8]

Religious Background:

An active humanist at a very young age, **Carpathia** admits to **Buck Williams** that he does not adhere to any religious creed. He has knowledge of eastern philosophies, telling Buck that the deaths of **Jonathan Stonagal** and **Joshua Todd-Cothran** were the result of his own good karma. He also describes his rapid move to power as almost enough to make an atheist believe in God, yet **Buck** reminds him that he said good karma was responsible for such events. ▣

Post-Rapture Journey:

As **Carpathia** rises from a member of the Romanian House of Deputies to secretary-general of the United Nations to potentate of the one world government that he establishes and names the Global Community, most of the world's population views him with fervent admiration. He promises the world peace in the midst of the turmoil created by the Rapture, gaining him many willing followers. Believers, however, come to realize that the world has given its allegiance to the Antichrist, a man who murders friends **Jonathan Stonagal** and **Joshua Todd-Cothran** and whose power enables him to alter the memories of witnesses, making them remember the event as a murder/suicide. ▣

For nearly 18 months, the peace **Carpathia** promised prevails, and **Carpathia** devotes himself to building the infrastructure of the Global Community and eradicating traditional religions, replacing them with the Enigma Babylon One World Faith. The interlude of peace is ended by WWIII, and in an effort to crush any resistance, **Carpathia** orders the bombing of nearly every major city in the United States and the United Kingdom. ▣ ▣ Famine and plagues of disease follow the world war until a quarter of the world's population is dead. ▣

The entire world is shaken in an earthquake foretold in Scripture as the wrath of the Lamb. **Carpathia's** city, New Babylon, is destroyed, but he escapes in a helicopter. When he lands, **Carpathia** finds that his most trusted aide, **Leon Fortunato**, has been killed in the quake. Fortunato claims that in an imitation of Jesus' resurrection of Lazarus, **Carpathia** tells **Fortunato** to "come forth" from the New Babylon rubble and raises him from the dead. **Carpathia** subsequently leads the world through divine judgments that scorch one-third of the earth's vegetation, destroy one-third of the earth's ships and fish, poison one-third of all rivers and springs, and cause the earth to be one-third colder and darker as a result of a judgment against the sun, moon, and stars. 4

After the judgment of cold weather is lifted, stinging locusts from hell torment **Carpathia's** staff and subjects, but **Carpathia** himself is unharmed. His former fiancée, **Hattie Durham**, is not so fortunate; she sustains several locust stings after recovering from the poisoning **Carpathia** orders when she refuses to abort their child. **Hattie** is strong enough to withstand the poison, but the unborn child is killed. In the next judgment, God sends 200 million fire-and-sulfur breathing horsemen to plague the earth, killing a third of the population. 5

Still more people are killed when an earthquake obliterates a tenth of the city of Jerusalem soon after the two witnesses, whom **Carpathia** murdered, rise from the dead and ascend into heaven. Despite the earthquake and the defeat he suffers when the witnesses rise, **Carpathia** makes an appearance at the opening of the giant Global Gala celebrating the halfway point of the peace treaty with Israel. At that celebration, his former pilot, **Rayford Steele**, tries to shoot him, but it is Jewish scientist **Chaim Rosenzweig** who succeeds in thrusting a blade into **Carpathia's** head and killing him. 6

In memory of the assassinated potentate, **Fortunato** commissions a statue of **Carpathia**. Before the funeral begins the statue speaks. That phenomenon is eclipsed when, in the middle of the funeral, **Carpathia's** body, now indwelt by Satan, rises from the casket, seemingly as healthy as ever. 7 **Carpathia** declares himself god and establishes the religion of Carpathianism in place of the Enigma Babylon One World Faith, which died out after **Peter the Second** was assassinated on **Carpathia's** orders. **Carpathia** appoints **Leon Fortunato** the Most High Reverend Father of Carpathianism. 6, 7

Fortunato passes a law mandating that every major world city have a statue of **Carpathia** and that all people bow before it 3 times every day. 8, 11 **Carpathia** further demands that all the world's people take a mark of loyalty to him or face death. Though **Carpathia** proclaims himself god, he is powerless to heal his subjects of the sores God sends in judgment on those who take the mark. 8

Carpathia does have power over Jews not in the protected city of Petra, and he orders those under him to persecute the Jews mercilessly, torturing them until they long to die but refusing them the mercy of death. When God causes the seas to become blood, much of **Carpathia's** remaining population base is killed, but **Carpathia** exhibits little concern over the state of the world's water. He stages an elaborate mockery of the Stations of the Cross, and he desecrates the temple in Jerusalem by murdering a man within the temple compound, throwing the blood of a pig onto the temple's altar, and setting up a throne for himself inside the Holy of Holies. **Carpathia** is not satisfied with these atrocities; he is desperate to destroy the remnant of Jews who have sought refuge in the protected city of Petra and orders fighter-bombers to 9drop concussion bombs on Petra as soon as messianic Jewish leader **Tsion Ben-Judah** arrives. **9**

Carpathia is enraged when God protects the people of Petra and no one is hurt by the blasts. He is enraged further by the drop in his public opinion ratings when freshwater sources become blood. Determined to show the world his power, he orders **Fortunato** to commission messiahs who will go all over the world and perform miracles in **Carpathia's** name, demonstrating that he has the same power believers claim God has. **Carpathia's** messiahs do many amazing things before the world's people, but neither they nor **Carpathia** can do anything to counteract the judgment God sends that causes the sun to burn unbelievers to death. **Carpathia** and his messiahs are equally powerless to light the city of New Babylon when God causes darkness to settle on it. The Antichrist himself is the only source of light, emitting a glow that extends several feet, but because no one else can see, he eventually has to lead his staff through the darkness to the light of nearby city Al Hillah. **10**

Shortly after **Carpathia** leaves New Babylon, the city is destroyed by insurgent GC armies. **Carpathia** acts quickly to crush the rebellion, sending 3 demons named **Baal**, **Ashtaroth**, and **Cankerworm**, who take on human bodies, to order his armies all around the world to the Valley of Armageddon. **Carpathia** plans to destroy Jerusalem and then Petra, wiping out the last strongholds of resistance against his authority as god of the world. **11**

As **Carpathia** waits for his forces to gain control of Jerusalem, he sets up his headquarters in Solomon's Stables beneath the Temple Mount. There, for a short time, Lucifer comes out of **Carpathia's** body, leaving him shrunken and appearing near death as a reminder that Lucifer is the source of his power. Soon after, **Carpathia** rides out on a giant black horse to join his army in the fight against Christ and the remnant in Petra. When Christ appears, **Carpathia's** army is slaughtered, and **Carpathia** is brought before Jesus for judgment. Jesus orders Lucifer to leave **Carpathia** for the last time. No longer indwelt by Satan, **Carpathia** kneels and acknowledges Jesus as Lord. Together with his False Prophet, he is thrown into the fiery pit. **12**

THE
LEFT BEHIND
CHARACTER
CONCORDANCE

CELEBRATING SECONDARY CHARACTERS AND BIT PLAYERS

It isn't just **Rayford**, **Buck**, **Chloe**, and **Carpathia** who live in the minds and hearts of the Left Behind readers. A vast tapestry of secondary characters helped bring the Left Behind story to life. These are, in their own ways, as essential to the story as the central characters. Here is a memory aid on the supporting cast.

ADON
Pudgy man of about 50 with slick, curly black hair and wire-rimmed glasses. He is a Greek believer, an artist, and a skilled craftsman. **Adon** speaks no English and is shy. He changes **Rayford Steele's** appearance and gives him a phony ID after the assassination of **Carpathia**. **7**

Agee, Thomas
Alias used by **Rayford Steele** in Le Havre while trying to find **Hattie Durham**. He poses as an import/export dealer. **6**

Ahmal
Part of **David Hassid's** GC staff. He mans the gate at **Carpathia's** funeral and has a confrontation with **Mr. Wong** over preferential seating. **7**

Akbar, Suhail
GC Security and Intelligence Director, replacing **Jim Hickman**. He is a Pakistani and a devout **Carpathia** supporter. **Akbar** is quiet and prefers to work behind the scenes, even though his experience and training surpass his former superior's. **8**

Akbar prominently appears with **Carpathia** on several occasions, including in Jerusalem. While there, he receives a giant, black 42 loyalty mark on his forehead. **Suhail** administers the lie detector test to many, including **Carpathia**, whose answers astound him. **9** He challenges **Carpathia** about certain issues but remains loyal to him. **10**

Akbar is given 2 main objectives: get the government running in Al Hillah and prepare for the huge leadership event in Baghdad. His final directive is to enlist all GC Peacekeepers and Morale Monitors into the GC One World Unity Army. **11**

After greatly disappointing **Carpathia** by mentioning New

Babylon, **Akbar** is sent to his quarters. **Carpathia** orders Commander **Tenzin** to torture **Akbar** with a rattan only to the point of near death, but when the zealots of Petra pirate the airwaves with **Chaim Rosenzweig's** teaching, **Carpathia** changes his mind and orders **Akbar's** death. [12]

Albie

Chief air traffic controller at Al Basrah airstrip tower. [6] He is a tiny, dark-faced, long-nosed man in his late forties. [4], [5] His real name is difficult to pronounce, so his friends call him **Albie**, shortened from Al Basrah. [6]

As a devout Muslim, **Albie** passionately hates the **Carpathia** regime and is one of the few Gentile non-Christians who steadfastly resists the Enigma Babylon One World Faith. [6] **Albie** becomes a believer after reading **Dr. Ben-Judah's** assessment of the difference between religion and Christianity. [7]

Albie flies for the Tribulation Force and, according to **Buck**, is the best black-market contact in the world. **Albie** superbly portrays GC **Deputy Commander Marcus Elbaz**, securing the safety of those at the safe house. [7] He is second in command at Operation Eagle, but must go into hiding when his **Marcus Elbaz** alias is blown. [9], [10]

Albie moves with **Mac** to Al Basrah after the Strong Building is deserted in light of news that nukes are coming to Chicago. Together with **Mac**, **Abdullah**, and **Rayford**, he watches the **false christ** in the desert near Petra. [10]

On a mission to hire wiretappers for Al Hillah meeting rooms, **Albie** ends up dead, double-crossed by fellow black marketer **Mainyu Mazda**. **Albie** is remembered for his love of God's love letter to him and for his street smarts. [11] At the judgment, **Albie** wears a white robe. He reconnects with **Mac** and is seen laughing and hugging him. [12]

Alex

Buck Williams's friend at the phone company who helps him figure out that the number on **Nicolae Carpathia's** business card is for the U.N. [1]

Alice

Verna Zee's secretary at *Global Weekly's* Chicago office. She is young and skinny with spiky dark hair and wears short skirts. She is engaged. Because of a misunderstanding about **Alice**, **Chloe** almost ends her developing relationship with **Buck**. **2**

Amy
Chloe Steele's roommate at Stanford. She is able to tell **Rayford Steele** that his daughter is on her way back to Mt. Prospect. She did not lose any family members in the Rapture. **1**

Anderson
Neighbors of the **Steele** family in Mt. Prospect. They assist **Chloe** after she realizes that the family home has been burglarized following the Rapture. **1**

Andre
Chaim Rosenzweig's driver. He is tall and dark-skinned and knows no English. **Chaim** has great confidence in his ability to drive defensively and in his awareness of any potential bombs. If ever under attack, **Andre** is ready to defend **Chaim** and himself. **3**

Andres
Shy, middle-aged man from the United South American States. He is afraid of the needle but gets a very small *o* for his loyalty mark. **Carpathia** is disgusted with this loyalist for his wimpy actions. **10**

Anis
Young border guard **Tsion Ben-Judah** encounters while trying to escape from Israel. **Tsion** is unsure whether he is a man or an angel, but either way recognizes that he was sent from God. **Anis** quotes Numbers 6:24-26 and sends **Tsion** and **Buck** on their way. **3**

Anis appears again as an armed guard at the Garden Tomb. He speaks the same passage of Numbers 6:24-26 to **Chaim** and **Buck** and adds "I will bless them" before he introduces himself as **Anis** and then disappears. **9**

Aristotle, Plato, and Socrates
George Sebastian's Greek captors. **Plato** is a big man with a French accent who poses as **George**. **Aristotle** is the leader of the group and tries to make **George** reveal the location of the Tribulation Force safe house. On guard duty in the woods, **Socrates** is met by **GC Senior Commander Howie Johnson (Mac McCullum)**, **Chloe Irene (Chloe Williams)**, and **Indira Jinnah (Hannah Palemoon)**. They threaten **Socrates**, forcing him to call in to **Aristotle** and **Plato**, then release him, having **Chloe** follow him. **Aristotle** and

Plato transfer **George** to a new location and imprison him in an elevator. The three "philosophers" go with **GC Commander Nelson Stefanich** for the attempted raid on the Greek co-op and follow **George**, **Mac**, **Chloe**, and **Hannah** to the airport. **Mac**, with angelic assistance, disables their plane, and the Tribulation Force team escapes. **10**

Arturo, Luís

Argentina co-op contact from Gobernador Gregores on the Chico River. This earnest, fast-talking man assists in the wheat/water transfer with India. **Luís** speaks fluent English from the years he spent in the United States during high school and college. He was also exposed to campus ministry groups during those years, so he knew what had happened at the Rapture. From the library of the little Catholic church he attended as a child, he found literature on how to trust Christ personally and started a new body of believers. **10**

Ashmore, Colonel Jonathan

A notable GC investigator nicknamed **Jock**. He is a tall, overweight man with an Australian accent and a tattoo of **Nicolae Carpathia's** face on his right hand. He first works at Stateville, then is transferred to San Diego to help deal with the Judah-ites. **Jock** wears his dress blues for **Chloe Williams's** beheading, but his moment of triumph is lessened by **Caleb's** appearance. **11**

Ashtaroth, Baal, and Cankerworm

Demonic spirits and **Nicolae Carpathia's** faithful underlings, they have been with Satan since his fall. **Carpathia** and **Leon Fortunato** breathe the froglike spirits into the bodies of 3 unusually pale, robotlike beings wearing black suits. **11**, **12** Once these empty shells are inhabited by the spirits, they begin to look very much like **Nicolae**. Six months before Armageddon, they are commissioned to deceive the nations and rally them to Megiddo to fight against God and his Son. **11**

At the judgment, Jesus sentences them to death and causes them to explode, burn, and eventually disappear. **12**

Ashton, Annie

Chloe Williams's hospital roommate after the wrath of the Lamb earthquake. Once **Buck** learns that **Annie** has died, he switches her hospital bracelet and chart with **Chloe's**. **Chloe** uses **Annie Ashton** as an alias to get out of the hospital. [4]

Athenas, Alex
Stocky, middle-aged Peacekeeper with a black crew cut and a high-pitched voice. He works at the detention center that incarcerates the underground Greek church. **Athenas** oversees the decapitation of **Mrs. Miklos**, **Pastor** and **Mrs. Demeter**, other Greek church believers, and those recently evangelized in prison. [8]

BAAL
See **Ashtaroth**.

Bailey, Stanton
Publisher of *Global Weekly* and boss of **Cameron Williams**. He requests that **Buck** take over **Steve Plank's** recently vacated job. When **Buck** supposedly misses an important meeting with **Nicolae Carpathia**, **Bailey** refuses to fire him and instead demotes him to staff writer in the Chicago office. [1]

When **Verna Zee** tries to get **Buck** in trouble over his insubordination, Bailey supports **Buck's** working from his home office. He calls **Buck's** article on the disappearances a masterpiece and plans to bring **Buck** back to New York in a year. He is fired after **Carpathia** takes over the media. [2]

Bakar
The director of the Global Community Academy of Television Arts and Sciences. From seeing the assassination tapes he realizes that **Nicolae Carpathia** was not killed by a bullet. **Leon Fortunato**, however, tells him what he must believe and report. At the viewing of **Carpathia's** body when it is lying in state, he collapses. [7]

Baker, Joe
Alias **Tsion Ben-Judah** gives himself when talking with GC men who question him while he waits for **Buck Williams** outside the hospital. While **Buck** is looking for **Chloe** after the wrath of the Lamb earthquake, **Tsion** poses as a Lithuanian who owns a bakery, and he offers the GC soldiers free doughnuts if they will come by his shop. [4]

Barnes, Bruce
One of only a few from New Hope Village Church in Mt. Prospect, Illinois, left behind after the Rapture. **Bruce** is a short and slightly overweight man in his early thirties with curly hair and wire-rimmed glasses. His wife and 3 children—ages 5, 3, and 1—were

all raptured. **Bruce** was a visitation pastor at New Hope, but he never truly believed the message of redemption in his heart. After the Rapture, he gives his life to Christ once he views the senior pastor's videotape. He makes every attempt to get the message of Christianity out, bringing **Rayford Steele**, **Chloe Steele**, **Buck Williams**, and many others to Christ. ▌1▐

Bruce becomes the leader of the Tribulation Force and one of the leading prophecy scholars among new believers ▌1▐, ▌2▐ He begins a ministry of house churches and travels all over the world teaching about Christ. After his evangelistic travels to Indonesia, he suffers from a deadly virus and lapses into a coma at Northwest Community Hospital. While he's there, the hospital is bombed. **Rayford** confirms **Bruce's** death soon after. ▌2▐, ▌3▐

The members of the Tribulation Force mourn **Bruce** but rejoice to discover thousands of pages of his writings and teachings, which they copy and distribute to believers. ▌3▐ **Hattie Durham** later reveals that **Nicolae Carpathia** actually arranged for **Bruce** to be poisoned long before the bombings, so **Bruce** could have been dead before the first bomb struck. ▌4▐

After the sheep and goats judgment, **Rayford** rejoices to see **Bruce** in a white robe at the throne of **Jesus**. ▌12▐

Ben-Judah Children

Teenage boy and girl. They are both very intelligent, and they attend a private school where they are exceptionally good students. **Tsion Ben-Judah** married their mother when they were 8 and 10. Both children become believers shortly after **Tsion** does. They are murdered with their mother after **Tsion** proclaims his beliefs on TV. ▌3▐ After the sheep and goats judgment, they are seen hugging their parents. ▌12▐

Ben-Judah, Mrs.

Widowed when a construction accident took the life of her husband, she remarried when her children were 8 and 10. She taught at the college level before her children were born. After **Tsion** makes his international presentation, she is concerned about what will happen to their family. Soon after her husband's presentation, she and her children are beheaded in the street in front of their home. ▌3▐ After the sheep and goats judgment she is seen hugging **Tsion** and their children. ▌12▐

Ben-Judah, Tsion

A fit man in his midforties with slightly graying, dark brown hair and facial features that give the impression of strength. [2], [4] His father was an Orthodox rabbi who raised his son to be a religious Orthodox Jew, but not a fundamentalist. **Tsion** knows 22 languages, is a former student of **Chaim Rosenzwieg**, and holds doctoral degrees in ancient languages and Jewish history. [2], [10] Because of his expertise as a rabbinical scholar, the Hebrew Institute of Biblical Research asked him to study messianic Scriptures and compile a report detailing the qualifications of the Jewish Messiah. [2]

Tsion reveals his belief in Jesus Christ as the Messiah on international TV, thus becoming a marked man. [2] His wife and two stepchildren are murdered, forcing him into hiding. **Michael Shorosh**, **Buck Williams**, and **Ken Ritz** help him escape to the United States of North America. He becomes the spiritual leader and teacher to the Tribulation Force. [3]

Tsion survives the wrath of the Lamb earthquake in an underground room of the church and moves to the **Donny Moore** safe house, where he remains a fugitive but continues his spiritual leadership. [4]

He speaks at the Meeting of the Witnesses in Jerusalem. [5] His scriptural teachings and warnings of doom prophesied in the Bible attract a large cyberspace audience, causing more than a billion people to visit his Web site every day. [6]

At the safe house with **Kenny Williams**, **Tsion** experiences a dream/vision that dramatizes several of the images of Revelation. When the safe house is compromised, he is dramatically rescued and brought to the Strong Building in Chicago. [7]

Tsion prepares **Chaim** for his role in Operation Eagle. [8] During the operation, **Tsion** remains stateside, offering prayer, comfort, support, and spiritual teaching to many. Later he leaves Chicago for Petra, where he addresses the crowds of Jewish believers as fighter-bombers approach and leads the people in worship when Petra is protected from the attack. [9]

Petra becomes **Tsion's** base of operations, where he continues his spiritual leadership and Internet ministry. Through it all, he remains humble, rejecting the adulation of the Petra millions. [10]

When **Rayford Steele** relocates to Petra, **Tsion** prefers that **Rayford** continue to head the Tribulation Force, with **Tsion** serving as chaplain. He performs the memorial service for **Chloe Williams** and **Albie**. **Chang Wong** helps present **Tsion's** message to the world on all GC airwaves, and **Tsion** prays for the removal of **Chang's** mark of the beast. Leaving the safety of Petra, **Tsion** goes to teach in Jerusalem, bringing many Jews to Messiah. He is killed there while defending the Lion's Gate and the northeastern corner of the Old City from **Carpathia's** army. [11]

At the judgment, Jesus spends time with **Tsion**, blessing him for his faithful labor. **Tsion** is seen hugging his wife and stepchildren. [12]

Bennett, Dan
Reporter from CNN stationed in Jerusalem while the prophets, **Eli** and **Moishe**, are preaching. He reports on their message and the unsuccessful attempt on their lives.

Berger, Pietr
Dr. **Eikenberry's** male assistant during **Nicolae Carpathia's** autopsy. He originally tells **Dr. Eikenberry** that he sees no bullet wound, but **Dr. Eikenberry** falsifies the autopsy results to say that **Carpathia** died of a single bullet wound. [7]

Berry, Marvin
Alias used by **Rayford Steele** while in Tel Aviv on his way to the Global Gala. He disguises himself in a green turban over a gray wig and dark sunglasses and wears a light, ankle-length robe. He discards the outfit after he fires at **Nicolae Carpathia**. [6]

Rayford uses the alias again when talking with **Laslos** about pickup time in Greece. While in Greece, **Adon** gives him a new look by adding glasses and leaving him with a quarter inch of dyed light gray hair and long stubble on his chin. Rayford thinks this makes him appear years older. When he lands at Kankakee, his new look catches even **Donna Clendenon (Leah Rose)** by surprise. [7]

When **Rayford** returns to Kankakee to pick up **Albie**, he uses the **Marvin Berry** alias. He also uses this name while he is acting as **Marcus Elbaz's (Albie's)** chauffeur at Pueblo. He causes commotion when the only GC employee by this name in the GC database turns out to be an elderly fisherman in Canada. [8]

Bihari
An underground church believer in India; he spearheads

the wheat/water exchange. He has a no-nonsense personality and is a capable, fast driver. **Bihari** is unable to see the angel **Michael** communicating with **Mac** at Rihand Dam. [10]

Billings, Dr. Vernon

Senior pastor at New Hope Village Church of Mt. Prospect, Illinois. He had made a tape about the Rapture and future events to be used to help people understand biblical teachings after the Rapture. **Bruce Barnes** continues his ministry by passing out these tapes to those left behind. **Dr. Billings's** wife, his 3 children, and their spouses were all raptured. [1], [2]

Blackburn, Claire

Receptionist at the reproductive clinic in Littleton, Colorado, where **Hattie Durham** stays. **Claire** is killed by a GC guard when **Buck Williams** and **Ken Ritz** attempt to rescue **Hattie**. **Hattie** is saddened by the news of her death. [4]

Blod, Guy

Temperamental but lauded painter and sculptor and minister of the creative arts for **Nicolae Carpathia**. **Guy** is commissioned to make a 24-foot bronze statue of the deceased **Carpathia**. He makes the statue nude, in keeping with his style of creating work as shocking and anti-God as possible. Although many consider **Guy** a genius, **David Hassid** thinks his work is profane and laughably gaudy. When the statue of **Carpathia** speaks, **Guy** shrieks and falls prostrate before it. [7]

Borland, James

The religion editor at *Global Weekly*. [1] He and **Buck Williams** argue about who is going to cover which news stories. **Stanton Bailey** agrees with **Buck** that **Borland** probably cannot handle the cover story of the peace-treaty signing. **Buck** and **Borland** air things out about **Borland** getting to do the treaty story. **Borland** believes that God is in everyone, and **Buck** hopes to share more with him someday soon. **Borland** is fired after **Carpathia** takes control of *Global Weekly*. [2]

Brewster

Florence's made-up 3-year-old son. [11]

Burton, Dirk

Former Princeton classmate of **Buck Williams**; a Welshman who worked in London's financial district. He warns **Buck** about the global currency changes. **Dirk** is considered a conspiracy theorist, suspicious of **Joshua Todd-Cothran's** involvement with international moneymen, including **Jonathan Stonagal**. **Buck** learns that **Dirk** was shot in the head, and suicide is suspected. **Buck** and **Alan Tompkins** know it is a setup, as **Dirk** was left-handed but shot in the right temple. **1**

CALEB

Angel who appears in China and Argentina with warnings against taking the mark and worshiping **Nicolae Carpathia's** image. Five years into the Tribulation, he is reported to be giving his warnings somewhere new almost every day. **Caleb** dresses in a robe and sandals. His hair and beard are short; his appearance and manner of speaking do not make his nationality apparent. **10**

Caleb appears to **Chloe Williams** in prison, helping her remember Scripture and encouraging her to sing. On the day of her beheading, he appears again, standing 15 or 16 feet high to confront **Jock**, preach to the undecided, and support **Chloe**. He blinds the world during some of the beheadings, including **Chloe's**. **11**

At the resurrection, **Caleb** is seen with **Gabriel**, **Michael**, **Christopher**, and **Nahum**. **12**

Cankerworm

See **Ashtaroth**.

Carmella

A heavyset Latina around 50 years old. Her mother died when she was a small child. She entered into the world of prostitution and drugs. **Shaniqua** shares a brochure with her and lets her know she is loved. That experience changes her life, and she begins to worship with The Place believers. **12**

Carpathia, Nicolae Jetty

See dossier on **Nicolae Carpathia**.

Cavenaugh, Helen

A 70-year-old survivor of the wrath of the Lamb earthquake. She lives next door to **Loretta** and sees **Chloe Williams** run outside **Loretta's** place when the earth shakes. **Mrs. Cavenaugh** is taken to the makeshift furniture-store "hospital," where **Buck** finds her and gets hopeful information about **Chloe**. **4**

Cenni, Detective Sergeant Billy

Policeman on the scene of the **Stonagal** and **Todd-Cothran** killings whose business card **Buck Williams** tries to use to prove his attendance at the pre-U.N. press-conference meeting. Both the business card and the policeman's name prove phony. **1**

Charles, Dr. Floyd

Heavyset African-American doctor in charge of the morgue at GC Hospital in Kenosha. In search of **Chloe** after the wrath of the Lamb earthquake, **Buck Williams** meets **Dr. Charles** and notices the mark of the believer on his forehead. **Dr. Charles** helps protect **Chloe** from GC staff. He regularly visits the Tribulation Force, checking on their injuries, and becomes a special friend to **Rayford**. **4**

    Dr. Charles shares with **Rayford** that his wife, **Gigi**, was raptured and their only daughter, **LaDonna**, died in a bus accident on the first day of kindergarten. The couple's grief ripped their marriage apart. They ultimately restored their marriage, but despite the love they shared, **Gigi** was unable to convince him of his need for Christ.

    Dr. Charles delivers **Chloe** and **Buck's** son, **Kenny**. As he assists a poisoned, pregnant **Hattie Durham**, **Dr. Charles** develops a deep love for her. **5** He contracts something that acts like cyanide poisoning when **Hattie** miscarries, and he dies about 6 months later. The Tribulation Force grieves and buries him in the backyard of the **Moore** safe house. **6**

    Rayford sees **Dr. Charles** at the judgment. **12**

Charles, Gigi

Raptured wife of **Dr. Floyd Charles**. After a miscarriage, **Gigi** gave birth to a little girl, **LaDonna**. **LaDonna** died when she was 5 years old. In his grief, **Dr. Charles** left **Gigi**, but her love eventually brought him back to her, although she could not convince him to make a decision for Christ before the Rapture. **5**

Charles, LaDonna

Five-year-old daughter of **Floyd** and **Gigi Charles**; she died in a bus accident on her first day of school. **5**

Chow, Chang

Male alias used by **Ming Toy**. **Z** gives her a man's haircut and lessons on behaving in a manly way. **Ming** uses her disguise to impersonate a low-level GC Peacekeeper. **10**

Christopher

1. See **Smith, Christopher**.

2. Angel who presents the gospel in China and Argentina. **Christopher** is a preacher of the gospel, setting the stage for the preacher who will come from the 144,000 Jewish evangelists to preach to the undecided. He brings the gospel to remote regions where the message of Christ has never been preached. **Christopher** dresses in a robe and sandals. His hair and beard are relatively short; his appearance and manner of speaking do not make his nationality apparent. **Christopher** appears to **Ming Toy**, promising her that she and her mother will celebrate the Glorious Appearing alive and on the earth. **10**

Ming sees **Christopher** again at the judgment; he appears at Jesus' throne along with **Gabriel**, **Michael**, **Nahum**, and **Caleb**. **12**

Christopher, Annie

Full name is **Angel Rich Christopher**. She is a trim Canadian woman with large, dark eyes, short dark hair, and beautiful teeth and skin. Originally she is the GC Condor 216 cargo chief, and later, after its destruction, she becomes the cargo chief of the Phoenix 216. She also becomes an intelligence analyst for the administrative branch of the GC. **Annie** loses her entire family in the wrath of the Lamb earthquake. She becomes a believer through **Dr. Ben-Judah's** Web site, influenced by reading "For Those Who Mourn." She meets and falls in love with **David Hassid**, and they plan to marry. **6**

Annie monitors sector 53 during **Nicolae Carpathia's** funeral and is killed when **Leon Fortunato** calls down lightning from heaven. **8** She is seen at the judgment. **12**

Cleburn

See **McCullum, Mac**.

Clendenon, Donna

Alias used by **Leah Rose** at the Belgium Facility for Female Rehabilitation, posing as **Hattie Durham's** aunt from California. **Leah** delivers the news that **Hattie's** sister, **Nancy**, has died. For this alias, **Zeke** transforms **Leah** with bleached blonde hair, darker contact lenses, and a dental appliance that gives her an overbite and slight buckteeth. **6FF**

Rayford Steele as **Marvin Berry** picks her up at the Kankakee Airport and surprises her with his new look. **7**

Conchita, Dr. Consuela

Director of Health Care for the Global Community. She tries to help people understand how to treat themselves for the sores judgment. **9** **Dr. Conchita** is promoted to Surgeon General of the GC. **Akbar** calls her **Connie** and requests that she supply heavy doses of sedative for 2 bomber pilots. **10**

Craig

A young GC guard at the hospital. He finds a marker for **Buck Williams** so **Buck** can change **Chloe's** hospital nameplate to **A. Ashton's** name. **4**

Crawford

Albie mentions North American States Midwest Regional Director **Crawford** in conversation with the GC at the safe house. He later confides to **Rayford Steele** that he had merely learned this name from a GC directory. **7**

Croix, Officer

Guard at Belgium Facility for Female Rehabilitation. He is about 6 feet tall with a French accent. **Leah Rose**, posing as **Donna Clendenon**, is unsuccessful in getting information from him other than that **Hattie Durham** has been transferred. **7**

D'ANGELO, Deputy Pontiff Francesca

Before the Global Gala crowd she, as assistant to Pontifex Maximus **Peter the Second**, announces his death from a highly contagious virus. By the next morning, she is relieved of her position and the Enigma Babylon One World Faith comes to an end. **6**

Daniel

Master of ceremonies at the Meeting of the Witnesses. He displays faithfulness, spiritual maturity, quickness in following directions, and bravery. **Daniel** also exhibits musical abilities, leading the crowds at Teddy Kollek Stadium in hymns. **5**

Dart, Olivia

Alias **Dwayne Tuttle** gives for his wife, **Trudy**, when they go to rescue **Mac McCullum** and **Abdullah Smith** from the Johannesburg ambush. She is called Liv for short. **6**

Dart

Alias **Dwayne Tuttle** uses when he and his wife go to rescue **Mac McCullum** and **Abdullah Smith** in Johannesburg. After landing the

Super J and using an Aussie accent, he boldly confronts **Leon Fortunato** about serving the Antichrist. 6

Datillo
GC squadron leader trained at Baltimore Area Leadership Training. **Deputy Commander Marcus Elbaz (Albie)** skillfully confronts him at the safe house, causing **Datillo** to leave the safe house cleanup to **Elbaz**. This allows the Tribulation Force to escape to the Strong Building. Later it is assumed that **Datillo** returned and torched the place, because **Rayford Steele** and **Albie see smoke coming from that area.** 7, 8

Delanty, Tyrola Mark (T)
Businessman and owner/director of the Palwaukee Airport in Wheeling, IL. 6 He is in his late thirties and is of African-American and Scottish-Irish descent. 7, 4 T's wife of 14 years, his 6 children, and everybody else he loved disappeared in the Rapture. T becomes suicidal, but he logs on to **Dr. Ben-Judah's** cyber class and starts attending a neighborhood church. He meets **Rayford Steele** when **Rayford** goes to the airport to collect **Ken Ritz's** belongings. **Rayford** and T become fast friends, encouraging one another in their new faith. 6

T makes many harrowing flights for the Tribulation Force. His last flight brings **Buck** and **Chaim** out of Israel into Greece. When he runs out of fuel, the Super J crashes and T is killed. The Tribulation Force members grieve the loss of this faithful friend. 7

Rayford sees T again at the judgment. 12

Demeter, Mrs.
Incarcerated when the Greek underground church, which her husband pastors, is discovered. After a prison guard hits **Mrs. Miklos** on the back of her head with a baton, **Mrs. Demeter** comforts her. Soon she too is hit by the same guard. Despite the intense pain, she lifts her hands to choose the guillotine rather than the mark. **Mrs. Miklos** briefly introduces **Mrs. Demeter** to **Buck Williams** before she boldly becomes a martyr for Christ. 8

Demeter, Pastor Demetrius
Christian friend of **Laslos** who helps pick up **Rayford Steele** on the run in Greece. **Demetrius** is around 30, tall and thin, with thick dark hair, olive skin, and black eyes. He

SUPPORTING CHARACTERS—D

179

speaks with a heavy Greek accent but is articulate in English. He was an Orthodox Jew before receiving Christ as Messiah and becoming instrumental in the growth of the underground church in Greece. His primary gift is evangelism, but he also is gifted with discernment. **7**

Faithful to the end, **Pastor Demeter** dies at the guillotine, but not before **Buck Williams** observes him leading several male detainees to Christ. **8**

Devlin, Patricia
Heavyset nurse at Northwest Community Hospital who helps identify the body of **Bruce Barnes**. After the bombing, she patiently looks for his body and closes **Bruce's** eyes for **Rayford Steele**. **2**

Diamond John
See **Stonagal, Jonathan**.

Donahue, Barbara
Financial editor at *Global Weekly*. She seems well informed about world markets. She concedes a big story to **Buck Williams**, hoping that the other *Global Weekly* editors will still be able to influence the story. **1**

Durham, Harriet (Hattie)
Beautiful, blonde senior flight attendant on Pan-Continental Airlines, working with **Captain Rayford Steele**. **Rayford** considers an affair with **Hattie** before the Rapture, which occurs while they are on a flight together. At her request, **Buck Williams** introduces **Hattie** to rising star **Nicolae Carpathia**. Despite **Rayford's** and **Buck's** warnings, **Hattie** becomes **Carpathia's** personal assistant and begins a relationship with him. **1** The two become engaged after it is announced that **Hattie** is pregnant, but **Hattie** is unhappy as she begins to see through **Carpathia**. Her growing suspicions about **Carpathia's** true nature prove accurate when she is demoted and later fired as his assistant. **Hattie** returns to the United States of North America, considering abortion. Her family and **Carpathia** encourage this decision, while **Rayford**, **Amanda**, and other members of the Tribulation Force beg her to reconsider and to open her heart to God. **3**

Hattie checks into a reproductive clinic in Littleton, Colorado, under the name **Li Yamamoto**, still considering abortion but growing attached to her unborn baby. Her life is threatened by **Leon Fortunato** and others in **Carpathia's** employ. **Buck** and **Ken Ritz** rescue **Hattie** and bring her back to the Mount Prospect safe house, but she has been poisoned by the GC and is deathly ill. **Buck** and **Chloe** witness to **Hattie**, but she cannot accept God's forgiveness for all she has done. ▪4

Although **Hattie** survives the poisoning under the care of **Dr. Floyd Charles**, she miscarries and no longer wants to live. Even after **Tsion Ben-Judah** witnesses to her, she does not want forgiveness. She is stung by the locusts and witnesses to her sister, **Nancy**, who was also stung, but still cannot accept God herself. She becomes obsessed with the thought of killing **Carpathia**. ▪5

After **Floyd** dies, poisoned by caring for **Hattie**, she disappears. The Tribulation Force learns that she is in custody in Brussels under the name **Mae Willie**, but she disappears again before they can reach her. She is seen in the crowd at **Carpathia's** assassination. ▪6

The Tribulation Force learns that **Hattie** is back in the States and worries that she may endanger the safe house. ▪7 She is recaptured by the GC and held in Pueblo, Colorado. **Rayford** and **Albie** go to her rescue and find that she has attempted suicide. They resuscitate her, and after hearing **Albie's** testimony, Hattie finally accepts Christ. ▪8

In Israel for Operation Eagle, **Hattie** is visited by the angel **Michael**, who makes it clear that she is to speak out against the Antichrist. She bravely confronts **Carpathia** at Golgotha and becomes a martyr when **Fortunato** brings fire from the sky that consumes her. Her death advances the cause of Christ by emboldening **Buck** and **Chaim Rosenzweig** to proclaim God's message. **Micah (Chaim)** gathers her ashes for a special remembrance at the safe house, and later the ashes are scattered at Petra. ▪9

At the judgment, Jesus gives **Hattie** a crystalline tiara and says, "Well done, good and faithful servant," ▪12

Dumas, Enoch

Spanish-American pastor of The Place. He carries a cheap hardbound Bible and promises **Chloe** that his people will pray for the Tribulation Force while they are on their mission in Greece. ▪8 **Enoch** relocates with his people from the Strong Building in Chicago to Palos Hills, Illinois, and continues to teach his growing flock until God miraculously transports them to Petra. ▪12

Dykes, James

Alias used by **Samuel Hanson** when he hides out with **Hattie Durham** (alias **Mae Willie**) in Le Havre. GC workers murder him for his involvement with **Hattie**. A man posing as **Dykes** nearly kills **Rayford**, but he is saved by **Trudy's** heroic measures after she is warned by **Mac McCullum**. 6

EARL

The husband videotaping the delivery of his child when the baby and the nurse disappear at the Rapture. 1

Edersheim, Alfred

Teacher of languages and Grinfield lecturer on the Septuagint. **Dr. Ben-Judah** quotes **Edersheim's** postulate that there are 456 messianic passages in Scripture supported by more than 558 references from the ancient rabbinical writings. 2

Edwards, Nicholas (Nick)

Rayford Steele's first officer at Pan-Con. He files a religious harassment complaint against **Rayford** for witnessing to him. **Leonard Gustafson** tells **Rayford** that **Edwards** has been promoted to captain. **Rayford** knows that **Edwards's** promotion helped shush the harassment complaint. 2

Eikenberry, Dr. Madeline

Forensic pathologist from Baghdad chosen to prepare **Nicolae Carpathia's** body for viewing. She falsifies **Carpathia's** autopsy report. 7

Elbaz, Deputy Commander Marcus

Alias used by **Albie**; he poses as a high-level GC Peacekeeper. His disguise includes a GC Peacekeeping Force uniform and weapon. His quick thinking and knowledge of the GC system enable him to secure the Tribulation Force's safety at the safe house. 7

David Hassid has **Elbaz** entered into the international GC database with name, rank, and serial number and assigned to the Chicago area of the United North American States, making it easy for **Albie** to continue to assist the Tribulation Force. 8

Albie's out on more flying missions when **Pinkerton Stephens** warns **Rayford Steele** that this alias has been revealed. 9

Elena

Georgiana Stavros imposter. **Elena** is tall and pretty with brown hair and light-colored skin. She carries a huge handgun with a silencer in a small, dark green satchel. **Elena** takes part in an ambush that results in the deaths of **K**, **Laslos**, and **Marcel**. Before he dies, **Marcel** pulls the cap from **Elena's** forehead, revealing the mark of the beast. [9]

Elena dies in an elevator at the hands of her captive, **George Sebastian**. **George** uses her phone, which proves fatal for the Greek co-op. [10]

Eli

One of the two prophets at the Wailing Wall declaring that Jesus Christ of the New Testament is the fulfillment of the Torah's prophecy of Messiah. [1] **Eli** speaks boldly and eliminates his attackers with fire. **Buck Williams** and **Tsion Ben-Judah** speak with him. Both **Eli** and **Moishe** are able to communicate without opening their mouths. [2]

The two witnesses are murdered by **Nicolae Carpathia**. Three days later, they are resurrected and rise into heaven. Their ascension is followed by an earthquake. [6]

Ernie

1. See **Kivistio, Lieutenant Ernest**.
2. Nineteen-year-old, red-haired mechanical whiz who pretends to be a believer, but has actually made a fake believer's seal. **Rayford Steele** discovers **Ernie's** deception when he goes to collect **Ken Ritz's** personal things. **Ernie** is stung by a demon locust and recuperates at Arthur Young Memorial Hospital in Palatine, Illinois. The Tribulation Force is concerned that he will find out where the safe house is. **Ernie** and **Hattie Durham** try to get **Abdullah Smith** to fly them to New Babylon. [5]

The Tribulation Force finds out that **Ernie** was burned up in California, probably the result of the horsemen. [6]

Evangelista, Phoebe

Name **Chloe Williams** gives the GC when they interrogate her in San Diego. [11]

Evangelista Jr., Phoebe

Name **Chloe Williams** gives as her child's during the GC interrogation. [11]

Ezer

Jewish butcher who provides free meat for the Tribulation Force's first post-manna meal. **Ezer** resists **Carpathia's** loyalty mark throughout the entire Tribulation, causing him to lose his house and his business. He does not, however, become a believer until just before the Glorious Appearing when he hears a rabbi preach to those trying to defend Jerusalem from **Carpathia's** Unity Army. After the Glorious Appearing, **Ezer** returns to his shop and, as a service to other believers, begins to butcher the animals God miraculously sends him. 12

FALSE CHRIST
See messiahs.

Feinberg, Rabbi Marc
A primary advocate of the initiative to reconstruct the Jewish temple. He predicts to **Buck Williams** that the temple will be rebuilt within the year. **Rabbi Feinberg** is a firm believer in the one true God of Abraham, Isaac, and Jacob, but is willing to tolerate other beliefs as long as he is allowed to keep his own. He confides to **Buck** that **Nicolae Carpathia** seems more like a messiah than Jesus. 2

Ferdinand
Tall, balding man with red cheeks who works at Carpathia Resurrection Field loyalty mark center. **Ginger** calls him to operate the facilitator (guillotine). He finds a corrugated, tinfoil-lined box to be used for catching **Steve Plank's** head after **Ferdinand** releases the blade. Also referred to as "Cheeks." 10

Fernandez, Conchita
Name given by one of the patients at the reproductive clinic in Littleton, Colorado. 4

Figueroa, Aurelio Sequoia
David Hassid's replacement on the GC staff. A tall, bony Mexican man who treats his superiors like royalty and his subordinates like servants. **Chang Wong** finds it amusing to tease him, especially about his full name, distinctive because each name contains all five vowels. **Figueroa** administers the lie-detector test to **Chang**. 9

   Figueroa invites his department's techies, including **Chang**, to watch the Petra bombing. He questions **Chang** about the mole situation but never figures out **Chang's** true role at the palace. When the heat judgment begins, he orders everyone to the basement. **Figueroa** takes credit for **Chang's** discovery that the rivers are no longer bloody when he reports to **Akbar**. 10

Figueroa is unaccounted for after the GC leadership leave New Babylon during the plague of darkness. **11**

Fitzgerald, Pauline
Alias **Leah Rose** uses when approached by GC in her garage. She claims to be a GC worker out of Des Plaines. **6**

Fitzgerald, Sergeant
Mac McCullum calls **Rayford Steele** by this name when confirming to **Rayford** that the plan is still on to evacuate **Buck Williams**, **Chloe Williams**, and **Chaim Rosenzweig** from Jerusalem after the Meeting of the Witnesses. **5**

Fitzhugh, Gerald (Fitz)
President of the United States. He is a fit, energetic man in his late fifties. **Fitzhugh** won *Global Weekly's* prestigious Newsmaker of the Year honor twice. **Buck Williams** enjoys the opportunity to interview **Fitzhugh**, opening a friendship between them. **1**

At the signing of the peace treaty with Israel, **Fitzhugh** sings **Nicolae Carpathia's** praises, much to **Buck's** surprise. **Carpathia** uses his power to take *Air Force One* from **Fitzhugh** and to convince the populace that the North American ambassador to the GC should supplant the sitting president. **Carpathia** reduces **Fitzhugh's** position to being in charge of enforcing **Carpathia's** global disarmament plan in America. **Fitzhugh** adamantly disagrees with the disarmament plan, and he plans an attack on Washington D.C. Friendship dictates that **Fitzhugh** warn **Buck** about these looming attacks. **2**

American militia factions, under the clandestine leadership of **Fitzhugh**, join forces with the United States of Britain and the former sovereign state of Egypt, and the militia attacks Washington, D.C. Later **Carpathia** announces that **Fitzhugh** was killed in the retaliatory attack. **3**

Fitzhugh, Wilma
Wife of President **Gerald Fitzhugh**. **1**

Florence
1. Stocky African-American night guard for **Chloe** at San Diego GC lockup. She gives **Chloe** a drugged chocolate shake and helps load her for transport to what was formerly known as Stateville. **11**

2. Middle-aged African-American woman who greatly influences The Place believers under the direction of **Enoch**. 12

Fortunato, Leonardo (Leon)

Sycophant from the New Babylon office who works very closely with **Nicolae Carpathia**. 3 He is short and stocky, with dark skin, hair, and eyes, notable for his buffoonish antics and clumsiness. When the wrath of the Lamb earthquake strikes, **Fortunato** claims to have died when GC headquarters collapses. He claims **Carpathia** brings him back to life by saying, "**Leonardo**, come forth!" The revived **Fortunato** is given a new title of Supreme Commander. 4 **Dwayne Tuttle** is the first to call him the False Prophet for telling others his resurrection story and worshiping **Carpathia**. 6

Fortunato is **Carpathia's** right-hand man and assumed successor when **Carpathia** is assassinated. He even tells GC workers to call him "Excellency," kneel before him, and worship him as they did **Carpathia**. 7 After **Carpathia's** resurrection, **Fortunato** returns to his role as the supreme commander. Later he becomes the Most High Reverend Father of Carpathianism and leads the world in worshiping **Carpathia** as the risen god. In his new role, "Neon Leon" wears flamboyant, gaudy, multicolored outfits covered with every religious symbol but those of Judaism and Christianity. 7, 8 **Fortunato** makes the statue of **Carpathia** speak and summons fire from the sky to destroy some who rebel against worshiping it. 7

Fortunato suffers from the sores judgment but remains close to **Carpathia** and all his activities. He is responsible for **Hattie Durham's** death as he again calls fire from the sky. During his speech announcing the mandate to worship **Carpathia's** statue, an angel of God appears, causing **Fortunato** to fall off his platform. 9

Carpathia commissions **Fortunato** to raise up **false christs** to preach and do miracles throughout the world and win allegiance to **Carpathia**. **Fortunato** is involved in top brass meetings with **Carparthia** and even calls a meeting of his own to discuss the bloody water situation, which **Carpathia** chides him for. He also debates **Tsion-Ben Judah**. 10

Fortunato remains by **Carpathia's** side during the Battle of Armageddon. 11, 12 After the Glorious Appearing, he is judged by Jesus. Fighting the angel **Michael** all the way, he is thrown into the lake of fire along with **Carpathia**. Then it seals up, and he is heard no more. 12

Francine
Secretary to **Earl Halliday**, **Rayford Steele's** supervisor at Pan-Con.
She takes the call regarding the bogus religious-harassment complaint filed by **Jim Long**. **2**

Frederick
Employee of **Nicolae Carpathia** who spotlights *Air Force One* for
Carpathia's and **Rayford Steele's** viewing. **2**

Friedrich
German confused about **Carpathia's** pig ride through Jerusalem.
He comments to another bystander that he thought **Carpathia** had
more dignity. **9**

GABRIEL
The announcer and pronouncer angel. **Tsion Ben-Judah** talks with
him during his vision/dream. **7** **Gabriel** appears with **Michael** at
various places around the world, making pronouncements for God
and standing in defense of his people. **10**

    Gabriel is present for the judgment of the Antichrist, the False
Prophet, and Lucifer, as well as the rewards of the saints. **12**

Ganter, Paulo
Inmate at the Greek detention center. **Buck Williams** uses his
name to help a young believer escape. **8** It is later revealed
that the real **Paulo Ganter** received the loyalty mark,
which helps the GC determine the true identity of the
young man released: **Marcel Papadopoulos**. **9**

Garfield, Jean
Supposed secretary to Pan-Con certification examiner
Jim Long of Dallas. She threatens to file a religious harassment
complaint against **Rayford Steele**—harassment that **Long**
claims happened while he was certifying **Rayford** on the 777.
Francine later confirms that there is no **Jean Garfield** at Pan-
Con Airlines, and **Hattie Durham** eventually confesses to
Rayford that she was behind the complaint, which she claims
was intended as a joke. **2**

Garner, Mrs.
GC secretary for **Pinkerton Stephens**. She reports that she
heard banging from **Hattie Durham's** room. She is told that
Hattie hanged herself and watches as **Hattie's** body is
loaded into the minivan. **8**

Ginger

A woman of about 60 with red hair who processes the undecided at Carpathian Resurrection Field loyalty mark center. **Steve Plank** shows her all the gory details of his injured body while she processes him. **10**

Goldman

Name **Chaim Rosenzweig** uses to reserve a room at The Night Visitors following **Carpathia's** assassination. **7**

Gonder, Jesse

Alias **Rayford Steele** uses in Al Basrah when he goes to pick up his Saber. **6**

Gustafson, Leonard

President of Pan-Con who meets with **Rayford Steele** in **Earl Halliday's** office. He strongly encourages **Rayford** to take the new job of flying for the president. **2**

Gustav, Dr. Od

The Scandinavian regional potentate. He signs **Peter the Second's** death certificate, and in his briefcase he carries the bag that will hold **Peter's** body. **6**

HAASE, DR. JURGEN

Head of the Global Community Emergency Management Association. He urges citizens to wear gas masks and work together to extinguish the fires after the 200 million horsemen arrive. **6**

Halliday, Earl

Pan-Con Airlines chief pilot at O'Hare and supervisor to **Rayford Steele**. He warns **Rayford** to stop witnessing because he is upset about complaints. **Earl** strongly encourages **Rayford** to fly *Air Force One*, especially since it is a job **Earl** has always wanted. **2**

Earl flies *Global Community One*, formerly *Air Force One*, into New York in **Rayford's** place and gets out before New York is attacked. He suspects that **Carpathia** wanted both him and the plane bombed while in New York and thinks **Rayford** set him up. Despite his anger, **Earl** must instruct **Rayford** on how to fly the Condor 216. He alerts **Rayford** to the bugging system that allows the pilots to hear anything going on in the rest of the plane, which proves invaluable in the Tribulation Force**'s** battle against

Carpathia. **Carpathia** sees **Earl** as only a "temporary necessity" and has him eliminated. **3**

Hamilton, Judy
Airstrip chief at Carpathia Memorial Airstrip. She is reluctant to help **Albie** (**Commander Elbaz**) and **Rayford Steele** until she reads the computer clearance straight from **David Hassid**. Upon seeing **Albie** and **Rayford's** clearance, she agrees to lend **Albie** her mini-van, and in exchange for **Albie's** promise not to report her insubordination, she offers to forget **Albie's** breach of protocol. **6**

Hannelore
Jacov's wife. She is a German-born Jew with sandy hair and shy blue eyes. She and **Jacov** had 2 small children who vanished at the Rapture. **Hannelore** becomes a believer after her husband receives Jesus as his Messiah at the Meeting of the Witnesses. Later she moves into **Chaim Rosenzweig's** estate to help take care of **Chaim** and **Jonas** after the demon locusts sting them. **5**

After **Nicolae Carpathia's** assassination, **Buck Williams** finds **Hannelore** murdered at the **Rosenzweig** estate along with her mother and **Stefan**. **7**

Hannelore's Mother
She has difficulty with the conversions of her son-in-law, **Jacov**, and her daughter. At first she wishes that **Stefan** and **Jacov** were still drunks and not "crazy religious people." However, she also becomes a believer after a demon locust stings her. **5**

Despite her pain, **Hannelore's mother** reads, studies, prays, and pleads with **Chaim Rosenzweig** and **Jonas** to come to Christ. She is murdered at the **Rosenzweig** estate along with her daughter and **Stefan**. **7**

Hans
Foundry foreman ordered to get supplies to **Guy Blod** for the sculpture of **Nicolae Carpathia**. **7**

Hanson, Beauregard (Bo)
Argues with **Rayford Steele** about **Ken Ritz's** personal items at Palwaukee Airport. According to **T Delanty**, **Bo's** father owned 5 percent of the business, but he died in a car wreck at the Rapture, and **Bo** became sole heir of that interest in the airport. **5**

Bo has a bleached crew cut and a muscular linebacker's physique. After being stung by the locusts, he tries to kill himself 3 times with no success. **5**, **6**

Bo develops a friendship with **Hattie Durham**, which eventually leads to the death of his brother, **Samuel**. After the news of **Sam's** death, **Bo** gets drunk, curses **Carpathia** and the world, and shoots himself to death. **6**

Hanson, Samuel

Brother of **Bo Hanson** and a Quantum pilot from Baton Rouge, Louisiana. He supposedly crashes somewhere off the shore of Portugal, carrying **Hattie Durham** on board. Later it is discovered that he did not crash the plane. **Samuel** dies in a gunfight when trying to protect **Hattie** from being subjected to GC interrogation. **6**

Harold

Elderly man raptured during **Rayford Steele's** flight to Heathrow. His wife is concerned that he is wandering the plane nude, because his clothes are left on his seat. **1**

Hassid, David

A young Jew from Eastern Europe, **David** has a dark complexion and dark hair and eyes. He's a computer genius, and he joins the GC because of his great respect for **Nicolae Carpathia**. **David** becomes a believer through **Tsion Ben-Judah's** Internet ministry. **Rayford Steele** is excited to meet this new believer and mentors him. **4**

David is a high-level administrator for the GC and works closely with the transportation of the fleet of GC airplanes and helicopters, reporting to **Leon Fortunato**. On occasion he even reports directly to **Carpathia**. **David** works for the Tribulation Force, providing them new computers and hand-sized units that can access the Internet and serve as solar-powered, satellite-connected global phones. **5**

David helps with the ill and the dead after the 200 million horsemen attack New Babylon. He falls in love with **Annie Christopher**, and they want to marry but fear it is too dangerous in their positions. **6**

David interacts with **Guy Blod** about **Carpathia's** statue and listens in on **Carpathia's** autopsy, learning the true cause of his death. He is present at **Carpathia's** funeral and witnesses both the statue speaking and **Carpathia's** resurrection. **7**

David continues to play an integral part in clearing the way for the Tribulation Force's work around the world. In the scorching heat of New Babylon, he suffers a spill requiring medical attention. **Nurse Hannah Palemoon** assists him, and she reports that, to the Tribulation Force, **David's** importance is surpassed only by **Dr. Ben-Judah's**. **David** is heartbroken by the news of **Annie's** death. 8

    David is presumed dead in the staged crash of the Quasi Two but is actually on his way to Petra to set up the communication center to serve the believers. **David** is killed by 2 GC soldiers in the hills around Petra. The Tribulation Force members are devastated by his death, especially **Hannah**. His phone, along with **Hattie's** ashes, is flown back to the States for a memorial. 9

    Rayford sees **David** at the judgment. 12

Hernandez, Captain Chico

Pilot who flies the 6-seater Learjet to Dallas with **Rayford** and **Amanda Steele** and **Nicolae Carpathia** on board during the insurrection. **Carpathia** tells **Rayford** he is sending **Chico** on assignment to the old National Security Agency Building in Maryland to fly only small aircraft, but in reality, **Carpathia** has him eliminated. 3

Hickman, Jim

GC intelligence analysis chief who comments on prophecy and the two witnesses. At first **David Hassid** considers **Hickman** brilliant but entirely too impressed with himself. 6 **Hickman** continues as GC intelligence director, arranging a forensic expert crew to study the **Carpathia** assassination evidence. 7

    Carpathia begins to consider **Hickman** a buffoon, recognizing that he was **Fortunato's** choice, not his. **Hickman** is given **Leon Fortunato's** old title, Supreme Commander, but he is never intended to be active in GC affairs. Under extreme pressure, **Carpathia** makes him reveal a source leak, someone who is later executed by **Carpathia**. Soon after, **Hickman** shoots himself. 8

Hill, Elva & Ian

Aliases used by **Dwayne** and **Trudy Tuttle** while dropping **Rayford Steele** off in Europe to find **Hattie Durham**. **Dwayne** uses a perfect British accent and shows **Rayford** two United States of Britain passports. 6

Holmes, Larry

Heavyweight champion of the world who lived in Easton, Pennsylvania. **Ken Ritz** mentions that **Holmes** defeated Muhammad Ali and claims that **Larry Holmes** would have punished those responsible for the disappearances were he still alive. Of course, at this writing Larry Holmes *is* still alive, but the series is set in the future. **1**

Hut, Loren

Global Community Morale Monitor chief from Calgary, Canada. He has dark hair, an athletic build, and is a decorated member of the GC. Hut confronts **Chaim Rosenzweig** and **Buck Williams** at the Temple Mount. A terrible reaction to the sores judgment makes him want to kill himself, but **Chaim** tells him not to. **Hut** has a difficult time showing proper respect to **Nicolae Carpathia**. His eventual disgust and disillusionment prompt **Carpathia** to kill him with **Akbar's** sidearm. **9**

IRENE, CHLOE

Alias **Chloe Williams** uses on the mission to rescue **George Sebastian**. She disguises herself as a high-level GC officer from Montreal. **10**

Ivins, Vivian (Viv)

Alleged to be **Nicolae Carpathia's** aunt and only living relative. **7**, **8** Although **Viv** helped raise **Carpathia**, he claims she is not a blood relative. **8** She is in her late sixties and typically dresses to match her blue-gray hair. **12**

Considered **Carpathia's** oldest confidante, **Viv** coordinates many GC activities and is prominent at **Carpathia's** funeral and resurrection. **7** She takes an active role in organizing the guillotines designed to help **Carpathia** control citizens by administering a mark of loyalty. **8**

As a member of **Carpathia's** inner circle, **Viv** appears prominently beside him in Jerusalem in high-level meetings. She kneels on the pavement to receive her *216* mark and creates a scene in her worship of **Carpathia**, crawling on the temple steps, hugging his statue, kissing his hands and feet, and anointing his shoes. In her one critical mistake, **Viv** goes to the temple to violate its traditions, and **Carpathia** hears that she may have gone into the Holy of Holies and sat on the throne. This enrages him, and though **Viv** begs for his forgiveness, he remains silent. **9**

Viv is with **Carpathia** when Petra is bombed, though he still treats her coldly. He chides her for complaining about her thirst during the heat judgment, then ridicules her. When temperatures return to normal, **Viv** is invited to a meeting of **Carpathia's** top brass, and **Carpathia** seems to have put it all aside. 10

Viv attends **Carpathia's** meeting at Solomon's Stables, confirming the photographers, taking steps to get **Chaim Rosenzweig** off the air, and bringing **Carpathia** water when he begins to fail. When Lucifer makes his presence known, she falls to the floor, making incoherent but ecstatic noises. 12

JACOV

Chaim Rosenzweig's driver and valet. He drives **Buck** and **Chloe Williams** and **Tsion Ben-Judah** to the stadium for the Meeting of the Witnesses, and he hears and receives the message and the believer's seal. He shoots Uzi bullets into the air to cause a diversion in order to get **Tsion** out of the stadium safely. He and his wife, **Hanelore**, had 2 small children who vanished in the Rapture. **Jacov** has a drinking problem before becoming a believer, but the first thing he does after coming to Christ is go to The Harem (a lewd bar) to preach on top of a table. He is mistaken for being drunk, but he is a changed man. **Jacov** witnesses to his wife and mother-in-law, who eventually accept Jesus as their Messiah. 5

Jacov picks up **Buck** from Ben Gurion Airport and later reports that **Chaim** has had a stroke. In what seems like a miracle, **Chaim** recovers, and **Jacov** gets him to the Global Gala stage. 6

After **Carpathia** is mortally wounded, **Jacov** tries to help **Chaim,** but his neck is broken by a blow struck to his head by the butt of a GC weapon. 7

Jaime

Tsion Ben-Judah's longtime driver. **Jaime** is close to receiving Jesus as his Messiah, but he dies in a car bombing the same day **Tsion's** family is murdered. 3

Janssen, Anika

A tall, blonde reporter working from the Temple Mount. She's mastered several languages, demonstrated when she guesses citizens' nationalities and begins interviews in their native languages. **Janssen** interviews some critical of GC personnel having received marks before those on pilgrimages did. She also interviews **Viv Ivins**. 9

Janssen breaks the news of **Chloe Williams's** capture as the GC news anchor out of Detroit. 11

SUPPORTING CHARACTERS—J

Jensen, Corporal Jack
Alias **Buck Williams** uses when accompanying **Albie** in search of the underground Greek church members incarcerated in Ptolemaïs. **Z** uses dark hair dye and dark contacts to disguise **Buck** as this GC Peacekeeper. **8** **Buck's Jensen** ID is left behind in the King David Hotel room, and **Chang Wong** destroys all record of Jensen. **9**

Jeoffrey
Hattie Durham's waiter at the Global Bistro. **3**

Jesse
Guard from the United South American States. He is dark skinned and has splendid teeth. **Jesse** guards **Chloe Williams**, and he accompanies **Chloe** and **Jock** to the former Stateville Correctional Facility. **11**

Jimmy
Dr. Charles phones this hospital contact and requests equipment to deal with **Hattie Durham's** miscarriage. **5**

Jinnah, Indira
Alias **Hannah Palemoon** uses on the mission to rescue **George Sebastian**. She learns an Indian accent and wears a high-level GC officer's uniform. **9**, **10**

Jock
See **Ashmore, Colonel Jonathan**.

Johnson, Howie
Alias **Mac McCullum** uses on the mission to rescue **George Sebastian** from Greece. His skin is altered to remove his freckles, and his red hair is darkened to brown. As **Johnson**, **Mac** wears glasses and the GC-issue camouflage of a senior commander. **9**, **10**

Johnson, Mary
One of the patients at the reproductive clinic in Littleton, Colorado. **Buck Williams** mistakenly thinks **Hattie Durham** is using this name. **4**

Jonas
Chaim Rosenzweig's gatekeeper and night watchman. **Buck Williams** rescues him from his outdoor booth and brings him inside **Chaim's** estate during the locust attack. **5**
    After being stung by a demon locust, **Jonas** comes to Christ.

Soon after, he is killed when a car strikes the gate booth. **Chaim** takes **Jonas's** death hard and claims that there is no truth in **Tsion Ben-Judah's** teachings. **6**

Jorge

Directed by **Leon Fortunato** to contact the guards at the loyalty enforcement center and order them not to allow the prisoners to sing. **10**

K

Member of the underground Greek church; his real name is **Kronos**. He is older than **Laslos** and speaks with difficulty because most of his front teeth are missing. He is murdered during the failed attempt to smuggle **Marcel Papadopoulos** and **Georgiana Stravros** out of Greece. **9 K** is remembered as one of the most beloved members of the Greek church. **10**

Karl

1. **Leon Fortunato's** Scandinavian cook on the flight to Johannesburg via Kuwait. He serves **Leon** eggs Benedict. He**'s** frantic when one of his workers is overcome with fumes from the 200 million horsemen. An emergency landing in Khartoum leaves him alternating between crying and bustling about arranging everything. In the ambush at Johannesburg, **Karl** dies from a bullet to the forehead. **6**
2. A mechanic in overalls at the Kozani airport whom an official tells to come see **Rayford Steele's** ID. **Karl** does not express much interest in **Rayford's** identification and appears to be irritated about being asked to leave his work. **7**

Kashmir

Mainyu Mazda's tattoo artist. She is small and young with large eyes and a *42* on her forehead. **Kashmir** is completely robed, and she wears rubber gloves as she tattoos. **11**

Katz, Herb

Alias **Buck Williams** uses when the Lincoln **Rayford Steele** is driving is stopped by **Carpathia's** guards. **Buck** tells a GC guard that he is an American businessman in Israel on pleasure. He tells another guard that he works for International Harvester. He uses this name again when checking into The Drake Hotel in Chicago, when checking into the King

David Hotel while trying to find **Tsion**, and throughout his mission to get **Tsion** out of Israel. **3**

After the wrath of the Lamb earthquake, **Buck** uses this name at Arthur Young Memorial Hospital when identifying himself to **Ken Ritz**, knowing **Ritz** will remember the name and associate it with **Buck**. **4**

Kerry
First GC bomber pilot to return to **Suhail Akbar's** office after the attack on Petra. He is proud of his "successful" bombing, not willing to accept responsibility for the failure. **Carpathia** orders his death. **10**

Kivisto, Lieutenant Ernest
GC officer in charge of getting earthquake survivors shelter. **Buck Williams** requests his assistance in finding **Chloe**. **4**

Kline, Dr. Samuel
Famous cardiovascular surgeon from Norway who **Rayford Steele** says is "in **Carpathia's** back pocket." **Kline** is on the news to report a proposal for measures to regulate the health and welfare of the Global Community. **Kline** calls **Buck Williams's** warning about the coming wrath of the Lamb earthquake an "interesting bit of fiction." In a private conversation with **Carpathia**, he discusses the reality of the water for temple ceremonies turning to blood, and he questions **Carpathia's** mention of using an atomic bomb on Israel if the two witnesses continue polluting the water. **Dr. Kline** also discusses with **Carpathia** establishing universal government funding of abortions and requiring amniocentesis for all pregnancies. **3**

Kollek, Teddy
Former mayor of Jerusalem who stood for peace, harmony, and statesmanship. The stadium used for the Meeting of the Witnesses is named after him. **5**

Kononowa
Potentate of the United Indian States who addresses the funeral crowds with great admiration for **Carpathia** and describes the one-world faith as **Carpathia's** "brilliant vision." **7**

Konrad, Deputy Commander
Alias **Chang Wong** uses over the phone to contact **Stefanich**, using a voice modulator that makes him sound like an elderly German

man. The alias is compromised when it is discovered that though chain of command indicates **Konrad** is Security and Intelligence Director **Akbar's** most important subordinate officer, **Akbar** has never heard of him. **10**

Kronos

1. See **K.**

2. A cousin of **K's** and part of the Greek co-op. He supplies firepower and a truck to **Mac McCullum**, **Chloe Steele**, and **George Sebastian** for their escape from Greece. Cousin **Kronos** goes with **Costas** and a few others to find out what happened to **K** and **Miklos** when they fail to return from helping **Marcel** out of Greece. Cousin **Kronos** and his wife are assumed dead after the raid on the Greek co-op. **10**

Krystall

Nicolae Carpathia's secretary. When **Carpathia** chides **Leon Fortunato** about his water meeting, she and others try to convince **Carpathia** of the issue's importance. She interrupts a meeting to let **Carpathia** know about strange heat-wave reports. During the heat judgment, **Krystall's** office is relocated under Building D, and she has to communicate with **Carpathia** via intercom. **10**

   Krystall helps the Tribulation Force by allowing **Otto Weser** to listen in on **Suhail Akbar** and learn his assignment in Al Hillah. **Rayford Steele** contacts **Krystall** to try to get information about **Chloe's** imprisonment, but she is unable to help. **Krystall** dies before the fall of New Babylon, possibly of poisonous gas. **11**

Kuntz, Sunny

Senior field supervisor, Global Community Relief, who assists in the paperwork for the rebuilding of Mt. Prospect following the wrath of the Lamb earthquake. He tells **Buck Williams** about **Helen Cavenaugh's** survival and directs **Buck** to the makeshift shelter. **4**

LAFITTE, GEORGES

Operative with Interpol. He calls **Buck Williams** about **Dirk Burton's** and **Alan Tompkins's** deaths. **1**

Lalaine, Dr.

To throw off GC workers, **Ken Ritz** uses this name while sitting at the hospital with **Chloe Williams**. **4**

Lars
Cocky, condescending GC worker who checks out **Chang Wong's** apartment and works to "fix" **Chang's** computer. He is one of **Chang's** coworkers. 9

Laslos
See **Miklos, Lukas.**

Leonard, Nigel
Supervisor of **Dirk Burton's** section at the London Exchange. He informs **Buck Williams** that **Dirk** has committed suicide. 1

Li
Seven-month-old son of an Asian woman aboard **Buck Williams's** plane to Tel Aviv. **Buck** introduces himself to her as **Greg North.** 6

Lie, Trygve
Former secretary-general of the U.N. mentioned in **Nicolae Carpathia's** United Nations speech. Originally from Norway. 1

Litewski, Caryn
Flight attendant. Her family had long been friends with **Cardinal Mathews**, who later becomes **Peter the Second. Caryn** was baptized by **Mathews.** 2

Litwala, Enoch
The United States of Africa potentate from Kenya. He voices his displeasure with **Peter the Second** to **Leon Fortunato. Carpathia** plants in **Enoch's** mind the plan to assassinate **Peter the Second.** 6
   One of the 3 insurgent kings. **Rayford Steele** suspects him of **Carpathia's** murder. 6 **Litwala** delivers a brief, bare tribute at **Carpathia's** funeral. He dies when **Fortunato** calls down fire from the sky, incinerating **Litwala** and the other opposing potentates. 7

Lloyd, Dr.
Tall, gray-haired doctor with glasses whom **Buck** pretends to know from a symposium at Bemidji. **Buck** tricks **Dr. Lloyd** into writing a prescription for Benzedrine to counteract the overdose of tranquilizers **Ken Ritz** has taken. 4

Lockridge, Dr. Shadrach Meshach
African-American preacher who gave a sermon entitled "My King Is . . ." **Chaim Rosenzweig** chooses this sermon for **Chang Wong** to broadcast on the GC television network to the undecideds, and millions respond. 12

Long, Jim

Fictitious Pan-Con certification examiner from Dallas. **Rayford Steele** is accused of witnessing to **Long**, and a threat is made to file a religious-harassment complaint against **Rayford**. **Hattie Durham** eventually confesses to **Rayford** that she was behind the complaint, which she claims was intended as a joke. **2**

Loretta

A parishioner of New Hope Village Church in Mt. Prospect, Illinois, who was left behind; all her family members were raptured. She came from a devout spiritual heritage but never knew Christ personally. After coming to Christ, she shows **Pastor Billings's** tape on the Rapture to everyone she can. **Loretta** becomes **Bruce Barnes's** secretary and assistant. **1**, **2**, **3**

Loretta deeply mourns the death of **Bruce Barnes**, and she works hard to get his work printed with the help of Tribulation Force members and **Donny Moore**. She is gifted with hospitality, sharing her home with those who have been left behind. **Loretta** dies in the wrath of the Lamb earthquake when her car comes down on top of her. **3**

Rayford Steele sees her in a white robe at Jesus' throne. **12**

MACK

Desk clerk at the Midpoint Motel. He relays a phone message to **Buck Williams**, turns off **Buck's** phone upon request, and provides him with a bandage. **Buck** tips him $20. **1**

Margaret

Leon Fortunato's secretary. **6** She assists **David Hassid** in securing good seats for the **Wongs** at **Carpathia's** funeral. **7**

Maria

Carpathianist and sister of **Jesse**, **Chloe Williams's** guard. **11**

Marianne

Alan Tompkins's sister. **Joshua Todd-Cothran** makes threats to **Alan** about her safety. **1**

Mathews, Cardinal Peter

A cardinal for more than 10 years and a prominent archbishop of Cincinnati. He is tall and dark-haired in his late forties. **Nicolae Carpathia** elevates **Mathews** to the position of pope of the one-world church. In his new role,

Mathews gains the title Pontifex Maximus. [2] He later rejects this title in favor of **Peter the Second**. [4]

Mathews leads the Enigma Babylon One World Faith, which combines elements and symbols of every religion willing to give up its claim to exclusive truth. Christianity and Judaism are, by definition, excluded from the One World Faith. [5]

Carpathia believes **Mathews** is a conspirator in the ambush at Johannesburg, scheming with **Rehoboth** to destroy **Carpathia** and take his position. **Leon Fortunato**, at **Carpathia's** command, organizes opposition to the 10 potentates, and they murder **Mathews**. A cremation covers the plot, and the Enigma Babylon One World Faith fades into oblivion. [6]

Mazda, Mainyu

Black-market contact of **Albie's** on Abadan Island. He is also known as Double-M because of a double-M tattoo on his neck for each murder he has committed, 13 in all. **Mazda** shoots **Albie** to collect the bounty of 20,000 Nicks on citizens with no loyalty mark and to steal the 30,000 Nicks **Albie** brought to hire **Mazda**. [11]

McCullum, Mac

Rayford Steele's copilot from New Babylon to Washington [3] Mac has reddish blond hair and a freckled, weathered face. He becomes a faithful friend to **Rayford**, helping him search for **Amanda**. When he asks **Rayford** for his thoughts on the vanishings, **Rayford** witnesses to him, and after some thought, **Mac** becomes a believer. [4]

Mac becomes chief pilot to **Nicolae Carpathia** and a vital source of inside information for the Tribulation Force, assisting them in life-and-death situations. [5] He becomes a hero saving **Leon Fortunato's** life during the Johannesburg ambush. [6]

The Global Community believes **Mac** dies in the crash of the Quasi Two, but he is not in that plane. He uses the crash to escape GC authorities. [8, 9] He is involved in Operation Eagle, flying and driving for the Tribulation Force. Under the alias of GC commander **Howie Johnson**, he travels to Greece to help rescue **George Sebastian**. [9] **Michael**, the archangel, shows up to help when **Mac** has trouble getting on the plane and out of Greece. After the Strong Building evacuation, **Mac** ends up in Al Basrah with **Albie**. [10]

Mac relocates to Petra after **Albie's** death, and he is instrumental in piloting believers to Petra. **Mac** and **Lionel Whalum** evacuate more than 150 people from New Babylon. As the Battle of Armageddon approaches, **Mac** flies reconnaissance missions over Al Hillah and gives **Rayford** an update on the enemy's weaponry. ▇11

Mac flies to Jerusalem in search of **Buck Williams** and witnesses the meeting in Solomon's Stables, during which Lucifer leaves **Carpathia's** body for a time. **Mac** returns to Petra, ready to fight, and rejoices with **Rayford** and **Abdullah Smith** over the victory. Like all the believers, **Mac** has one-on-one time with Jesus, during which Jesus calls him by his real name, **Cleburn**. At the judgment, **Mac** is reunited with his good friend, **Albie**. ▇12

McGillicuddy, B.
Name on the first-class airplane ticket provided for **Buck Williams** to get him from Chicago to New York to see **Nicolae Carpathia**. ▇2

Medvedev, Vasily
Steve Plank's right-hand man. **Medvedev** resents that he took the mark and is therefore unable to decide for Christ. After **Plank's** beheading, he commits suicide, shooting himself in the head. ▇10

messiahs
False christs commissioned by **Nicolae Carpathia** and sent out by **Leon Fortunato**. One of these **messiahs** is seen by **Rayford Steele**, **Mac McCullum**, **Abdullah Smith**, and **Albie** in the desert near Petra. **Mac** thinks the **messiah** resembles a young **Fortunato**. The **false christ** performs several miracles, including cloud cover, turning water to blood, raising from the dead, and multiplying food. He is referred to as "a type of Christ." After deceiving and killing many, the **messiah** disappears. ▇10

Micah
Name used by **Chaim Rosenzweig** in his role as spokesperson for and witness to the Jews. For his role as **Micah**, **Chaim's** skin and hair are darkened, and he grows a thick beard. He wears brown contact lenses instead of his glasses, a small mouth appliance that makes his chin protrude, and a brown robe similar to a monk's. As **Micah**, **Chaim** confronts the Antichrist, leads Israeli believers to Petra, and preaches to the remnant. *Micah* is an anagram of *Chaim*. ▇GFF

Michael

1. See **Shorosh, Michael**.
2. The archangel; the general of the angelic army. **Michael** shows images from Revelation to **Tsion Ben-Judah** during his vision. **7** **Michael** appears to **Hattie Durham** and makes clear to her that she is to speak out against **Carpathia**. He also appears to **Rayford Steele**, restoring **Rayford's** hearing and his energy. **Michael** also protects a helicopter full of Tribulation Force members and encourages the crowd at Petra just before the GC armies attack. **9**

On the mission to rescue **George Sebastian**, **Michael** appears in the plane and helps **Mac McCullum** get on board. At the Rihand Dam, **Michael** takes water that has turned to blood and makes it clean for **Mac**. **10**

Michael plays an integral role in Jesus' judgment of the wicked. He brings **Nicolae Carpathia**, **Leon Fortunato**, **Ashtaroth**, **Baal**, and **Cankerworm** before Jesus. Once Antichrist and the False Prophet have been judged, **Michael** pushes the two of them into the lake of fire. He also brings Lucifer before Jesus. Lucifer wrestles with **Michael** as a lion, a serpent, and a dragon. After Lucifer is judged, **Michael** chains him and flies him into the abyss. **12**

Miklos, Lukas

A Greek contact of **Ken Ritz**, nicknamed **Laslos**. He is a lignite supplier for GC thermoelectric plants. He is short and stocky with dark, curly hair. **Laslos** and his wife offer hospitality to **Rayford Steele** and **Tsion Ben-Judah**, who give them news of **Ken's** death. Later, **Buck Williams** meets with **Laslos** to discuss his role in the International Commodity Co-op, and **Laslos** decides to throw his energy into increasing the value of his lignite business and selling it to the GC before they decide to take it from him. **5**

Laslos carries out his plan and begins building a new operation that will have the appearance of a shipping business but will in reality ship commodities for the co-op. He and his wife are part of the growing underground church in Greece. **6**

Despite the danger, **Laslos** and fellow church members hide and minister to **Rayford** after **Carpathia's** assassination, providing him with a disguise and an identity to get him out of Greece. **7**

When the Greek church is raided, **Mrs. Miklos** is incarcerated with other underground church members. Shortly before she is beheaded, **Laslos** sends a message through **Buck**, telling her that she has been a wonderful wife and that they will be reunited in heaven. **Laslos's** wife, the **Demeters**, and other believing friends are killed in the GC detention centers for refusing to take **Carpathia's** mark. [8]

Laslos, in hiding and feeling guilty for not being present when his church was raided, lives in a 1-man underground shelter north of Ptolemaïs. He spends his days sleeping and his nights secretly visiting other believers. **Rayford** and **Laslos** devise a plan to get **Marcel Papadapolous** and **Georgiana Stravros** out of Greece, but the plan fails. **Laslos** and **Marcel** are murdered, and it is suspected that **Georgiana** has been killed and replaced by a GC impersonator named **Elena**. [9]

At the judgment, **Rayford** sees **Laslos** and his wife again. [12]

Miklos, Mrs.

Laslos's wife; she is heavyset and speaks broken English. [5, 6] **Mrs. Miklos** is a quiet woman, but she is also fearless, unwaveringly stating and defending her convictions. **Mrs. Miklos** enjoys the danger involved in being a part of the growing underground church and takes pleasure in assisting the Tribulation Force members. Before she becomes a martyr for Christ, **Mrs. Miklos** prays boldly with a group of women, continuing even after the GC beat her. She chooses to go to the guillotine rather than receive the mark of loyalty. [8]

Rayford sees **Mrs. Miklos** accept a martyr's crown at the judgment. [12]

Miller, Carolyn

Widow of **Eric Miller**. She contacts **Buck Williams** about her husband's suspicious drowning. [1]

Miller, Eric

A press colleague of **Buck Williams**; he works for *Seaboard Monthly*. He tries to weasel in on Buck's meeting with **Nicolae Carpathia**. **Miller** drowns after falling from a Staten Island ferry. His wife finds this suspicious because of the cold night, which should have driven **Eric** to the indoor area of the ferry, and his swimming skills. **Buck** finds that **Miller** had been writing for the past 2 years about the reconstruction of New Babylon with the help of **Jonathan Stonagal's** finances, and he suspects that **Carpathia** or **Stonagal** may be responsible for **Miller's** death. [1]

Moishe

One of the two prophets at the Wailing Wall declaring that Jesus Christ is the fulfillment of the Torah's prophecies of Messiah. The two witnesses, **Eli** and **Moishe**, wear burlap robes and no shoes, and both have long gray hair and unkempt beards. **1-6** Listeners are able to understand **Eli** and **Moishe** in their own tongues. **2** One attacker is killed by fire that comes from **Moishe's** mouth. **5**

    Nicolae Carpathia murders **Eli** and **Moishe** at the Wailing Wall. They resurrect 3 days later and rise into heaven, and an earthquake follows. **6**

Moon, Walter

Intelligence enforcement chief for the GC. He tells **Leon Fortunato** that **Hattie Durham** has been captured and taken to Brussels. **6**

    Moon is present at **Carpathia's** assassination as security chief and sends the EMTs away after **Carpathia** shows no vital signs. **7**

    A Caparthian loyalist, **Moon** asks to be given the mark before anyone else. **Carpathia** appoints him supreme commander, replacing **Jim Hickman**. **8**

    As supreme commander, **Moon** follows **Carpathia** around in Jerusalem. When **Moon** confronts **Carpathia**, telling him that an attack on the messianic Jews could cause a return of the afflictions, **Carpathia** mocks him. Later, when **Moon** talks to **Carpathia** about the water turning back to blood, **Carpathia** warns him that his second-guessing is likely to result in his death. **Moon's** fatal error is not getting **Tsion Ben-Judah's** pirated broadcast off the air as fast as **Carpathia** would like. **Carpathia** borrows **Suhail Akbar's** gun and shoots each of **Moon's** hands, then continues to shoot until **Moon** falls silent. **Aurelio Figueroa** reports to **Chang Wong** a rumor that Indian stewards killed **Moon** outside **Carpathia's** plane. **9**

Moore, Donny

Small blond with an astronomical IQ. **4 Donny** is good at fixing electronic equipment and uses his computer savvy to assist the Tribulation Force. He sets up nontraceable phones and deluxe computers, and also helps **Loretta** get **Bruce Barnes's** work in print. **3**

    Donny and his wife, **Sandy**, become believers soon after the Rapture. The **Moores** dig a shelter in their backyard in preparation for the coming judgments and trials. **Donny** and **Sandy** are killed in the wrath of the Lamb earthquake, but their duplex becomes a safe house for the Tribulation Force. **4**

Many of **Donny's** possessions become important to the Tribulation Force, including his telescope, which they use to monitor the heavens. **5**

Moore, Sandy

Married to **Donny Moore**. **Sandy** and **Donny** become believers after their baby is raptured. **Sandy** is killed in her duplex during the wrath of the Lamb earthquake, and **Buck Williams** and **Tsion Ben-Judah** bury her in the backyard. The **Moore** duplex becomes a safe house for the Tribulation Force. **4**

Mother Doe

Name given **Chloe Williams** upon being picked up by Ambu-Van after the wrath of the Lamb earthquake. Through this name, **Buck** learns that **Chloe** is pregnant. **4**

Murphy, Jeremy

George Sebastian's chopper instructor. He witnessed to **George** before the Rapture and then vanished. **George** thought **Jeremy** was crazy and got him in trouble for trying to proselytize on the job. Later **George** seeks out **Jeremy's** church for answers. **9**

NAGUIB, ATEF

Rayford Steele's Egyptian alias; he poses as **Abdullah Smith's** brother when taking **Tsion Ben-Judah** to Petra. To change his appearance, he puts on glasses and Egyptian robes, grows a mustache, and has **Z** make his skin darker. **10**

Nahum

Angel who appears in China and Argentina, predicting the destruction of New Babylon. He dresses in a robe and sandals, and his hair and beard are relatively short; his appearance and manner of speaking do not make his nationality apparent. **Nahum** brings warnings to the undecided, sometimes with **Christopher**. **10**

At the judgment, **Nahum** is seen at **Jesus'** throne along with **Christopher, Caleb, Gabriel,** and **Michael**. **12**

Nancy

Hattie Durham's sister. She works in an abortion clinic. After **Nancy** is stung by a locust, **Hattie** pleads with her to believe in Jesus, but **Nancy** refuses. **5**

After the judgment of the 200 million horsemen, **Chloe Williams** discovers **Nancy** on the list of those killed. 6

Ng, Li
Woman who worked for Channel 7 News and was raptured along with her whole household. She lived in **Rayford Steele's** neighborhood. 1

Ng, Suzie
Name of a client at the reproductive clinic in Littleton. 4

Ngumo, Mwangati
Secretary-General of the United Nations and president of Botswana; he steps down and **Nicolae Carpathia** takes his place. **Ngumo** allows this because he is promised his country will be allowed to use **Dr. Rosenzweig's** formula to bring fertility to Botswana. 1

    Carpathia does not follow through on his promise, however, and **Ngumo's** countrymen grow to hate him. **Rehoboth, Ngumo's** rival, becomes regional potentate, and **Ngumo** is forced to live under his rule. **Leon Fortunato** arranges for **Ngumo** to meet with **Carpathia**, but instead **Fortunato** appears alone at the meeting site, the Condor 216. The plane is ambushed, and **Ngumo** is killed by **Rehoboth's** insurgents. 6

Nigel
A young guard at the San Diego GC lockup. He delivers **Jock's** breakfast and opens a prison window at **Jock's** request. After **Chloe Williams** is drugged, **Nigel** helps load her into a hearse, then into a plane. 11

North, Greg
Identity of a deceased GC worker that **Z** gives to **Buck Williams**. **Buck** uses this identity on the way to Tel Aviv when he introduces himself to **Li** and his mother. He also uses it in Greece when he meets with the **Miklos** family. 6

    Buck uses the **Greg North** alias again when he calls the **Rosenzweig** estate after **Nicolae Carpathia's** assassination. 7

ORESKOVICH, GEORGE
Alias **Buck Williams** uses in Britain to fly home after **Alan Tompkins's** car-bombing murder. **Buck** is able to travel undetected as a naturalized Englishman from Poland. **Buck** also uses this name for his press credentials after he is reported dead in the bombing. 1

Oritz, Juan

Chief of the international politics section of *Global Weekly* angry that **Buck Williams** is going to cover the summit conference. **Ortiz** questions **Buck's** ability to find a common denominator between the 4 simultaneous and crucial international meetings. **1**

Otterness, Scott M.

Aging, heavyset guard at the Plaza Hotel who gives **Nicolae Carpathia** his gun. **Carpathia** uses the gun to kill **Jonathan Stonagal** and **Joshua Todd-Cothran**, then brainwashes **Otterness** to believe **Stonagal** stole the gun and killed himself. **1**

PAFKO, ANDREW

Alias **Rayford Steele** uses when he is approached by GC Peacekeeping troops in **Leah Rose's** garage. His ID says he is a GC Peacekeeper based in Des Plaines, Illinois. The 200 million horsemen arrive and kill the GC guards before their suspicions about **Rayford's** authenticity get him into trouble. **6**

Palemoon, Hannah

Nurse at the **GC's** New Babylon hospital, who grew up on a Cherokee reservation. Although she heard about Jesus on the reservation and in college, **Hannah** is angry with God for rapturing so many people and leaving her alone. When **Tsion Ben-Judah** warns about the earthquake and **Hannah's** entire family is subsequently killed, **Hannah** begins to think seriously about **Carpathia's** leadership qualities and **Tsion's** religious claims. Finally, after **Tsion** demonstrates accuracy in his warnings about the plagues, **Hannah** makes a decision for Christ. She meets **David Hassid** in the hospital, where she treats his head wound and develops a strong friendship with him. **Hannah** is with **David Hassid, Mac McCullum, Abdullah Smith**, and **Leah Rose** when the Quasi Two crashes. **8**

The GC erroneously assumes the Quasi Two crash has resulted in **Hannah's** death, but **Hannah** and **Leah Rose** soon arrive at Mizpe Ramon and assist those needing medical attention. **Hannah** reacts emotionally when **David** decides not to return to the United North American States at the end of Operation Eagle. Before his death, **David** sends an e-mail apology, complimenting her love for God and work for Christ. **Hannah** is devastated upon hearing of **David's** death. She provides medical assistance at Masada and does general volunteer work at Petra before returning to the States for a time of remembrance. ⁹

Disguised as a New Dehli Indian named **Indira Jinnah**, **Hannah** flies out on the mission to rescue **George Sebastian**. ⁹ She assists in the Greek rescue by driving the jeep, scoping out the co-op with **Chloe Williams**, and shooting the GC with a DEW. After the rescue, **Hannah** returns temporarily to the Strong Building until it is evacuated. She then heads with **Leah** to Long Grove, Illinois, where she helps with co-op business. 10

Hannah remains in Long Grove until **Lionel Whalum** brings her to Petra for **Albie** and **Chloe's** memorial service. As the battle of Armageddon approaches, she mans a weapon on the perimeter of Petra. 11

Hannah works in the infirmary at Petra until Christ appears and the sick are instantly healed. She is awed by Jesus at the Glorious Appearing and heads for Jerusalem with all the believers. 12

Papadopoulos, Marcel

Fifteen-year-old boy **Buck Williams** frees from the loyalty mark center in Ptolemaïs, Greece. **Buck** calls him **Paulo Ganter** and tells the GC he is deporting **Ganter** to the United North American States. ⁸

When the GC finally realize the deception and track down **Marcel's** true identity, he becomes an international fugitive. With the help of Tribulation Force members, **Laslos** devises a plan to get **Marcel** to the States. **Marcel** is killed along with **K** and **Laslos** when the GC sends two imposters to impersonate **Georgiana Stavros** and **George Sebastian**. ⁹

Pappas, Costas

Young man from the **Mikloses'** underground church who serves as lookout in front of the laundry. **Costas** and Cousin **Kronos** risk their lives to recover the bodies of **Miklos**, **Kronos**, and **Marcel Papadopoulos**. **Costas** wants to go with the Greek rescue team, but he is told to stay behind and is killed in the co-op raid. 10

Pappas, Mrs.

Costas's mother; she works for the Greek co-op under the name Mrs. P. The co-op members provide food, weapons, a truck, and prayer for the Greek rescue team. **Mrs. Pappas** is killed when the GC raid the co-op on the night of the rescue team's escape from Greece. 10

Peter the Second
See **Mathews, Cardinal Peter**.

Plank, Steve
Senior executive editor of *Global Weekly* and **Buck Williams's** boss before becoming **Nicolae Carpathia's** international press secretary and spokesman. **1**

Plank becomes publisher of the *Global Community East Coast Daily Times*, the paper that results from a merger between the *New York Times*, the *Washington Post*, and the *Boston Globe*. **2**

The GC believes **Plank** dies in the wrath of the Lamb earthquake, but he survives, though horribly deformed, and becomes GC Peacekeeper **Pinkerton Stephens**. He reveals his true identity to **Rayford Steele** and **Albie**, telling them he became a believer at the first tremor of the earthquake. After a year of recovery from his injuries, **Plank** secured a place in the GC hierarchy, determined to use his position to destroy **Carpathia**. After telling his story, **Plank** helps **Rayford** after **Hattie Durham's** attempted suicide and arranges for their escape. **8**

Still as **Pinkerton Stephens**, **Plank** warns **Rayford** that the Strong Building and **Albie's Marcus Elbaz** alias are no longer safe. He helps **Rayford** devise a plan to get the Tribulation Force members home after the **Sebastian** rescue mission. **9**

Plank becomes a martyr when he refuses to take the mark of the beast. **10** Rayford sees him receive a crown at the judgment. **12**

Plato
See **Aristotle, Plato, and Socrates**.

Pope John XXIV
Serves as Pope for 5 months before being raptured. **2**

Potter, Marge
Steve Plank's matronly secretary; she helps **Buck Williams** with messages and allows **Buck** and **Steve** to come to her house to watch **Nicolae Carpathia's** interview. **Marge** serves as **Buck's** secretary from the time **Steve** moves on until **Buck** is forced to move to Chicago. **1**

Marge tells **Buck** she thinks **Carpathia** is the messiah. She is fired when **Carpathia** takes over the media. **2**

Pudge

President's **Fitzhugh's** Secret Service agent. **Pudge** takes **Buck** to see **Fitzhugh** and helps **Buck** leave the meeting with **Fitzhugh** unseen by **Carpathia's** people. 2

RASHID

Cameraman wearing a turban who accompanies **Corporal Riehl**. He intends to film **Loren Hut** executing **Micah (Chaim)**, but **Hut** is unable to even harm **Micah**. **Rashid** continues to film **Carpathia** and **Chaim's** discussion about the loyalty mark and the sores judgment. **Carpathia** corrects **Rashid** when he films loyalists suffering from the sores judgment, and soon **Rashid** begins to suffer from the same sores. 9

Razor

Hispanic military-trained man; he got his nickname from a snowmobile accident in which his helmet saved him from being decapitated by a razor wire. At the Battle of Armageddon, **Razor** is on the perimeter of Petra, ready to defend the city. 11

    Razor helps rescue **Rayford Steele** when he is injured on the outskirts of Petra. **George Sebastian** teases **Razor** about his proper salute and his adherence to military etiquette. When everyone gathers in Jerusalem after the Glorious Appearing, **Razor** helps **Abdullah** cook a delicious first meal of meat, fruit, and vegetables after months of manna. 12

Rehoboth, Bindura

Regional potentate of the United States of Africa. He is from Sudan, a country whose people despise him for his misuse of public funds. His unpopularity eventually forces him to relocate to the GC regional palace in Johannesburg. He becomes regional potentate rather than **Mwangati Ngumo**, increasing the friction between them. **Rehoboth** conspires with **Peter the Second** to overthrow **Nicolae Carpathia** and install **Peter** in his place, with **Rehoboth** promised **Fortunato's** role. **Rehoboth** is found dead in his office, along with his staff. The GC also kill all of his family members, but it is reported that their deaths were related to the plague of 200 million horsemen. 6

Rice, Bernadette

Newswoman at the Temple Mount in Jerusalem; she records the attempted execution of **Micah (Chaim)**. The execution fails, and when **Nicolae Carpathia** arrives on the scene, **Bernadette** is on the ground, shaking with fear. As **Chaim** confronts **Carpathia**, **Bernadette** moves away on her hands and knees. 9

After reporting on the failed execution, **Bernadette** decides to follow **Micah** and is airlifted to Petra after disguising herself and attending the Masada meeting. Eventually **Bernadette** makes a decision for Christ. 10

Riehl, Corporal
GC corporal who confronts **Chaim Rosenzweig** at the Temple Mount and is incapacitated, unable to shoot **Chaim**. **Loren Hut** directs **Riehl** to summon a cameraman so they can get **Chaim's** (**Micah's**) assassination on camera. 9

Ritz, Kenneth
Tall, lean pilot who owns **Ritz's** Charter Service. A resourceful and reliable flyer, he takes **Buck Williams** from Waukegan, Illinois, to New York the day after the Rapture. 1 **Ken** is also called upon to fly **Buck** and **Tsion Ben-Judah** out of Egypt. 3

After the wrath of the Lamb earthquake, **Ken** works with **Buck** to rescue **Chloe** from the hospital before the GC can capture her. **Ken** observes the way the Tribulation Force members love each other and asks **Buck** more about what he believes. **Buck** directs him to the Bible and **Tsion's** Internet site. The next time **Ken** meets with the Tribulation Force, he shows them the new seal of the believer on his forehead. **Ken** moves into the **Donny Moore** safe house basement. 4

Ken uses his wealth and economic expertise to plan what later becomes the International Commodity Co-op. He flies to Israel with **Rayford** to rescue **Tsion**, **Buck**, and **Chloe**, and is shot and killed by GC Peacekeepers while trying to board the plane home. **Buck** and **Chloe** name their son **Kenny** after their dear friend and brother in Christ. 5

At the judgment, Jesus praises **Ken** for using his God-given mind and abilities to thwart the works of the enemy and encourage other Christians. 12

Rob
President Fitzhugh's adviser; he is continually apologizing. 2

Rogoff, Tobias
Alias **Chaim Rosenzweig** uses in Greece following the assassination of **Nicolae Carpathia** and his escape from

Israel. He poses as a retired librarian from Gaza on his way to the United North American States. **7**

Root Beer Lady

A reference to **Amanda White Steele**; her initials—A.W.—resemble a brand of root beer. The reference appears in an e-mail to **Bruce Barnes** in an attempt to cast doubt on **Amanda's** loyalty to the Tribulation Force. **4 Hattie Durham** later reveals that she, on **Carpathia's** orders, had been the one behind the attack on **Amanda's** credibility. **5**

Rose, Leah

Head administrative nurse at Young Memorial Hospital in Palatine, Illinois, who assists **Dr. Charles** during **Hattie Durham's** miscariage. **5, 6 Leah** tells the Tribulation Force that she became a believer after her 2 sons were raptured, her husband committed suicide, and her own suicide attempt failed. She takes over some of the cooking for the safe house occupants and begins screening all of **Tsion Ben-Judah's** correspondence. **Leah** travels to Brussels as **Donna Clendenon** to check on **Hattie**, inform her of her sister's death, and find out if she has compromised the Tribulation Force. **6**

In Belgium **Leah** meets **Ming Toy**, who tells her **Hattie** has been released by the GC. **Leah** fears **Hattie** will inadvertently allow the GC to follow her to the safe house, so she flies back to the States to warn the Tribulation Force. **Leah** later goes with **Rayford Steele** and **Chloe Williams** to investigate the Strong Building and to pick up **Chaim Rosenzweig**. When the safe house is compromised, **Leah** is with the group that rescues **Tsion** and **Kenny**. **7**

Leah helps **Chloe Williams** with the International Commodity Co-op but eventually becomes bored. **8** She is eager to assist with Operation Eagle and drives the 4 "victims" of the Quasi Two crash from Amman to Mizpe Ramon. **8 Leah** remains in the Middle East, assisting the Tribulation Force with her driving abilities and nursing skills. Finally she heads home to the United North American States and settles in at the Strong Building in Chicago. **9**

When the Strong Building is compromised and evacuated, **Leah** goes with **Hannah Palemoon** to live with **Lionel** and **Felicia Whalum** in Long Grove, Illinois. God prompts **Leah** to pray for **Lionel** and those with him on assignment in Argentina, and her prayers prove critical to the crew's well-being. **10**

Leah remains in Long Grove until traveling to Petra for **Albie**

and **Chloe's** memorial. She begins to help **Lionel**, **Ming**, and **Hannah** with the co-op in Petra. 11

When **Rayford** is badly injured outside Petra, **Leah** is among those who go to rescue him. She uses her nursing skills to assist the sick and injured at Petra until all are healed at the Glorious Appearing. **Leah** travels to Jerusalem with all the believers and stays at the home of **Eleazar** and **Naomi Tiberias**. 12

Rose, Shannon

Leah Rose's husband; **Leah** tells the Tribulation Force that after their 2 children were raptured, **Shannon** committed suicide by leaving his car running in the closed garage. 6

Rosenzweig, Dr. Chaim

A highly regarded Israeli botanist; he wins the Nobel Prize in chemistry and is named *Global Weekly's* "Newsmaker of the Year" for developing a fertilizer that causes even the Israeli desert to produce lush vegetation. His formula becomes vital in **Nicolae Carpathia's** negotiations for the Israeli peace treaty. **Chaim** is warm and humble with an almost childlike naïveté. He befriends both **Carpathia** and **Buck Williams**. 1-3 After **Tsion Ben-Judah's** family is murdered, **Chaim** tries to enlist **Carpathia's** help for **Tsion**. 3

Chaim opens his home to **Buck** and **Chloe Williams** and **Tsion Ben-Judah** when they travel to Jerusalem for the Meeting of the Witnesses, though he continues to reject their message about Christ. After **Buck** is injured while attempting to board the plane back to the States, he returns to **Chaim's** house. In a TV appearance, **Chaim** boldly points people to **Tsion Ben-Judah's** Web site for answers to the disappearances and the judgments. But **Chaim** still refuses to come to **Christ**, even after being stung by a locust and seeing several of his staff become believers. 5

After the death of his gateman, **Jonas**, **Chaim** is angry with God and concludes that there is no truth in **Tsion's** teachings. He is increasingly disillusioned with **Carpathia** and becomes obsessed with a plan to kill the potentate. **Chaim** pretends to have a stroke so that he will not be viewed as a threat and spends his time creating and sharpening a blade to use against **Carpathia**. **Chaim** is invited as a guest of honor to the Global Gala in Jerusalem. He is on the stage when

Rayford Steele fires his gun, causing **Carpathia** to duck and fall directly onto **Chaim**. [6]

Chaim flees the Global Gala and is eventually found and rescued by **Buck**. He is devastated to learn that the GC have executed his staff. **Chaim** confesses to **Buck** that he killed **Carpathia** by pushing his blade into the potentate's head when he fell. On a flight to Greece with **Buck**, **Chaim** finally humbles himself before God and accepts Christ as his Messiah as the plane crashes. **Buck** and **Chaim** survive the crash, but their pilot, **T**, is killed. [7]

After the crash, **Chaim** spends time healing from his injuries and learning from **Tsion**. He experiences deep guilt over his rejection of God, **Carpathia's** assassination, and the deaths of his staff. Later plans are made for **Chaim** to return to Israel in a new teaching role. [8]

Chaim takes on the role of **Micah**, a Moses figure. He witnesses **Hattie Durham's** death in Jerusalem, which gives him the courage to confront **Carpathia**. After the confrontation, **Carpathia** instructs **Loren Hut** to kill **Chaim** with nine shots, but though **Hut** fires at **Chaim**, the bullets do not harm him. **Chaim** negotiates with **Carpathia** for the departure of messianic Jews from Israel, leading them to safety in Petra. [9]

Once in Petra, **Tsion** and **Chaim** preach daily to the undecided. **Chaim** gathers with new believers each night and listens to their testimonies. [10] When **Tsion** goes to preach to the Jews in Jerusalem, he leaves those at Petra in **Chaim's** hands. [11]

Just before the Glorious Appearing, **Chaim** preaches to the largest-ever international audience, and millions choose Christ. He and **Rayford** wait together for Christ's return until **Rayford's** wounds are miraculously healed. After the Glorious Appearing, **Chaim** relocates to Jerusalem with the believers and teaches about the prophecies still to be fulfilled. [12]

SAHIB

Tall, thin man who guards **Mainyu Mazda**; **Sahib** was **Mazda's** brother-in-law until **Mazda** murdered his wife, **Sahib's** sister. [11]

Sandra

An assistant to **Nicolae Carpathia** and **Leon Fortunato**. She shares an office with **Jim Hickman**. **Sandra** is deeply devoted to **Carpathia** and wants to bow and worship him whenever she comes into his presence. [8] **David Hassid** tells **Chang Wong** to access **Sandra's** files to keep current on **Carpathia's** schedule. [9]

Santiago, Ramon

GC Peacekeeper who tells **Jim Hickman** that **Nicolae Carpathia** will shortly be in the market for a pig. Because he violates GC rules by divulging confidential information, **Ramon** is put to death. Much to **Hickman's** distress, **Carpathia** shoots **Ramon** in the forehead. 8

Schnell, Hilda

Head of Global Community Cable News Network. She provides coverage of **Nicolae Carpathia's** funeral on numerous large screens. 7

Scholten, Kiersten

Young woman who assists **Dr. Eikenberry** with **Nicolae Carpathia's** autopsy. 7

Schultz, Mrs,

Chloe Steele's ninth grade PE teacher; after the Rapture, **Chloe** finds **Mrs. Schultz's** name in the New Hope Village Church directory. 2

Seaver, Gerri

Alias **Z** provides for **Leah Rose**. For this alias, **Leah** bleaches her hair blonde, changes the color of her contacts, and uses a dental appliance. This name confuses **Ming Toy** when she calls to warn **Buck Williams** about the threat to his father and brother. As **Gerri Seaver**, **Leah** is questioned by the GC while waiting for **Rayford** and **Chloe**. 7

Sebastian, Beth Ann

George and **Priscilla Sebastian's** daughter. 11FF

Sebastian, George

Lead chopper pilot for Operation Eagle. **George** is tall and large with blond hair, blue eyes, and a deep tan. He lives in San Diego with his wife and daughter. **George** tells **Rayford Steele** that a chopper instructor named **Jeremy Murphy** kept telling him that Jesus was coming to take the Christians to heaven. After the Rapture, **George** found **Jeremy's** church and prayed to receive Christ. When **George** is finished telling his story, he shows **Rayford** weapons left over from the U.S. stockpile, and they pack the weapons for storage. **George** plays an integral role in Operation Eagle, and after its completion, he agrees to fly 2 young Greek believers to the United

North American States. They are ambushed and **George** is taken captive by the GC. [9]

George escapes the GC and meets up with **Chloe Williams**, **Mac McCullum**, and **Hannah Palemoon**, who are in Greece to rescue him. He returns to his family in San Diego and flies missions for the Tribulation Force, including taking Argentinean wheat to India. [10]

George is a vital part of the Tribulation Force in San Diego, and he takes part in the mission to bug the Baghdad conference rooms. He is valued for his military experience and excellent weapons training abilities. Once the compromised San Diego safe house compound is evacuated, **George** helps **Mac** and **Otto Wesser** evacuate New Babylon believers before the city is destroyed. Later he serves on the front lines against the GC on the outskirts of Petra. [11]

After witnessing the Glorious Appearing and the defeat of the GC, **George** settles with his family at the **Tiberias** home in Jerusalem. [12]

Sebastian, Priscilla (Priss)

Wife of **George**, mother of **Beth Ann**. **Priscilla** is one of the busiest people in the San Diego compound though she is rarely fully healthy. She and **George** set up a command center in the San Diego compound after **Chloe Williams** is taken by the GC. Priscilla is evacuated to Petra where she attends **Albie** and **Chloe's** memorial service. She continues to live in the safety of the red city and helps babysit **Kenny** while **Buck Williams** and **Rayford Steele** are on missions. [11]

Priscilla relocates with her family to the **Tiberias** home in Jerusalem after the Glorious Appearing. [12]

Shaniqua

African-American woman from The Place who witnesses to **Carmella**. **Carmella** accepts Christ and joins the Place believers. [12]

Shivte family

Elderly Jewish couple with 2 sons in their forties; the whole family are believers in Christ. **Tsion Ben-Judah** and **Buck Williams** stay with the **Shivtes** in Jerusalem. **Mr. Shivte** and his sons defend the city with **Buck** and **Tsion**. [11]

Shorosh, Michael

Boat owner from Jericho who takes **Buck Williams** up the Jordan River to find **Tsion Ben-Judah**. **Michael** became an exuberant follower of Jesus through the teachings of **Eli**, **Moishe**, and **Tsion Ben-**

Judah and was very involved in **Tsion Ben-Judah's** stadium ministry. **Michael** sells **Buck** an old school bus so **Buck** and **Tsion** can escape Israel. He is arrested and possibly martyred for his involvement in freeing **Tsion**. 3

Smith, Abdullah (Smitty)

Contact of **Mac McCullum's** who had been a fighter pilot for the Jordanian military. **Abdullah** is a believer in his early thirties with dark skin, eyes, and hair. 6 He flies **Buck Williams** from Amman, Jordan, to northern Greece, and then flies **Buck** to Chicago just in time for **Kenny's** birth. 5

Abdullah reveals that he divorced his wife when she became a Christian, but after she was raptured, he reread her letters about Christ and became a believer. He becomes **Mac's** first officer on **Carpathia's** Phoenix 216. 6

Abdullah lives in New Babylon and continues to fly for **Carpathia**, but he looks for opportunities to assist the Tribulation Force. His death is faked in the Quasi Two crash, and he travels to Mizpe Ramon. 8

Because of his military training, **Abdullah** has a valuable understanding of weaponry. He travels to Petra disguised as the brother of **Atef Naguib (Rayford Steele)**. 9, 10 Later he sees the archangel **Michael** and is miraculously protected by God when GC munitions pass through his helicopter without harming the craft or anyone on board. 9

After the bombing of Petra, **Abdullah** chooses to remain there. He learns to communicate with Tribulation Force members by computer, and he uses his piloting skills to fly missions for the believers in Petra. **Abdullah** flies a helicopter with **Albie** and **Mac** aboard and sees the false christ. He also joins these two men in delivering water from India to Argentina in exchange for wheat. He continues to work on his English and his sense of humor. 10

Abdullah flies to New Babylon with **Rayford** to rescue **Chang** and is a principal pilot for the airlift from New Babylon to Petra. 11

Abdullah locates Rayford after his ATV crash outside Petra and helps with his rescue. When believers resettle in Jerusalem after the Glorious Appearing, he helps make the first post-manna meal at **Chaim's** compound and assists in teaching about events to come. 12

Smith, Christopher

First officer for Captain **Rayford Steele**; he is flying with **Rayford** when the Rapture occurs. After landing in Chicago, **Christopher** slits his wrists when he learns that his sons have disappeared and his wife has been killed in a wreck. **1**

Smitty

See **Smith, Abdullah.**

Socrates

See **Aristotle, Plato, and Socrates.**

Stallion

Bouncer at a nightclub in Israel who supplies **Buck Williams** with a turban and a scarf. **5**

Staub, Russell

Alias **Buck Williams** uses to fly into Israel to visit **Chaim. 6** Leah **Rose** gives the name **Russell Staub** as the owner of the Range Rover she is using when she is questioned by the GC. After the plane crash in Greece, **Buck** gives this name to the GC. **7**

Stavros, Georgiana

Sixteen-year-old girl who escapes the loyalty mark center in Ptolemaïs, Greece, with the help of **Buck Williams** and **Albie. 8**

Georgiana makes contact with the underground Greek church and plans to escape to the United North American States. The plan goes awry, and she is captured by the GC. She gives up information to the GC and then is killed. **9**

Steele, Amanda White

Second wife of **Rayford Steele**. She is handsome and wealthy, with salt-and-pepper streaked hair. **Amanda's** first husband and 2 daughters were raptured. When she meets **Rayford, Amanda** tells him she had been in a Bible study with **Rayford's** raptured wife, **Irene**, and became a Christian after the Rapture through her memories of **Irene's** teachings. **Amanda's** relationship with **Rayford** deepens, and they are married in a double ceremony with **Buck Williams** and **Rayford's** daughter, **Chloe**. After her wedding, **Amanda** moves to New Babylon to be with **Rayford**, and she starts an import/export business. **2** Back in Chicago to meet with the Tribulation Force, **Amanda** meets with **Hattie Durham** to offer her support and counsel about her pregnancy. **3**

Nicolae Carpathia reports to **Rayford** that **Amanda** was killed in a plane crash during the earthquake. **4** Evidence surfaces that she was a traitor to the Tribulation Force, but **Rayford** refuses to believe stories of **Amanda's** death or treachery. He continues to search for her, finally finding her body in a plane at the bottom of the Tigris River. **4**

It is eventually discovered that **Amanda** was a genuine believer and trustworthy member of the Tribulation Force. **5** **Hattie** apologizes for disseminating the lies, invented by **Carpathia**. **6**

Rayford sees **Amanda** again at the judgment. She is also reunited with **Irene**, and the two get along without difficulty. **12**

Steele, Chloe

See dossier on **Chloe Steele Williams**.

Steele, Irene

First wife of **Rayford Steele**. She is raptured along with her son, **Rayford Jr. Irene** met **Rayford Steele** in Reserve Officer Training Corps in college. They eventually had two children, **Chloe** and **Rayford Jr. Irene** was an active member of New Hope Village Church. After she is raptured, **Rayford** wishes he had listened to her message about God. **1**

Rayford is reunited with **Irene** at the judgment, where she meets her son-in-law, **Buck Williams**, and her grandson, **Kenny**, for the first time. **Irene** also sees **Rayford's** second wife, **Amanda**, whom she had taught in a Bible study before the Rapture. **12**

Steele, Rayford

See dossier on **Rayford Steele**.

Steele, Rayford Jr. (Raymie)

Twelve-year-old son of **Rayford** and **Irene Steele**. He is raptured along with his mother. Before the Rapture, **Irene** faithfully prayed **Raymie** would never stray from his strong, childlike faith. **1** **Raymie** is reunited with his father and sister and meets his brother-in-law, **Buck Williams**, and nephew, **Kenny**, at the judgment. **12**

Stefan

Part of **Chaim Rosenzweig's** valet staff and the man **Jacov** habitually drinks with. At **Jacov's** invitation, **Stefan** attends the Meeting of the Witnesses and believes in Jesus as his Messiah. His driving ability secures the Tribulation Force's safety after the meeting. When **Buck** falls from the Gulfstream and is unable to escape Israel, **Stefan** provides covert hospitality and friendship. He later moves into **Chaim's** residence, along with **Jacov** and **Hannelore**, to care for **Chaim** and **Jonas** after they are attacked by locusts. **5**

In fear of **Carpathia**, **Stefan** refuses to drive **Chaim** to the Gala. **6** When **Buck** arrives at **Chaim's** estate after **Carpathia's** assassination at the Gala, he finds **Stefan**, **Hannelore**, and her mother murdered. **7**

Stefanich, Nelson

GC soldier at headquarters in Ptolemaïs and head of the **George Sebastian** situation. He went to Madrid Military School with **Suhail Akbar**. **Stefanich** leads the attempted raid on the Greek co-op along with **Aristotle**, **Plato**, **Socrates**, and several other GC. He is also at the airport when the Greek rescue team escapes with **George** after **Michael** appears and blinds the GC. **10**

Stephens, Pinkerton

Identity assumed by **Steve Plank** after he survives the wrath of the Lamb earthquake. His appearance is altered enormously by his injuries. One of his legs is missing, the fingers of his right hand are only nubs, and vivid burn scars mark his left hand. His neck, cheekbones, and ears are deeply scarred as well. A toupee covers his head, and a prosthesis covers most of his face, hiding the gaping cavity left by his injuries. He takes off the prosthesis so **Rayford Steele** and **Albie** can see the mark of the believer on his deformed forehead. **8**

Stonagal, Jonathan

Power broker with almost unrivaled wealth. **Stonagal** advocates streamlining the world currency to the American dollar. As the owner of major banks around the world, he helps finance **Nicolae Carpathia's** rise to power. **Buck** views "Diamond John" as a murderous, behind-the-scenes schemer. **Carpathia** murders **Stonagal**, then brainwashes witnesses. Official reports state that **Stonagal** committed suicide over his involvement in 2 murders. **1**

Strong, Thomas

Strong made a fortune in insurance and built an 80-story tower in Chicago to house his international headquarters. The building is badly damaged in the Chicago bombing but becomes the United North American States safe house for the Tribulation Force. **7**, **8**

Sullivan, Captain
Alan Tompkins's superior officer at Scotland Yard. When **Tompkins** is killed, **Sullivan** tries to frame **Buck Williams** for the murder. [1]

Sullivan
Name **Rayford Steele** uses as the GC commander who has ordered a cleanup of **Leah Rose's** garage. [6]

Suzie
Attendant at the Pan-Con Club who reprimands a doctor for performing his "Rapture Special" (minor stitches) on **Buck Williams** in front of the other guests. She suggests they use the washroom instead. [1]

T
See **Delanty, Tyrola Mark**.

Tangvald
Name of someone registered at The Night Visitors for the same night **Chaim Rosenzweig** registers under the name **Goldman**. [7]

Tenzin
Unity Army commander from India; **Nicolae Carpathia** orders him to beat a soldier named **Ipswich** with a rattan to the point of near death and then to kill him. **Tenzin** is also told to beat **Chief Akbar** until he is near death; after **Chaim Rosenzweig** appears on international TV, Tenzin is told to kill **Akbar**. [12]

Theodore, Wallace
Nightline host who conducts a live interview with **Carpathia** the same day **Carpathia** gives 2 press conferences and a speech to the United Nations. [1]

Tiber, Clancy
Personal assistant to Global Community Supreme Commander **Leon Fortunato** on the trip to Johannesburg. When the Condor 216 falls under attack from **Rehoboth's** insurgents, **Fortunato** uses **Clancy** as a shield, and he is shot to death. [6]

Tiberias, Eleazar
Elder at Petra and father of **Naomi**. Before she died of cancer, **Eleazar's** wife encouraged him to study the prophecies

about Messiah in the Jewish scriptures, and after the Rapture, **Eleazar's** reading leads him to trust in Christ. At Petra, he keeps a watchful eye on his daughter's blooming romance with **Chang Wong.** 11

Eleazar opens his home to single women and married couples when believers relocate to Jerusalem after the Glorious Appear - ing. 12

Tiberias, Naomi

Daughter of **Eleazar Tiberias**; she was 13 at the time of the Rap- ture. **Naomi** and her father began to study Jewish prophecy after the Rapture and soon received Jesus as their Messiah. 11 The only language she knows is Hebrew, but believers are miraculously able to understand her. She uses her genius with computers to teach **Rayford Steele** and others to navigate world news sources and information databases, and she scares **Chang Wong** into thinking his cover has been blown by tapping into GC palace computers and tripping an alarm. 10

At Petra, **Naomi** leads the computer center with humor and self- confidence. She goes with **Rayford** on the mission to bring **Chang** out of New Babylon; after finally meeting face-to-face, **Chang** and **Naomi** soon fall in love. They man the tech center in Petra as the Battle of Armageddon approaches. 11

Naomi and **Chang** are together at the Glorious Appearing. Her home in Jerusalem is one of those used to house believers. 12

Tiffany

1. Candy striper at Arthur Young Memorial Hospital who greets **Buck Williams** when he tries to find **Ken Ritz**. She tells him that her sister and brother-in-law were killed in the recent earthquake. 4 2. **David Hassid's** assistant. 8 When interviewed about the Quasi Two crash, she expresses shock and sadness about **David's** reported death. She does not enjoy working with her new boss, **Aurelio Figueroa**, and especially dislikes his smoking cigars in his office. 9

Todd-Cothran, Joshua

Head of the London Exchange. **Nicolae Carpathia** tells his staff that **Todd-Cothran** will be the ambassador of the Great States of Britain, a territory extending throughout most of Europe. **Carpathia** then gives the same title to the man sitting beside **Todd-Cothran**, caus- ing **Todd-Cothran** to assume **Carpathia** has simply misspoken. Later in the meeting, however, **Carpathia** murders **Todd-Cothran** and **Jonathan Stonagal**. Witnesses are brainwashed to believe that **Stonagal** killed **Todd-Cothran** and himself. [1]

Tompkins, Alan
Thin man with dark hair who works for Scotland Yard; **Tompkins** has concerns about world financiers. After meeting with **Buck Williams**, he is killed by a car bomb in London. His superior, **Captain Sullivan**, describes **Tompkins** as "one of the finest men and brightest investigators it has been my privilege to work with." [1]

Tony
Hattie's coworker who vanishes on the flight to Heathrow. His blazer, shirt, tie, and trousers lay on the floor of the plane. [1]

Toy, Ming
See **Woo, Ming Toy**.

Tung
GC local leader in Zhengzhou who leads the raid on a group of Muslim worshipers. He is in charge of about 30 Peacekeepers. [10]

Tuttle, Dwayne
Large blond from Oklahoma who sells and demonstrates aircraft and does acting work whenever he gets the opportunity. He and his wife, **Trudy**, become believers after their 4 sons are raptured. As **Dart** and **Olivia**, they answer the distress signal **Mac** sends out during the Johannesburg ambush, and later they become the key South Sea operatives for the International Commodity Co-op. As **Ian** and **Elva Hill**, they join **Rayford Steele** in the attempt to find **Hattie Durham** in Le Havre. Later they are murdered by GC in Al Basrah as they sit in a café waiting for **Rayford**. [6]

Tuttle, Trudy
Wife of **Dwayne Tuttle**; she is tall and dark-haired and from Oklahoma. She accompanies her husband on several missions to assist the Tribulation Force. She becomes **Olivia Dart** when her husband lands in Johannesburg in response to **Mac's** distress signal, and she saves **Rayford's** life as **Elva Hill** by telling him to abort the mission when he unknowingly is met by a GC assassin. She is later killed along with her husband as she sits in a café in Al Basrah waiting for **Rayford**. [6]

UNCLE GREGORY

Krystall's uncle; according to **Krystall**, he is her last living relative who hasn't taken **Carpathia's** mark. **Rayford Steele** tells **Krystall** to direct her uncle to **Tsion Ben-Judah's** Web site. Later **Rayford** pretends to be **Uncle Gregory** so he can talk to **Krystall** on the phone. ▇11

Uri

GC pilot who drops a concussion bomb on Petra. His plane is equipped with a video camera, and he catches the bombing on tape. **Uri** is the first to realize that the people of Petra have survived. Back in **Suhail Akbar's** office, **Uri** discusses with **Kerry** the success of their mission. **Uri** and **Kerry** are soon sedated and cremated so they will not be able to dispute the GC's claim that the mission failed due to pilot error. ▇10

VAJPAYEE, RAMAN

A GC employee; he is at the initial New Babylon meeting in **Nicolae Carpathia's** suite of offices. He interrupts the meeting, and **Carpathia** kills him by breaking his neck. ▇11

Viktor

First of the regional potentates to speak at **Nicolae Carpathia's** funeral. **Viktor** is from the United Russian States. ▇7

WASHINGTON, LUCINDA

The Chicago bureau chief for *Global Weekly*; she is raptured. **Lucinda** talked to **Buck Williams** about God 3 days before the Rapture. ▇1

Weser, Otto

German who leads a group of believers about 6 miles from New Babylon. After his people are safely taken to Petra, he helps **Mac McCullum** evacuate 150 more believers right before the fall of New Babylon. He and some of those from his group man the perimeter of Petra. ▇11

Otto is on the front lines alongside **George Sebastian** and **Razor** on the outskirts of Petra. After the Glorious Appearing, he settles in an abandoned hotel in Jerusalem with the rest of his people. ▇12

West, Sue

San Diego GCNN reporter who reports on **Albie's** death and **Chloe Williams's** arrest. ▇11

Whalum, Felicia

Wife of **Lionel Whalum**. She becomes a Christian immediately after the Rapture, along with her husband. They live in Long Grove, Illinois, and open their home to **Leah Rose** and **Hannah Palemoon** after the Strong Building is evacuated. ⏹ **Felicia** relocates to Petra for **Chloe Williams** and **Albie's** memorial service. ⏹

Whalum, Lionel

Wealthy businessman and skilled pilot from Long Grove, Illinois. He and his wife, **Felicia**, were churchgoers whose children witnessed to them, but they didn't become believers until immediately after the Rapture. **Lionel** becomes a pilot for the International Commodity Co-op. **Leah Rose** and **Hannah Palemoon** move into the **Whalums'** house after the Strong Building is evacuated. **Lionel** assists in the co-op's wheat/water exchange, and **Leah's** prayers lead him to an unsecured wheat pallet that could have endangered the flight. ⏹

Lionel arranges for planes and pilots to evacuate the Tribulation Force from San Diego. He flies **Felicia**, **Hannah**, and **Leah** to Petra for **Chloe Williams** and **Albie's** memorial service. He takes over the co-op, assisted by **Ming Toy**, **Leah**, and **Hannah**. ⏹

Lionel continues to run the co-op until the Glorious Appearing. He goes to **Chaim Rosenzweig's** house in Jerusalem for the first post-manna meal. ⏹

White, Amanda

See **Steele, Amanda White**.

Williams, Cameron (Buck)

See dossier on **Buck Williams**.

Williams, Chloe

See dossier on **Chloe Steele Williams**.

Williams, Jeff

Buck Williams's brother from Tucson. **Jeff's** wife, **Sharon**, and their children are raptured while in the mountains. ⏹

Jeff is eventually murdered by the GC, and the house where he and his father live is burned down. He becomes a believer before his death. ⏹

Williams, Kenneth Bruce (Kenny)

Buck and **Chloe Williams's** baby son. He is named for martyred believers **Kenneth Ritz** and **Bruce Barnes**. ⏹

The Tribulation Force members enjoy watching **Kenny** grow, with **Tsion**, **Ming**, **Priscilla**, and others pitching in to take care of him when his parents are away. **7**, **11**

Kenny's "Gampa," **Rayford**, and his friends at Petra care for him and keep him busy after the deaths of his parents. As the Glorious Appearing approaches, 4 ½ -year-old **Kenny** is excited to see Jesus. At the judgment, he is reunited with his parents and meets his young Uncle **Raymie** and his Grandma **Irene** for the first time. **12**

Williams, Mr.

Buck Williams's father. He has a strained relationship with **Buck**. **Mr. Williams** has a trucking business, which his son **Jeff** joins. He believes that going to church and Sunday school is enough to make one a Christian. **1**

Mr. Williams and **Jeff** are murdered by the GC. **Buck** later learns that his father had become a believer and attended an underground church. **7**

Williams, Sharon

Wife of **Jeff Williams**; **Buck's** sister-in-law. **Sharon** is raptured while driving to pick up her children from a retreat. The children are also raptured. **1**

Willie, Mae

Alias **Hattie Durham** uses in Le Havre, France, and at the Belgium Facility for Female Rehabilitation. **6**

Wilson, Duke

At the peace-treaty signing, the caption "Duke Wilson, former writer, *Newsweek*" appears with **Buck Williams's** picture. **2**

Wong, Chang

Ming Toy's brother; he becomes a believer through the witness of friends. **Chang** resides in China but travels to New Babylon with his parents for **Nicolae Carpathia's** funeral. **7**

Chang's father forces him to go to work for the GC in New Babylon. **Chang** is distraught over receiving the *30* mark of the beast, but with his dual marking, he is in a unique position to work for the Tribulation Force. As a new employee at Global Community Headquarters in New Babylon, **Chang** is left to hold down the fort while **David Hassid** escapes with **Mac McCullum**, **Hannah Palemoon**, and **Abdullah Smith** via the Quasi Two crash story. **8**

Chang becomes despondent over receiving the mark, but later discovers that he was drugged during its administration. Despite his mark, **Chang** is spared from the sores judgment. He alerts Tribulation Force members to **Carpathia's** movements and builds dossiers on everyone traveling to Greece or Petra. **Chang** learns through his mother's e-mails that both his parents have turned to God. 9

Continuing his strategic role inside the palace, **Chang** provides life-and-death information to the Tribulation Force. When the plague of darkness hits, he begins to plan his escape from New Babylon. 10

Rayford Steele and **Naomi Tiberias** rescue **Chang** and bring him to safety in Petra. **Chang** and **Naomi** fall in love, but they are advised not to become engaged until after the Glorious Appearing. **Chang** uses his computer genius to help in the tech center at Petra. **Tsion Ben-Judah** prays over **Chang**, and the mark of the beast is miraculously removed from his forehead. 11

Chang helps get **Chaim Rosenzweig** on the international air-waves to be seen by the largest audience ever. His relationship with **Naomi** continues to grow, and the two witness the Glorious Appearing together. Once in Jerusalem he settles at **Chaim's** home. 12

Wong, Mr.

Chang Wong and **Ming Toy's** father. He travels to New Babylon for **Nicolae Carpathia's** funeral. **Mr. Wong** is arrogant and admires **Carpathia**. His business contributes more than 20 percent of its profits to the Global Community. 7

In his zeal for **Carpathia**, **Mr. Wong** wants his son, **Chang**, to be the first to receive the loyalty mark. 8 **Chang** later discovers that his father had him tranquilized so he could be given the mark. **Mr. Wong** becomes disillusioned with **Carpathia** and turns to God. He and his wife decide they will do whatever is necessary to avoid taking the mark of the beast, and **Mr. Wong** is nearly suicidal because of his guilt over making **Chang** take the mark. 9

When **Ming** travels to China, she learns her father was discovered by the GC and killed. 9

Wong, Mrs.

Chang Wong and **Ming Toy's** mother. She travels to New Babylon for **Nicolae Carpathia's** funeral. 7 **Mrs. Wong**

fears that if she speaks against her husband's zeal for **Carpathia** or if her children admit they are Judah-ites, she will lose **Chang** and **Ming**. In an
e-mail to **Chang**, **Mrs. Wong** reveals that she has been accessing **Tsion Ben-Judah's** Web site and learning about God. She tells **Chang** that she and her husband will do whatever is necessary to keep from taking the mark of the beast and asks him to pray. 9

When **Ming** travels to China, she finds her mother grieving the death of her husband. **Ming** wants to take her back to San Diego, but **Mrs. Wong** insists on staying in China. The angel **Christopher** tells **Ming** that she and her mother will be alive on earth when Christ returns. 10

Woo, Ming Toy

Guard at the GC's Belgium Facility for Female Rehabilitation (Buffer). She meets **Leah Rose** when **Leah** comes to Buffer looking for **Hattie Durham**. **Ming** tells **Leah** that her husband was killed in a commuter train wreck when the Rapture occurred. She joined the GC after the peace-treaty signing but trusted Christ after reading letters from her brother, **Chang Wong**. **Ming** becomes a helpful source of GC information for the Tribulation Force. She is assigned to **Nicolae Carpathia's** funeral in New Babylon and meets up with her family there. She gives **Leah** the information that **Buck Williams's** father and brother have been killed. 7

David Hassid arranges for **Ming** to be reassigned to the United North American States, and **Albie** and **Buck** take her back to the Strong Building. Because she is AWOL from the GC, she remains at the safe house during Operation Eagle. 8

Ming remains in Chicago, helping with **Kenny**, reviewing **Tsion Ben-Judah's** Web site messages, and working with **Tsion** and **Chang** on **Tsion's** TV presentation.

Under the identity **Chang Chow**, a young, male GC Peace-keeper, **Ming** travels to Long Grove, Illinois, and Pawleys Island, South Carolina. Pilot **Ree Woo** takes her on to China, where she finds her mother and learns of her father's death. In her disguise, **Ming** is able to get GC information and help believers escape before their locations are raided. She is told by the angel **Christopher** that she and her mother will be alive on earth when Christ returns. **Ming** moves back to San Diego, where her friendship with **Ree** continues to grow. 10

Ming babysits **Kenny** and **Beth Ann Sebastian** during the search for **Chloe Williams**. When the Tribulation Force is evacuated from San Diego, she moves to Petra and assists **Lionel Whalum** with the co-op. **Ming** marries **Ree Woo** soon after **Chloe** and **Albie's** memorial service. She and **Ree** help guard the perimeter of Petra before the Battle of Armageddon. **11**

As **Christopher** promised, **Ming** is alive to witness the glorious appearing of Christ. **12**

Woo, Ree

Pilot trainer who specializes in small, fast, maneuverable craft. When he meets **Ming Toy**, **Ree** tells her that he moved to America as a teenager, and after the Rapture he read the Bible to the point of exhaustion, eventually becoming a Christian. After piloting **Ming** to and from China and flying other missions for the co-op, **Ree** serves on **Rayford Steele's** crew in Argentina. **Luís Arturo** takes a special liking to him. Meanwhile, **Ree's** relationship with **Ming** continues to develop. **10**

Ree marries **Ming** in Petra. His official papers state that he is a GC loyalist who runs a company named Woo and Associates, and under this guise he bugs **Carpathia's** Baghdad conference room while he is supposedly wiring it for sound. **Ree** also assists in recruiting pilots for the airlift to Petra. As Armageddon approaches, **Ree** helps guard the perimeter of Petra. **11**

Ree meets Jesus while holding hands with his wife. Later he accompanies **Ming** as they relocate to Jerusalem. **12**

Wyatt

Soldier working as manifest coordinator at Ben Gurion Airport. With small talk and attempts to follow regulations, **Wyatt** delays **Rayford Steele's** takeoff in the Gulfstream after **Nicolae Carpathia's** assassination. **7**

YAMAMOTO, LI

Alias **Hattie Durham** uses at the reproductive clinic in Littleton, Colorado. For her disguise, she cuts her hair short, dyes it black, and wears colored contact lenses. **4**

Z

See **Zuckermandel Jr., Gustaf.**

Zee, Verna

Takes over **Lucinda Washington's** job at the Chicago bureau of *Global Weekly* after **Lucinda** is raptured. When **Buck Williams** is demoted and sent to Chicago, she becomes his superior, taking pleasure in making **Buck** miserable. **2**

Buck and **Verna** do not get along even after the Tribulation Force extends hospitality to her when World War III breaks out. **Verna** sees **Tsion Ben-Judah** at **Bruce Barnes's** funeral and threatens to reveal his location and **Buck's** faith, but **Buck** and **Chloe** force her to back down. **3**

Verna lends **Buck** her car after Chicago is attacked, but he has to replace it after he abandons it in search of **Chloe**. **Buck** eventually becomes the publisher of *Global Community Weekly* and has opportunity to fire **Verna**, but he chooses not to. **Loretta** witnesses to **Verna** but this only makes **Verna** think **Loretta** is odd. **3**

Zhizaki

An Asian man who works with **Guy Blod**; **Zhizaki** has 2-inch-long green nails. He presents to David Hassid a computer-generated schedule for the production of **Nicolae Carpathia's** statue. **7**

Zuckermandel, Gustaf (Zeke)

Operates a gas station in Des Plaines, Illinois, where he and his son make fake IDs in the basement. **Zeke's** wife and 2 daughters are killed in a fire after the Rapture. A truck driver leads **Zeke** to Christ, and he becomes active in a local underground church. **6**

Zeke is taken by the GC, charged with black-market activity, and beheaded for refusing to take the loyalty mark. **8**

Zuckermandel, Jr. Gustaf

Zeke's son; he helps with the black-market gas station. He is sometimes called **Z** or Little **Zeke**, though he is bigger than his father. **Z** is a former drug addict who comes to Christ through the witness of a long-haul trucker. He helps the Tribulation Force with his skill at creating disguises and forging documents. **6**

Z continues to provide the Tribulation Force members with disguises while coping with the disappearance and beheading of his father. He moves into the Strong Building safe house. **8** After the Strong Building is evacuated, he moves to Avery, Wisconsin. **9** Eventually there is little need for him to create disguises, but as a result of his intensive study of the Bible, **Z** becomes the assistant pastor of the underground church in Avery. **10**

Little **Zeke** relocates to Petra and creates disguises for **Ree Woo's** Baghdad mission. As the Battle of Armageddon approaches, he helps guard the perimeter of Petra. ⑪

After the Glorious Appearing, **Z** travels to Jerusalem with other Tribulation Force members. ⑫

By definition, the characters in the series are people who had not come to Christ when the Rapture occurred. But over the course of the books many become believers and develop personal relationships with Christ. The books are clear that such a life-changing moment can happen at any time, in any place,.through any situation. All it takes is a heart willing to listen and a soul willing to receive Christ's salvation. The characters pray and ask Christ into their lives in all kinds of places and circumstances. Here are some of the highlights.

CONVERSIONS

IT CAN HAPPEN ANYWHERE:
WHEN AND WHERE DID EACH CHARACTER COME TO CHRIST?

Abdullah Smith:
In his military quarters in Amman, Jordan, reading over his raptured, divorced wife's letters about Jesus. **6**

Amanda White:
In church after attending a Bible study with Irene Steele the day of the Rapture. **2**

Annie Christopher:
After her entire family died in the earthquake, she read Tsion's Web site, especially "For Those Who Mourn." **6**

Bernadette Rice:
Inside Petra, after seeing Loren Hut try to shoot Micah in Jerusalem and disguising herself to get into Petra. **10**

Bruce Barnes:
New Hope Village Church—he raced there and watched Pastor Billings's Rapture tape after his family disappeared. **1**

Buck Williams:
A U.N. washroom immediately before Carpathia's meeting. **1**

Carmela:
Working as a prostitute in Chicago. Shaniqua from The Place gave her a brochure and told Carmela someone loved her. **12**

Chaim Rosenzweig:
On a plane, right before it crashes in Greece. **7**

Chang Wong:
In China, through the urging of friends. **7**

Chloe Steele:
On a plane after praying that God would give her a personal sign that he cares, then opening her eyes to find Buck. **1**

David Hassid:
At the GC complex, reading "Romans Road" on Tsion's Web site. **4**

Dwayne and Trudy Tuttle:
In church after their 4 sons were raptured. **6**

Ezer:
Through Tsion's last-minute preaching in Jerusalem. **12**

Floyd Charles:
Reflecting on his raptured wife, Gigi's, faithful comments. **5**

George Sebastian:
At Jeremy Murphy's church shortly after the Rapture. 9

Hannah Palemoon:
In New Babylon, reading "Romans Road" on Tsion's Web site. 8

Hannelore:
Through the coaxing of her husband in Jerusalem following the Meeting of the Witnesses. 5

Hattie Durham:
In a Montana motel after Albie's account. 8

Jacov:
On the pavement outside the Meeting of the Witnesses. 5

Jonas:
At Chaim's compound while suffering from a locust sting. 5

Ken Ritz:
Through Buck's urging and Tsion's Web site. 4

Leah Rose:
At home after attempting suicide; she read a "Don't Be Left Behind" tract she had found at a day care center. 6

Lionel and Felicia Whalum:
About 10 minutes after the Rapture of their 3 kids and entire neighborhood Bible study. 10

Lukas Miklos:
In Jerusalem, watching Tsion Ben-Judah on TV. 5

Luís Arturo:
In the library of his tiny Catholic church in Argentina. 10

Mac McCullum:
At the GC shelter in New Babylon after Rayford's sharing. 4

Ming Toy:
Through Chang's letters while she was assigned to the GC reconstruction administration in the Philippines. 7

Rayford Steele:
In his Mt. Prospect home watching Dr. Billings's videotape. 1

Ree Woo:
When he was given an easy-to-understand Bible while stationed in San Diego. 10

Shivte men:
During Tsion's last day preaching in Jerusalem. 11

Stefan:
After Jacov's story and the Meeting of the Witnesses in Jerusalem. 5

Steve Plank:
In a collapsing building during the wrath of the Lamb earthquake. 8

Tsion Ben-Judah:
After a 3-year messianic prophecy study convinced him Jesus was the Messiah. 2

Zeke Zuckermandel and Zeke Jr.:
At their gas station, led to Christ by a long-haul trucker. 6

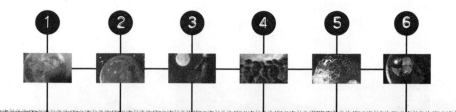

LOCATION, LOCATION, LOCATION!

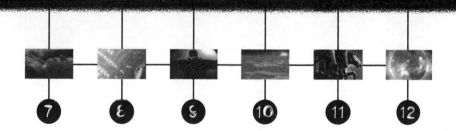

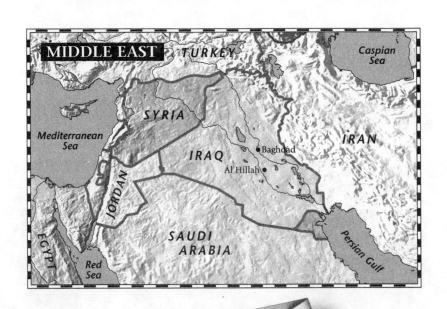

MIDDLE EAST

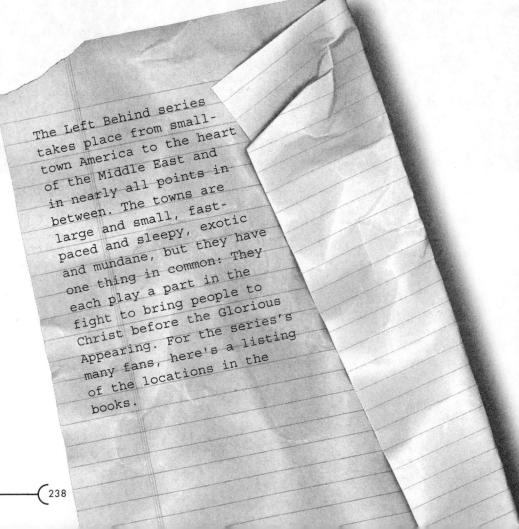

The Left Behind series takes place from small-town America to the heart of the Middle East and in nearly all points in between. The towns are large and small, fast-paced and sleepy, exotic and mundane, but they have one thing in common: They each play a part in the fight to bring people to Christ before the Glorious Appearing. For the series's many fans, here's a listing of the locations in the books.

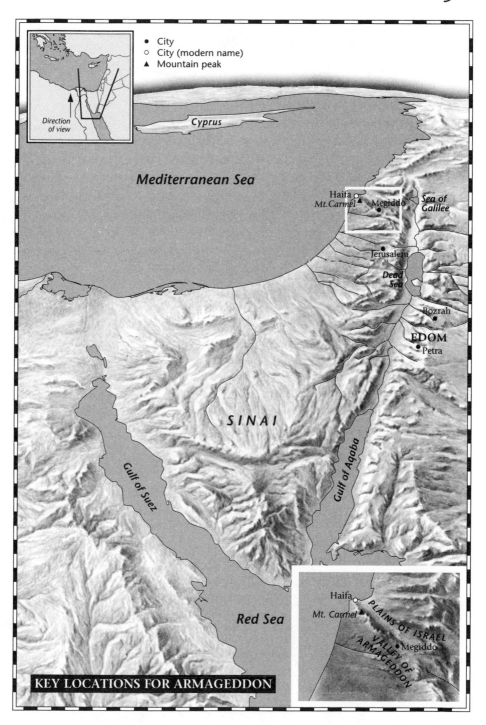

KEY LOCATIONS FOR ARMAGEDDON

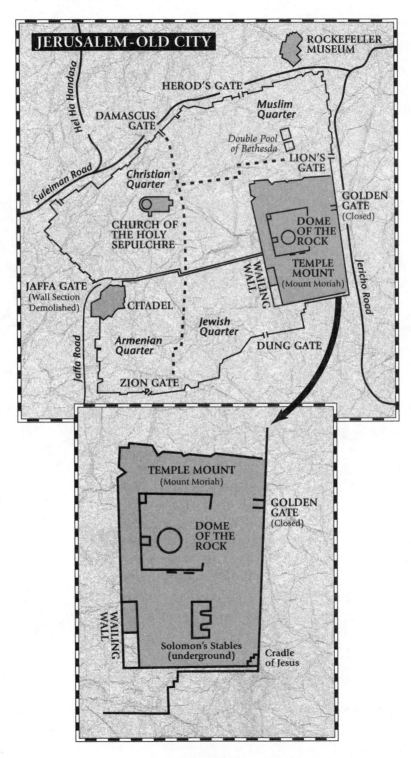

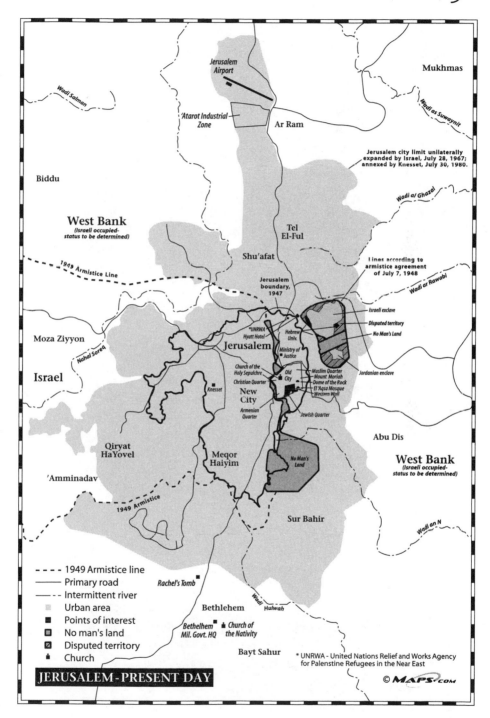

Mukhmas

Wadi Salman

Jerusalem
Airport

Wadi as Suwaynit

'Atarot Industrial
Zone

Ar Ram

Biddu

Jerusalem city limit unilaterally
expanded by Israel, July 28, 1967;
annexed by Knesset, July 30, 1980.

West Bank
(Israeli occupied-
status to be determined)

Wadi al Ghazal

Tel
El-Ful

Shu'afat

1949 Armistice Line

Jerusalem
boundary,
1947

Lines according to
armistice agreement
of July 7, 1948

Wadi ar Rawabi

Moza Ziyyon

Nahal Soreq

Jerusalem

*UNRWA
Hyatt Hotel

Hebrew
Univ.

Israeli exclave

Disputed territory

No Man's Land

Ministry of
Justice

Jordanian enclave

Israel

Church of the
Holy Sepulchre

Christian Quarter

Old
City

Muslim Quarter
Mount Moriah
Dome of the Rock
El 'Aqsa Mosque
Western Wall

Knesset

**New
City**

Armenian
Quarter

Jewish Quarter

Abu Dis

Qiryat
HaYovel

Meqor
Haiyim

No Man's
Land

West Bank
(Israeli occupied-
status to be determined)

'Amminadav

1949 Armistice

Sur Bahir

Wadi an N

- - - 1949 Armistice line
——— Primary road
—-—- Intermittent river
▢ Urban area
■ Points of interest
▣ No man's land
▨ Disputed territory
♠ Church

Rachel's Tomb

Wadi
Hulwah

Bethlehem

Bethlehem
Mil. Govt. HQ

♠ Church of
the Nativity

Bayt Sahur

* UNRWA - United Nations Relief and Works Agency
for Palestine Refugees in the Near East

JERUSALEM - PRESENT DAY

© MAPS.com

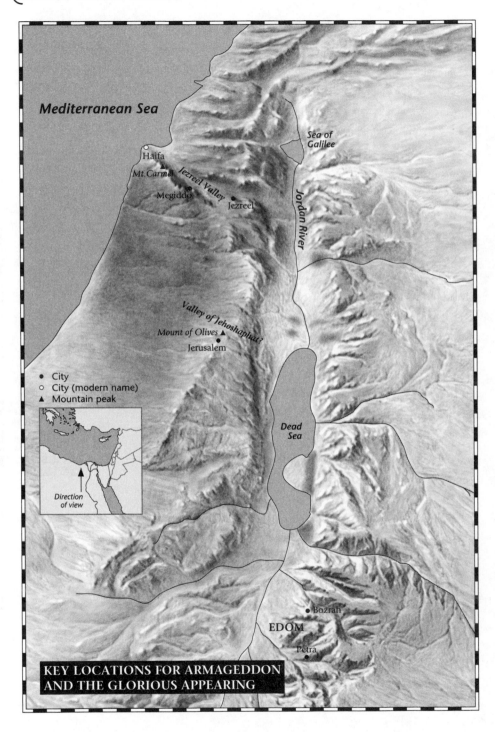

Mediterranean Sea

Sea of
Galilee

Haifa
Mt. Carmel
Megiddo
Jezreel

Jezreel Valley

Jordan River

Valley of Jehoshaphat?
Mount of Olives
Jerusalem

● City
○ City (modern name)
▲ Mountain peak

Direction
of view

Dead
Sea

Bozrah

EDOM

Petra

**KEY LOCATIONS FOR ARMAGEDDON
AND THE GLORIOUS APPEARING**

CITIES, STATES, AND COUNTRIES

ABADAN
City on Abadan Island; on the **Shatt al Arab** in southwestern **Iran**, 30 miles from **Al Basrah**. Albie goes to **Abadan** to meet Mainyu Mazda. **11**

Addis Ababa
Capital city of **Ethiopia**. Nicolae Carpathia and pilot Mac McCullum discuss whether to land in **Addis Ababa** after the 200 million horsemen begin to kill those aboard the plane to **Johannesburg**. **6**

Al Arish
City near the **Israeli-Egyptian** border on the coast of the Mediterranean. It is famous for its beautiful shores and palm-lined beaches. Tsion Ben-Judah and Buck Williams flee to **Al Arish** in a school bus after Tsion's family is murdered, and Ken Ritz meets them there with his Learjet. At the city's airstrip, Buck and Tsion evade GC patrol cars and the GC roadblock by setting their bus on fire. With this diversion, Buck and Tsion are able to board the Learjet headed for **Palwaukee Airport**. **3**

Al Basrah
Major Iraqi city 550 kilometers southeast of **Baghdad**. It is **Iraq**'s second-largest city and has an international airport where Albie controls the tower. **4** Albie and Rayford Steele go to the **Al Basrah** desert for target practice, and when they return, they discover that Dwayne and Trudy Tuttle have been murdered in an open **café**. **6**

Al Basrah is Albie's and Mac's base for flying co-op missions after the **Strong Building** evacuation. ⑩ After Albie is murdered by Mainyu Mazda, Mac has to clean out their **Al Basrah** appartment. ⑪

Al Birah
City west of **Jericho** with an airstrip that serves **Jerusalem**. According to Michael Shorosh, the airstrip is large enough enough to handle a Learjet. ③

Alexandria
Major Egyptian city. Buck Williams hopes to smuggle Tsion Ben-Judah out of the Middle East through the **Alexandria** airport. The idea is discarded, and the airport in **Al Arish** is used instead. After the airport in **Cairo** is destroyed, **Alexandria** becomes the hub of Egyptian air travel. ③

Al Hillah
Roughly 100 kilometers south of **Baghdad** on a branch of the **Euphrates River** in central **Iraq**. Rayford Steele sees the city while in a chopper with Mac McCullum. ④

Al Hillah becomes the storage facility for a vast arsenal of nuclear weaponry. World leadership under Nicolae Carpathia moves to **Al Hillah** during the darkness judgment in **New Babylon**. The weaponry is disbursed to the newly formed One World Unity Army, and 6 months later Carpathia leaves **Al Hillah** for **Baghdad**. ⑪

After Carpathia has Suhail Akbar executed, he orders that Security at **Al Hillah** be called and informed of their boss's death. Carpathia further demands that Security take over the television broadcasting center and kill 1 leadership figure in the center for every 60 seconds that the signal continues to be pirated by Chang Wong. ⑫

Amarillo
City in Texas. Rayford Steele lands at an abandoned airstrip just east of **Amarillo** and awaits a call from Leon Fortunato after aborting a trip to pick up Hattie Durham. ④

Amman
Capital city of **Jordan**. Abdullah Smith recounts how he cried out to God from his quarters in **Amman** after his wife and 2 children were raptured. ⑤ Later, Carpathia has a missile launched from **Amman** to ensure **Petra's** destruction after his fighter-bombers drop their payloads. ⑨

Argentina
South American country. Rayford Steele and his team go to **Argentina** to pick up co-op wheat bound for India. There he meets Luís Arturo

and other believers and hears the angels Christopher, Nahum, and Caleb speak. Before he leaves, freshwater sources turn to blood. **10**

Arlington Heights

Fashionable suburb roughly 25 miles northwest of Chicago. Buck Williams and Chloe Steele take a late-evening walk through **Arlington Heights** while they air out their miscommunications. **Northwest Community Hospital** is in **Arlington Heights,** as is the underground church that Zeke Zuckermandel and his son, Z, attend. **2, 6**

Ash Shawbak

Jordanian city halfway between **Buseirah** and **Petra.** Carpathia and his generals fly to **Ash Shawbak** in a cargo plane to begin the **Petra** offensive. **12**

Athens

Greek city Buck Williams plans to stop in on the way back to the United North American States from **Israel.** The billowing cloud of smoke that blankets the sky over **Jerusalem** affects daylight, causing Buck's flight to **Athens** to be cancelled. Later, Abdullah Smith plans to land in **Athens** until Buck points out that they're going to Ptolemaïs. **5**

Atlanta

Rayford Steele flies a **747** to **Atlanta** with Chloe as a passenger. Over lunch here, Rayford confesses to Chloe that he considered having an affair with Hattie Durham before the Rapture. **1**

Australia

At a funeral in **Australia,** most of the attendees and the corpse vanish in the Rapture, but at another Australian funeral, few of the attendees vanish and the corpse remains. **1** Bruce Barnes tours **Australia,** preaching about the Rapture and biblical prophecy. **2**

Avery

Town in western Wisconsin, not far from the Minnesota border. Z relocates here after the **Strong Building** evacuation. Although his disguise business is seldom needed anymore, he serves fellow believers by assisting the pastor of an underground church. **10**

BABATPUR

A town in India about 100 miles north of the **Rihand Dam.** Albie lands here for the co-op wheat/water exchange. **10**

Babylon
Major city of the ancient world, roughly 50 miles south of present-day
Baghdad, Iraq. The ruins of this city become the site of Nicolae
Carpathia's one-world government headquarters. The city is renamed
New Babylon. 2

Baghdad
Capital city of **Iraq.** It is 600 miles from **Jerusalem** and 50 miles north
of **Babylon,** on the banks of the **Tigris River. Baghdad** is *Global Community One*'s closest landing site to **Babylon** while that city is being
rebuilt. **2**
    Not long before Armageddon, Carpathia gathers world leaders in
Baghdad to strategize the final solution to the Jewish problem. The
meeting rooms are located where the Iraq Museum once was. **11**

Baltimore
City in central Maryland. Rayford Steele makes several flights out of
Baltimore. On one of these flights, he speaks of his faith to his copilot,
Nick Edwards, who later files a complaint against Rayford. **2**
    Leah flies to **Baltimore** from **Brussels,** Belgium. She must rush back
to Illinois to warn the Tribulation Force that Hattie Durham may com-
promise the **safe house. 7** Ming Toy suggests this city as a possible site
for her to work as a prison guard. **8**

Beersheba
An Israeli city. Michael Shorosh suggests a route through **Beersheba** for
Buck Williams and Tsion Ben-Judah's escape from **Israel.** Buck is ques-
tioned by the GC 10 kilometers south of **Beersheba. 3**

Belgium
See **Belgium Facility for Female Rehabilitation.**

Bethlehem
Birthplace of Jesus. At **Masada,** Micah (Chaim Rosenzweig) proclaims
Jesus as the Messiah, born to a virgin in **Bethlehem. 9**

Boston
Capital of Massachusetts. Rayford Steele makes several flights here for
Pan-Con. **1** Steve Plank relocates to **Boston** to run the *Global Community East Coast Daily Times,* and Hattie Durham flies to **Boston** just
before the wrath of the Lamb earthquake. **3**
    Amanda Steele takes a flight out of **Boston** to **Baghdad;** she is
killed when the plane crashes into the **Tigris River** during the earthquake. **4**

Botswana

In southern Africa between South Africa, Namibia, Zimbabwe, and Zambia, the **Kalahari Desert** makes up most of this country. U.N. Secretary-General Mwangati Ngumo is promised Chaim Rosenzweig's formula to make **Botswana** fertile in exchange for surrendering his position to Nicolae Carpathia. [1]

Botswana does not get the formula, nor does the Global Community aid in reconstruction efforts here. [6]

Bozeman

City in southwest Montana. Rayford Steele and Albie land at a tiny airstrip here to rest after rescuing Hattie Durham. They find a nearly deserted motel and rent 2 rooms. Hattie receives Christ during their stay. [8]

Bozrah

Modern day **Buseirah, Jordan**. **Bozrah** is a remote village in the mountains 20 miles north of **Petra** and was the capital of the ancient land of **Edom**. The Battle of Armageddon extends south to this area, and Jesus soils his robe in the blood of **Bozrah** as prophesied. [11], [12]

Brussels

Capital city of Belgium. **Brussels** is the site of the **Belgium Facility for Female Rehabilitation**. [7]

Buseirah

Remote city in the mountains of **Jordan**, about 30 miles southeast of the **Dead Sea** and 20 miles north of **Petra**. **Buseirah** is the site of the ancient city of **Bozrah** in **Edom**. After Jesus appears and the slaughter of the Unity Army begins, Nicolae Carpathia retreats to **Buseirah** with the remainder of his forces. Jesus leads believers to **Buseirah**, where GC forces attack but are killed by Jesus' words. Jesus descends and walks on the battlefield, then leads believers to **Jerusalem**. [12]

CAIRO

Capital city of **Egypt**. It is destroyed by GC retaliatory strikes during WWIII. **Alexandria** takes **Cairo**'s place as the hub of Egyptian air travel. [3]

California

Both Hattie Durham's family and Chloe Steele are in **California** when the Rapture occurs. [1] Ernie is killed in **California**. [6]

Chicago

Major city in Illinois. Rayford and Chloe Steele live just outside **Chicago**. Buck Williams also works here after being demoted from his position in **New York City**. [2]

Downtown **Chicago** is bombed shortly after WWIII begins, and Buck frantically searches for Chloe, who barely escapes the **Drake Hotel**. 3

Chicago is evacuated after the bombings, but when the Tribulation Force learns there is no radiation, they move into the abandoned **Strong Building** downtown. 7, 8 The believers of The Place also find refuge in **Chicago** until they and those in the **Strong Building** evacuate just before the city is bombed with nuclear weapons by the GC. 10

China

Dirk Burton tells Buck Williams that Carpathia is being introduced to key people all over the world, including in **China**. 1 Ming Toy travels to **China** in search of her parents, finally finding her mother 50 miles west of **Zhengzhou**. 10

Cincinnati

An Ohio city. Buck Williams meets Cardinal Peter Mathews here and interviews him on a flight to **New York City**. 2

Cluj

One of the larger university towns in Romania and birthplace of Nicolae Carpathia. 1

Crete

Island in the Mediterranean. A contact from the Jordanian co-op agrees to lend his plane to the Tribulation Force in exchange for being dropped off in **Crete** and later returned to **Jordan**. 9

Cyprus

An island in the Mediterranean south of Turkey. Tsion speaks at a huge rally in **Larnaca**, **Cyprus**, and his sermon is twisted by the GC news to make it seem that he murdered his family. 8 When the Unity Army assembles at Armageddon, they are supported by airbases on **Cyprus**. 11

DALLAS

Large city in Texas; it has a military strip where Rayford Steele is recertified to fly 777s and the Condor 216. He later flies Carpathia out of this strip just before the retaliatory strikes during WWIII. 3

Denver

The Mile High City, it is Colorado's capital and most populous city. Hattie Durham flies to **Denver** after briefly seeing Amanda Steele in **Chicago**. She later takes a nonstop flight to **Denver** from **Boston** before the wrath of the Lamb earthquake. Hattie tells people she has family to visit here, but her family is really from Santa Monica, **California**. 3

Des Plaines

Illinois city largely destroyed in the wrath of the Lamb earthquake. 7 Hattie Durham's **condo** is here, and she takes a chopper to the **Des Plaines** Police Department after the Rapture. 1

 Amanda White's clothing store and Zeke Zuckermandel's gas station are in **Des Plaines**. 2, 6

EASTON

City in eastern Pennsylvania. Ken Ritz flies Buck Williams to **Easton** after the Rapture, allowing Buck to make his way to **New York City** from here. 1 Ken stops in **Easton** to top off the tank when flying Buck to **Tel Aviv**. 3

Edom

Ancient land prophesied to be protected from Antichrist. It is in modern-day **Jordan**, and included within its borders is the city of **Petra**. 5

Egypt

Middle Eastern country centered on the Nile River. **Egypt** becomes part of the **Middle Eastern Commonwealth** under Nicolae Carpathia's global administration. But U.S. President Gerald Fitzhugh tells Buck Williams that **Egypt** and Britain are cooperating with U.S. militia against Carpathia. Egyptian forces marching on **New Babylon** are attacked and defeated by the GC, and **Cairo** is destroyed in GC retaliatory strikes. 2

 In a dream, Buck is told by an angel to flee into **Egypt**. He takes Tsion Ben-Judah from Israel and helps him escape the Middle East on a plane piloted by Ken Ritz. 3

England

One of the countries of Great Britain. **England** is the heart of an island nation. Dirk Burton and Alan Tompkins are murdered in **England**, and it is initially reported that Buck Williams was also killed in the car bombing. 1

 U.S. President Gerald Fitzhugh tells Buck **England** has agreed to assist the U.S. militia in overthrowing the Global Community. Major English cities are bombed in retaliation. 2

Enid
Northern Oklahoma city. Chloe Steele's post-Rapture trip from **California** to **Mt. Prospect**, Illinois, takes her through **Enid**. **1**

Ethiopia
Nation in northeastern Africa that has a secret alliance with **Russia** and assists **Russia** in its surprise attack on **Israel**. **1**

Evanston
Illinois city 13 miles north of **Chicago**. Buck Williams travels here when searching for Chloe after **Chicago** is bombed. **3**

GABORONE
Capital city of **Botswana**. Since only helicopters can land here after the wrath of the Lamb earthquake destroys the airport, the meeting between Leon Fortunato and Mwangati Ngumo is scheduled for **Johannesburg**. **6**

Gobernador Gregores
A city on the **Chico River** in southern **Argentina**. Luís Arturo lives here. The city's main runway was reportedly destroyed in the war, although from the air it looks like the original runway is still viable for air traffic. The angels Christopher, Caleb, and Nahum speak in this area, and Rayford Steele and George Sebastian hear them. The GC arrive but are banished by the angels. **10**

Great States of Britain
Established by Nicolae Carpathia; it expands Great Britain to include much of Western and Eastern Europe. Both Joshua Todd-Cothran and another man are named ambassador of this region, a discrepancy clarified when Carpathia murders Todd-Cothran. **1**

Greece
Mediterranean country that becomes part of the **United Holy Land States**. A vital underground church grows here after the Rapture, and Greek believer Lukas Miklos organizes his countrymen into an important branch of the International Commodity Co-op. **6**

Hannah Palemoon, Chloe Williams, and Mac McCullum land at an abandoned airstrip in **Greece** to rescue George Sebastian. **9** Shortly after the Tribulation Force members leave **Greece** with Sebastian, a GC raid destroys the Greek co-op. **10**

Greenland
Island nation in the northernmost reaches of the Atlantic Ocean. After the Rapture, Rayford Steele tries unsuccessfully to make contact

with **Greenland**. **1** Abdullah Smith proposes **Greenland** as a final refueling stop for Buck Williams's flight home before the birth of his son. **5**

HAIFA

Israel's third-largest city, 30 kilometers northwest of the **Plain of Megiddo**. Buck Williams meets with Chaim Rosenzweig on the outskirts of **Haifa**. **1** Chaim later cites **Haifa** as an example of the way society is worsening under the Enigma Babylon One World Faith. Mac McCullum arranges for a chopper to be ferried from **Haifa** for the Tribulation Force after the Meeting of the Witnesses. **5**

Leon Fortunato announces that **Haifa** has complied with the order to erect statues of Nicolae Carpathia. **8**

When GC armies gather for the Battle of Armageddon, those from the west land at **Haifa** and head for the **Valley of Megiddo**. **11**, **12**

Haiheul

A small town just north of **Hebron**; Buck Williams and Tsion Ben-Judah pass through on their way out of **Israel**. **3**

Hawalli

City in eastern Kuwait. A huge body of underground believers, many of whom are professionals, is here. Abdullah Smith and Mac McCullum smuggle surplus foodstuffs and 144 sophisticated computers to **Hawalli** believers while they refuel the Condor 216 for their trip to **Johannesburg**. **6**

Hebron

The first Jewish city in the land of **Israel**, south of **Jerusalem**. Buck Williams and Tsion Ben-Judah travel through **Hebron** on their way out of **Israel**. **3**

Holy City

See **Jerusalem**.

Holy Land

See **Israel**.

Hudson

A small and scenic Wisconsin city near the Minnesota border. Mac McCullum picks up Z from **Hudson** to fly him to **Petra**. **11**

INDONESIA

Country made up of a series of islands in the Pacific. At the Rapture, most of the spectators and all but one of the players at a Christian high school soccer game here disappear. **1** Bruce Barnes takes a missionary trip through **Australia** and **Indonesia**. He becomes ill after the trip from what appears to be a bug or virus, but in reality he has been poisoned by Nicolae Carpathia. **3**

Iran

Oil-rich Middle Eastern country. The GC gains control of all oil rights here. **3**

Iraq

Middle Eastern country with a hot, desert climate. The Egyptian militia heads toward **Iraq** but is quickly eliminated by GC air forces before reaching **New Babylon**. **2** The GC owns the rights to oil in **Iraq**. **3**

Israel

Country bordering the Mediterranean Sea; location of the Holy Land. After the development of Chaim Rosenzweig's formula, the **Israeli** desert blooms with flowers and produce. The formula brings peace and prosperity to this country and turns it into one of the richest nations in the world. **Israel** is attacked by **Russia** in an attempt to gain control of the formula, but the **Holy Land** is miraculously protected. The wreckage of the Russian planes provides **Israel** with 6 years' worth of combustible material for fuel. Nicolae Carpathia arranges a 7-year peace treaty with **Israel** in exchange for the right to franchise Rosenzweig's formula. **1**

Buck Williams travels through **Israel** with Tsion Ben-Judah, rescuing him after the murder of his family and escaping to **Egypt**. **3** **Israel** is the only region spared the destruction of the wrath of the Lamb earthquake. **4** This nation becomes part of the **United Carpathian States**. **7**

During the plague of boils, **Israel** is declared a no-fly zone, and Carpathia declares martial law. **10**

The Global Community Armies amass in **Israel** for the Battle of Armageddon. **11** All of **Israel**, except for **Jerusalem**, is leveled in the earthquake after the Glorious Appearing. **12**

Istanbul

In northwest Turkey; it is the only city in the world located on two continents—Europe and Asia. **Istanbul** is where the GC guillotines are manufactured and then shipped to **Greece** and **Iraq**. **8**

JACKSONVILLE

City in northwest Florida. Mac McCullum and Rayford Steele refuel here on the trip back to **San Diego**. **11**

Jericho

East of **Jerusalem** on the road to **Amman**, **Jericho** is one of the cities attacked in the Russian Pearl Harbor. **1**

Buck Williams sets out north on the **Jordan River** with Michael Shorosh near **Jericho** to search for Tsion Ben-Judah. They put ashore on the east side halfway between **Jericho** and **Lake Tiberius**. After Buck and Tsion's escape, Michael's home in **Jericho** is raided by the GC. **3**

Jerusalem

The Holy City of **Israel**, also known as the Eternal City. **Jerusalem** is sacred to the Jewish, Christian, and Muslim faiths. It is home to the **Old City**, including the **Temple Mount** and the **Citadel**. **Jerusalem** experiences peace and prosperity thanks to Chaim Rosenzweig's formula. It is one of the cities attacked in the Russian Pearl Harbor. The two witnesses preach here at the **Wailing Wall**, and no rain falls in **Jerusalem** from the time of the Rapture. **1**

The signing of the peace treaty with **Israel** takes place in **Jerusalem**, as well as the rebuilding of the **temple** and the Meeting of the Witnesses at **Teddy Kollek Stadium**. **2**, **4** Nicolae Carpathia's assassination also takes place in **Jerusalem**. **6**

After his resurrection, Carpathia talks of **Jerusalem**'s importance to Judah-ites and makes plans to visit. **Jerusalem** is the only city that resists making and worshiping a statue of Carpathia. **8** He travels to **Jerusalem** and desecrates many of its holy sites, including the **temple**. **9** Although Carpathia wants to target Jews in **Jerusalem**, the 144,000 witnesses have great success here in bringing the undecided to faith. **10**

During the GC siege of **Jerusalem**, Buck Williams and Tsion Ben-Judah go to **Jerusalem** to preach and fight. Much of the city is destroyed, and both Tsion and Buck are killed in the fighting. **11**

After the Glorious Appearing, the remnant follows Jesus to **Jerusalem**. The city is raised 300 feet above the ground in an earthquake while the surrounding land is flattened. Although **Jerusalem** had been in ruins from the fighting, it is miraculously clean and the foliage is in full bloom when Jesus enters. **12**

Johannesburg

South African city where Regional Potentate Rehoboth resides in a beautiful **palace**. Abdullah Smith and Mac McCullum fly Leon Fortunato to **Johannesburg**, where the plane comes under fire from Rehoboth's insurgents and is attacked by the 200 million horsemen. Dwayne and Trudy Tuttle land in a Super J to assist Mac and Abdullah. **6**

Jordan
Middle Eastern nation east of **Israel**, bordered by the **Jordan River**, Syria, **Iraq**, and **Saudi Arabia**.

KENOSHA
City in southeast Wisconsin. Area victims are taken to hotels turned into hospitals in **Kenosha** after the wrath of the Lamb earthquake. Chloe Williams is treated at the **GC hospital** here. ▪4

Khartoum
Capital city of Sudan, the largest country in Africa. Mac McCullum and Abdullah Smith land the Condor 216 here after some of the 200 million horsemen attack the unrepentant on the plane. The ailing and dead are taken off the plane and the Condor 216 is fumigated before continuing to **Johannesburg**. ▪6

Kozani
An administrative province in **Greece**. Rayford Steele lands here after fleeing **Israel** following the assassination of Nicolae Carpathia. The **Kozani** airport is 25 miles south of **Ptolemaïs**. Rayford is taken to a rustic **cabin** in the woods some 20 kilometers south of **Kozani** where fellow believers refresh him. T is flying Buck Williams and Chaim Rosenzweig when he runs out of gas as he approaches this airport. The Super J crashes and T dies. ▪7

David Hassid plans for Ming Toy to fly into **Kozani** on the way to the **United North American States**. Albie and Buck fly here on their trip to encourage the incarcerated members of the underground church. ▪8

A GC plane with the "philosophers" on board flies from the **Kozani** airport to try and stop the Sebastian rescue. ▪10

LAGUNA GRANDE
Argentine town 60 miles south of **Gobernador Gregores**. The GC has a loyalty mark facility here. ▪10

Larnaca
City on the island of **Cyprus**. Tsion Ben-Judah once preached at a huge rally in **Larnaca**, and the GC uses a video of the rally to identify Michael Shorosh. ▪3

Abdullah Smith lands at what is left of the **Larnaca** airport, one of the least patrolled airstrips in the **United Carpathian States**. From here, Rayford Steele and others return to the States and Mac McCullum, Chloe Williams, and Hannah Palemoon head for **Greece**. ▪9

The Greek rescue team considers flying home through **Larnaca** but dismisses the idea. 10

Le Havre

City on the English Channel in France. Hattie Durham is supposedly here with Samuel Hanson. Rayford Steele and the Tuttles go to **Le Havre** and look for Hattie in **apartment 323.** 6

Liberal

A small town in the southwest corner of Kansas. Rayford Steele lands in **Liberal**, stalling on his mission to find Hattie Durham for the GC. 4

Libya

A northern African nation. **Libya** and **Ethiopia** have a secret alliance with **Russia** and assist in the attack on **Israel.** 1

Littleton

Colorado city just south of **Denver**. Hattie Durham goes to a **reproductive clinic** in **Littleton.** 4

Lod

City in Israel 9 miles southeast of **Tel Aviv.** David Ben Gurion International Airport is in **Lod.** 2

London

Capital of Great Britain, in southeast **England**. Rayford Steele is flying a **747** to **London** when the Rapture occurs. Buck Williams travels to **London** to meet with Dick Burton 1 The city is bombed by the GC in retaliation for its alliance with the U.S. militia. 2

Long Grove

Illinois city, northwest of **Chicago**. Ming Toy (as Chang Chow) gets a ride from **Chicago** to **Long Grove**. Lionel Whalum and his family live here, and Leah Rose and Hannah Palemoon settle in with the Whalums after the **Strong Building** is evacuated. 10 They remain in **Long Grove** until they go to **Petra** for Albie and Chloe's memorial service. 11

Los Angeles

Major city in Southern **California**. Rayford Steele discovers through the bugging system in the Condor 216 that Nicolae Carpathia plans to bomb this city. 3

MANHATTAN

One of 5 boroughs in **New York City**. The island of **Manhattan** is one of the world financial capitals and home to the **United Nations.**

The Jewish Nationalist conference is held in Manhattan. ▎1 Buck Williams has a palatial **Manhattan** office until he is demoted to the **Chicago** branch of *Global Weekly.* ▎2 **Manhattan** is hit hard in the WWIII bombings. ▎3

Mecca
City in western **Saudi Arabia**; **Mecca** is the birthplace of Mohammed and the center of the Islamic world. The Muslim sacred city is leveled by the GC. ▎10

Megiddo
City in northern **Israel**, about 100 kilometers north of **Jerusalem**. The **Plain of Megiddo** is immediately to the west and takes its name from this city. **Megiddo**'s strategic location made it the site of more wars than any other place in the world; the city was destroyed and rebuilt 25 times. The Unity Army command post for the Battle of Armageddon is in **Megiddo**. ▎12

Mexico City
Capital of Mexico. **Mexico City** is bombed as an object lesson for Nicolae Carpathia's opposition. ▎3

Middle Eastern Commonwealth
Region established by Nicolae Carpathia; it includes the former sovereign state of **Egypt**. ▎2 This region is later renamed the **United Holy Land States**. ▎7

Minneapolis
Minnesota city; sister city to St. Paul. Chloe Williams is taken to **Minneapolis** after being treated for her earthquake injuries. Ken Ritz flies Buck here to get Chloe. ▎4 Later the GC reports that Chloe is an American subversive who escaped from **Minneapolis**, where she had been detained for questioning. ▎5

Mizpe Ramon
Small Israeli town in the **Negev Desert**. Albie and Rayford Steele fly into **Mizpe Ramon** as part of Operation Eagle. They supervise the completion of a remote airstrip and refueling center for the airlift. ▎8

David Hassid arranges for the GC database to indicate that the work at **Mizpe Ramon** is a GC exercise, so the Tribulation Force is initially able to move freely. Messianic Jews are airlifted 50 miles to **Petra** from here. After the mission is accomplished, Tribulation Force members fly out of **Mizpe Ramon** to the **United North American States** via **Larnaca**. ▎9

Montreal

City in Quebec, a province in eastern Canada. Nicolae Carpathia names **Montreal** one of the cities that will be bombed as an object lesson for those who oppose him. **3**

Mt. Prospect

An Illinois city northwest of **Chicago**. The Steele family's **house**, **New Hope Village Church**, Loretta's **house**, and the **Donny Moore safe house** are in **Mt. Prospect**. **1-7** Because of its location near the northern Illinois epicenter of the wrath of the Lamb earthquake, **Mt. Prospect** sustains massive damage and loss of life. **4**

NAIROBI

The capital of Kenya. At the **Nairobi** airport, Leon Fortunato invites Enoch Litwala, new regional potentate for the **United States of Africa**, to the Global Gala in **Jerusalem**. **6**

Nanjing

City in eastern **China** on the bank of the Yangtse river. Chang Wong told his parents that there was an underground church in **Nanjing**, so Ree Woo takes Ming Toy to **Nanjing** to look for them. Ming and Ree meet an old woman who tells them the church has relocated to **Zhengzhou**. **10**

New Babylon

City rebuilt over the ruins of **Babylon** in **Iraq**, south of **Baghdad**. Much of the rebuilding is financed by Jonathan Stonagal. Nicolae Carpathia decides to move the United Nations to **New Babylon**. **1**

New Babylon becomes the **Global Community headquarters**, designed by Carpathia himself. Thousands make pilgrimages here to see the magnificent headquarters. Ten percent of the world's weaponry is shipped to **New Babylon**. **2**

After he goes to work for Carpathia, Rayford Steele and his wife, Amanda, have a sprawling **condo** in **New Babylon**, though they never feel it is home. Mac McCullum also lives here. The **GC headquarters** and much of the city lies in ruins after the wrath of the Lamb earthquake. **3**

The city is rebuilt as the capital of the world—the center of banking and commerce, headquarters of the Global Community, and new holy city when the Enigma Babylon One World Faith relocates here. **4** It is described as the most magnificent city ever built, with massive, crystalline buildings and a stunning skyline. **5**, **6** Carpathia's funeral is held in **New Babylon**, and Annie Christopher is there, patrolling sector 53. This area is hit by lightning at the end of the service. Ming Toy is also on assignment at the funeral, and her parents and brother, Chang Wong, attend. During the funeral, Carpathia's body is indwelt by Satan and resurrects. Hannah Palemoon works as a nurse in **New Babylon** and treats David Hassid at the **palace hospital** after the funeral. **7**

By faking their deaths in the Quasi Two crash, Hannah, David, Mac, and Abdullah Smith escape **New Babylon**. **8** After David is gone, Chang takes over his job and works for the Tribulation Force from inside the **palace**. He orchestrates Buck Williams's ability to film Chaim Rosenzweig during Carpathia's desecration of the **temple**. Carpathia returns to **New Babylon**, demanding that the 10 regional potentates join him here. Leon Fortunato is speaking in the beautiful **Church of Carpathia** outside the **palace** in **New Babylon** when an angel appears and disrupts his speech. From his office in **New Babylon**, Carpathia watches bombers headed for **Petra**. **9**

New Babylon falls into complete darkness in one of God's judgments, and many die in the chaos. Carpathia relocates his government to **Al Hillah** just before **New Babylon** is destroyed by 2 invading armies, as prophesied. **11**

New York City

In southeast New York; one of the major world cities. The *Global Weekly* **Building** and the **United Nations headquarters** are in **New York City**. **1** The city sustains massive damage and is shut down in the WWIII bombings. **3** Because of the United States' role in the rebellion, New York is last on Carpathia's refurbishing list. **5**

Northern Ireland

The mainly Protestant segment of Ireland; the country is part of the United Kingdom. Scotland Yard reports that the **London** bombing that killed Alan Tompkins appeared to be the work of **Northern Ireland** terrorists and might have been a case of retribution. **1**

OAKLAND

City in western **California** on the **San Francisco** Bay. Nicolae Carpathia arranges for this city to be bombed following the insurrection. **3**

Old City

Walled city of ancient **Jerusalem**; the **Old City** is only 1 kilometer square and divided into quarters—Muslim, Jewish, Christian, and Armenian. There are 11 gates into the **Old City**, which contains the **Temple Mount**. The **Old City** is Nicolae Carpathia's main objective in the siege on **Jerusalem**. ⏹ Much of the fighting takes place here. The walls of the **Old City** are leveled in the earthquake that reshapes **Jerusalem**, and Jesus leads the remnant inside. ⏹

PALATINE
City in Illinois, a short distance from **Mt. Prospect**. The city is almost destroyed in the earthquake, except for **Arthur Young Memorial Hospital**. ⏹

Palos Hills
In northeastern Illinois. Enoch, leader of The Place, relocates here after receiving word that **Chicago** is going to be nuked by the GC. ⏹ Enoch continues leading a small band of believers that grows to 100. They meet in an abandoned shopping mall and laser-tag park 10 miles from Enoch's home in **Palos Hills** until they are miraculously transported to Petra. ⏹

Paris
Capital of France. Just after the Rapture, Rayford Steele tries to make contact to land at **Paris** but is told to go back to **Chicago**. ⏹ On a later trip, Rayford buys Amanda White an expensive diamond necklace in **Paris**. ⏹

Park Ridge
Chicago suburb with a rebuilt section of new pavement and a couple of working traffic lights that Buck passes on his way to rescue Z. ⏹

Pawleys Island
City on the east coast of South Carolina. Ming Toy stops here before flying to **San Diego**, then **China**. ⏹

Persia
Ancient name for the modern country of **Iran**.

Petra
The Rose Red City, about 50 miles southeast of **Mizpe Ramon** in **Jordan**. It is an ancient rock city, carved by hand into a sandstone canyon. **Petra** is chosen as the new home for Jews airlifted as part of Operation Eagle. Scholars, including Tsion Ben-Judah, believe God intended **Petra** for this purpose from the beginning of time. ⏹

David Hassid travels to **Petra** before Operation Eagle to set up its communications center and sees GC forces assembling outside the city. Rayford Steele, Mac McCullum, George Sebastian, Abdullah Smith, and Albie head to **Petra**, and the GC troops are driven out, but David is killed by 2 remaining Peacekeepers. Operation Eagle is successful, and a million people are brought to **Petra**. The GC surround the city again, but the archangel Michael preaches to and comforts those inside **Petra**, and a massive crater opens a mile in every direction to swallow the attacking army. 9

Nicolae Carpathia's GC forces launch an air attack on **Petra**, but no residents are killed. They are engulfed in flames but not hurt. The city becomes the nucleus for Tsion Ben-Judah's and Chaim Rosenzweig's ministries. A group of godly men, the elders, surrounds Tsion and Chaim. God provides for the needs of those in **Petra**, giving them water and manna, putting them under his protection, and even keeping their clothes from wearing out. Rayford Steele continues to lead the Tribulation Force from **Petra** before relocating to **San Diego**. Abdullah flourishes here, and Mac and Albie visit him often. 10

The Whalums, Leah Rose, and Hannah Palemoon eventually relocate to **Petra**. The memorial service for Albie and Chloe Williams is held here. Chang Wong moves to **Petra**, and **New Babylon** believers travel here before **New Babylon**'s destruction. From **Petra**, Chang broadcasts Tsion's teachings live all over the world. Chang and Naomi Tiberias train others on the computers so responses to Tsion's teachings can be answered. Tsion hands over the leadership of **Petra** to Chaim when he leaves to fight and preach in **Jerusalem**. As the Battle of Armageddon approaches, GC forces once again surround **Petra**, but the city is protected by God. 11

Rayford Steele is badly injured on an ATV outside **Petra** but is rescued and brought back inside. Just before the Glorious Appearing, a cross appears in the sky, and Rayford and all the injured at **Petra** are miraculously healed. After Jesus appears, the remnant leaves **Petra** and follows him to **Jerusalem**. 12

Prudhoe Bay

North of Alaska. The second-largest reserve of oil in the world is just above this bay, and Nicolae Carpathia plans to pipe the oil out to the international market. 3

Ptolemaïs

City in northern **Greece**. **Ptolemaïs** has large quantities of lignite, used to power thermoelectric plants. Lukas Miklos works in **Ptolemaïs** as a major lignite supplier. Rayford Steele, Chloe Williams, and Tsion Ben-Judah land in **Ptolemaïs** on the way home from the Meeting of the Witnesses and visit Laslos and his wife. Abdullah Smith and Buck

Williams also land in **Ptolemaïs**, and Buck meets briefly with Laslos before continuing on to the States. **5**

After Nicolae Carpathia's assassination, Rayford plans to land in **Ptolemaïs**, but the airport is closed and dark so he travels to **Kozani**. **Albie** flies to **Ptolemaïs** to pick up Buck and Chaim Rosenzweig after the Super J crash. **7**

Ptolemaïs is home to the largest underground church in **Greece**. Believers fall under heavy persecution from the GC, and Buck and Albie fly into **Ptolemaïs** to meet with believers imprisoned in the GC **detention center**. **8**

Laslos, K, and Marcel pick up the Georgiana Stavros imposter, Elena, just outside **Ptolemaïs**. She murders the 3 men in K's car, and George Sebastian is taken captive. Mac McCullum, Hannah Palemoon, and Chloe travel to **Ptolemaïs** to rescue him. **9**

When Mac, Hannah, and Chloe arrive, they find **Ptolemaïs** looking as though it's been through a war. But one of the strongest branches of the International Commodity Co-op is still headquartered in **Ptolemaïs**, and believers meet clandestinely under a **pub**. The GC also has a headquarters in **Ptolemaïs**—a dingy, poorly staffed building. George Sebastian is imprisoned here in a broken elevator until he kills Elena and escapes. The Greek rescue team flies out of an abandoned airport 80 miles west of **Ptolemaïs**, avoiding the **Ptolemaïs** airport to evade the GC. With the help of the archangel Michael, the team makes it out of **Greece**. Soon after, the Tribulation Force learns that the remaining underground believers in **Ptolemaïs** have been killed by the GC. **10**

Pueblo
Colorado city about an hour south of Colorado Springs. Hattie Durham is confined here in a GC **bunker**. She makes contact with Rayford Steele, and Albie and Rayford go to rescue her. **8**

QAR
Communications site used to help relay messages to **New Babylon** from **Al Basrah**. **4**

RAFAH
City on the Egyptian border on the Gaza Strip. **Rafah** is one of 4 places suggested by Michael Shorosh for Buck Williams to escape from **Israel** with Tsion Ben-Judah. It is heavily patrolled. **3**

Rantoul
Eastern Illinois city. The **Rantoul** GC base sends a chopper, unknowingly

for use by the Tribulation Force. **7** This chopper is used by Rayford Steele and Albie in their rescue of Hattie Durham. **8**

Rome

Italian city once the center of the ancient world and is now home to the **Vatican**. Rayford Steele and Mac McCullum fly Leon Fortunato to **Rome** to pick up Peter Mathews. **3** Mathews is picked up from **Rome** several times before he moves to **New Babylon**. **4** After Mathews's death, all holy texts are shipped from **Rome** to **New Babylon**. **7**

The International Commodity Co-op has an airstrip south of **Rome** where fuel is stockpiled. The Greek rescue team stops here to refuel on the way home. **10**

Rose Red City

See **Petra**.

Russia

Nation stretching across eastern Europe and northern Asia. **Russia** has a devastated economy and spends its resources stockpiling weaponry. In an attempt to benefit from Chaim Rosenzweig's formula and dominate the Middle East, **Russia** launches a surprise attack on **Israel**. The invading forces are destroyed in a miraculous protection of **Israel** that becomes known as the Russian Pearl Harbor. **1** Once Rosenzweig's formula is licensed by Nicolae Carpathia, **Russia** is able to grow grain in the frozen Siberian tundra. **3**

SALT LAKE CITY

Chloe Steele flies Air California to this Utah city, one of her many stops on the trip home to Illinois after the Rapture. **1**

San Diego

Major city in southwest **California**. Buck, Chloe, and Kenny Williams relocate to the **San Diego compound** with the Sebastian underground church after the **Strong Building** is evacuated. **10**

The GC has a headquarters in **San Diego**, one of the largest in North America. Chloe is taken there and held in a cell—a cage in the corner of a larger room—before being transferred to **Stateville Correctional Center**. **11**

San Francisco

Port city in western **California** on the San Francisco Bay. Earl Halliday tells Rayford Steele that Mac McCullum will meet him in **San Francisco** to help copilot the Condor 216. Rayford learns that Nicolae Carpathia is going to bomb **San Francisco**, so he stalls here until he knows Amanda is out of the city. The airport and most of the Bay Area are destroyed in the bombing. **3**

Saudi Arabia

Middle Eastern nation and a major oil producer. The GC acquires the rights to the oil in **Saudi Arabia**. **3**

Shanghai

A major Chinese city. Ree Woo delivers co-op goods to **Shanghai** before flying Ming Toy 200 miles west to **Nanjing**. **10**

Siberia

Extremely cold region in northern **Russia**. Chaim Rosenzweig's formula allows the frozen tundra to produce grain. **3**

Springfield

Capital of Illinois. Chloe Steele travels through **Springfield** on her way home following the Rapture. **1**

Staten Island

Small island at the mouth of the Hudson River in southeast New York. It is reported that Eric Miller drowned off the **Staten Island** ferry and his body washed up on **Staten Island**. **1**

TA'IZZ

City north of the Gulf of Aden in southern Yemen. The co-op has an airstrip just east of **Ta'izz**, and Abdullah Smith flies here with a shipment for **Petra**. **10**

Tamel Aike

City on the **Chico River** in southern **Argentina**. The GC has mark application sites in **Tamel Aike**, 60 miles from where Rayford hears the angel Christopher speak. **10**

Tel Aviv

Large city in **Israel** 35 miles from **Jerusalem**. Buck Williams is in **Tel Aviv** when the Russian Pearl Harbor occurs. **1**

   David Ben Gurion Airport is 9 miles southeast of **Tel Aviv** in **Lod**. Peter Mathews is staying in the penthouse suite of a 5-star hotel in **Tel Aviv** when Buck tries to contact him about the two witnesses. **2**

   Under Nicolae Carpathia's rule, **Tel Aviv**, as well as **Jerusalem** and **Haifa**, shows moral decline despite the rebuilding of the **temple** and the establishment of the Enigma Babylon faith. **5**

   Rayford Steele stays in a seedy hotel on the west side of **Tel Aviv** when in **Israel** for the Gala. **6**

Tel Aviv citizens build a statue of Carpathia, as ordered by Leon Fortunato. **Tel Aviv** is the location of the first loyalty mark application site; the Quasi Two crash occurs during the site's inauguration. 8

Hattie Durham receives a visit from the archangel Michael in her **Tel Aviv** hotel room and learns she is to confront the Antichrist and the False Prophet. 9

Tennessee
After the wrath of the Lamb earthquake, only the *Global Community Weekly* presses in **Tennessee** and southeast Asia have printing capabilities. 4

Tucson
An Arizona city. Buck Williams's father and brother, Jeff, live in **Tuscon**. After the Rapture, Buck gets word that they are still there and doing well. 1 Mr. Williams and Jeff join an underground church in **Tuscon**. They are eventually killed by the GC and their home is burned. 7

UNITED AFRICAN STATES
One of the 10 regions of the Global Community; it is represented by the number 7. Enoch Litwala becomes regional potentate after Bindura Rehoboth is killed. At Nicolae Carpathia's funeral, Litwala is killed by lightning. 7

United Asian States
Global Community region represented by the number *30*. 7

United Carpathian States
New name given to the **United Holy Land States** after Nicolae Carpathia's assassination. It is represented by the number *216*. 7 **Ptolemaïs, Greece**, is home to the largest underground church in the **United Carpathian States**. 8

United European States
One of 10 regions in the Global Community, represented by the number *6*. 7

United Great Britain States
One of 10 Global Community regions, represented by the number *2*. 7

United Holy Land States
Global Community region that encompasses the Middle East. It is renamed the **United Carpathian States**. 7

United Indian States
One of the 10 Global Community regions, represented by the number *42*. ⑦

United North American States
Global Community region represented by –6. ⑦

United Pacific States
Represented by the number *18*; one of the 10 Global Community regions. ⑦

United Russian States
World region represented by the number *72*. ⑦

United States of Africa
One of 10 world regions. Bindura Rehoboth is the first regional potentate for this area. ⑥ The region is renamed the **United African States**. ⑦

United States of Asia
One of the 10 world regions. ②–⑦ It is renamed the **United Asian States**. ⑦

United States of Britain
See **United States of Great Britain**.

United States of Great Britain
The former **Great States of Britain**. ②–⑥. Renamed the **United Great Britain States**. ⑦

United States of North America
One of the 10 world regions established by Nicolae Carpathia. ② This region is renamed the **United North American States**. ⑦

United South American States
One of the 10 Global Community regions, represented by the number *0*. ⑦

VATICAN CITY
Independent region within the city of **Rome**. Cardinal Mathews heads for **Vatican City** for the papal vote after the treaty signing. The newly forming religion, Enigma Babylon One World Faith, is headquartered here. ② Later Mathews moves to **New Babylon**. Leon Fortunato gathers the 10 regional potentates in **Vatican City**. He destroys every evidence of Christianity in the **Vatican**. ⑧

WADI MUSA

A town in **Jordan**, just east of **Petra**. Mac McCullum and Albie fly their Operation Eagle charges to this village. **9**

Washington, D.C.

Capital of the United States of America; it becomes the capital of the **United States of North America** under Nicolae Carpathia. After the change, President Fitzhugh and the vice president are headquartered in the old Executive Office Building in **Washington**, **D.C.** The east coast militia, with the aid of the **United States of Britain** and the former sovereign state of **Egypt**, launches an attack that leaves **Washington, D.C.** in ruins. **2**

ZHENGZHOU

A large Chinese city, over 300 miles northwest of **Nanjing**. The Chinese underground church relocates here. Ree Woo takes Ming Toy to **Zhengzhou** to find her parents and promises Ming that he will add the small underground church here to the co-op's list. Ming finds out that her father was killed by the GC and her mother is 50 miles west in mountains. While undercover as a male Peacekeeper, Ming witnesses a raid on a Muslim group in **Zhengzhou** and hears the angels Christopher, Nahum, and Caleb preach. **10**

Zion

Reference to the city of **Jerusalem**. The two witnesses, Eli and Moishe, use this term. **1**

BUILDINGS AND STRUCTURES

AL-KHASNEH
"The Treasury," **Al-Khasneh** is cut from the rock of the Jordanian city of **Petra**. It is reported to have held the riches of Pharaoh during the Exodus. ⑨

Amman Airport
See **Queen Alia International Airport, Resurrection International Airport.**

Amphitheater
Large open-air auditorium. In **New Babylon**, evidence regarding Nicolae Carpathia's assassination is stored and inspected in a room under the **amphitheater**, and during the funeral, seating is provided in the **amphitheater**. ⑦ Later a makeshift **amphitheater** is constructed in **Tel Aviv** to house mark application equipment. ⑧

Angola
Common name for the Louisiana State Penitentiary. To capture Tribulation Force rescuers, the GC claims Chloe Steele has been imprisoned here. Chloe is actually confined in **Stateville Correctional Center.** ⑪

Armitage Arms
London pub. Buck Williams and Alan Tompkins meet here before Tompkins is killed by a car bomb in front of the pub. ①

Arthur Young Memorial Hospital

In **Palatine**, Illinois, where Ken Ritz and Chloe Steele are taken after the wrath of the Lamb earthquake. **4** Leah Rose is head administrative nurse, and Dr. Charles periodically works here and assists members of the Tribulation Force. **6**, **4** Hattie Durham is taken to this **hospital** before her miscarriage, and after they are stung by locusts, Bo Hanson and Ernie are also treated at **Arthur Young**. **5** Leah and Buck Williams take Dr. Charles to this hospital just before he dies. **6**

BAGHDAD AIRPORT

After WWIII erupts, Nicolae Carpathia has Rayford Steele land here to pick up 3 ambassadors. Rayford lands at **Baghdad Airport** after the wrath of the Lamb earthquake and sees much destruction. **3**

Belgium Facility for Female Rehabilitation (BFFR or Buffer)

GC detention center in **Brussels, Belgium**. Hattie Durham is briefly imprisoned here. Leah Rose pretends to be Hattie's aunt and tries to visit her, but Hattie has already been released. Leah does, however, meet Ming Toy, a believer who works at **Buffer** as a guard. **6**, **7**

Ben Gurion International Airport

See **David Ben Gurion International Airport**.

Bethesda Pools

See **Pools of Bethesda**.

Building 5

Part of the GC **detention center** in **Ptolemaïs, Greece**. **Building 5** is designated for those caught without Carpathia's loyalty mark and the worst criminals. Pastor Demeter is imprisoned and executed here. **8**

Building D

Maintenance facility several hundred yards from the **New Babylon palace**. In **Building D** Chang Wong is forced to receive the loyalty mark. **9** During the heat judgment, Krystall, Nicolae Carpathia's secretary, has to be relocated to a cooler room beneath **Building D**. She communicates with Carpathia via intercom. **10**

Bunker

Underground GC facility an hour south of Colorado Springs in **Pueblo**. Hattie Durham is imprisoned here and tries to commit suicide before Albie and Rayford Steele rescue her with the help of Pinkerton Stephens (Steve Plank), undercover as a GC officer here. **8** From the **bunker**, Stephens tells Rayford about George Sebastian's capture and helps

Rayford get Buck Williams, Abdullah Smith, Hannah Palemoon, and Leah Rose to safety in the **Strong Building**. 9

CABIN

20 miles south of **Kozani**; members of the Greek co-op take Rayford here to encourage him and allow him to rest. The **cabin** can be reached only by traveling an unpaved road. 7

Café

Buck Williams and Tsion Ben-Judah meet in a small **Jerusalem café** just before Tsion broadcasts his findings on the prophecies concerning Messiah. 2 Buck and Abdullah Smith meet in an outdoor **café** to discuss a flight from **Amman**, and Rayford Steele and Dwayne and Trudy Tuttle await Albie in a bustling outdoor **café**. Later the Tuttles are killed at the **café** as they wait for Albie and Rayford to return. 5, 6

Capital Noir

Luxury hotel in **Washington**, **D.C.** leveled at the beginning of WWIII. Nicolae Carpathia stays in **Capital Noir**'s presidential suite the night before it is destroyed. 2

Carlisle Hotel

New York City hotel that Rayford Steele enjoys visiting. Rayford, Chloe, Hattie Durham, and Buck Williams meet for an elegant dinner here. During their meal, Buck interviews Rayford about the disappearances, and Rayford presents his testimony. 1

Carpathia Memorial Airstrip

In Colorado Springs; Albie and Rayford Steele land here when rescuing Hattie Durham from the GC **bunker** in **Pueblo**. 8

Carpathia Resurrection Field

Airport south of Colorado Springs, Colorado. There is a loyalty mark application center in the north wing of the airport. Steve Plank is beheaded here. 10

Cellar, The

Dank, underground eatery in **Jerusalem** visited by Chaim Rosenzweig and Buck Williams. 5

Central Park

A centerpiece of **Manhattan**. Buck Williams and Steve Plank walk through the park as they discuss Dirk Burton, Alan Tompkins, Eric Miller, Jonathan Stonagal, Joshua Todd-Cothran, and Nicolae Carpathia. 1

Chalet
Retreat in France where world financial leaders assemble for secret meetings about world monetary currencies. 1

Church of Carpathia
Just outside the **palace** in **New Babylon**. Leon Fortunato speaks in the sanctuary, announcing that the grace period for taking the mark has expired and reminding people of the requirement to worship Nicolae Carpathia's image 3 times a day. As the speech ends, the lights go out in the church, causing chaos. An angel appears on the GC broadcast and warns against taking the mark. 9

Church of the Flagellation
One of the Stations of the Cross. On **Jerusalem's Via Dolorosa**, the **Church of the Flagellation** is in the **Old City** west of the Muslim quarter. Buck Williams and Tsion Ben-Judah make plans to meet here when they are separated during the fight against the Unity Army for **Jerusalem**. 11 The church is used as a staging area for the Unity Army as the battle continues. 12

Citadel
Fortress on the western side of the **Old City**, just south of the **Jaffa Gate**. It is the highest point on the southwestern hill of **Jerusalem**. Tsion Ben-Judah wants Buck Williams to take the elder Shivte to the **Citadel**. Many scared men are holed up here. It is a stronghold for the Jewish rebels fighting the Unity Army. 11

Cradle of Jesus
Chamber approximately 50 by 70 feet beneath the southeast corner of **Jerusalem's Temple Mount**. Both a basilica named for Saint Mary and a mosque were previously located in that chamber. On Carpathia's instructions, the sanitation system for **Solomon's Stables** is designed to empty into the **Cradle of Jesus**. 12

Crematorium
Place where Peter the Second's body is burned to cover up his assassination by the 10 regional potentates. 6

DALLAS/FT. WORTH AIRPORT (DFW)
15 miles from **Dallas** and 18 miles from Fort Worth, Texas, **DFW** has 4 terminals and is one of the busiest airports in America. It closes briefly after the Rapture. 1

WWIII destroys all but one of the airport's major runways. Captain

Hernandez flies *Global Community Three* into **DFW** with Leon Fortunato, Nicolae Carpathia, and Rayford and Amanda Steele on board. **3**

Only half this airport is functional after the wrath of the Lamb earthquake, but the rest is quickly rebuilt. Mac McCullum and Rayford fly into **DFW** to pick up a former Texas senator who has become the ambassador from the **United States of North America**. Soon after, Rayford aborts his mission to pick up Hattie Durham in **Littleton**, Colorado, and returns to **DFW**, knowing the mission is a setup for his and Hattie's murders. **4**

Damascus Gate

On the north side of **Jerusalem**'s **Old City**, this gate opens onto the ancient road to Damascus. The Shivte brothers believe the Unity Armies will come from the northwest through this gate. After taking the elder Shivte to the **Citadel**, Buck Williams returns to this area, looking for Tsion Ben-Judah and the Shivte brothers. **11** Mac McCullum later goes through the **Damascus Gate** on horseback in disguise as a Unity Army officer. **12**

David Ben Gurion International Airport

In the city of **Lod** 9 miles southeast of **Tel Aviv**, **Ben Gurion** is the busiest civil airport in the Middle East. Rayford Steele flies Nicolae Carpathia into this airport for the signing of the peace treaty with **Israel**, and Ken Ritz flies Buck Williams in to witness the signing. The newly repainted *Air Force One* sits on display here as well. **2**

Ken flies Buck into **Ben Gurion** again for the rescue of Tsion Ben-Judah. **3** Rayford and Mac McCullum fly into **Ben Gurion** for the Meeting of the Witnesses, and the Condor 216 is hangared here. When Ken assists the Tribulation Force in escaping from the **Rosenzweig estate**, he tells pursuing Chopper Two that he will see him at **Ben Gurion**. **5**

Buck flies into **Ben Gurion** to see Chaim and attend the Global Gala. Rayford also enters **Israel** through this airport, thinking the high level of traffic will allow him to get through undetected. **6** After Carpathia's assassination, Rayford flies out of **Ben Gurion** in the Gulfstream without clearance. **7**

Mac McCullum is supposed to land at **Ben Gurion** after performing an air show. Instead he flies the plane by remote and crashes it into the beach, faking his and 3 other Tribulation Force members' deaths. **8**

Denver International Airport

Buck Williams tells the GC he flew into this Colorado airport when he speaks with Hattie Durham's guards at the **reproductive clinic** outside **Littleton**, Colorado. Actually, Ken Ritz flew him into **Denver's Stapleton Airport.** 4

Detention Center

In **Ptolemaïs, Greece**; Greek believers are beheaded here by GC guillotines. The **detention center** is a complex of 5 former industrial buildings. The windows are covered with bars, and the perimeter is a tangle of fence and razor wire. It houses approximately 900 prisoners. Buck Williams and Albie fly to the **detention center** on a research trip for *The Truth*. Disguised as GC officers, they free Marcel Papadopoulos and Georgiana Stravros. ₹ See **Building 5**.

DFW

See **Dallas/Fort Worth Airport.**

DIA

See **Denver International Airport.**

Doctor Pita's

Restaurant in **Jerusalem**. Abdullah Smith is eating here when Mac calls him after Carpathia's assassination. 7

Dome of the Rock

Huge, beautiful mosque on the **Temple Mount**. The **Dome of the Rock** is considered the second-holiest Muslim religious site after Mohammed's birthplace, **Mecca**. Nicolae Carpathia persuades the Muslims to take their shrine and the sacred section of the rock to **New Babylon**, allowing the Jews to rebuild their **temple** on its original location. 2

Drake Hotel, The

Chicago hotel overlooking **Lake Michigan**. Buck and Chloe Williams stay at **The Drake**. They invite Bruce Barnes and Rayford and Amanda Steele to join them for lunch in the Cape Cod Room. 2

The hotel sustains heavy damage during the retaliatory strikes on **Chicago** during WWIII. 3

Dulles

See **Washington Dulles International Airport.**

DuPage County Jail

Former name of the Illinois facility used by the GC for mark applications. Zeke Zuckermandel Sr. is executed here. ₹

Dung Gate

Southern gate in **Jerusalem** closest to the **Western Wall**; one mile from the **Damascus Gate**. The Jewish rebels in **Jerusalem** gain control of a GC battering ram and take it inside the **Dung Gate**. **11** In disguise as a GC officer, Mac rides a horse in this area. **12**

EASTERN GATE

See **Golden Gate**.

Eastern Wall

East wall of the **Old City**, containing the **Lion's Gate** and the **Golden Gate**. The **Mount of Olives** is half a mile from the **Eastern Wall**. **12**

FAITH PALACE

Site of Peter the Second's office in **New Babylon**. **6**

Flower Gate

See **Herod's Gate**.

GARDEN TOMB

Traditional site of Jesus' entombment and resurrection. Nicolae Carpathia's sow ride down the **Via Dolorosa** ends at the **Garden Tomb**. Carpathia speaks here and declares himself god on earth. The crowds then continue to the **Temple Mount**. **9** Unity Army troops gather in the garden for the siege on **Jerusalem** **12**

GC Grand Hotel

See **Global Community Grand Hotel**.

GC Hospital

In **Kenosha**, Wisconsin. The makeshift **hospital** was converted from a couple of hotels. In his search for Chloe, Buck Williams meets Dr. Charles, who is head of the **hospital's morgue**. Buck learns that Chloe was treated here before being transferred to **Minneapolis**. **4**

Glenview Naval Air Station

In the center of Glenview, Illinois, about 20 miles north of **Chicago**. Ken Ritz tells Buck Williams about when his instruments went wacky near **Glenview**, making him better able to believe those who attribute the Rapture to aliens. **1**

The **Glenview Naval Air Station** is where Rayford Steele meets Nicolae Carpathia after the insurrection. Rayford thought that the station had been closed for years, but Hernandez tells him the big runway is still open. **3**

Dr. Charles tells Buck about GC plans to fly Chloe out of **Glenview** after the earthquake. 4

Global Bistro

A restaurant in **New Babylon** frequented by Nicolae Carpathia and Hattie Durham. Hattie helped conceive the **Global Bistro**, and the menu carries international cuisine, mostly American. Hattie meets Rayford Steele here and laments her deteriorating relationship with Carpathia. 3

Global Community Grand Hotel

A fancy new hotel in **Jerusalem**, a quarter mile from the **King David Hotel**. Peter the Second is murdered here with "feathers" from an ice sculpture. All 10 regional potentates are housed at the **GC Grand Hotel** during the Global Gala. 6

Global Community Headquarters

In **New Babylon**. Nicolae Carpathia designs the magnificent **headquarers** for his international government, and huge numbers make pilgrimages to see the new building. Carpathia lives in **Suite 216** on the top floor of the 18-story **headquarters**. The building also has a helipad on the roof. Rayford and Amanda Steele meet with Carpathia here. 2

Carpathia operates the Global Community out of the New Babylon **headquarters**, in an area surrounded by upscale houses. Mac McCullum, Rayford, and Carpathia escape in a chopper from the **headquarters** roof as the wrath of the Lamb earthquake hits. The building is leveled. 3

Leon Fortunato claims he was killed in the collapse of **GC headquarters** but was soon resurrected by Carpathia. The Global Community operates out of a massive **shelter** in **New Babylon** until the new **headquarters**—this time a **palace**—is completed. 4, 5

Global Weekly Building

In **New York City**. Buck Williams works on the twenty-seventh floor in a small, cluttered office. Steve Plank, Buck, and *Global Weekly* reporters meet here and discuss whether Buck should be allowed to cover the U.N. and Jewish Nationalist meetings. Buck is called into Stanton Bailey's impressive office here and offered Steve Plank's job. Buck accepts the promotion and works in the New York office until he is demoted to the *Global Weekly* **Chicago bureau office** for supposedly blowing the U.N. story. 1 The *Global Weekly* **Building** is destroyed in the New York bombings, and its headquarters are rebuilt in an abandoned warehouse. 4

Global Weekly Chicago Bureau Office

Lucinda Washington had an office here before she was raptured. Verna Zee takes over when Lucinda disappears. After being demoted from his position in New York, Buck Williams is briefly assigned an office here—a cubicle containing the communal coffeepot. He is quickly given permission to work from home by Stanton Bailey, *Global Weekly*'s publisher. **2**

Golden Gate

Also called the Eastern Gate or the East Gate, it is one of the ancient gates into the **Old City** of **Jerusalem**, east of the **Temple Mount**. The gate was sealed in A.D. 810. Jewish tradition says that in the end times, Messiah and Elijah will lead the Jews to the **temple** through a gate from the east. Tsion Ben-Judah shows Buck Williams a cemetery built outside the **Golden Gate** by Muslims in an attempt to prevent this triumphal entry. **2** Tribulation Force members speak of the **Eastern Gate** as a promise that they will see each other again when Jesus returns. **7**, **10**, **11**.

During the siege on **Jerusalem**, Buck believes GC troops will storm the **Golden Gate** to reach the **Temple Mount**. **11** The cemented-over gate is opened in the earthquake that elevates **Jerusalem**, and Jesus leads believers through the Eastern Gate into the newly clean city. **12**

Greek Detention Center

See **Detention Center**.

HAREM, THE

Seedy bar in **Israel** where Jacov goes to tell of his faith after he receives Christ. It has a neon sign. **5**

Heathrow Airport

In **London, England, Heathrow** is the world's busiest international airport. Rayford Steele is heading here when the Rapture occurs. **Heathrow** is closed after the Rapture. Buck takes a flight into **Heathrow** after it is reopened to see Alan Tompkins about Dirk Burton's death. In spite of authorities swarming this airport, Buck flies out undetected. **1** A 100-megaton bomb destroys **Heathrow** in Nicolae Carpathia's attack on **London**. **2**

Heathrow is rebuilt into a high-tech and efficient but smaller airport. Abdullah Smith lands here to refuel on his trip to get Buck home for Kenny's birth. **5**

Herod's Gate

Sometimes called the Flower Gate, this is the northernmost gate in the **Old City** and is about an eighth of a mile from the **Church of the Flagellation**. Tsion Ben-Judah preaches here, then runs toward the **Lion's Gate**, where a bullet mortally wounds him. Buck Williams defends the wall near this gate; he is on top of the wall when a GC bomb hits it. 11 Mac McCullum approaches **Herod's Gate** and finds Buck's lifeless body. He kills a soldier who is trying to steal Buck's boots. 12

Hilton

A well-known chain of hotels. Buck Williams checks into the Frankfurt **Hilton** under an assumed name while awaiting a flight home. 1

Holman Meadows

New York candy store where Rayford Steele buys Windmill Mints for Chloe. 2

Hospital

David Hassid searches the GC **hospital** in **New Babylon** for Annie Christopher. David suffers heatstroke and dehydration and ends up in the **palace hospital** under Hannah Palemoon's care. 8

During Operation Eagle, Hannah and Leah Rose set up several makeshift **hospitals**, including one just outside **Mizpe Ramon** and **Masada**. Makeshift medical tents are erected to service loyalists during the sores judgment. 9

See also **Arthur Young Memorial Hospital**, **GC Hospital**, **Northwest Community Hospital**.

Hostel

Upon arriving in **Jerusalem** for the Gala, Buck Williams stays in a **hostel** under the alias Russell Staub. 6 Ming Toy and Ree Woo stay in a **Zhengzhou hostel** while Ming searches for her mother. 10

JAFFA GATE

On the west side of the **Old City** of **Jerusalem**, near the **Citadel**. It is well fortified with many rebel troops, and Buck Williams guesses correctly that Carpathia's army will storm an easier gate. 11 Leon Fortunato and Nicolae Carpathia enter the **Old City** in a Humvee through the **Jaffa Gate**. 12

JFK

See **John F. Kennedy International Airport**.

John F. Kennedy International Airport

In Queens, New York. Rayford Steele considers landing at **JFK** after the Rapture but is told no planes can land here. Buck Williams flies from Germany to **Kennedy** after his trip to **London**. As he sits in **JFK**, he reads his own obituary. Steve Plank meets Buck at the airport. Rayford plans to meet Hattie Durham at the **Pan-Con Club** here, and Buck surprises Chloe Steele on a flight out of **JFK**. [1]

On Nicolae Carpathia's instructions, Buck flies into **JFK** and interviews Rabbi Feinberg before the rabbi flies out. *Air Force One* is kept in an auxiliary hangar at **Kennedy**. It is reported that the militia fighting against the Global Community is threatening nuclear war on **New York City**, and on the airport in particular. [2]

KANKAKEE AIRPORT

In Kankakee, a small Illinois city roughly 60 miles south of **Chicago**. After an unsuccessful trip to see Hattie Durham, Leah Rose flies to **Kankakee** where Rayford meets her in the Gulfstream. **Kankakee** becomes a safe airport for the Tribulation Force, although it is tiny. Albie sets up a small, private transport company out of this airport. [7]

Many flights go in and out of here, including the one delivering Hattie's "body." [8] George Sebastian is scheduled to fly Marcel and Georgiana into this airport. [9] Eventually the GC tightens security and **Kankakee** is no longer safe for the Tribulation Force. [10]

Kennedy Airport

See **John F. Kennedy International Airport**.

Kibbutz

Hebrew word for a communal settlement. Buck Williams meets with Chaim Rosenzweig at a **kibbutz** on the outskirts of **Haifa**, and they discuss Rosenzweig's formula. [1]

King David Hotel

Luxurious hotel in downtown **Jerusalem** where Buck Williams stays while covering the peace-treaty signing. [2] He stays here again, under the name Herb Katz while trying to contact Tsion Ben-Judah. [3]

The Tribulation Force's reservations at this hotel are bounced when Nicolae Carpathia's group commandeers the top floor during the Meeting of the Witnesses. [5] Carpathia reserves 2 entire floors for the Global Gala. [6]

Chaim stays at the **King David** as he waits to confront Carpathia before Operation Eagle. [8] Later the GC checks Chaim's and Buck's rooms and finds fingerprints and IDs to discern their true identities. [9]

Knesset

Israeli government building in **Jerusalem**. It has a single chamber with 120 seats. The **Knesset** Building is chosen for the peace-treaty signing, and President Fitzhugh is interviewed by Buck Williams here. **2**

Nicolae Carpathia sets up his **Jerusalem** headquarters in the **Knesset**. While there with Buck, Chaim Rosenzweig confronts Carpathia about letting messianic Jews head for **Petra** in exchange for the ceasing of the sores plague. Carpathia continues to hold high-level meetings with his staff in the **Knesset** until he suspects the building is bugged and moves to the Phoenix 216. **9**

Kollek Stadium

See **Teddy Kollek Stadium**.

LA GUARDIA

In Queens, New York; one of the busiest airports in the world. After the Rapture, Buck Williams contemplates taking a plane out of **La Guardia** to **London**. Nicolae Carpathia flies into **La Guardia** before holding a press conference and addressing the United Nations. **1**

La Petit Hotel

A hotel south of **Le Havre**, France, where Rayford Steele and the Tuttles stay while trying to find Hattie Durham. An expensive, secluded place. **6**

Lion's Gate

In the **Eastern Wall** of the **Old City** of Jerusalem. Tsion Ben-Judah is shot as he runs toward the **Lion's Gate**. **11**

MANHATTAN HARBOR YACHT CLUB

Where Buck Williams meets Chaim Rosenzweig for lunch. They enjoy salmon together. **2**

Midpoint Motel

Fleabag motel on **Washington Street** near the **Waukegan**, Illinois, airport. Buck Williams stays here while awaiting a flight to New York. **1**

Midway

One of **Chicago**'s airports, second to **O'Hare** in size. Buck Williams is supposed to take a nonstop flight from **Greece** to **Midway** to get home for the birth of his child. His flight is cancelled due to the smoke affecting daylight in **Jerusalem**. **5**

Military Compound

Buck Williams stays in a **military compound** when in **Haifa** to meet with Chaim Rosenzweig. From here he witnesses the Russian Pearl Harbor. **1**

Mitchell Field

Airport in Milwaukee, Wisconsin. Amanda Steele flies into **Mitchell Field** from **San Francisco**. Buck Williams receives a phone message to pick her up here. Rayford Steele flies to **Mitchell Field** from **Iraq**. Hattie Durham calls the Tribulation Force, and they meet her at **Mitchell Field**. **3**

Morgue

Morgues report missing corpses at the Rapture. **1** Rayford Steele finds Bruce Barnes in the makeshift outdoor **morgue** of what was once **Northwest Community Hospital**. **2**

Buck Williams meets Dr. Charles, a believing doctor in charge of the **GC Hospital's morgue**. Buck takes Miss Ashton's body to the **morgue** with Chloe's Mother Doe wristband on it. **4**

David Hassid has to transport bodies to the **morgue** after the 200 hundred million horsemen arrive. **6**

Nicolae Carpathia's body is taken to the **palace morgue**. **7**

Jim Hickman is delivered to the **morgue** after a self-inflicted gunshot wound to the temple. David has Hannah Palemoon see if Annie Christopher ended up in the **New Babylon morgue** after sector 53 receives a lightning strike during Carpathia's funeral. **8**

NEW HOPE VILLAGE CHURCH

In **Mt. Prospect**, Illinois. The Steele family attended here. After the Rapture, visitation pastor Bruce Barnes continues to hold services for those seeking answers. He shows Senior Pastor Billings's tape on the Rapture to teach people what is ahead and how to become a Christian. Many attend services here and come to Christ. **1**

Bruce instructs the original Tribulation Force members here, and his memorial service is held at the church. **2**, **3**

A shelter, 24 by 24 feet, is built under the church. It has a bedroom with 4 sets of bunk beds, a kitchenette, a living room/study, and a full bath. When Tsion Ben-Judah flees **Israel**, he stays in this underground safe house until the wrath of the Lamb earthquake destroys the church. Donny Moore and Loretta are killed on church grounds in the earthquake. **4**

Night Visitors, The

Seedy hotel where Chaim Rosenzweig and Buck Williams stay the night after Nicolae Carpathia's assasination. **7**

Nike Base

Near **Northwest Community Hospital** in Arlington Heights, Illinois.

The old base is taken over by U.S. militia to store contraband weapons. It is bombed by Nicolae Carpathia's forces. **2**

Northwest Community Hospital

Hospital in **Arlington Heights,** Illinois. Rayford Steele disembarks here from his helicopter flight after the Rapture. It is about 5 miles from his home. **1**

Bruce Barnes is taken to **Northwest Community Hospital** with what appears is a deadly virus. The **hospital** is bombed in the WWIII attacks. **2**.

O'HARE INTERNATIONAL AIRPORT

The busiest airport in America before the Rapture, in **Chicago**. Has only 2 runways open after the Rapture. Rayford Steele is told to land here. **1**

Nicolae Carpathia arranges for Buck Williams to fly out of **O'Hare**, and Rayford flies out of **O'Hare** to **Dallas** for his recertification on the 777. Earl Halliday has an office at **O'Hare**. **2**

Carpathia has this airport bombed in WWIII. **3**

Orly

Airport outside **Paris**, France; it lost air-traffic controllers and ground controllers in the Rapture. **1**

PALWAUKEE AIRPORT

At the Rapture, 2 crashes occur at this northern Illinois airport. Ken Ritz flies frequently out of **Palwaukee** and has 2 Learjets based here. **1** He flies Buck Williams to **Israel** from here, then flies Buck and Tsion Ben-Judah back to **Palwaukee** from **Egypt**. The airport does not normally process international travelers, so Tsion goes unnoticed. **3**

The airport becomes a virtual ghost strip, and Ken considers making an offer on it. He dies before he can complete the deal. Rayford Steele finds out T is the major owner of **Palwaukee Airport**. T decides to allow the Tribulation Force to run the co-op airlift operation out of **Palwaukee**. **5**

At this airport, T fuels the Gulfstream, readies the charts, and stocks the refrigerator for Rayford, Buck, and Leah Rose's trip to Europe and the Middle East. **6**

Albie flies Buck and Chaim Rosenzweig out of **Greece** to **Palwaukee**. When the safe house in **Mt. Prospect** is evacuated, Tribulation Force members drive here to board the helicopter supplied from **Rantoul**. After T's death, the Tribulation Force plans to use **Kankakee Airport** more. **7**

Pan-Con Club

At **John F. Kennedy Airport**; Pan-Continental employees and their frequent fliers come here to relax. Rayford and Chloe Steele meet Hattie Durham at the **Pan-Con Club**. Rayford talks with Hattie here, apologizing for their near affair and sharing his faith with her. ▌1

Parking Garage

A cabbie takes Chloe and Rayford Steele by a 6-story **parking garage** in **Atlanta**. The Rapture had occurred just after a late ball game, and the place became jammed when some of the drivers disappeared. ▌1

Pizza place

Noisy eatery in the **Mt. Prospect** area. Bruce Barnes and Buck Williams eat here and discuss Buck's possible trip to see Nicolae Carpathia. ▌2

Plaza Hotel

Famous hotel in **New York City** used for many important meetings. Jonathan Stonagal lives here for the 10 days of U.N. discussions. Buck Williams meets Nicolae Carpathia at the Plaza and runs into Eric Miller here the day before Eric dies. ▌1

Buck stays at the **Plaza Hotel** when he travels to New York to interview Rabbi Feinberg. ▌2

Pools of Bethesda

Built by the Romans as healing baths north of the **Temple Mount** in **Jerusalem**. Buck Williams drags Tsion Ben-Judah toward the **Bethesda pools** during the fighting, then brings him to a small chamber in the building after Tsion is shot. ▌11 After Tsion's death, Jewish rebels construct a makeshift shrine to him at **Bethesda**. ▌12

Pub

In **Ptolemaïs, Greece**. The Greek co-op meets in a laundry under the **pub**. Chloe Williams and Hannah Palemoon meet the co-op believers here and get information about Geoge Sebastian. Mac McCullum finds George here after George escapes from the GC. Later that night, the **pub** is raided by the GC and the Greek believers are killed. ▌10

QUEEN ALIA INTERNATIONAL AIRPORT

South of **Amman, Jordan**. Abdullah Smith flies Buck Williams out of this airport in an Egyptian fighter jet; he takes off without clearance from air traffic control. The airport had recently reopened after repairs for earthquake damage. ▌5 The airport is renamed **Resurrection International Airport**. ▌8

REPRODUCTIVE CLINIC

In **Littleton**, Colorado. Part of a GC testing laboratory in a former Enigma Babylon church. The lab does cloning and tissue research on fetuses from the clinic. Hattie Durham goes to the **clinic**, considering an abortion. Buck Williams and Ken Ritz rescue her, barely evading the GC. ◼4

Resurrection Field

Airport south of Colorado Springs, Colorado. Steve Plank arranges for GC records to say Rayford Steele landed at **Resurrection Field** but doesn't intend for Rayford to actually fly here. ◼9

Resurrection International Airport

In **Amman, Jordan**, the Tribulation Force uses in Operation Eagle. Formerly **Queen Alia International Airport**. ◼8 Leah Rose meets David Hassid, Abdullah Smith, Hannah Palemoon, and Mac McCullum here and transports them to **Mizpe Ramon**. ◼9

Two GC fighter-bombers take off from **Resurrection Airport** for the attack on **Petra**, and a missile is launched at **Petra** from the airport. ◼10

Rihand Dam

On the Rihand River in central India. The biggest underground church outside of America is Bihari's group in this area. Mac McCullum, Abdullah Smith, and Albie visit the dam during the co-op's wheat/water exchange and see the water turned to blood. Mac meets the angel Michael by the dam and is given fresh water to drink. ◼10

Rockefeller Museum

In **Jerusalem** just outside the walls of the **Old City**. An incendiary device is hurled over it onto the wall Buck Williams is standing on. ◼11

SHACK

George Sebastian is taken to a small, wood **shack** in the woods northwest of **Ptolemaïs, Greece**. He is held in the cramped, damp cellar until taken upstairs the next day and fed at a small wooden table. The GC hold him captive here until they take him to their **Ptolemaïs** headquarters. ◼10

Shelter

Nicolae Carpathia has an enormous **shelter** built just outside **Baghdad**. It is deep, made of concrete, and able to withstand bombs and radiation. The **shelter** is 30 feet below ground and has supplies, plumbing, lodging, and cooking areas. It floats on a membrane filled with hydraulic fluid and sits on a platform of spring shock absorbers. The **shelter** is large enough to hold the Condor 216. Carpathia operates out of the **shelter** after the wrath of the Lamb earthquake. Rayford Steele and Mac McCullum meet with Carpathia here, and Carpathia tells Rayford that Amanda is dead. ■4

Solomon's Stables
40 feet beneath the **Temple Mount**. The **Stables** are a series of pillars and arches that once supported the southeastern platform of the courtyard. The halls are a little over 30 yards wide, 60 yards long, and nearly 30 feet high. Mac McCullum sees at least 100 of Nicolae Carpathia's men, not in uniform, tending more than 1,000 horses. ■12

Stanford University
College in Palo Alto, **California**, where Chloe Steele attended before the Rapture. She leaves **Stanford** when the disappearances occur and travels home to **Mt. Prospect**. ■1

Stapleton Airport
In **Denver**. Ken Ritz and Buck Williams land here in a Learjet on their mission to rescue Hattie Durham from the reproductive clinic. ■4

Stateville Correction Center
In Joliet, Illinois. **Stateville** houses a GC loyalty mark center and one of the largest international prisons. Chang Wong doctors GC files to indicate that Lionel Whalum received the mark at this center. ■10 Chloe Williams is incarcerated and eventually beheaded here after she tells of her faith and the angel Caleb speaks. ■11

Suite 216
Carpathia's opulent office complex, covering the top floor of the **Global Community headquarters** in **New Babylon**. The suite includes a massive office, conference rooms, private living quarters, and an elevator to the helipad. **Suite 216** is destroyed with the rest of **Global Community headquarters** in the wrath of the Lamb earthquake. ■2-4.

TAVISTOCK HOTEL
In **London, England**. Buck Williams checks into the **Tavistock** while investigating the death of Dick Burton. After Alan Tompkins is killed by a car bomb, Buck heads back toward the **Tavistock** but goes straight on to **Heathrow** when he sees squad cars surrounding the hotel. ■1

Teddy Kollek Stadium
Soccer stadium in **Jerusalem** named after one of the city's most prominent mayors. Eli, one of the two witnesses, is invited by Tsion Ben-

Judah to speak in this stadium. ◼2 Both Eli and Moishe appear and speak in unison to the crowds. ◼3

Kollek Stadium is the site of the gathering known as the Meeting of the Witnesses. A crowd of 50,000 crams the stadium, with twice as many outside, and many come to Christ as their Messiah through the preaching of Tsion and the witnesses, including some of Chaim Rosenzweig's staff. Leon Fortunato, Nicolae Carpathia, and Peter the Second make uninvited appearances at the gathering. When the two witnesses arrive, Carpathia's voice fails and the water he drinks turns to blood. ◼5

Temple

The Jewish place of worship. A Jewish Nationalist conference meets in New York to discuss rebuilding the **temple** in **Jerusalem**, and it is announced that Nicolae Carpathia will assist. ◼1 Under Carpathia's influence, Muslims agree to move the **Dome of the Rock** from the **Temple Mount**, allowing the **temple** to be rebuilt on its original site. Work begins on the **temple**, with prefabricated walls shipped in, and the building is quickly finished. The two witnesses appear at the reopening of the **temple** and speak against it. They predict that Carpathia will one day defile the **temple** he helped rebuild. Here the witnesses first turn water to blood. ◼2

Carpathia learns that Orthodox Jews have gone back to the old ways of sacrificing animals in the **temple** and forbids it, saying this practice violates the Enigma Babylon One World Faith's policies. ◼5,6 Although not a religious Jew, Chaim Rosenzweig is horrified by Carpathia's intrusion into **temple** affairs. ◼7

As predicted by the two witnesses, Carpathia plans to desecrate the **temple**. ◼8 After his ride down the **Via Dolorosa** and appearances at the **Garden Tomb** and **Calvary**, he stands in a white robe on the **temple** steps and watches as loyalty marks are administered. The next day, Carpathia enters the **temple**, murdering a man and driving the priests out. He cuts through the veil in front of the Holy of Holies, slaughters a pig, and throws its blood on the altar. When the statue of Carpathia is brought into the Holy of Holies, crowds outside riot. Later, Carpathia learns that Viv Ivins entered the **temple** and sat on the throne, and he is furious. ◼9

In his siege on **Jerusalem**, Carpathia announces plans to destroy the **temple** and build his **palace** over its site. Chaim teaches that the first 30 days after the Glorious Appearing will be used to prepare the **temple** for Jesus. ◼12

UNITED NATIONS HEADQUARTERS

In **New York City**. Buck Williams becomes a believer here. Nicolae Carpathia calls a pre-press conference meeting at the **U.N. headquarters** to announce his 10 leaders. During the meeting, Carpathia murders Joshua Todd-Cothran and Jonathan Stonagal and brainwashes witnesses. **1** Carpathia announces that the **United Nations headquarters** will move to **New Babylon** and the government will be renamed the Global Community. **2**

Urn Tomb

Area at **Petra** that has a pillared portico in its courtyard. **11**

VATICAN

Papal headquarters in **Rome**. Peter Mathews initially operates the Enigma Babylon One World Faith out of the **Vatican**. **2** Eventually Mathews relocates to **New Babylon**. Leon Fortunato gathers the 10 regional potentates and destroys every relic and piece of artwork in the **Vatican**, demolishing every evidence of Christianity. **8**

WAILING WALL

Known to Jews as the Western Wall, it is the only part of Herod's **Temple** that still stands. It is on the western side of the **Temple Mount**. Jews assemble here for prayer and lamentation, and the two witnesses, Eli and Moishe, preach before it. **2-6** Tsion Ben-Judah and Buck Williams talk with Eli and Moishe here. **3**

Nicolae Carpathia murders the two witnesses at the **Wailing Wall**. Three days later, they are resurrected and rise into heaven. **6**

As Micah, Chaim Rosenzweig challenges men from the **Wailing Wall** to consider Jesus. **9**

In the earthquake reshaping the earth, the **Wailing Wall** falls. Jesus stands in its place and speaks to the remnant. **12**

Washington Dulles International Airport

In **Washington, D.C.** *Air Force One* is delivered here and then flown to New York on its maiden voyage. Rayford Steele flies his wife, Amanda, on a nonstop flight from **New Babylon** to **Dulles**. The airport is obliterated in WWIII. **2** Rayford tells Buck Williams that **Dulles** is a pile of debris and there are no plans to rebuild it. **4**

Waukegan Airport

Ken Ritz flies Buck Williams out of this tiny airstrip in northern Illinois following the Rapture. **1** Ken also has a Learjet available here after the wrath of the Lamb earthquake, although the airport suffered much damage. Later the Tribulation Force uses this airport for various trips. 4FF

Western Wall
See **Wailing Wall**.

YAD VASHEM HISTORICAL MUSEUM

Jerusalem museum dedicated to the memory of Holocaust victims. Buck Williams and Tsion Ben-Judah are informed that it has been destroyed. 11

ZION GATE

In the south wall of the **Old City**. The Unity Army plans to leave the **Old City** through the **Zion Gate** and head for **Petra**. 12

GEOGRAPHIC
FEATURES

Armageddon
See **Valley of Armageddon**.

Bering Strait
Separates North America from Asia. Fishermen from the **Bering Strait** work with the International Commodity Co-op. **5** One of the co-op's projects is harvesting the ocean beneath the **Bering Strait**. **6**

Calvary
Rocky hill outside **Jerusalem**; it is also called **Mount Calvary** or **Golgotha**. **Calvary** was the site of Jesus' crucifixion. Nicolae Carpathia visits **Calvary** in his mockery of the Stations of the Cross, and Leon Fortunato encourages the crowds to worship Carpathia here. Hattie Durham confronts Carpathia and Fortunato at the base of **Golgotha**, and Fortunato calls lightning down from the sky to engulf her. Chaim Rosenzweig later returns to **Calvary** to gather Hattie's ashes. **9**

Cavern
Giant crevice in the earth hundreds of feet deep that miraculously opens and swallows GC Peacekeepers pursuing Mac McCullum's vehicle during Operation Eagle. An even larger **cavern**, stretching a mile in every direction around **Petra**, engulfs the attacking GC army. **9**

Chico River
Running through southern **Argentina**, the **Chico River** gets more and more polluted as the Tribulation progresses. The Argentine co-op, led by Luís Arturo, believes the GC is intentionally polluting the river. Eventually, the state of the river compels believers living along it to exchange wheat for clean water from India. **10**

Dead Sea
Body of water touching both **Israel** and **Jordan**, about 15 miles east of **Jerusalem**. The **Dead Sea** is salty, extremely deep, and well below sea level. Michael Shorosh tells Buck Williams that the bodies of Tsion Ben-Judah's would-be attackers will be burned by salt when they reach the **Dead Sea**. **3**

Euphrates River
Waterway running through **Iraq** and Syria. It dries up shortly before Armageddon, allowing the kings of the East to transport their weapons into **Israel** across dry land. Industries dependent on the river face ruin. **11**

Golgatha
Hebrew name for **Calvary**; **Golgotha** translates roughly as "Place of the Skulls."

Gulf of Aqaba
Gulf on the east coast of the Sinai peninsula. Troop transport ships are based here to support GC ground troops preparing for battle. **11**

Gulf of Suez
On the west coast of the Sinai peninsula. Troop transport ships are based here to support GC ground troops. **11**

Jehoshaphat Valley
See **Valley of Jehoshaphat**.

Jezreel Valley
See **Valley of Armageddon**.

Jordan River
Runs into the **Sea of Galilee** and from there between **Jordan** and **Israel** to the **Dead Sea**. The main source of fresh water for both **Israel** and **Jordan**. Buck Williams asks how to get up the **Jordan River** in his attempt to find Tsion Ben-Judah. Michael Shorosh takes him up the **Jordan** to **Lake Tiberius**. **3**

Kalahari

Desert in **Botswana**. There is great hope that Mwangati Ngumo will return home with Rosenzweig's formula and bring fertility to the **Kalahari.** ▮

Lake Geneva

Lake in southern Wisconsin. Buck Williams is offered a vacation home here if he will become the president and publisher of the *Chicago Tribune.* ▮

Lake Michigan

One of the Great Lakes; both **Chicago** and Milwaukee are on the shores of this lake. Fresh water is harvested from **Lake Michigan** in northern Wisconsin, so the GC is unconcerned about nuking **Chicago.** ▮

Lake Tiberius

See **Sea of Galilee**.

Masada

Mesa-shaped mountaintop in **Israel**, 1,300 feet above the western shore of the **Dead Sea**. An ancient fortress here was the final Jewish outpost in the A.D. 66–73 rebellion against **Rome**. At **Masada**, Chaim Rosenzweig addresses searching Jewish people, and many receive Jesus as their Messiah. Nicolae Carpathia orders his GC troops to shoot to kill at **Masada** even though he had cleared the area as safe for a time. ▮

Mount Calvary

See **Calvary**.

Mount Megiddo

See **Valley of Armageddon**.

Mount Moriah

Hill in eastern **Jerusalem**. The **Temple Mount** is built over **Mount Moriah**, where Abraham expressed his willingness to God to sacrifice his son Isaac. ▮

Mount of Olives

Hill half a mile from the **Eastern Wall** of the **Old City**; also called Mount Olivet. Even though the two witnesses are ordered to stay on the **Temple Mount**, they preach here. ▮

Chaim Rosenzweig instructs thousands of Jewish believers to go to the **Mount of Olives** for the airlift to **Petra**. Nicolae Carpathia instructs

GC troops to shoot to kill even after he gives temporary safety clearance in exchange for relief from the sores judgment. ⑨

After the Glorious Appearing, Jesus touches the **Mount of Olives** and it splits from east to west, forming the **Valley of Jehoshaphat.** ⑫

Mount Olivet
See **Mount of Olives**.

Mount Zion
Site of the ancient **temple** in **Jerusalem**. Tsion Ben-Judah teaches that a deliverer will come out of **Mount Zion.** ⑪

Negev Desert
A region in southern **Israel**. In his escape from **Israel** with Tsion Ben-Judah, Buck Williams passes near the northern edge of the **Negev.** ③ **Mizpe Ramon** and **Petra** are in the **Negev**, and Nicolae Carpathia's false messiahs perform miracles here. ⑩

Plain of Megiddo
See **Valley of Armageddon**.

Plain of Esdraelon
See **Valley of Armageddon**.

Plain of Jezreel
See **Valley of Armageddon**.

Sea of Galilee
The only natural freshwater lake in **Israel**. The two witnesses tell Buck Williams to go to **Galilee** in search of Tsion Ben-Judah. He is told that the **Sea of Galilee** is now called **Lake Tiberius**. With the help of Michael Shorosh, Buck finds Tsion halfway between **Jericho** and **Lake Tiberius** on the east side of the **Jordan River.** ③

Shatt al Arab
The **Tigris River** becomes the **Shatt al Arab** at **Al Basrah.** ④

Sinai Desert
The Sinai peninsula, between **Egypt** and **Israel**. Buck Williams and Tsion Ben-Judah travel through **Sinai** on their escape from **Israel.** ③

Temple Mount
The biblical name of a hill in east **Jerusalem**, within the **Old City**. It was the site of Solomon's **temple**. The **Temple Mount** houses the Muslim mosque called the **Dome of the Rock** until it is moved to **New Babylon** and the Jewish **temple** is rebuilt. It is a holy place in

Jerusalem where the two witnesses speak. ▌2▐ They call upon God to allow it to rain for 7 minutes only on the **Temple Mount.** ▌3▐

Nicolae Carpathia orders the two witnesses to leave the **Temple Mount** within 48 hours or they will be shot. Tsion Ben-Judah tells Chaim Rosenzweig that the GC has planned a terrorist attack at the **Temple Mount** the next day. A 10-second hailstorm interrupts the assassination attempt on the two witnesses. ▌5▐

At the Global Gala, there is a confrontation at the **Temple Mount** between the GC and the two witnesses. Carpathia assassinates Eli and Moishe at the **Wailing Wall.** ▌6▐

The winning statue of Carpathia is moved to the **Temple Mount** so people can worship it as well as receive their marks of loyalty. Tens of thousands of loyalists wait here to receive their marks, and finally Suhail Akbar, Walter Moon, and Viv Ivins get theirs. Later Chaim confronts Carpathia at the **Temple Mount** as Carpathia sees his followers writhing from the sores judgment. After Carpathia desecrates the **temple**, the **Temple Mount** is swarmed by angry citizens. Chaim addresses the crowds, telling messianic Jews where to go for the airlift to **Petra,** instructing Orthodox Jews to go to **Masada** for further teachings, and inviting the undecided to consider Jesus as Messiah. ▌9▐

The **Temple Mount** is the last stronghold of the rebels in the siege on **Jerusalem**. Finally the Unity Army guarding this area is decimated by the words of Jesus. ▌12▐

Tigris River

Near **Baghdad**; with the **Euphrates**, it bordered the ancient Fertile Crescent. Amanda Steele's **747** crashes into the **Tigris** after the wrath of the Lamb earthquake. Mac McCullum helicopters Rayford Steele to the river. On his dive into the **Tigris**, Rayford finds Amanda's body in the wreckage of the plane. ▌4▐

Valley of Armageddon

A 350-square-mile valley roughly 70 miles from **Jerusalem**. This region is also called the Plain or Valley of Megiddo, the Plain of Esdraelon, and the Plain of Jezreel or the Jezreel Valley. The name *Armageddon* is from Hebrew words meaning Mount Megiddo. Two hundred thousand mounted GC troops assemble here for the battle known as Armageddon, though the actual fighting takes place in **Petra** and **Jerusalem**. After Jesus speaks Scripture to the soldiers assembled at Armageddon, their bodies rupture, causing blood to flow 4 feet deep for nearly 200 miles until God sends a hailstorm that freezes over the mess. ▌11▐, ▌12▐

Valley of Jehoshaphat

It is prophesied that the fighting of Armageddon will end in this region. ▮ The valley is created by the splitting of the **Mount of Olives** after the Glorious Appearing. The name means "Jehovah judges." On the day of the judgments, believers feel compelled to head for the **Valley of Jehoshaphat**. Here Jesus judges the sheep and the goats and rewards the Old Testament and tribulation saints. ▮

RESIDENCES

Apartment 323

Apartment in **Le Havre**, France, where Rayford Steele goes in search of Hattie Durham and Samuel Hanson. A GC assassin is waiting for Rayford in the apartment, but Rayford escapes after receiving a last-second warning from Trudy Tuttle. **6**

Condo

Hattie Durham has a **condo** in **Des Plaines**, Illinois. **1** Buck Williams moves to a beautiful **condo** midway between the *Global Weekly* **Chicago bureau office** and **New Hope Village Church** in **Mt. Prospect**. **2** Rayford and Amanda Steele have a sprawling 2-story **condo** in **New Babylon**. **3**

Donny Moore Safe House

Donny and Sandy Moore's duplex in **Mt. Prospect**. It becomes a **safe house** for the Tribulation Force after the Moores' deaths. Half the duplex is unusable due to earthquake damage, but it has a usable garage and an underground shelter in the yard. Sandy Moore and Dr. Charles are buried in the backyard. **4-6**

Members of the Tribulation Force live here until the **safe house** is compromised and they must move to the **Strong Building**. **7** After the evacuation, the GC burns the **Donny Moore safe house** to the ground. **8**

House

The Steele family has a huge, spotless **house** in **Mt. Prospect**. Rayford returns here after the Rapture and finds Irene's and Raymie's clothes.

Chloe leaves **Stanford University** and returns to the **Mt. Prospect house**. The **house** is robbed in the chaos after the Rapture. **1** Rayford and Chloe continue to live in the **house**, although Rayford considers downsizing and is lonely here, surrounded by reminders of Irene. He sells the **house** for his move to **New Babylon**. **2**

Loretta has a stately, 5-bedroom, 2-story **house** in **Mt. Prospect** that becomes the first Tribulation Force **safe house**. Verna Zee briefly stays here before moving in with friends. After the New York bombing, Chloe and Buck Williams live with Loretta. Hattie Durham meets with Amanda, Chloe, Loretta, and Buck here. The **house** is leveled in the wrath of the Lamb earthquake. **3**

Stefan has a **house** in a lower middle-class neighborhood of **Jerusalem**. Buck Williams stays here following his attempt to escape **Israel**. **5**

After the Glorious Appearing, single women and married couples stay at the lovely Tiberias **house** in **Jerusalem**. **12**

Palace

The new **GC headquarters**, built in **New Babylon** after the wrath of the Lamb earthquake. Nicolae Carpathia marshals energy for the **palace** while the world suffers in the cold judgment. **5**

Leon Fortunato lives in opulent quarters on the entire seventeenth floor of the new **palace**, and Carpathia occupies the eighteenth floor. The sprawling **palace** complex has every convenience, including its own airstrip, and thousands of employees, including David Hassid, Mac McCullum, and Annie Christopher. With the arrival of the 200 million horsemen, 15 percent of palace employees are killed. The assassinated Carpathia lies in state at the **palace**. **6**

Under sweltering heat, Carpathia's funeral and resurrection take place in the **palace** courtyard. **7** Chang Wong comes to work at the **palace** and becomes a valuable asset for the Tribulation Force as a mole. Loyalty enforcement facilitators are not displayed at the **palace**. **8**

When the darkness judgment falls on **New Babylon**, Carpathia relocates from the **palace** to **Al Hillah**. **10**

Regional Potentate Rehoboth has a **palace** in **Johannesburg**. It is nearly as large as the GC **palace** in **New Babylon**. The GC takes over the **palace** after Rehoboth's insurgents attack the Condor 216 and kills Rehoboth's family. They find the regional potentate and many of his staff dead in the **palace**. Mac and Abdullah Smith are brought to Rehoboth's **palace** for treatment. **6**

Penthouse

Buck Williams has a beautiful **penthouse** apartment on **Fifth Avenue** in **New York City**, and he and Chloe move here after they are married. [2] The **penthouse** is destroyed in the WWIII bombings. [3]

Quonset Hut

Rounded metal buildings made famous in World War II. The metal building Ken Ritz uses for parking at the **Waukegan Airport** is a **Quonset hut**. [1]

Ken lives in the corner of a **Quonset hut** at **Palwaukee Airport** and stores his gold bullion underground. [4], [5]

Pinkerton Stephens works in a **Quonset-hut**-style building deep off the road near **Pueblo**, Colorado. [6]

Rosenzweig Estate

Chaim's walled and gated home, within walking distance of the **Old City** in **Jerusalem**. The compound was formerly an embassy. Tsion Ben-Judah and Buck and Chloe Williams stay here during the Meeting of the Witnesses and escape from the helipad on the roof. Buck returns to Chaim's house to recuperate after he falls from the Gulfstream, then moves to Stefan's **house**. He cares for Chaim at his **estate** after the locusts attack. Finally Buck leaves for the States, arriving just in time for Kenny's birth. [5]

After Nicolae Carpathia's assassination, Buck goes to Chaim's house, trying to find him. He finds the house pillaged by the GC and Chaim's staff slaughtered. [7]

After the Glorious Appearing, single men are housed at Chaim's **estate**. All the damage done by the GC is miraculously gone. [12]

Safe House

See **House, Donny Moore Safe House, Strong Building**, San Diego Compound.

San Diego Compound

Underground shelters like **Quonset huts**. Buck, Chloe, and Kenny Williams move here, where George Sebastian and his family live with an underground group of believers, after the **Strong Building** evacuation. Rayford Steele, Ming Toy, and Ree Woo also relocate to the **San Diego compound**. Chloe continues to run the International Commodity Co-op from here, and Rayford flies between **San Diego** and co-op centers. [10]

On watch at the **San Diego compound**, Chloe sees something on surveillance monitors and is picked up by the GC when she goes outside to investigate. She is able to call Rayford with a coded message to get the **San Diego** believers to **Petra**, and the **compound** is evacuated. **11**

Strong Building

Eighty-story tower in **Chicago** that housed the Strong Insurance Company's international headquarters. This 5-year-old building was considered a technical marvel and was wholly solar-powered. Neither the foundation nor at least the first 35 stories are compromised by the earthquake. **7**

The **Strong Building** becomes an amazing gift to the Tribulation Force, and they relocate here after the **Donny Moore safe house** is compromised. They darken the windows to keep themselves hidden. The garage of the **Strong Building** proves a treasure chest of vehicles, and Buck Williams appropriates a Humvee. **8**

From the **Strong Building**, Tsion Ben-Judah prays for Chaim Rosenzweig and encourages Chang Wong. Chloe meets the belivers of The Place and invites them to the **Strong Building**. After Operation Eagle, Rayford returns to the **Strong Building** with Buck, Albie, Mac McCullum, Abdullah Smith, Leah Rose, and Hannah Palemoon. **9**

The **Strong Building** serves as the Tribulation Force's **safe house** until news comes that **Chicago** is going to be nuked. **10**

White House

The official residence of the president of the United States of America. President Fitzhugh and his wife invite Nicolae Carpathia to spend the night at the **White House. 1**

ROADS

Algonquin Road
Runs through the northwest suburbs of **Chicago**. A woman picks Rayford Steele up on this road and gives him a ride home after the Rapture. **1**

Fifth Avenue
One of the most famous streets in the world, running through **Manhattan**. Buck Williams's **penthouse** apartment is on **Fifth Avenue**. **2**, **3**

Hel Ha Handasa
Road leading to the **Old City** in **Jerusalem** where Buck sees troops amassing. **11**

Jaffa Road
Leads from the south into the **Old City** through the **Jaffa Gate**. Buck sees Unity Army forces on the **Jaffa Road**, though they ignore the **Jaffa Gate**. **11** The Unity Army cavalcade, with Mac McCullum, later approaches the **Old City** on the **Jaffa Road**, and Nicolae Carpathia and Leon Fortunato enter through the **Jaffa Gate**. **12**

Kennedy
Expressway out of **Chicago** that Buck Williams travels in his search for Chloe. **3**

Lake Shore Drive
Running along **Lake Michigan** in Chicago. Chloe Williams drives on **Lake Shore Drive** after the bombing of **Chicago**. Buck also drives this road trying to find Chloe. **3**

LSD
Short for **Lake Shore Drive**. ₃

Mannheim Road
North-south roadway near **Chicago**. After the Rapture, livery compa-
nies move their communications centers to a median strip near the
Mannheim interchange. Buck Williams acquires expensive transportation to **Waukegan** from here. ₁

Michigan Avenue
One of **Chicago's** ritziest roadways. **Michigan Avenue** is destroyed in
the WWIII bombing. ₃

Rue Marguerite
The street Samuel Hanson and Hattie Durham live on in **Le Havre**,
France. ₆

Sheridan Road
Buck Williams takes this barricaded but unguarded road near the lake
in **Chicago** to try and find Chloe after the bombings. ₃

Siq
The principal route into **Petra**. The walls of the Siq are lined with
channels to carry drinking water to the city. Inside, the **Siq** narrows
to little more than 5 meters, with walls towering hundreds of meters
on either side. The floor was originally paved but is now covered with
soft sand. ₁₀

Suleiman Street
Runs around the north side of the **Old City**. Unity Army troops amass
here for the siege of **Jerusalem**. ₁₁ The army later travels down **Suleiman Street** to the **Damascus Gate**. ₁₂

Via Dolorosa
The Way of the Cross—the traditional route in **Jerusalem** that Christ
took to **Calvary** on the day of his crucifixion. As masses line the path-
way, Nicolae Carpathia desecrates this route by traveling it on the back
of a massive pig. ₉

Washington Street
Near the **Waukegan airport**. Soon after the Rapture, Buck Williams
stays in the **Midpoint Motel** on **Washington Street** while awaiting his
flight with Ken Ritz to New York. ₁

Willow Road
The road taken by Buck Williams to get from the airport to the **safe house** in **Chicago** for the birth of his child. It still has a giant concrete pile left, which Buck has to swerve to avoid. **5**

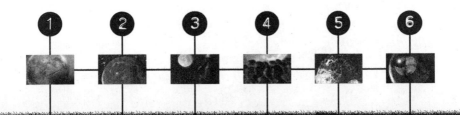

PLANES, TRAINS, AND AUTOMOBILES

GETTING AROUND IN THE LEFT BEHIND WORLD

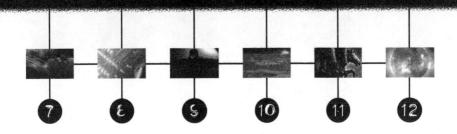

LEFT BEHIND begins in a **Boeing 747** over the Atlantic. By the end of *Glorious Appearing*, characters travel to virtually every corner of the globe, fighting their way through the chaos caused by the Rapture, evading the roadblocks of Carpathia's power structure. In many ways, the Left Behind series is about using faith and mobility to combat the Antichrist. From Rayford Steele's fateful flight across the Atlantic until the gathering of the surviving faithful at the *Glorious Appearing*, the Left Behind books move fast, and the characters move even faster. Here's a summary of how the characters make their way around the world and back.

NOTE TO READERS:

If you're detail-oriented, you will notice a change in Nicolae Carpathia's plane, Global Community One. The plane was originally a 757 . . . then careful readers pointed out that a 757 is too small to be the plane described. As Jerry Jenkins says, "You've got to remember this is set in the future. Who knows what the 757s of tomorrow will look like?" But for technology-minded readers of today, in later printings the plane was changed to a 777. Hold on to those 757 editions, though—they'll be collectors' items!

PLANES

2-engine Fixed-wing
Small plane Rayford Steele carries in the cargo hold of the **Condor 216** to ensure access to smaller airports. 4

2-seater Jet
Rayford Steele and Buck Williams fly in a **2-seater jet** after the Tribulation Force is evacuated from San Diego. They fly this plane to Petra when they realize they can't prevent Chloe's execution. 11

747
See **Boeing 747**.

777
See **Boeing 777**.

II One
Peter the Second's plane; it is 50 percent larger and costs twice as much as the **Condor 216**. Carpathia takes the plane for himself and renames it the **Phoenix 216** after Peter the Second is killed and the **Condor 216** is destroyed in the ambush at Johannesburg. 6

Air California
Airline Chloe Steele takes on one of the many legs of her post-Rapture trip home. 1

Air Force One
President Gerald Fitzhugh's plane; Nicolae Carpathia is picked up by *Air Force One* in New York City for his trip to Washington, D.C. Fitzhugh intends to make this plane *Air Force Two*, the vice president's plane, after

the new *Air Force One*—a brand-new 777 with the latest in technology, communications, security, and accommodations—is completed. He offers to lend the new *Air Force One* to Carpathia and his U.N. contingent for the flight to the peace-treaty signing in Jerusalem. Fitzhugh even christens the plane *Global Community One* for Carpathia's voyage. Carpathia publicly thanks him for the "gift" of the plane and never gives it back. **2**

Boeing 747

The world's fastest subsonic jetliner, with capacity for 416 passengers. Rayford Steele is flying a 747 from Chicago to London when the Rapture occurs and more than 100 passengers disappear. **1** Rayford flies 747s until he is recertified to fly 777s. **2**

A British Airways 747 collides with a **DC-10** at Baghdad Airport when the wrath of the Lamb earthquake hits, and Rayford helps passengers to safety before searching the airport for his wife, Amanda. He finally finds Amanda's plane, also a 747, at the bottom of the Tigris River. **4**

Boeing 777

A wide-body twinjet plane. The 777 is smaller than the 747 but more fuel efficient and aerodynamic. The new *Air Force One*, soon renamed *Global Community One*, is a 777. Rayford is trained on the 777 and calls it the Jaguar of airplanes. **2**

Bombers

See **Fighter-bomber**.

British Airways 747

See **Boeing 747**.

Challenger 3

About the size of a **Learjet**, but nearly twice as fast. After the wrath of the Lamb earthquake, Mac McCullum finds it in the middle of an airstrip. He replaces an antenna, installs a new tail rudder system, and loads it into the **Condor 216**'s cargo hold. Later Mac teaches Rayford Steele how to fly it. **4**

Chopper

See **Helicopter**.

Chopper One

GC **helicopter** used to fly Nicolae Carpathia to the first night of the Meeting of the Witnesses. Ken Ritz picks up Tsion Ben-Judah and Buck and Chloe Williams in **Chopper One** and flies to the airport for their escape from Jerusalem. **5** Mac McCullum and David Hassid fly on **Chopper One** with 144 computers to be delivered to the **Condor 216**. **7**

Chopper Two

GC **helicopter** flown in pursuit of Ken Ritz, Chloe and Buck Williams, and Tsion Ben-Judah in **Chopper One**. **Chopper Two** pursues them all the way to the Jerusalem airport. **5**

Concorde

The only commercial supersonic **jet**, capable of traveling at more than twice the speed of sound. It can carry 100 passengers from New York to London in just over 3 hours. Rayford Steele makes contact with a **Concorde** pilot right after the Rapture. The pilot reports that nearly 50 of his passengers are missing. **1**

Condor 216

Hybrid plane; the cockpit is identical to a **777**, but the plane handles more like a **747** despite being bigger and heavier. The **Condor 216** flies at 33,000 feet at speeds of more than 700 miles per hour and can fly on autopilot. It is built to fly Nicolae Carpathia and his entourage. Carpathia claims to have designed the **Condor 216**, although Earl Halliday practically built the plane and installed a bugging system to allow the pilots to hear everything happening in the passenger compartment. During the WWIII bombings, Rayford Steele flies the **Condor 216** carrying Carpathia and his ambassadors to Baghdad. **3** The plane survives the wrath of the Lamb earthquake and is taken to Carpathia's shelter. **4** During the plague of locusts, David Hassid jams the **Condor 216**'s cargo hold with copies of Tsion Ben-Judah's studies, and believers unload and distribute them wherever Mac McCullum flies. **5** On a flight to Johannesburg, the 200 million horsemen appear, and the plane makes an emergency landing. The **Condor 216** is bullet riddled and finally destroyed in an ambush. **6**

Copter

See **Helicopter**.

DC-10

Rayford flies a **DC-10** into Milwaukee with Hattie Durham. **3** A **DC-10** collides with a **747** on the east-west runway of Baghdad Airport during the wrath of the Lamb earthquake. **4**

Egyptian Fighter Jet

Secured by Abdullah Smith to fly Buck Williams home for the birth of his child. The **jet** can fly nearly 2,000 miles an hour at high altitudes but has a shorter-than-usual fuel range. Abdullah's has an enlarged fuel tank and a small cargo hold. David arranges for Albie to land the **Egyptian fighter** in Palwaukee. **5** This plane is later used to ferry Buck and Chaim Rosenzweig home after T crashes the **Super J. 7**

Fighter-bombers

Huge planes used by the GC to bomb Petra. They have the tallest gear of any fighter ever, and the interior allows room for a 15,000 pound bomb 11 feet long and 4½ feet in diameter. The GC reports the planes shot down by Judah-ites, but they are actually returned to GC hangars and their serial numbers are replaced. **10**

GC Fighter

Plane Rayford and Albie fly from Kankakee to Colorado to secure Hattie Durham's safety. **8**

Global Community One (GC One)

President Fitzhugh's new *Air Force One*; he christens it *Global Community One* when he lends it to Nicolae Carpathia for the flight to the peace-treaty signing. Carpathia calls the plane a gift and keeps it. *Global Community One* has a room containing high-tech security and surveillance equipment and backup communications. It also has a private apartment for the pilot. The plane is destroyed in the attack on New York City. Carpathia's next 2 planes, the **Condor 216** and the **Phoenix 216**, are also called *Global Community One*. **2**

Global Community Three

Plane Chico Hernandez flies to DFW airport with Nicolae Carpathia, Leon Fortunato, and Rayford and Amanda Steele. He has to land the small **Learjet** at a nearby military strip because DFW has been bombed. **3**

Gulfstream Jet

Small plane procured by Ken Ritz for the Tribulation Force's trip to Israel. He also uses it to fly Rayford Steele out of Tel Aviv and teaches Rayford about the **Gulfstream**. Rayford gets Chloe Williams and Tsion Ben-Judah out of Israel in the **Gulfstream**. T gives the **Gulfstream** to the Tribulation Force after Ken Ritz's death. **5**

Rayford uses the **Gulfstream** to fly out of Tel Aviv after Carpathia's assassination, refueling in Greece before touching down at Kankakee Airport. This type of plane is also flown in the prepations for Operation Eagle. Albie and Rayford plan to fly the fighter and the **Gulfstream** to Mizpe Ramon. **7**

Gulfstream IX

Plane Rayford and Abdullah fly to New Babylon to rescue Chang. Mac flies Rayford back to San Diego in the **Gulfstream** and also flies Zeke to Petra. ▮11

Hajiman

Smaller version of the **Concorde**, but just as fast. Buck wonders if he and Abdullah will be flying home on it, but Abdullah boards the **Egyptian fighter jet** instead. ▮5

Helicopter

Often called **choppers**, these appear frequently in the Left Behind series. After the Rapture, Rayford Steele and Hattie Durham are flown to their homes in a **chopper**. ▮1 Mac McCullum lands a **chopper** on the roof of the GC international headquarters in New Babylon, rescuing Rayford and Nicolae Carpathia before the wrath of the Lamb earthquake. Although people run and grab the **helicopter**'s rudders, Carpathia insists that Mac take off, causing many to fall to their deaths. ▮3 After the earthquake, Mac trains Rayford on a **chopper**. Then they fly around rescuing earthquake victims and searching for Rayford's wife, Amanda. As a result of their conversation on this flight, Mac becomes a believer. ▮4 Carpathia arrives via **chopper** at the Meeting of the Witnesses, creating a dramatic and unexpected entrance. ▮5 **Choppers** are also involved in the massive airlift known as Operation Eagle, during which George Sebastian acts as **chopper** lead. Two **helicopters** arrive at the Temple Mount for the confrontation with Chaim Rosenzweig and Buck Williams, with Carpathia the only civilian on board. Michael, the archangel, appears on a Tribulation Force **helicopter** while it is under attack from the GC. ▮9 At the Glorious Appearing, Carpathia and Fortunato escape in a **helicopter** and fly north as the Unity Army is slaughtered. ▮12

Jet

Stefanich, the 3 philosophers, and a pilot arrive in a heavily armed **jet** to prevent the rescue of George Sebastian, but God intervenes. ▮10

Jordanian Fighter Plane

Albie takes off in this refurbished **jet** to bring Buck Williams and Chaim Rosenzweig home from Greece. ▮7

Juliett

See **Super J.**

Learjet (Lear)

After the Rapture, Ken Ritz tells Buck Williams he has **Learjets** at Palwaukee and Waukegan, and he uses one to fly Buck near JFK airport. **1**

Carpathia, Leon, Rayford, and Amanda are flown in *Global Community Three*, a six-seater **Learjet,** by Chico Hernandez to Dallas/Fort Worth military strip. Ken flies Buck and Tsion out of Egypt on his **Learjet.** **3**

After the earthquake, Buck helps Ken get his **Lear** out of Waukegan Airport, and Ken flies Buck near Minneapolis to find Chloe. Ken later flies the **Lear** to Stapleton Airport, Denver, in search of Hattie, then flies her to the safe house. **4**

One of Lionel Whalum's people leaves a **Lear** at the Petra strip, and Abdullah flies it to the new co-op strip. **10**

Multi-million-Nick Aircraft

See **Fighter-bomber**.

Ozark

Chloe Steele flies on this airline from Enid, Oklahoma, to Springfield, Illinois, to the Chicago area on her way home after the Rapture. Rayford remembers an airline-industry joke that **Ozark** spelled backward is Krazo. **1**

Pan-Continental

Airline Rayford Steele and Hattie Durham work for. Captain Steele is one of their top pilots, and Hattie is a flight attendant who often works Rayford's flights. Other **Pan-Con** employees in the series are Tony, Christopher Smith, Earl Halliday, and Nick Edwards. **1, 2**

Pan-Con 747

See **Boeing 747**.

Phoenix 216

After Peter the Second's death, his plane is rechristened and taken by Nicolae Carpathia to replace the **Condor 216** lost in the ambush at Johannesburg. Mac McCullum is Carpathia's pilot for the aircraft, and Annie Christopher is the cargo chief. The **Phoenix 216** is 50 percent larger and costs twice as much as the **Condor 216**. David Hassid installs new metal detectors, and David, Annie, Abdullah, and Mac plant a sophisticated bugging device that can be accessed even outside the plane. Leon Fortunato tells David about plans to take this plane to go see the 10 regional potentates. Mac and Abdullah fly Carpathia's entire administrative team to Israel for the Gala. **6**

After receiving a head wound from Chaim Rosenzweig, Carpathia is pronounced dead on the plane. **7**

David Hassid mentions to Walter Moon that this plane will be flying to Tel Aviv, where the resurrected Potentate Carpathia and his VIPs will inaugurate the first loyalty mark application site open to the public. David supervises the loading of the **Phoenix 216**'s cargo, which includes the largest **pig** in the GC database. **8** The **Phoenix 216** is also the scene of several important meetings, monitored by the Tribulation Force through the bugging system. **9**

Quantum
Like a huge **Learjet**. Rayford suspects Hattie may be escaping in a **Quantum** to kill Carpathia. There is a report that this airplane, owned and piloted by Samuel Hanson, went down with Hattie near the shores of Portugal. **6**

Quasi Two
Very expensive jet Mac McCullum plans to fly into Tel Aviv, with a huge load of guillotines and skids of biochips and injectors for the GC. The **Quasi Two** is considered a marvel of modern technology and can be flown by remote control. Abdullah Smith, Hannah Palemoon, David Hassid, and Mac McCullum are scheduled on board, but the "Fatal Four" fake their deaths, having Mac fly the plane remotely and crash it into the Mediterranean. **8**

Rooster Tail
High-speed, transatlantic 4-seater; Chang Wong authorized George Sebastian to fly it to the United North American States. **7** After George is taken captive in Greece, Mac asks to see the **Rooster Tail** and orders it gassed up, but later finds that the gas tank has been drained. **10**

Super J (Super Juliet)
Plane Dwayne and Trudy Tuttle fly to rescue Mac McCullum and Abdullah Smith in Johannesburg. It is sleek, black, and incredibly aerodynamic, with power to burn and lots of room. In Brussels, Rayford Steele boards the **Super J** just in time with the help of the Tuttles, and the 3 of them fly to Al Basrah. T kids Rayford about the **Super J**, saying it is to the **Gulfstream** what a Porsche is to a Chevy. **6**

T flies the **Super J** into Israel to rescue Chaim Rosenzweig and Buck Williams. The plane runs out of gas while attempting to land in Greece and crashes. T dies, but Buck and Chaim survive. **7**

Supersonic Plane

Any plane capable of flying faster than the speed of sound. Rayford Steele asks Abdullah Smith to secure a **supersonic plane** to pick up Tsion Ben-Judah and transport him and others to the Middle East. **9**

Surveillance Planes

Surveillance planes are blown off course by the shock wave following the falling star. **5** Rayford and Chloe worry that **surveillance planes** may spot them while they are checking out the Strong Building. **7**

Transport Plane

Lionel Whalum takes a huge **transport plane** to take wheat from Argentina to India for the co-op. **10**

Turboprop

A small, low-speed propeller plane. Chloe Steele takes a **Pan-Con turboprop** for the last leg of her journey home after the Rapture. **1**

Warplanes

Thousands of Russian **warplanes** attacking Israel slam into the earth; the miraculous protection of Israel is called the Russian Pearl Harbor. **1**

Whirlybirds

See **Helicopter**.

TRAINS

TRAINS ARE RARELY MENTIONED in the Left Behind series, but:

When the Rapture occurs, 6 **trains** are involved in head-on collisions, causing many deaths. Several **trains** also run into the backs of others. It takes days to clear the tracks and replace the **train** cars. **1**
Ming Toy's husband is killed in one of these **train** accidents. **7**

Buck needs to take a **train** into New York. After Ken Ritz drops him off, he has to walk about 2 miles to the **train** platform and wait 70 minutes for the **train**. Because of the chaos caused by the Rapture, the **train** stops 15 miles short of Buck's destination, so he has to make the last leg of the commute to his office on a yellow bike. **1**

After the locusts arrive, people in Jerusalem jump in front of **trains** but are unable to kill themselves, although many are maimed. **5**

AUTOMOBILES

4-door
Ming Toy drives a compact **4-door** in Belgium. Lukas Miklos drives a small, white **4-door to** pick up Rayford Steele in Greece following Carpathia's assassination. **7**

4-wheel Drive
Jeff Williams takes a **4-wheel drive** vehicle to look for the scene of his wife's accident after the Rapture. Ken Ritz picks up Buck in a **4-wheel drive** after the Rapture. **1** Nearly all Operation Eagle vehicles are **4-wheel drive** and can pick their way around any obstacle. **9**

All-terrain Vehicle (ATV)
Four-wheeled vehicles; Rayford drives one to reach Mac on the outskirts of Petra. He is thrown from the **ATV** and badly injured. **11** Razor and Leah Rose ride **ATV**s to rescue Rayford. Chang and Naomi also take **ATV**s to survey Petra. **12**

Black Vehicles
In Jerusalem, three oversized **black vehicles** carry Carpathia's entourage, including regional dignitaries, Most High Reverend Father Leon Fortunato, Suhail Akbar, Walter Moon, and Viv Ivins. **9**

BMW
Rayford's car; when he returns to Chicago after the Rapture, it is waiting for him in the parking garage with a full tank of gas. The **BMW** has a car phone Rayford retrieves. **1**

Bus

Buck buys Michael Shorosh's old school **bus**; it smells of fish and paint. He and Tsion barely escape Israel in the **bus**. 3

Cab

Cabs appear frequently in the Left Behind series. After the Rapture, several **cabs'** motors are still running and drivers' clothes are lying on the seats. Volunteer drivers have to move the **cabs** out of the way. **Cab** rides rise to premium cost after the Rapture. Buck Williams uses **cabs** in New York and in London. Steve Plank and Buck take one together. A cabbie shows Rayford and Chloe Steele the aftermath of a 6-story parking garage wreck where everything got jammed during the Rapture. 1 Buck gets an interview on temple history and the rebuilding of the temple from Rabbi Feinberg while they share a **cab** ride. 2

After Buck falls from the **Gulfstream** and is injured, he is picked up by a **cab** and shares his faith with the driver. He also buys a Bible and clothes from the cabbie and is directed to medical help. 5

After Carpathia's assassination, Buck takes a 100-Nick **cab** ride in Jerusalem to find Chaim Rosenzweig. He secures another **cab** ride for 150 Nicks to get Chaim and him to The Night Visitors. 7

Carpet-Service Minivan

Likely the vehicle used to transport the Steeles' household and garage items after the robbery. 1

Cousin Kronos's Truck

Four-wheel drive, 5-speed manual transmission, very heavy and powerful. It's not new or fast. George Sebastian and Mac McCullum use it to help in their escape out of Greece; they leave it as a roadblock. 10

Dump Truck

Removes broken chunks of asphalt from the road after the earthquake. 4 A **dump truck** full of gravel brings Rayford Steele and Mac McCullum to the airstrip in Al Basrah. 4

Fire Truck

After Chicago is bombed, **fire trucks** and other emergency vehicles are everywhere. 3 **Fire trucks** are also on hand for rescues after the wrath of the Lamb earthquake. 4

Foam Truck

Puts out the fire when Ken Ritz drives a burning car to Stapleton Airport on the mission to help Hattie Durham escape Littleton, Colorado. 4

Ford Truck
Stefan owns an old, green, English **Ford truck**, which Chaim Rosenzweig recognizes at The Harem. 5

Forklift
The food and 144 computers on board the **Condor 216** are unloaded by **forklift** and smuggled to believers. 6 A monstrous **forklift** is called in to move the statue of Nicolae Carpathia. 6

Fuel Truck
Gets in Albie's way during the earthquake and causes him to twist his foot. 4

Golf Cart
David Hassid uses a **golf cart** to get the Wong family through the crowds at Nicolae Carpathia's funeral. Someone steals the cart during Carpathia's resurrection, so David has to call for another. Once he gets another cart he frantically searches for Annie. 8

Hearse
Used by Chloe Williams's GC captors to transport her to the airport. 11

Hummer/Humvee
Buck and Chloe Williams acquire a white **Hummer** from the Strong Building's parking lot. Buck finds it surprisingly comfortable, predictably powerful, and amazingly quiet. Thanks to the **Hummer's** low center of gravity and wide wheelbase, almost nothing can make it tip. Buck takes the Hummer to rescue Zeke Jr. and has to rig the brake lights so he can manually turn them on in regular traffic but not have them going on during the rescue. 8

Chloe drives the **Humvee** to a tiny airstrip near Lake Michigan to meet Buck and the others returning from the Middle East. Buck drives Chloe and the others to the airport in the **Humvee** on their way to the Sebastian rescue in Greece and the Petra mission. 9

Buck and George take the **Hummer** to search for Chloe after she is captured by the GC and pick up Rayford Steele and Mac McCullum on the outskirts of San Diego. 11 A big, royal **Humvee** transports Nicolae Carpathia and Leon Fortunato around the battlefield of Armageddon. They stand on the hood and top, and Carpathia even stands on it as it is driven. When the **Hummer** goes through the bloody battlefield, it gets stuck and Fortunato has to get out and rock it. The vehicle is filthy for its arrival in Jerusalem; Carpathia forgot to ask anyone to clean it. 12

Jeep

One of Rayford Steele's vehicles. [1] A GC **Jeep** delivers Rayford and Mac McCullum to their hotel in Jerusalem. The GC escort for the Meeting of the Witnesses is 2 **Jeeps** with flashing yellow lights and 4 armed guards. Another GC **Jeep** trails Jacov on the way to the Meeting of the Witnesses. T Delanty owns a red **Jeep** and lends it to Dr. Charles to transport an oxygen tank to the safe house. [5]

David Hassid is to appropriate a GC **Jeep** for Albie and Rayford, and Hamilton offers either her car or the **Jeep** to Albie once the clearance David provides suddenly appears. At Bozeman, Albie secures a **Jeep** to transport Hattie Durham and Rayford. [8]

George Sebastian borrows a **Jeep** to transport Marcel and Georgiana, but the plan goes awry and GC in **Jeeps** apprehend him. [9] Mac has to hot-wire a GC **Jeep** to transport Chloe Williams and Hannah Palemoon in Greece. When Mac gets out, Hannah takes over driving. The "philosopher" group also carts George around in a GC **Jeep**. Caravans of **Jeeps** unload GC personnel in Argentina. [10] In the Petra area, a Jeep shines a beacon to illuminate Carpathia as he stands on a **truck**. [12]

K's Car

Tiny, white car. Marcel Papadopoulos, Lukas Miklos, and K are killed by Elena in the car. [9]

Land Rover

See **Range Rover**.

Late-model Luxury Car

Owned by Lukas Miklos. [5]

Limo

After the Rapture, Buck Williams pays well to have a **limo** take him to the northern suburbs of Chicago. At the U.N. press conference Buck observes VIPs being dropped off by **limos**. [1]

Buck is told to take a flight from O'Hare and then take a **limo** to meet Nicolae Carpathia for lunch. Instead the black stretch **limo** takes him to the Manhattan Harbor Yacht Club to meet Chaim Rosenzweig, by Carpathia's design. A **limo** takes Rayford Steele and Carpathia to a hangar where Rayford sees *Air Force One* being repainted as *Global Community One*. [2]

A flag-bedecked Botswanian **limo** full of armed men meets the **Condor 216** at Johannesburg International Airport. [6]

Lincoln
White, late-model car rented from O'Hare and driven by Rayford
Steele. After Nicolae Carpathia whisks Rayford away, Buck Williams
drives it to the **Land Rover** dealership, and the sales manager reluc-
tantly agrees to return it to O'Hare. **3**

Luxury Motor Coaches
Transport Carpathia and his entourage from Tel Aviv to Jerusalem
for the peace-treaty signing. **2** Carpathia rides in one to confront the
two witnesses and try to negotiate getting the sun to shine normally
again. **5**

Mercedes
Tsion Ben-Judah's driver picks up Buck Williams in a white **Mercedes**
and takes him to the Wailing Wall, then picks up Tsion and Buck after
Tsion's TV message. **2** Hattie Durham's driver picks Rayford Steele up
in New Babylon in a white stretch **Mercedes**. **3** Chaim Rosenzweig
owns a **Mercedes van**, which Jacov drives to pick up Tribulation Force
members from the King David Hotel and take them to Chaim's home.
He also drives them to the Meeting of the Witnesses in the **van**. The
next night, Stefan drives the **van** to the Meeting and later gets Chaim,
Tsion, Chloe, and Buck away from the stadium. **5**

Military Transport
Ming Toy takes a **military transport** to New Babylon for Carpathia's
funeral. **7**

Military Truck
A camouflaged, canvas-covered **military truck** transports the sow
for Nicolae Carpathia's ride down the Via Dolorosa. **9**

Minivan
Bihari drives a **minivan** at more than 70 miles per hour during the
co-op's wheat/water exchange. **10**

Motor Scooter
Small and light enough to be stored indoors or hidden in the woods.
Albie and Mac ride them in the Al Basrah and Abadan areas, usually
after dark. **11**

Personnel Transport/Carrier
New vehicle from France driven in by a co-op volunteer. It becomes one
of Mac McCullum's vehicles for Operation Eagle. It has a 6-speed transmission and can be driven in automatic or manual. Mac transports

Hannah Palemoon, Leah Rose, and other believers to Petra in this vehicle and nearly drives them into a canyon as they evade the GC. ⑨ Chloe spots a GC **personnel carrier** outside the Tribulation Force compound in San Diego. George Sebastian later concludes this vehicle was a decoy. **Personnel carriers** also advance on the battlefield of Armageddon. ⑪

Pickup

Albie, Mac McCullum, and Rayford Steele take a **pickup** to get food after the wrath of the Lamb earthquake. It has a clutch, which forces Mac to drive it since Albie has injured his foot in the earthquake. ④ Later Albie and Rayford take the pickup to go practice shooting a Saber. ⑥ Rayford becomes concerned when a **pickup** arrives at the cottage in Greece, but Laslos reassures him. ⑦

Public Address Trucks

GC **trucks** that roll through the street after the resurrection of the two witnesses with announcements that volunteers are needed and closing ceremonies of the Gala will go on as planned. ⑥

Range Rover

Fully-loaded vehicle purchased by Buck Williams from a **Land Rover** dealership after the outbreak of WWIII. Sometimes called the **Land Rover** or the **Rover**. The **Range Rover** has 2-wheel drive, 4-wheel drive, all-wheel drive, independent suspension, and the ability to switch between manual and automatic transmission—it will go anywhere and is seemingly indestructible. The **Rover** is also equipped with phone, citizen's band radio, fire extinguisher, survival kit, and flares. ③

The **Range Rover** survives even after it and Chloe Williams are thrown into a tree in the attack on Chicago. ③ Buck drives it through the wrath of the Lamb earthquake and uses its built-in compass to navigate his search for Chloe. ④

Rayford Steele and Leah Rose take the **Range Rover** to retrieve money from the safe at Leah's house. The tinted windows prevent the GC from noticing Leah until they look through the windshield. ⑥ Leah drives the **Range Rover** to get Chaim Rosenzweig, Rayford, Chloe, and Albie to the safe house, and later it is driven to rescue Tsion Ben-Judah and Kenny Williams after the safe house is compromised. ⑦ Chloe and Buck park the **Range Rover** in the basement of the Strong Building and replace it with a **Humvee**. ⑧

Rental Car

Buck Williams and Ken Ritz squish inside a red subcompact car—the only **rental** available—to search for Chloe after the earthquake. ④

Rover
See **Range Rover**.

Sedan
Alan Tompkins's Scotland Yard issue, light green **sedan** is bombed. **1** Chaim Rosenzweig owns an ancient **sedan** with a manual transmission and bald tires. Buck Williams drives it to find Jacov at the Harem and later takes it to the Wailing Wall. **5**

Suburban
Ken Ritz owns a **Suburban,** used by the Tribulation Force after Ken's death. Ernie works to keep it running. Rayford Steele plans to take the **Suburban** to T Delanty to be used by his small church, but instead must drive it to find Hattie. **5, 6** Rayford, Leah Rose, and Chloe Williams leave it at the ersatz bar after GC officers start asking questions. **7**

SUV
Chloe is thrown into the backseat of a large **SUV** with wire mesh on the windows and no locks or door handles inside for transport to the Stateville prison. The **SUV** is escorted by a phalanx of GC motorcycles and squad cars. **11**

Tow Truck
After the Rapture, **tow trucks** remove cars left without drivers. **1**

Truck
During the earthquake, Buck watches as **trucks** flip over. **4** The GC cart guillotines through the streets in open **trucks** to show people the consequences of thinking for themselves. Albie sees these **trucks** in Ptolemaïs. **8** Miklos owns hundreds of **trucks**, used to assist the Greek underground church. Several **trucks** bring Jews to Petra for Operation Eagle. **9**

Mac runs over Elena's cell phone with a **truck**. Large **trucks** haul the water and wheat for the co-op exchange. **10** When Chloe leaves the San Diego underground compound, she has to pretend she is out jogging as 2 GC **trucks** start to follow her. They eventually haul her to the GC's San Diego headquarters. **11**

Van
Rayford Steele travels in a **Pan-Continental** courtesy **van** on his way to DFW airport. **2** The murderers of Tsion Ben-Judah's family escape in a nondescript **van**. **3** Buck Williams and Ken Ritz tamper with a GC **van** in Littleton so the GC can't follow them in their attempt to free Hattie Durham. **4** A rented **van**, driven by Leah Rose, transports the "Fatal

Four" to Mizpe Ramon. ⟨ Greek GC Peacekeepers in a **van** fly past Mac and flash an obscene gesture. When they notice his GC uniform, they drive back and claim to have been waving. 10

Verna's Car

Junky old import; Verna Zee lets Buck Williams borrow it during the WWIII attack on Chicago. Buck has to abandon it while searching for Chloe. He replaces **Verna's car** with one left behind by a parishioner of New Hope Village Church. 3

OTHER MODES OF TRANSPORTATION

Horse

Buck Williams sees cops on horseback as he travels through New York City; they are among the few who can travel efficiently in the chaos caused by the Rapture. ▌ The 200 million horsemen ride huge, dark **horses** with faces like lions; they breathe fire and smoke and are visible only to believers. Unbelievers are trampled by the **horses** or die from the yellow-and-black smoke they exhale. Leah Rose is the first member of the Tribulation Force to see the horsemen; they slaughter GC Peacekeeping Forces questioning Leah and Rayford Steele. 6

At the Battle of Armageddon the Unity Army surrounds Petra, with hundreds of thousands of the soldiers on horseback. Many **horses** and riders are burned by DEWs. Nicolae Carpathia rides a massive black **horse**, 2 hands taller and 100 pounds heavier than the others. Mac McCullum rides a huge, black **horse** with the group flanking Carpathia. The Unity Army's **horses** are spooked by lightning and thunder before the Glorious Appearing, and the **horses** buck and rear when the heavens light up just before Jesus appears. Many GC riders are thrown. Jesus and the armies of heaven appear on white **horses**. Thousands of GC **horses** are slaughtered along with their riders at the sound of Jesus' words. 12

Pig

Nicolae Carpathia rides an enormous sow down the Via Dolorosa in Jerusalem. Leon Fortunato even has a saddle made for the **pig**. The sow is clearly drugged, and eventually her legs buckle; Carpathia's aides must rush to keep him from falling off. The next day, Carpathia slaughters the **pig** inside the temple. **9**

Oceangoing Vessels
Buck Williams, Leah Rose, and Z discuss the number of 1,000-ton or larger vessels Chloe has on record before the seas turn to blood. **10**

Wheelchair
After the wrath of the Lamb earthquake, Buck Williams helps Ken Ritz, suffering from a head wound, into a **wheelchair** at the hospital. **4** Chaim Rosenzweig purchases a motorized **wheelchair** to aid in the deception that he has had a stroke. **6** After Nicolae Carpathia's assassination, Chaim leaves the **wheelchair** at the Global Gala. **7** Pinkerton Stephens uses an electric **wheelchair** after sustaining major injuries in the earthquake. After David Hassid's heatstroke and head injuries, he needs a **wheelchair** on the way to the morgue. **8**

Yellow Bicycles
Buck finds a **yellow bicycle** in New York City after the Rapture. The bike's sign reads, "Borrow this bike. Take it where you like. Leave it for someone else in need. No charge." **1**

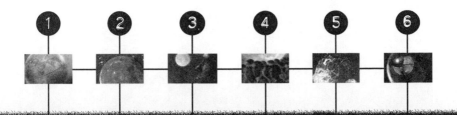

WEAPONS

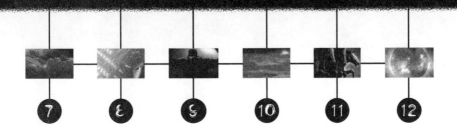

WEAPONS

FROM THE BEGINNING of the Left Behind series, when Nicolae Carpathia commits his first murders with a borrowed gun, to the end, when the greatest battle of all time culminates in Christ's Glorious Appearing, weapons of all kinds appear in the books. Of course, the most lethal "weapons" are the words of Christ, which slay Unity Army soldiers where they stand. But other weapons wreak havoc during the Tribulation. Here's a look at the various means of destruction and protection characters use throughout the series.

9 mm
Albie carries a **9 mm** gun in a holster to rescue Hattie Durham in Pueblo. ⒏ In Petra, Rayford Steele hands Mac McCullum a **9 mm**. Mac carries it when he transports messianic believers to Petra during Operation Eagle. Rayford advises him not to use it but to depend on God to protect them. ⒐

12-gauge Shotgun
Short-range shoulder weapon belonging to George Sebastian. Mac McCullum finds it on the rescue mission in Greece and gives it to Hannah Palemoon. Hannah uses the shotgun to shoot out the door of the "philosophers'" shack. ⑩

38-caliber Police Special
Gun belonging to Scott M. Otterness, an aging guard at the Plaza Hotel. It has a 4-inch barrel and is loaded with high-velocity, hollow-point shells. Carpathia borrows and uses it to kill Jonathan Stonagal and

Joshua Todd-Cothran, then brainwashes Otterness to remember that
Stonagal had ripped the gun out of the holster and killed himself before
Otterness could react. **1**

.44 Revolver
Sahib's gun. Mainyu Mazda uses it to kill Albie **11**

.45
A 45-caliber weapon. Mac McCullum gives Leah Rose this gun to use
in the rescue of David Hassid. **9**

50-caliber Rifle
4 feet long, at least 35 pounds, with a built-in bipod. The rifles have
a range of 4 miles and take 7 seconds to hit a target 2 miles away.
George Sebastian arranges for 100 of these **rifles** to be shipped to
Mizpe Ramon. A team armed with **50-caliber rifles** heads for Petra in
search of David Hassid. Firing one of the **rifles** leaves Rayford dazed,
his ears ringing, head buzzing, and hands vibrating. Some have incendiary tips that make the casing separate when it hits soft material like
flesh. **9**

George hides one in the Rooster Tail, which Mac later discovers in
the secret-panel cargo hold. Mac uses the **rifle** to shoot the gas tank
of a GC car and create a diversion. Later he ditches it because it is too
cumbersome when he has to run a great distance. **10**

Along with **DEWs**, **50-caliber rifles** cause several dozen casualties
on the perimeter of Petra. **12**

Baton
Club often used by law enforcement. A guard at the detention center
in Greece beats Mrs. Miklos savagely with her **baton** for refusing
to stop praying. Pastor Demeter is also hit with a guard's **baton** for
sharing his faith with fellow inmates. **8**

Battering Ram
In the siege on Jerusalem, the GC army moves a colossal **battering ram**
toward the Wailing Wall. Jewish rebels charge and take the **battering
ram** inside the wall. With a second **battering ram**, GC forces break
through the northeastern wall of the Old City. The rebels fight fiercely
and nearly gain control of this **battering ram** too, but the GC return
with high-powered automatic weapons, a **grenade launcher**, and a
bazooka. **11**

When approaching the Old City of Jerusalem after the Glorious
Appearing, Carpathia shouts to make way for the missile launchers

and **battering rams**. Before the Unity Army can attack, the soldiers are slaughtered and Jerusalem shifts in a massive earthquake. **12**

Bazooka
A lightweight antitank weapon. The Unity Army uses a **bazooka** against rebel forces in Jerusalem. **11**

Beretta
Firearms manufacturer. Ken Ritz carries a 9 mm automatic **Beretta** every time he flies for Buck Williams. He uses it to help Buck and Hattie Durham escape from the reproductive clinic in Littleton, pulling the **Beretta** from an ankle holster and squeezing off shots just above ground level to keep GC guards away. **4**

Big Blue 82s
See **Concussion Bomb**.

Bomb
GC peacekeeping forces drop a 100-megaton **bomb** on Heathrow Airport, destroying it and causing radiation fallout. **2** Nicolae Carpathia has several key world cities bombed, including Chicago. Northwest Community Hospital takes a direct hit in the bombing of Chicago. **2**, **3**

A nuclear **bomb** hits Chicago 3 days after the last occupants of the Strong Building evacuate. **10**

While fighting in Jerusalem, the wall Buck is on is hit by a **bomb**, leaving him mortally wounded. **11**

See also **Car Bomb**, **Concussion Bomb**.

Car Bomb
Alan Tompkins is killed when a **bomb** explodes in his Scotland Yard vehicle. Buck Williams is reported dead in the bombing and suspects that it is related to the connection between Nicolae Carpathia, Jonathan Stonagal, and Joshua Todd-Cothran. **1**

Jaime, Tsion Ben-Judah's driver, is close to receiving Jesus as his Messiah when he is killed by a **car bomb** the same day Tsion's family is murdered. **3**

Concussion Bomb
Set off at the Johannesburg ambush, sending Mac McCullum, Abdullah Smith, Leon Fortunato, and others running from the Condor 216. **6**

Two massive **concussion bombs**, 4.5 feet in diameter, 11 feet long, and 15,000 pounds each, are prepared for the attack on Petra. Most of their weight is made up of gel consisting of polystyrene, ammonium nitrate, and powdered aluminum. These **bombs** are also called Big Blue

82s or daisy cutter bombs and are designed to detonate a few feet above the ground and create a fireball 6,000 feet in diameter, killing anything in a 2,000-acre area. The **concussion bombs** are dropped on Petra, and despite a direct hit, residents are unharmed. 10

Daisy Cutter Bomb
See **Concussion Bomb**.

DEW
See **Directed Energy Weapon**.

Directed Energy Weapon
A lightweight, nonlethal **rifle** often called a **DEW**. With a maximum range of a little under half a mile, a **DEW** shoots a concentrated beam that penetrates clothing and heats moisture on the skin to 130 degrees in seconds. George Sebastian has **DEWs** sent to Operation Eagle sites. 9

Hannah Palemoon uses a **DEW** on 2 GC Peacekeepers at the road-block in Greece to distract them from checking Mac's and George's marks. 10

George coordinates about 100 **DEW** operators around the perimeter of Petra to shoot at Unity Army horses, causing temporary mayhem. Later another **DEW** attack throws the Unity Army into chaos, but they recover and return fire on Petra. 11 George's occasional volleys from **DEWs** continues to be a nuisance for Unity Army troops, causing several dozen casualties. 12

Gatling Gun
Machine gun with revolving barrels that each fire once per revolution. Inside Jerusalem, the Unity Army has them mounted on massive caissons. Mac McCullum guesses the **Gatling guns** could fire 50-caliber shells. 12

Glock
Popular firearms manufacturer. Hannah Palemoon packs a 9 mm **Glock** at the Greek pub. 10

While in New Babylon for Chang's rescue, Abdullah Smith carries a 45-caliber **Glock** to guard Chang's door. 11

Grenade Launcher
Shoulder-fired weapon that shoots small missiles containing explosives. The GC issues Ming Toy a **grenade launcher** in China, but she vows she won't use it and fortunately doesn't have to. 10 The GC Unity Army opens fire with a **grenade launcher** in the siege on Jerusalem. 11 The Unity Army also uses a **grenade launcher** for the ineffective attack

on Petra. At least 1 of these is destroyed by a chunk of ice in the hailstorm following the Glorious Appearing. 12

Guillotine
Weapon used for beheading; called loyalty enforcement facilitators by the GC. Each **guillotine** is simply constructed from wood, screws, blade, spring, and rope. The machine lets gravity pull down a sharpened blade onto a victim's neck, making the execution process quick and foolproof. One **guillotine** is installed at each GC mark application site; the machines are used to behead those who refuse to receive the mark of the beast. Many believers are martyred at the **guillotines**, including Mrs. Miklos, Pastor and Mrs. Demeter, Zeke Zuckermandel Sr., Steve Plank, and Chloe Williams. 8-11 At the judgment, all the believers who died at the **guillotines** receive martyrs' crowns. 12

Ice-sculpture Feathers
The 10 regional potentates break "feathers" off an ice sculpture depicting Peter the Second as an angel and stab Peter to death with them. His body is cremated, and it is reported that he died of some fast-moving disease. 6

Knife
One of the two witnesses' attackers carries a bayonet-type **knife** that appears to have come from an Israeli-issue military rifle. When he tries to attack the witnesses, he falls dead. 1 When another man with a **knife** leaps at the witnesses, he seems to hit an invisible wall and falls dead. 5

Lance Missile
A short-range ballistic missile, propelled 5 to 75 miles by a liquid-fueled rocket engine. A **lance missile** is launched at Petra after 2 **concussion bombs** are dropped. Despite a direct hit by the missile, the only result is a geyser that extinguishes the flames and supplies water for residents. 10

Lightning
Leon Fortunato calls down **lightning** from heaven at Nicolae Carpathia's funeral, killing 3 regional potentates and many in sector 53, including Annie Christopher. 7 Fortunato calls **lightning** down again at Calvary and kills Hattie Durham. 9

Loyalty Enforcement Facilitator
See **Guillotine**.

Luger

A favored German **pistol** issued in WWII. Chloe Williams carries her father's ancient **Luger**, which he considers a keepsake, when she leaves the Strong Building to find the source of the light she sees through a telescope. Before going out, she experiments with the **Luger** until she figures out how to load it and how the safety works. Thankfully, she never has to use it. 9

Chloe carries a **Luger** again at the Greek pub. She also packs a **Luger** and an **Uzi** while in the woods. 10

Mortar Cannon

Used to shoot at high angles. The GC's **mortar cannons** are bigger than usual, and Rayford Steele is surprised by the distance they achieve as shells fall around him on Petra's perimeter. One of these lands in front of Rayford and sends his ATV out of control, leaving him badly injured. 11

Pistol

Mac McCullum and Abdullah Smith carry contraband **pistols**. At the Johannesburg ambush, Leon Fortunato asks if any weapons are on board. Mac knows the **pistols** are in the cargo hold but he can't get to them. 6 Miklos has a **pistol** at his 1-man underground shelter, but he does not carry it outside. 9

Poison

While Bruce Barnes is on an international evangelistic mission, Nicolae Carpathia has him **poisoned**. Bruce makes it back to the States just before the outbreak of WWIII. Initially it is unclear how Bruce dies, but it is believed he died from **poisoning** just before the hospital was bombed. 2

Hattie Durham is also **poisoned** by Carpathia's people, causing her unborn child to die. 5 Hattie survives, but Dr. Charles dies from the **poison** transferred to him from Hattie. 6

Rattan Rod

A flexible stick about 1 inch thick and 4 feet long. On Nicolae Carpathia's orders, Commander Tenzin beats Ipswitch nearly to death with his **rattan rod**. 12

Rifle

A long gun that has rotating grooves cut into the inside of the barrel to make the bullet spin at high speed. A mercenary soldier charges the two witnesses with a high-powered **rifle** and is incinerated. Another would-be attacker carries a bulky, high-powered sniper **rifle**. The assassins are vaporized, their **rifles** turned to sizzling liquid. **5**

Saber
Gun Albie supplies to Rayford Steele. The **Saber** is a semiautomatic with no safety. It disassembles into a rectangular block of black metal, about 10 inches long, 5 inches wide, and an inch and a half deep. Albie tells Rayford the **Saber** was so named because it appears to be a sword in its sheath. Nicolae Carpathia uses a **Saber** to kill the two witnesses. At the Global Gala, Rayford aims his **Saber** at Carpathia, and the gun goes off when Rayford is bumped in the crowd. **6** Later Rayford's **Saber** is found with his fingerprints on it, and it is reported that he is the assassin, though Carpathia's wounds prove to be from a **sword**. **7**

Semiautomatic
A man posing as Jimmy Dykes greets Rayford Steele with a **semiautomatic pistol**. **6** Loren Hut carries a **semiautomatic** handgun with a 9-round clip. He fires it unsuccessfully at Chaim Rosenzweig, but a scoffer nearby is killed by one bullet. Hut discards his **semiautomatic** when the sores judgment overtakes him. **9**

Submachine Gun
Automatic firearm fired from the shoulder or hip. A GC guard points a **submachine gun** at Mac McCullum and his loaded vehicle headed for Petra, but Mac eludes him. **9**

Sword
Chaim Rosenzweig creates a 15- to 18-inch **sword**, which fits perfectly into the tubing of his wheelchair. He conceals the **sword** this way at the Global Gala, then uses it to assassinate Nicolae Carpathia. After the **sword** is removed from Carpathia's body it is given to Minister Blod by Dr. Eikenberry. Blod is told to put it inside the statue of Carpathia. Mention of the **sword** is omitted from the autopsy report. **7**

Carpathia carries an ornate, oversized silver **sword** with gold inlays and a garish handle for the Battle of Armageddon. He swings the **sword** around and uses it to hold himself up when trying to exit a vehicle. Carpathia's Unity Army also carries swords.

Used symbolically in reference to God's Word, which Revelation 1:16 calls "a sharp two-edged **sword**." When Jesus returns, he slays the Unity Army with this "**sword**" from his mouth. **12**

Uzi

An Israeli-designed **submachine gun**, small and lightweight. In Jerusalem, someone attacks the two witnesses, firing an **Uzi**; it appears to jam and the attacker falls and dies. **1**

Buck Williams encounters an **Uzi** in Littleton while attempting to rescue Hattie Durham. The GC guards carry **Uzis** and fire upon the receptionist at the reproductive clinic, killing her. Buck hits one of the GC guards, and his **Uzi** clatters to the marble floor. **4**

At the Meeting of the Witnesses, Jacov creates a diversion by hiding his **Uzi** under his clothes, then firing it into the air to get Chloe Williams and Tsion Ben-Judah to safety. **5**

On the last day of the Global Gala, Jacov is killed when he is hit with the butt end of an **Uzi** and knocked into the crowd. **7**

The underground Greek co-op is armed with **Uzis**. The Greek rescue team—Hannah Palemoon, Chloe Williams, and Mac McCullum—also carry them. **10**

Chloe takes an **Uzi** when she leaves the San Diego compound. When pursued by GC, she ditches it. Buck and George Sebastian are armed with **Uzis** when they search for Chloe. Tsion trains on one before heading to Jerusalem, and he describes it as being like shooting with a garden hose. In Jerusalem, Buck carries 2 **Uzis** after Tsion dies; when the wall is hit he loses both and is left injured and unarmed. **11**

In Jerusalem, Mac kills about a dozen GC soldiers with an **Uzi**. **12**

ABOUT THE AUTHORS

Jerry B. Jenkins (www.jerryjenkins.com) is the writer of the Left Behind series. He owns the Jerry B. Jenkins Christian Writers Guild (www.ChristianWritersGuild.com), an organization dedicated to mentoring aspiring authors, as well as Jenkins Entertainment, a filmmaking company (www.Jenkins-Entertainment.com). Former vice president of publishing for the Moody Bible Institute of Chicago, he also served many years as editor of *Moody* magazine and is now Moody's writer-at-large.

His writing has appeared in publications as varied as *Time* magazine, *Reader's Digest, Parade, Guideposts,* in-flight magazines, and dozens of other periodicals. Jenkins's biographies include books with Billy Graham, Hank Aaron, Bill Gaither, Luis Palau, Walter Payton, Orel Hershiser, and Nolan Ryan, among many others. His books appear regularly on the *New York Times, USA Today, Wall Street Journal,* and *Publishers Weekly* best-seller lists.

He holds two honorary doctorates, one from Bethel College (Indiana) and one from Trinity International University. Jerry and his wife, Dianna, live in Colorado and have three grown sons and three grandchildren.

Dr. Tim LaHaye (www.timlahaye.com), who conceived the idea of fictionalizing an account of the Rapture and the Tribulation, is a noted author, minister, and nationally recognized speaker on Bible prophecy. He is the founder of both Tim LaHaye Ministries and the Pre-Trib Research Center.

He also recently cofounded the Tim LaHaye School of Prophecy at Liberty University. Dr. LaHaye speaks at many of the major Bible prophecy conferences in the U.S. and Canada, where his prophecy books are very popular.

Dr. LaHaye earned a doctor of ministry degree from Western Theological Seminary and an honorary doctor of literature degree from Liberty University. For twenty-five years he pastored one of the nation's outstanding churches in San Diego, which grew to three locations. During that time he founded two accredited Christian high schools, a Christian school system of ten schools, and Christian Heritage College.

There are almost 13 million copies of Dr. LaHaye's fifty nonfiction books that have been published in over thirty-seven foreign languages. He has written books on a wide variety of subjects, such as family life, temperaments, and Bible prophecy. His current fiction works, the Left Behind series, written with Jerry B. Jenkins, continue to appear on the best-seller lists of the Christian Booksellers Association, *Publishers Weekly, Wall Street Journal, USA Today,* and the *New York Times.* LaHaye's second fiction series of prophetic novels consists of *Babylon Rising* and *The Secret on Ararat,* both of which hit the *New York Times* best-seller list and will soon be followed by *Europa Challenge.* This series of four action thrillers, unlike *Left Behind,* does not start with the Rapture but could take place today and goes up to the Rapture.

He is the father of four grown children and grandfather of nine. Snow skiing, waterskiing, motorcycling, golfing, vacationing with family, and jogging are among his leisure activities.

Tyndale House would like to thank Sandi Swanson and Denise Little with Tekno Books for their hard work in making this book possible!

SANDI L. SWANSON, with her husband of over thirty years, James, has cared for eleven special-needs children while raising their three biological children in the small town of Sandy, Oregon. Besides being a fan of (and expert on) the Left Behind series, Sandi's interests include women's Bible studies and aiding James as a biblical research assistant.

DENISE LITTLE worked for Barnes & Noble/B. Dalton Bookseller for ten years as a bookstore manager all over Texas, then for four more years as their national book buyer in New York City for science fiction, fantasy, and romance. She was selected as Bookseller of the Year by *Romantic Times* and by the Virginia and New Jersey chapters of Romance Writers of America. She launched the company's genre magazine, *Heart to Heart*, and wrote it for its first two years of existence. She also was closely involved in launching its fantastic fiction magazine, *Sense of Wonder*. Denise then joined Kensington Publishing, where she ran her own imprint, Denise Little Presents, as well as editing fiction and nonfiction projects throughout the list, including books by a number of best-selling authors. Several of the romances she edited and published under her imprint were nominated for RITA Awards by the Romance Writers of America. Since 1997, she's been executive editor at Tekno Books, working for Dr. Martin H. Greenberg. Her books, published and forthcoming, include *Perchance To Dream*, *Twice Upon a Time* (winner of the New York Public Library's 100 Best Books of the Year Award), *Constellation of Cats*, *The Quotable Cat*, *Murder Most Romantic*, *Alaska: True Adventures in the Last Frontier* (with Spike Walker), *Creature Fantastic*, and *The Nora Roberts Companion*. Her short fiction is included in *Civil War Fantastic* and *Alternate Gettysburgs*. Denise has been a Christian as long as she can remember—and as she's moved around the country, she has found her spiritual home in many wonderful churches. She lives in Green Bay, Wisconsin.

What People Are Saying about the Left Behind Series

"This is the most successful Christian-fiction series ever."
—**Publishers Weekly**

"Tim LaHaye and Jerry B. Jenkins . . . are doing for Christian fiction what John Grisham did for courtroom thrillers."
—**TIME**

"The authors' style continues to be thoroughly captivating and keeps the reader glued to the book, wondering what will happen next. And it leaves the reader hungry for more."
—**Christian Retailing**

"Combines Tom Clancy–like suspense with touches of romance, high-tech flash and Biblical references."
—**The New York Times**

"The most successful literary partnership of all time."
—**Newsweek**

"Wildly popular—and highly controversial."
—**USA Today**

"Christian thriller. Prophecy-based fiction. Juiced-up morality tale. Call it what you like, the Left Behind series . . . now has a label its creators could never have predicted: blockbuster success."
—**Entertainment Weekly**

"They can be fun and engaging, with fast-paced plotting, global drama, regular cliffhanger endings, and what has to be the quintessential villain: Satan himself."
—**abcnews.com**

"Not just any fiction. Jenkins . . . employed the techniques of suspense and thriller novels to turn the end of the world into an exciting, stay-up-late-into-the-night, page-turning story"
—**Chicago Tribune**

Tyndale House products by
Tim LaHaye and Jerry B. Jenkins

The Left Behind® book series
Left Behind®
Tribulation Force
Nicolae
Soul Harvest
Apollyon
Assassins
The Indwelling
The Mark
Desecration
The Remnant
Armageddon
Glorious Appearing
The Rising

Other Left Behind® products
Left Behind®: The Kids
Devotionals
Calendars
Abridged audio products
Dramatic audio products
Graphic novels
Gift books
and more . . .

Other Tyndale House books by
Tim LaHaye and Jerry B. Jenkins
Perhaps Today
Are We Living in the End Times?
The Authorized Left Behind Handbook
Embracing Eternity

For the latest information on individual products, release dates, and future projects, visit www.leftbehind.com

Tyndale House books by Tim LaHaye	Tyndale House books by Jerry B. Jenkins
How to Be Happy Though Married	*Soon*
Spirit-Controlled Temperament	*Silenced*
Transformed Temperaments	
Why You Act the Way You Do	

IN ONE CATACLYSMIC MOMENT
MILLIONS AROUND THE WORLD DISAPPEAR

Experience the suspense of the end times for yourself. The best-selling Left Behind series is now available in hardcover, softcover, and large-print editions.

1
LEFT BEHIND®
A novel of
the earth's last
days . . .

2
TRIBULATION FORCE
The continuing
drama of those
left behind . . .

3
NICOLAE
The rise of
Antichrist . . .

4
SOUL HARVEST
The world
takes sides . . .

5
APOLLYON
The Destroyer is
unleashed . . .

6
ASSASSINS
Assignment:
Jerusalem,
Target: Antichrist

7
THE INDWELLING
The Beast takes
possession . . .

8
THE MARK
The Beast rules
the world . . .

9
DESECRATION
Antichrist takes
the throne . . .

10
THE REMNANT
On the brink of
Armageddon . . .

11
ARMAGEDDON
The cosmic battle
of the ages . . .

12
GLORIOUS APPEARING
The end of
days . . .

FOR THE MOST ACCURATE INFORMATION VISIT
www.leftbehind.com

ABRIDGED AUDIO Available on three CDs or two cassettes for each title. (Books 1–9 read by Frank Muller, one of the most talented readers of audio books today.)

AN EXPERIENCE IN SOUND AND DRAMA Dramatic broadcast performances of the best-selling Left Behind series. Twelve half-hour episodes on four CDs or three cassettes for each title.

GRAPHIC NOVELS Created by a leader in the graphic novel market, the series is now available in this exciting new format.

LEFT BEHIND®: THE KIDS Four teens are left behind after the Rapture and band together to fight Satan's forces in this series for ten- to fourteen-year-olds.

LEFT BEHIND® > THE KIDS < LIVE-ACTION AUDIO Feel the reality, listen as the drama unfolds. . . . Twelve action-packed episodes available on four CDs or three cassettes.

CALENDARS, DEVOTIONALS, GIFT BOOKS . . .

FOR THE LATEST INFORMATION ON
INDIVIDUAL PRODUCTS, RELEASE DATES,
AND FUTURE PROJECTS, VISIT

www.leftbehind.com

Sign up and receive free e-mail updates!

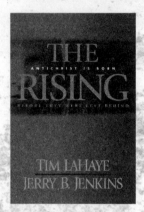